MEĻAĻ

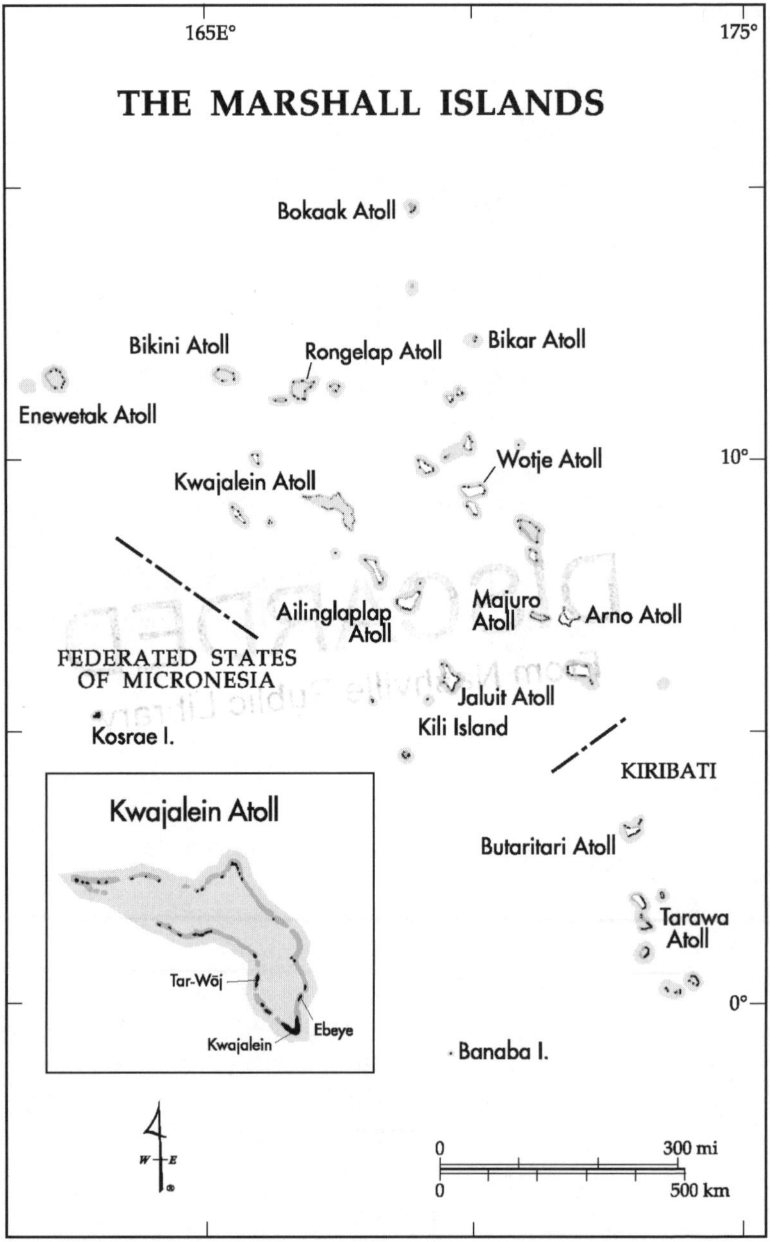
THE MARSHALL ISLANDS
165E°
175°
10°
0°
Bokaak Atoll
Bikini Atoll
Rongelap Atoll
Bikar Atoll
Enewetak Atoll
Wotje Atoll
Kwajalein Atoll
Ailinglaplap Atoll
Majuro Atoll
Arno Atoll
FEDERATED STATES OF MICRONESIA
Jaluit Atoll
Kili Island
Kosrae I.
KIRIBATI
Butaritari Atoll
Tarawa Atoll
Banaba I.
Kwajalein Atoll
Tar-Wōj
Ebeye
Kwajalein
W
E
0
300 mi
0
500 km

MEĻAĻ

Robert Barclay

University of Hawai'i Press
Honolulu

Printed in the United States of America
02 03 04 05 06 07 6 5 4 3 2

Library of Congress Cataloging-in-Publication Data

Barclay, Robert.
Meļaļ / Robert Barclay.
p. cm. —
ISBN 0–8248–2591–8 (paper)
1. Marshall Islands—Fiction. I. Title. II. Talanoa.
PS3602.A77 M45 2002
813'.6—dc21 2001058301

Map by Manoa Mapworks.
Courtesy of Center for Pacific Islands Studies.

Text art: *Once Before Time*, by Pia Stern.

University of Hawai'i Press books are printed on acid-free paper and meet the guidelines for permanence and durability of the Council on Library Resources.

Designed by Argosy Publishing

Printed by Versa Press

For Ken and Bobbi

Meļaļ. ARCHAIC. Playground for demons; not habitable by people.

Contents

Part One
Fallout Demonic

We believe in peace and love, not in the display of power to destroy mankind. If maintaining peace means killing and destruction of the fruits of man's efforts to build himself a better world, we desire no part of it.

—From a 1968 petition signed by a majority of the displaced islanders of Kwajalein Atoll, asking that they be allowed to return to live on their islands

Home

On Good Friday in 1981 Rujen Keju was the second one awake of fourteen clan members and eight family members in his Army-built, concrete blockhouse on the Marshallese island of Ebeye. He was a strong man, five and a half feet tall, thick with muscles in his chest and arms and legs. He crept like a soldier or a criminal with a pellet gun in one hand and a plastic flashlight in the other. His electricity had been out for two days. No breeze had blown for three. The night before had been a night of flying roaches. Sweat slicked his shooting hand, the aim of his pistol lingering at shapes he imagined in the shadows. Grains of sand and grit stuck to the bottoms of his feet, and at every sixth or seventh step, his toes feeling their way over and between mats lumped with dark breathing bodies, he would brush his feet off on his calves and become unbalanced.

Rujen had not slept well, the night's heat having deviled his brain into producing some feverish, seemingly crucial debate of which he could remember nothing beyond the excited rise and fall of too many voices. He woke tense, finding his hands balled into fists, not for fighting but as if he were gripping something getting away.

He ran the beam of his light like a prison's steady spotlight along the concrete ledge, that likely place where the tin roof joined the concrete wall, but the light passed only crumbling chunks of boric acid, a bald and armless Black Barbie, and sleeping flies upside-down on the stalks of plastic flowers in Pepsi-can vases. Farther on a small electric fan aimed at the sleepers, its blue blade paralyzed within a rusted cage. Just under the ledge and past a row of open wooden louvers was a velvet painting of Jesus Christ. Wedged into one corner of the frame was a black-and-white instant photograph of Rujen's wife, Iia, holding a baby boy, Nuke, named after the most powerful thing on Earth. Now twelve, Nuke lay asleep on a mat beside his brother, Jebro, named after the king of the stars, the greatest hero ever in the Marshall Islands. He was born with six fingers on his left hand—a long extra pinkie without the nail. It had no strength, but Jebro boasted he could bring fish by wiggling it in the water. He called it his magic finger. Iia was dead, buried in the cemetery out behind the kitchen. In the painting the right hand of Christ cupped a radiant, floating heart, and the left, displaying its wound, pointed up through a yellow halo toward flypaper swatches hanging from the rafters. Some of the lighter colors in the painting were flourescent and the eyes glowed when the light moved away.

Rujen passed quietly through the warm sour air of his blockhouse, turning side to side with his light and gun, going slowly from the long room then carefully sideways through a bead curtain into the small room where his mother and most of the elder people slept. From there he took a long quick stride into his kitchen. His focus was broad, his eyes not blinking as they followed the course of the light, but the only life he found was a group of four German roaches who bumped into each other and then changed direction before scuttling out of sight. A trickle of water ran from a styrofoam cooler and channeled into fractures on the concrete kitchen floor, pooling under a burlap rice sack that hung from the roof by a black polypropylene rope. Behind it dead yellow termites were stuck by salt slime to a Plexiglas window that viewed a cemetery and Rujen's silhouette amid the blurred reflection of his light. He noticed a child's drawing of a shark smeared in the slime, its tail curved like a crescent moon around a length of duct tape that covered a crack.

Rujen wedged the barrel of his gun into his armpit so he could dry his sweaty palm on his briefs. He scratched at mosquito bites on his thigh. Somebody sneezed. A gecko chirped its alarm. After returning the gun to his hand he flung open the door to the toilet room, as was his custom most every morning, and sighted along the floor. He stayed crouched for one, two, three, four, five seconds, shining his light, but nothing moved. It had been two weeks since he shot the last rat, and although he liked not finding rats in the morning, he sometimes almost wished he did because shooting one seemed like good luck to start the day. It had to be the new poison being spread around the island, he thought as he sat on his concrete toilet. The rats were too smart for the traps, and the old poison killed only cats and dogs. After Rujen dumped a bucket of saltwater into his toilet, smelling as it did because it was connected straight to the iron main rusting to pieces just a couple feet below, he found a few moments later that sewage had bubbled up into his concrete kitchen sink. "Jesus Christ," he said, and then he wondered why he suddenly became—or suddenly remembered that he should be—angry with his son.

Going Fishing

NOT LONG AFTER Rujen Keju had clipped his Kwajalein Missile Range ID badge to the collar of his overalls, slung his boots over his shoulder, and left his home for the pier, his two sons, Jebro and Nuke, were up and headed in the same direction. Jebro carried a large gray duffel bag. Nuke had a small one-strap backpack. Each held a one-gallon jug of water. Around them, red morning light caught lingering smoke from the dump and the air seemed charmed with a magic pastel glow. Hinges squeaked. Water splashed. Bodies coughed and spat. Calico cats moved low and quick past helter-skelter cemeteries where snoozing mongrel dogs lay by concrete crosses that bore, in English, the names and dates of the dead.

The brothers walked unhurried, two among dozens spilling from shacks and blockhouses along nameless puddled alleys, passing on their way the one-room concrete jail, the Seventh Day Adventist missionary school, one-room scrap-wood bars and stores, the Kitco store, Hideo Milne's boat shop, the pink walls of the Islander Disco, and the quiet tin shack of the power plant that stank of oil and a damp dead fire. The brothers' path met the paths of others, most everyone converging toward the pier to meet the ferryboat, headed for work three miles up the east reef to the Army base on Kwajalein. The holiday, Good Friday, cut their numbers by a third, most of them men this morning since maids did not work on base on holidays. Dusty taxi cars and pickup trucks squeaked and rattled over the coral gravel roads in low gear, some of the vehicles reconstructed with plywood and two-by-fours where the salty winds had rusted parts of them away. A wave of the hand and a car would stop—twenty-five cents a ride.

From not too far away came the deep diesel drone of the ferryboat, the *Tarlang*. Jebro smiled at his yawning younger brother and handed him a slice of dried fish. "You better eat, Nuke," he said. "I need you strong today."

Jebro had been back to Ebeye only a week. For almost two years he had been helping the family of his mother's dead brother on Ailinglaplap, an island in an atoll of the same name lying two hundred miles to the south. Jebro helped them build a store on the side of their house, and it was he who suggested they buy and repair the broken, kerosene-powered freezer offered for sale by a trader on the *Micro Pilot* supply ship. Parts from the dump made for a free but less-than-perfect fix of the freezer's guts, and the cut-to-fit hull of a beach-washed dinghy was an awkward but efficient replacement for the rusted-through lid. Although the freezer made it the noisiest store on Ailinglaplap, it was also very successful for its size because it sold the cheapest fish—fish caught by Jebro and the children who followed him, mostly young nieces and nephews but their friends too. At seventy-five cents a pound, Jebro's fish were cheaper than paying a dollar and a half for six ounces of canned tuna which were sold by the other family stores, and cheaper than two to eight dollars a pound for frozen fish sold in the Robert Reimers chain store. Jebro's plan worked, and he liked giving people a good deal on fish, and when they came they often bought other merchandise such as corned beef or menthol cigarettes.

Jebro had returned to Ebeye because his father, Rujen, who was the highest Marshallese worker at the Kwajalein sewage plant, had talked his boss into giving Jebro the recently vacated, entry-level position of Waste Worker III. The job was forty-eight hours a week, paying American minimum wage, and he would start on Monday. Like his father and all Marshallese who worked there, Jebro would need to catch the *Tarlang* to Kwajalein in the morning and then back again before six in the evening (unless specifically authorized for overtime) or be fined for trespassing—a fine more than twice his daily pay. He would not be allowed in the American stores or restaurants, and he would be searched at a checkpoint before leaving. Not even a Pepsi bought from a machine was allowed on the boat back to Ebeye.

Jebro had wondered, when he went for his orientation on Wednesday, if a sign outside of one of the American clubs was a joke, a mistake, or a serious warning. It read, in Marshallese but not in English:

> NO MARSHALLESE ALLOWED ON THESE PREMISES. ANYBODY CAUGHT WILL FACE IMPRISONMENT AND WILL BE RUINED.

The sign had made Jebro angry and he wanted to do something about it, but he knew the money he could get from the job, a guaranteed check every two weeks, was better than any other opportunity around.

During his week back on Ebeye, Jebro had been repairing his father's boat, a fifteen-foot aluminum skiff with a twenty-five horsepower outboard. The hull had a few holes, but the seams were tight—some epoxy putty made it sound. The engine was frozen, but only from disuse. A little taking apart and putting back together, new oil and a new plug, and it was running well enough even though it smoked maybe more than it should. It was loud too, but Jebro could tell, having a feel for things, that the engine would not fail. On Thursday he put the boat in the water and moored it near the pier. He would take his brother turtle fishing—something Nuke had never done—and spend the weekend with him before starting work on Monday.

Ebeye's concrete pier was broken open in places on the top and the sides, exposing twisted rusting rebar and coral rubble used as fill. From where Jebro and Nuke approached, stepping around milky puddles, the pier listed just a little to the left, toward Kwajalein. In shallow oily water to the right, aluminum skiffs and about a dozen plywood power boats lay at anchor just outside a broken strand of sulfur-colored sand, the beach, which stretched in patches from the pier and past the round gray tanks of Mobil gas to the dump at the end of the island. Beyond the dump's smoldering mounds of trash the reef lay strewn with rusting twisted piles of cars and trucks and heavy machinery, some of it looking to be the remains of bulldozers and a crane, all of it blistered and fusing together in different shades of orange and black and casting long jagged shadows. Above the beach, weathered wooden slum shacks stood on stilts, and behind them, past the road, stood other shacks of wood and tin in different shapes and sizes. Power lines draped across, between, and down from wooden poles, connecting most all the stores and homes and bars and churches.

The *Tarlang*, an Army transport given two welded upper decks to accommodate its hundreds of passengers, throttled down and glided in for docking. Jebro watched Annie, a tan and muscular American woman, one of the *Tarlang*'s deck hands, climb over the rail and stand ready with a rope. Then he saw his father, who did not look happy, break from his place near the front of the boarding line and walk quickly toward him and Nuke.

Nuke nodded at something said to him by another boy and unslung his backpack. He dropped it next to the duffel bag at Jebro's feet then put his water jug beside it.

"You never told me you planned to camp on Tar-Wōj," Rujen said to Jebro. "You cannot. You know that."

Nuke left to join a group of boys who had begun throwing rocks from the end of the pier.

Jebro made eye contact with his father then looked down at his feet. "Tar-Wōj misses her family," he said.

"You won't trick me with that kind of talk, Jebro," Rujen said. "Swear to me, now, you'll stay away from Tar-Wōj."

Jebro winced as though he were in pain. "I swear I had a dream telling me to go." He grabbed his father's hand.

"You cannot!" Rujen said loudly, attracting the attention of several nearby people. "That's the law." He freed his hand and looked over his shoulder at the approaching *Tarlang*. "Stop this—just ask a landowner for permission to go to Loi, Ningi, some other island on this side of the reef. Maybe you and Nuke—"

"Nuke has never seen his home island," Jebro said. "Maybe that's more of a crime than a law."

Rujen's eyes moved from one to another of the people gathering around. He leaned forward and whispered, "I told you—" What he was about to say was interrupted when the *Tarlang* bumped against the pier and caused a tremor.

Jebro took his father's hand again, this time looking into his eyes. "My grandfather would tell me to go."

An old man cleared his throat. "He's right," he said, "Ataji would be going too." One of his eyes was mostly closed, drooling a thin white liquid.

"Let them go, Rujen," another old man said.

Jebro tightened his grip.

Rujen pulled back, but he could not free his hand. "My father was a troublemaker!" he nearly shouted. "He and Handel Dribo—always making trouble with the islands. You," he said to Jebro, "the helicopters will see you—you'll be reported for trespassing, and they'll never give you the job!" Rujen jerked his hand free and raised his palm to hush Jebro from speaking. "No! You cannot. That's my boat and—"

"Your boat?" a woman asked. "*Eguuuk!* What did you ever catch but rainwater with that boat?" She laughed loudly at her own joke, inciting others.

"It is your boat," Jebro said calmly, smiling, but raising his voice just a little. "So I'll just leave it here, find some other way to the island of my birth, where coconuts, pandanus, and breadfruits fall to the ground and rot because that is the Americans' law." Jebro whistled for Nuke, who was hiding something in his hand. "Get over here, Nuke. Now I have to swim you to Tar-Wōj on my back!"

"Enough, Jebro!" Rujen scolded.

Two young girls in floral dresses stood behind Rujen, both making funny angry faces. Jebro winked at them. "You're right," he said to his father. "Nuke and I can always stay here and catch Pampers from the pier, or, even better, we can race beer can boats in puddles on the reef, just like the rest of the children. I was champion once—remember?"

Rujen's lips moved as if words were stuck behind his teeth. He jerked around and faced the two giggling girls. They screamed and ran away, one pulling the other. He looked back at Jebro. "You were never such a troublemaker," he said, then he glanced at the crowd as if to see who was on his side. He shook his head. "I think you're risking too much, but if you think you can do it without getting caught, go ahead, go to Tar-Wōj."

The man with the rheumy eye assured Rujen that he had made the right decision. Another man said, "Jebro will use his magic finger to make the helicopters look away."

Jebro restrained a smile and looked seriously at his father. "Come with us. Somebody can tell the boss you got sick." People looked to Rujen. Rujen looked across the lagoon. Nuke came over and stood next to Jebro, pushing the duffel bag a little with his foot. He chewed gum and he smelled of cigarette smoke.

"No." Rujen said, fiddling with the ragged plastic at the edge of his badge, "I'm needed today . . . at the church. Today's Good Friday." He smiled at his sons, then gave Jebro a pat on the shoulder before joining the rear of the boarding line. "Monday," he said sternly without looking back, "you come with me."

Jebro elbowed out of his shirt and pushed it into Nuke's chest. He waved his arms and whistled to clear a path, then flexed his muscles in an exaggerated pose for Nuke's admiration before he ran, laughing, and dived off the pier. He broke the water fingers first and swam quickly, dolphin style, just above the dead coral bottom. A few moments later, in one strong movement, he shot out of the water and pulled himself over the stern of his father's boat.

Nuke hauled the gear to the bottom of some narrow concrete steps and waited, talking to some younger children above him while Jebro started the engine and brought the boat toward the pier. The bottom step was covered with a thick film of algae, skid marks on it where earlier people had slipped.

When Jebro bumped the boat to a stop, the children above Nuke jumped over him and bombed into the water on the other side of the boat.

Nuke laughed, almost slipping when he handed Jebro the gear.

"Sit to the left up front," Jebro ordered, pulling on his shirt. He checked to make sure that everything was in place, that the boat was balanced, that no children were near the path of the prop, then he told Nuke to push off from the bow.

As they cut a clean wake away from Ebeye, after waving good-bye to an unexpectedly large group of people watching, Jebro's eye caught a bright flash overhead that came from the east. He first thought it was one of the American missiles streaking toward the lagoon, but the burning glow and vapor trail looked different, erratic, prismatic, and seeing it brought on a strange sense of familiarity or kinship which at first, because it initially seemed dangerous, he tried to deny. It could only be a meteor, or something . . . but when it disappeared just after he got the attention of Nuke, who did not see it, Jebro thought it was best just to say, "Keep an eye out for birds," because the familiar feeling had become very strong, and it made him sure that the thing in the sky was not a meteor or a missile but a—he couldn't figure it out. The *Tarlang*'s horn bellowed three times, a final boarding call.

Another Dimension

ETAO REENTERS THE atmosphere at a burning speed and dives for the center of the lagoon. He nails the water and rockets to the bottom, tickling the kooch of a nurse shark before surfacing to hover, in the fading red glow of the morning, just above a small splashing chop. His body is lean, muscular, and deep dark brown, a body in perpetual youth. His hair is black, wavy soft and long, dripping water. A piece of turtle shell (the neck plate of an upper shell) hangs by sennit rope from his neck. Below white eyebrows, white as the forehead spot on the pejwak bird, blink his large almond-shaped eyes, deep like polished black stones, coldly revealing nothing but an alluring gleam like that in the eyes of a feral tom cat. His nostrils flare with each of his quick excited breaths, and his slick skin pulls tight over his round chin and brings up the buttons of his cheekbones as he grins—teeth flashing white as the foam of the sea.

Etao the troublemaker, the trickster hero, has been called home after sailing away a very long time ago. He surveys the atoll, his grandfather's creation, and looks toward the island of Tar-Wōj, where N̦oniep lives, the dwarf who speaks in dreams.

Then, with just a thought, Etao changes himself into a blue-spotted grouper and hovers still for a moment more before he drops nose-first into the lagoon, causing a single tear-shaped drop of water to fly up and fall back after him. He slurps down a little fish as he cuts around a coral head, somersaults, and then nudges two dolphins into the southern distance as he finds his bearings and swims without hurry for Tar-Wōj.

On Tar-Wōj N̗oniep dreams of demons who paddle from the west. They come to steal his soul. They serve Wūllep and his cohort, L̗ajibwinām̗ōn̗, whose hateful curses seep and reach from the invisible island of Ep like the fingers of a scummy slick, a sick streak—if it could be seen—staining the water as if from a thin green gruel leaking out from under a bloated corpse on the beach, spreading the disease of their evil, the curse of their infectious misery, the pollution and perversions with which they corrupt the nature of mortal living things.

N̗oniep, last of the little jungle people whose laughter once tickled the ears of Marshallese children and whose charms once seduced women who wandered the jungles alone, dreams of the legion of demons long since thick on Ebeye: Soul stealers, decay makers, child eaters, sickness spreaders, brain suckers, the foulest of all conjurable demons clinging to people and things like sea slugs sucking the reef, feverishly intent in the service of their masters on wringing death from life, on replacing everything pure and natural and pleasurable with stinking rot and ruin, a living death, life inside-out.

N̗oniep dreams of demons he has fought and destroyed, of how until now he has escaped their masters' detection. He dreams of a plan, a hope, a small and unrealistic chance of stopping what looms like a monstrous wave risen to a precarious height. N̗oniep the dwarf, the sorcerer, the healer, sleeps alone and dreams and knows his long, long life has reached its end. Now, as the treetops fill with the cries of birds who rise and fly away to feed at sea, his dreaming ends and he wakes, intentionally so, because he has little time before the demons come to steal his soul, less time before the coming of the two he has called by speaking in their dreams, Jebro and Etao.

N̗oniep rises within the frond-covered ribs of his pandanus tree home, pushes away a crab that creeps across his sleeping mat, then ties his long black hair into a topknot. He drinks from a coconut and eats a handful of mashed taro, then he walks a short distance to sit in front of an incredibly large breadfruit tree and begins chanting into it the rest of everything he knows.

The Value of a Seat

When Rujen found that his usual seat on the *Tarlang* had been taken by Caleb Aini, a construction laborer from Jaluit, he did nothing but stand nearby and stare at grains of sand embedded in the fresh gray deck paint. Many other seats were empty, even the aisle seat on Rujen's bench where in the middle sat his friend, Juda, a delivery man employed by Surfway, Kwajalein's grocery store. Juda, admired by some for his exceptionally long earlobes, played pipito with Caleb and two more of Rujen's friends, Jiem and Bottomly, whose wide rear ends covered most of the facing bench. They looked up at Rujen then back down at the game, none of them seeming to be aware of what Rujen saw as a discourtesy.

Rujen scratched his flip-flops across the sandpapery deck. Two dagger-shaped sun beams faded and brightened as they stabbed in rhythm with the gentle rolling of the boat, back and forth across his feet. He did not want to speak first.

The seating areas near the bow were relatively free of engine noise and fumes and that was reason enough for choosing to sit there, but Rujen's particular seat was also out of the glare of the rising sun, on the leeward side which meant no salt or spray on rough windy mornings, and being on the second deck it was also covered against rain. He could see the islands across the lagoon from his seat and watch birds diving at schools of fish. The hiss and slap of water meeting the steel hull often eased him into a short nap. He and his friends mostly played pipito only on the return trip.

Long ago it may have been a deliberate effort by Rujen and his friends to board early and be among the first at the bow, but over time it had simply become habit and Rujen could not think of any other time when he had found somebody in his seat. He had boarded late this morning, having lost his place in line to speak with Jebro, and although he knew there was no such thing as having rights to any particular seat, he was aware of where other people usually sat and it seemed proper to him that such arrangements be respected. It bothered Rujen that Juda and Jiem and Bottomly were not aware of the problem. They had accepted Caleb's company as if whoever sat in that seat was as interchangeable as a light bulb.

Rujen knew something about the man in his seat, about how Caleb's house had been a place where his American and Filipino coworkers could visit and drink with him and screw young Marshallese *kokan*—whores—who Caleb found for them. Not too long ago, Caleb had smacked his wife with a piece of wood after drinking too much. He was supposed to be different now after a weekend in jail, a missionary man who never drank or swore or hit his wife. Rujen looked down at him, trying to think of something clever but not too rude that would give him reason to sit elsewhere.

Juda slapped his hand on the bench and told Rujen to sit down and join the card game. "Listen to this story Caleb told about Marquez, that fat Guamanian he works for," Juda said, waving Rujen closer. "He fired his foreman—you know Mark who owns that big boat? So—it was Wednesday—Marquez tried testing the plumbing himself in the female apartments and he flooded it. Tell him, Caleb." But Caleb just smiled, so Juda finished the story. "Water was shooting up the shower drains and sinks, because Marquez thought he was supposed to put a hose down the vent on the roof. When those women came home screaming and yelling, Marquez kept backing up and he fell into a trench! Now he has to pay all of them money for new carpets and things, and he might even get fired by the big boss in Hawai'i."

"Tell Rujen about that big rubber cock you found in one of their rooms," Jiem said to Caleb.

Rujen tried, but he couldn't suppress a small laugh. He covered his mouth with his hand when he looked down at Caleb's badly shaven head. Stubby black hairs grew at different lengths there, and some small scabby sores were dusted white with powder, making Caleb's scalp look scorched and bomb-blasted like a scene from a black-and-white war movie.

Caleb smiled awkwardly, meeting Rujen's eyes for just a second. "I hear your boys are going camping," he said, his smile widening over a broken front tooth. "Charlemagne, my oldest, keeps telling me he wants to go sometime."

Rujen, ignoring Caleb, saw that his friends were oblivious to his problem. He felt sure they might never understand until they too found Calebs in their seats. Saying he needed to use the toilet, a lie, Rujen dropped his boots by the bench and walked away. He was still determined to regain his seat, but he feared that if he remained standing or took the aisle seat next to Juda, then he might say or do something rash, drawing attention, and make himself appear as the scoundrel instead of Caleb. Still fresh in his mind was his argument with Jebro and the crowd they had attracted. Jebro had once told him that a good way of solving a problem was to think about something else for a while. Rujen would try this and wait for a plan to come into his mind.

Vibrations from the engines ran like an electric charge up Rujen's legs as he wandered aft, and when he could go no farther and both his hands gripped the stern rail, his whole body shook and his lips went numb. He looked for his sons in the direction of Tar-Wōj, and he thought he saw the boat once, but it was hard to tell because of the swirling black exhaust rising from just above the stern's churning white waterline. The engines' thrumming noise and loud vibration became strangely comfortable, like not having to think, a feeling he knew might eat away an hour in just a moment if he let it.

Rujen could not see well through the smoke, and it stung his eyes each time it caught back-drafts and filled the deck with dancing black ghosts. Just for an instant he feared his heart was racing in time with the vibration, and the sudden fright made him release the rail as if it were hot. He moved quickly backward without looking, turned around, and climbed the stairs to a spot behind the pilothouse. From there he looked again across the lagoon for his sons.

His first thought upon not seeing the boat—it was not the best of boats—was that it had sunk and that he should tell the captain right away so that a rescue could be made. He peered into the rear window of the pilothouse. One of the crew, Annie, looked back at him and they stared blankly at each other for a moment. Then Rujen felt embarrassed, smiled, and looked away. He realized then that even if the boat had gone under, Jebro would know what to do. Rujen had never seen Jebro panic or lose his temper or even very often fail at anything he did, and if such traits were not so admirable, then Rujen might think there was something very unnatural about his son. He was frequently complimented about Jebro, and while he tried to take credit (they looked very alike in the face), he was not really sure how his son had become the young man that he was. He certainly resembled his grandfather, Ataji, as far as taking charge and deciding things, although Ataji had a bad temper and never seemed very happy unless he was causing trouble with the Americans—or the Japanese if one believed all the stories he told. Jebro's disposition was more like that of Iia's, his mother's, a quiet strength and a happiness so infectious that when the two of them were together, years ago, it was enough to cause even the most sour of people to smile.

Iia had been evacuated to Kwajalein atoll from Rongelap when she was nine, after her island accidentally received too much fallout from one of the atomic bomb tests at Bikini—the Bravo test. She was burned, and had some of the other trouble, but not nearly as bad as most because she had been sick that day and had remained inside her house. After their stay at Kwajalein, after the doctors said they had recovered, Iia could have moved on with the other Rongelap people who were relocated to Ejit at Majuro, but her mother, widowed, and two of her sisters stayed on at Kwajalein with the family of some clan members. She married Rujen eight years later despite the objections of his family. They had wanted him to marry another girl who had good land rights on the main island of Kwajalein, but Iia's sunny charm and optimism instilled in Rujen a happiness he was powerless to abandon.

Jebro was Rujen and Iia's first born and they had wanted more, a girl, but she had miscarried once before giving birth to Jebro, three times before Nuke, and then the one after. The miscarriages were things she scarcely spoke about—one day she would be pregnant and the next she would be gone, to stay at one of her sisters' homes for a while, and when she returned—it was understood. Rujen never asked much about what had happened, because he believed that in that unspoken language between man and wife she seemed to say she wanted it that way.

But there was no hiding from that last miscarriage before Nuke, no Rujen pretending for Rujen's sake, as if ignoring it made it so it never happened and would not happen again, because it did, because during a sudden sun shower in the afternoon Rujen had seen her on her knees digging in the corner of the cemetery out behind the kitchen, not so crowded then as it later became, and what had once been out of sight and spared from mind suddenly became very real, very present, and to have denied himself the pain of it in the past, to have let her bear it by herself, made him feel very much like a criminal. She had looked frightened. Something wrapped in rags lay beside her.

Beyond her, out over the ocean, was what looked like half of an upside-down rainbow. The long, windblown hairs of another rainstorm either in front or behind made the rainbow appear to be whirling. Rujen had looked back and forth between Iia and the rainbow tornado, wanting to shout for her to look, wanting to comfort her with its beauty and his company, but at the same time—knowing—having heard described what comes out of Rongelap women sometimes, he became a coward, ashamed at the thought of having to see the thing his wife was burying and to know that he had put it in her—of having her hate him for it.

He did go to her though, realizing that he could not keep staring and that he could not walk away, but as if she had sensed his hesitation she asked him, softly, to leave as soon as he put his hand upon her back. Iia finished her business while Rujen waited quietly a short distance away. He sat on a bucket, his back against a broken Japanese washing machine, looking from his wife's shoulders hunched over and working to the rainbow tornado slowly being swallowed by the rain. Iia never spoke about that day and did not mark or tend the grave. She stayed a while with the family of her eldest sister.

In time she regained her sunny personality—so strong was that part of her, so indestructible—and then there was Nuke, a perfect, beautiful baby, but a final miscarriage caused a hemorrhage and killed her when Nuke was three.

Rujen asked to be alone a bit with her that day and held her lifeless hand. He said that he was sorry. He had at first convinced himself that his seed was poison, but he knew, because every year the Brookhaven doctors came and took her to their ship to examine her and take her blood, and once they took a little piece of bone from her chest. The doctors never said, though, that Iia better not try having any babies; they said that Iia was one of the lucky ones, not like other radiated people they examined from Rongelap and Utirik and Ailinginae and Likiep and Rongerik, many of them with cancer and some taken to America never to come back—but Rujen knew, he had to, because of the way they said she was a lucky one every time every year the Brookhaven doctors came and took her to their ship.

He knew, but who was he going to confront and accuse, the U.S. Army, the Navy, the entire American country? He had heard the rumors that they did it on purpose, because they wanted to know what things their bombs could do, but Rujen never believed that and neither had Iia. How could he believe that? For the President and the Army and the Navy and all the leaders of America to think together to do something so awful on purpose to peaceful Christian people, while at the same time they fought the evil powers and gave the Marshallese so much and strived to fill the world with peace and good and freedom—all of them, thousands of them together, would have to be completely *wūdeakeak*, insane. It made no sense.

No, he could only blame himself, for nights when he had whispered how much he wanted one more child—because he knew, he had always known, and because he was too blind to have known any better. In the days following Iia's death he did not talk or eat or leave the house, and twice he had tied then untied a rope into a noose.

It was young Jebro, finally, who spoke to him and coaxed him out to join the wake. Rujen could not remember what Jebro had said to him, only that it was as if Iia's soul had been behind Jebro's eyes, almost teasing him for feeling so gloomy. They put a concrete cross atop the grave and painted it white, and filled two china bowls with multicolored shards of beach-washed glass. Rujen never remarried, never even wanted to.

He scanned the lagoon again, thinking, but not too worried, that not enough time had passed for his sons to be out of sight. Annie came out of the pilothouse, half of a glazed doughnut glazing her fingers and her lips. "Looking for another shooting star?" she asked. "I don't think ones like that come in pairs—too light now anyway."

"No," Rujen said, not sure what she was talking about. "My boys went fishing, but—it's okay—I was just looking . . . for my boat." He felt nervous, almost guilty for having to keep secret his sons' destination. He looked into Annie's light blue eyes, the color of shallow water over sand.

"See ya," she said, and passed him on her way down the stairs. She smelled strongly of deodorant.

Rujen gripped the banister and leaned over the stairs. He wanted to ask about the shooting star, but Annie walked away before he could think of how to frame the question. He heard laughing, and when he brought himself upright he saw the captain and two of his men grinning at him from behind the pilothouse window. Rujen turned away, feeling a little hot in the face as he scanned again where he thought his sons should be.

Tar-Wōj was too far to see, but Rujen knew exactly where it lay, and he knew the water played tricks, making you see things not really there, so he figured it must be true too that it could make you *not* see things, such as your two sons in a small boat, that really were right in front of you. He picked a point on the horizon, and he believed his sons to be somewhere near a line from himself to that point. He knew Jebro had also picked a point on the horizon, and he knew it would be true to Tar-Wōj. Jebro might now be showing Nuke how to memorize that point, and be telling him about such things as the whereabouts of octopus holes and secret fishing techniques and how to swim with sharks without being eaten, things Rujen's father had told Jebro and Rujen had not.

Rujen knew the horizon possessed a spot, a different spot for each place a boat might be coming from, that would lead a boat to Tar-Wōj, to where Ataji Keju had died five years before, while sitting in the shade of a breadfruit tree. Ataji had gone that last time, even though his heart had been giving him pains, as part of one of his many protest re-occupations. He had been protesting ever since he was removed from the island in 1965, when the Americans took most of the lagoon and several of the surrounding islands to be used as a bull's-eye for ballistic missile testing. Although Ataji had always taken the American money given to him each year for Tar-Wōj, he had never respected the American law that forbade him to go there, and he had always said that he would not die on Ebeye. He had been beaten once by police for trespassing on the base at Kwajalein and refusing to get inside the jail—one eye had always been red after that. Many years earlier, he had been shot twice by Japanese soldiers, leaving one circular scar high on his leg and one just above his backside over a bullet that was never removed. He had swum all the way across the lagoon with those wounds, so he claimed, escaping by night after refusing to work any longer at building airstrips, tunnels, and bunkers.

Rujen had always shown his father respect, even admired him, although sometimes he had considered him and his politics an embarrassment. One day, maybe a year before his father's death, upon expressing this embarrassment to his uncle, he learned that his father was sometimes embarrassed by him as well. They were two entirely different people. Often, this meant a relationship of silence, of avoiding eyes, of living together as if the other was not there. When Ataji had died—the news broadcast from Tar-Wōj by marine radio—Rujen knew better than to make arrangements for the body to be brought back to Ebeye. Because no missile shots were planned that week, and given the tropical climate, the Army did not interfere with a burial in the old family cemetery at Tar-Wōj. Marshallese custom was that clan and family members remain six days after a burial, whereupon the soul comes up from the ground, finds the sun rising in the east, and walks to the water to wash. At this moment the soul leaves the earth and a graveside wake is held in the dead person's honor. Of course, it was not a Christian practice, but some of the churches on Ebeye accepted it. Rujen had no problem with it, particularly with respect to his father who, unlike his mother, had never been a churchgoer, had never been baptized, and had never spoken of Christ as his lord and savior.

Rujen and his mother prayed, nonetheless, at the grave and asked God to forgive Ataji for these things, to accept him for being a good man who, despite his lawlessness and angry tirades, always shared what he had and cared for the well-being of his family, his clan, and those who came to him for help. Had he not been undevout, he might have passed for a very good Christian. They cleared the cemetery of some of the overgrowing vines and grasses, and placed a wooden cross at the head of Ataji's grave, his name and dates carved in deep and painted green (the only paint they had at the time). Although Rujen talked about coming back some day to place a better cross of concrete or cinder blocks, he never did.

Rujen looked along the imaginary line he had created from himself to the horizon, and knew Jebro to be in a boat near that line not only going after fish and maybe making some money from them, but also going after something to put inside himself and his brother, a thing Ataji had showed him of the old ways, something Rujen had never bothered to believe existed or even cared about if it did. It came to Rujen that if he or any other Marshallese on the *Tarlang* did not get paid, then they would have no reason to work, but that if Jebro did not catch fish, or made only enough money over many years to keep the boat from sinking, he would still find profit each day in practicing what Ataji had taught him. He wondered if his son, who would begin earning paychecks on Monday, would be able to endure the pull of two different ways of living, and if he could not, which would he choose—if he had any choice at all. It also came to Rujen that he now knew how to get Caleb Aini out of his seat.

When Annie returned to the pilothouse, Rujen stood waiting for her and handed her a five dollar bill. She must have thought him to be somewhat goofy, but she did take the money and agreed to do as he asked. The boat was nearing Kwajalein, but there was still enough time for Rujen to work his plan.

He found his friends and Caleb Aini still at their card game, and he laughed along when the usual jokes were made about a man returning from an exceptionally long trip to the bathroom. "Caleb," he said, "I was just talking to Annie, and she was looking for you. She wants to give you some money—I don't know why."

Caleb squinted, cocking his head to one side. "Ahhhhh—you lie! She—"

"I shit you not," Rujen said in English. "I swear by God she has some money for you."

"Go, Caleb," Juda said, "and then come tell us what happened before we get to Kwajalein."

"I think this is some kind of joke," Caleb said, but he got up and headed aft, twice looking back before he climbed the stairs.

Juda began scooting toward the bulkhead, but Rujen reached out and squeezed his shoulder. "That's *my* seat," he said, and stepped over Juda's legs. He sat down and closed his eyes, wanting a little rest before the boat docked at Kwajalein. He was a blink away from a light sleep when Caleb returned.

"She found this by the candy machine," Caleb said. He passed around the five dollar bill. Written in the margin, in English: *This money buys out Caleb Aini.*

The Beginning

In a white but lightless time even before time itself, but not long before N̦oniep the dwarf and Etao the troublemaker, there was only Ļowa, master of empty spaces. He created for himself a home, the sea, which was bordered on one side by an extensive low shelf, and on the other side by a swamp of thick, tangled mangroves. Ļowa called out, "Receive your fishes and your reefs!" and then amid the fishes many reefs grew out of the sea. He said, "Receive your sand and your soil!" and then islands appeared on the reefs. Ļowa said to the islands, "Receive your plants and your trees, your animals and your birds!" All this came to be. Ļowa then asked Keār, a white seabird, to fly up and spread out the sky, the stars, and then the sun, which she did just as a spider weaves her web between two bushes. At the four directions of the new world, Ļowa placed four potent spirits: Iroojrilik, Master West, spirit of fertility; Ļōkōm̧raan, the Daymaker Man of the east; Ļōrōk, Sir South, a handsome spirit of kindness, and keeper of Ewerōk, the invisible island to be the home of the souls of the dead; and Ļajibwinām̧ōn̄, Last in the North, a spirit of wickedness.

When he deemed his world hospitable, Ļowa came out of the sea and made himself comfortable on the invisible island of Ep. After refreshing himself with coconut milk, he hollered up to create the moon. He gave the moon two wives: One that fed him well, and one that encouraged him to fast. Ļowa then created the Rimakaiio, invisible sleeping giants whose steady breathing became the trade winds, and Kwōjenmeto, a demon of the sea, and Lino, spirit of the surf, and Kabinge, spirit of lightning and guardian of the thunder bird, Jourur. Ļowa thought of the people who should live in his world, and while he formed an idea of these people in his imagination, a tree grew up out of his head. When the idea was complete, the tree split his skull and out rolled two beings: Wūllep, who was as much a worm as he was a man, and his sister Limdunanij, a very attractive woman who was pregnant. When the tree took root in the soil and his skull regained its former shape, Ļowa said to his children, "Where there is kindness, there will be life."

"I don't understand," Wūllep said, curling around his father's feet. Ļowa patted his son's head.

Limdunanij wedged herself between Wūllep and Ļowa. She looked up at her father and asked, "What do you mean?"

Ļowa smiled at the confused faces of his children. He gently squeezed the shoulders of Limdunanij, who probed with both hands the bulge of her belly. "I will tell you a story," Ļowa said, "one about the nature of the soul, and then you will understand." He smoothed an area in the sand so that he could draw pictures to accompany his story. "Not long from now," he began, using his little finger to draw a navigational chart, "Iroojrilik, Master West, will have a daughter of marriageable age. He will inform his cousins, Ļōrōk of the south, Ļōkōm̧raan of the east, and Ļajibwinām̧ōn̄ of the north, and they will sail their canoes to Iroojrilik's island. Iroojrilik's daughter, Kiji, is to choose among them for her husband. Ļajibwinām̧ōn̄ arrives first, and, thinking it is a race, he runs up the beach shouting, 'I win! I win! I'm here to take Iroojrilik's daughter as my prize!'

"'You're mistaken, cousin,' says Iroojrilik, 'and in your rush you have neglected to bring a single gift. I don't think my daughter will want you at all.'

"Ļajibwinām̧ōn̄ goes to sulk in some bushes, and from there he watches his cousins arrive in their canoes. Ļōrōk is the last to pull his canoe up on the beach, because his is the heaviest with gifts of shell necklaces and poles full of bananas and pandanus and breadfruits. Ļōrōk is very handsome, and Kiji soon chooses him to be her husband. There is a feast, and Ļajibwinām̧ōņ pretends to accept his defeat honorably, but the next day, as Ļōrōk leads Kiji to his canoe, Ļajibwinām̧ōņ reaches out from his hiding place in the bushes and steals her soul. Kiji and Ļōrōk are unaware of the theft, and they sail away to Ļōrōk's island. Ļajibwinām̧ōņ goes to his own island, and once there he cannot help but play with his stolen possession, Kiji's soul, which is like a little fluid ball, jellylike like a jellyfish or a fish egg, and clear because her soul is pure. Ļajibwinām̧ōņ is not very careful, and he soon scratches the soul, causing it to leak. When Kiji dies years later on Ļōrōk's island, it is a double death because there is no soul to inhabit her ghost."

Ļowa looked up from his drawings in the sand and saw that his children were no longer listening. Limdunanij had moved to lay by some bushes, and she was giving birth. Wūllep, still below his father, stared at the wet hairy head of a baby pushing out from between his sister's legs. Ļowa thought it was best not to interfere, so he bid good-bye to his children and to all he had created, saying, "Yokwe, love to you," as he flew up into the sky. He looked back one last time, thought for a moment, then called down to his creations, "Things happen very quickly, so watch out!" He blinked and vanished, gone forever to continue his making of new worlds wherever there exists nothing but empty spaces.

Limdunanij gave birth to two sons, Ļanej and Ļewōj, and the three of them and Wūllep lived peaceably on Ep for a short time, but, as the two brothers grew older, they could not help but develop a dislike of their uncle. One day the four beings happened to be sitting on the stalks of arrowroot, when suddenly the plants grew incredibly fast and shot the four of them up into the sky. This new position offered vast powers to master, although Wūllep, who considered himself ruler of all, was lazy and did very little but sleep.

Ļanej and Ļewōj created three women and sent them down to populate the Earth with human beings. The oldest was Lijenenbwe, who they sent to live at Namu, and it was her gift to teach her sons the power of divination. The second was Lōktañūr, who they sent to live at Ailinglaplap, and it was her gift to teach her sons the power of navigation and how to be leaders of other men. The youngest was Limejokeded, whom they sent to live at Majuro, and it was her gift to teach her sons the power of deception.

Before long, the brothers plotted to kill their uncle so that they and their mother would be rulers among the stars. Wūllep overheard their plans, and, fearing an attack, he stared so hard at his nephews for such a long time that his eyes exploded and he fell back down to Earth. He landed on Imroj, an island of Jaluit atoll. The crash he made was loud enough to catch the attention of Iroojrilik, who set sail from his home in the west. He found Wūllep at Imroj and asked the worm-man what had happened.

Wūllep only moaned, complaining about his fall and loss of sight.

Iroojrilik built a hut and led Wūllep inside. "You can rest here," he said, "and then you will think of what to do." Iroojrilik stayed with Wūllep for three months and brought him food, then left after he began to dislike him. In those three months, a large painful boil grew bigger and bigger on Wūllep's side. When it broke, out came two little boys. One was older and his name was Jemāluut. The younger, a mischievous little boy who had eyebrows white like the forehead spot of the *pejwak* bird, was named Etao.

When Jemāluut and Etao had grown from little boys into young men, their father, Wūllep the worm-man, instructed them to find a witch named Lijepake who lived on the island of Bikar, and to get from her a magic piece of turtle shell and a magic drink. "These things," Wūllep said, "will give me what power I need to defeat my nephews and regain control in the sky. You, my sons, will do this for me and be rewarded as I see fit. Now go," he said, flicking his wormy tail in the direction they should sail, "and waste no time."

Etao did not object when his brother demanded leadership of the quest. He let Jemāluut sail the canoe and read the navigational signs and stars and currents that would lead them north to Bikar, and while Jemāluut did all the work, Etao rested, once in a while using the reflective surface of the water to practice smiles of seduction. The ocean was very rough in the north, and the single pass that led into the lagoon at Bikar was too full of giant waves to enter. "We can bring the canoe close to the ocean side of the island and tie to the bottom," Jemāluut said, "and from there we can swim through the breakers to get to the witch."

Etao clapped his hands. "And I was ready to give up, wise brother!" he said. "Your plan is brilliant, but don't you think I should stay with the canoe and bail water?"

"Good idea," Jemāluut said. "I was thinking the same thing," He sailed as close as he could to the island, to a spot where spray from the giant crashing breakers was so thick that it was hard to see from one end of the canoe to the other. The spray made it impossible to see the shoreline of the island. The sun too was hidden by the spray, and if not for the ocean swells springing the canoe high and low, then it would seem as though they were within a cloud in the sky. "Maybe I should rest first," Jemāluut said over the booming surf. "In a little while the water may be calmer."

"It may be rougher," Etao said. "Should I be the one to fetch the magic for our father?" He made as if to dive over the side of the canoe.

"No! I will go. Just keep the canoe from sinking."

Jemāluut dived while the canoe teetered at the peak of a swell. Etao cheered him on: "Stroke! Stroke! Keep your head above water!" But the breakers pounded Jemāluut against the coral, cutting him, and he had to swim back to the canoe.

"You almost made it!" Etao shouted, patting the knuckles of his brother's hands clinging tightly to the rail. "Just one more try and I am sure you will make it over the reef."

"Wait . . . res . . ." Jemāluut's knees knocked the bottom of the canoe with each rise and fall.

"The waves get bigger as we speak!" Etao said. "We must tell our father that we failed." Jemāluut looked into his brother's eyes then pushed off from the canoe and tried again for the island. This time, Etao had to dive in and drag him back. "I guess I'd better try now," Etao said, after helping Jemāluut into the canoe. "Name this reef after me if I never return!" Etao swam with steady strokes toward the island, and when the first breaker was just about on top of him, he dived down and grabbed the bottom. When the wave had passed, he rose for air and stroked, then dived again. Down and up, down and up, Etao made his way past the surge channels and over the reef until he could slosh and walk his way to the beach.

He could smell the foul odor of the witch right away, and it led him straight to the center of the island to where he could hear her raspy breathing coming from within her sleeping house, a square thing on posts with a loft and a pandanus thatch roof. The house was almost invisible within a tall thicket of brushwood. The dense tangle of branches overhead created an atmosphere of night, with dots of sunlight like stars winking through high and clicking wind-blown leaves. "Hey witch! Hey hey!" Etao shouted. "Come out and give me some magic!"

A pale woman not young or very old, tall and potbellied and her body covered with sores, dropped out the loft and shook a stumpy finger at Etao. There was blood around her mouth, maggots too, but she had perfect teeth. Her eyes were bright but wholly black, and the heavy curls hanging from her head seemed covered with fish slime. "Who's this?" the witch demanded. "Why don't you know of no coming here?—no coming back and forth, no coming, no leaving!—but you—tell me how you got here!"

The witch stepped so close to Etao that he could feel her rotten cold breath on his forehead, but his eyes remained fixed on her firm and freshly oiled breasts, breasts ripe enough for giving milk. He smiled up at her, his practiced smile of seduction, not wanting to show the least discomfort. He knew the witch could kill him in an instant. "We came to get a magic drink and a magic piece of shell for our father."

"Who is *we*?" The witch glanced around Etao. "Who is the father, huh? Say his name who knew to send you here. And name your mother too. That is what I want to know!" The witch sniffed at the top of Etao's head and probed his ear with a fingernail.

"I have no mother," Etao said, keeping his head still, "nor does my older brother who waits for me in the mist behind the breakers. We came from a boil on the side of our father, Wūllep, who is blind and fell from the sky. He sent us here for the magic."

"Hmmmm . . ." the witch moaned, seemingly interested in something she found in Etao's ear. "But why does your brother stay in the canoe, huh? That is what I want to know."

"He is tired from trying to swim, from getting beaten by the waves. Now give me the magic so I can go before he sinks our canoe." Etao kept the smile on his face.

"I think your brother is pretending. I think he detests me and that is why he waits in the canoe. Or are you tricking him, keeping him from the island? That is what I want to know!" The witch spat blood into the dirt, studied Etao's face for a while, then grinned. "You think I don't know your mind? You detest me too, smiling just to fool me. Yes?"

Etao tried to look hurt. "I smile only because I want to think of you as the mother I never had!"

"Ayyyyyyyaa!" the witch howled, then roughly rubbed Etao's cheek. "You are the kind I like, one whose soul is murky like mine. Wait here. I'll get the magic you need." The witch took long strides into her cookhouse, and when she returned she held in her hands a neck plate from the upper shell of a turtle and some rotten pandanus cones. Etao held out his hands.

"Wait!" the witch shrieked, causing maggots to fall like lost teeth from her mouth. "Do you know the power of this magic?

Maybe you are tempted to have it for yourself, to have power over your father and brother, over other people as you wish? Hmmmm?"

"My father is a worm. I never once thought of bringing him this magic. Now give it to me!"

The witch laughed so hard that the sores on her body began to bleed thick black blood. "I knew it all the time!" she shrieked. "You did well keeping your secrets to play this trick on your father and brother." She held out the cones. "First, here is the drink. Suck the juice from these pandanus cones I prepared for you."

Etao took the cones. They were covered with maggots, thick with slime like that found on the scales of barracudas. The witch looked down at him, motioning for him to put the cones in his mouth. Etao suspected he may be the victim of a trick, so he hesitated for a moment, but then he held his nose and closed his eyes and sucked the cones dry while he thought of nothing but the sweetest bananas he ever ate. He felt stray maggots wiggling in his mouth, and he bit them before he swallowed. He felt no different, no power, only an increasing sickness that made him drop to his knees. "You tricked me!" he shouted.

"Tricked me! Tricked me!" the witch echoed. "Aaaghh, you should have known that such powerful magic can kill! Maybe you die, hmmmm, maybe not. Here," she said, tossing him the piece of turtle shell, "wear this around your neck and see what happens next—or let me watch you, my only son—Ayyyyyaa!—lay there and die."

Etao took the shell and did as he was told. At once he was blind, dizzy, hearing nothing but the witch's laughter whirling around in his head, and then he was forgetting himself, losing his senses—so much confusion, like the mix of too many colors turning black. He tried to reach out but he could not move and he could not shout and at times he felt as though his body had been stretched and snapped and divided into countless pieces, but then, like shooting a canoe out of the cold shadow of a trough into sunlight, Etao found himself lying, alert and very alive but trembling from the lingering cold, on a mat inside the witch's cookhouse. Across from him, looking at him, was a hawksbill turtle, about medium sized with its head raised high and its top shell clean of algae and polished to a wet-looking shine. Its beak looked as though it were filed to an unnatural sharpness, and within it crawled maggots. Etao knew it was the witch.

"When you and your brother wander on and become hungry," the turtle said solemnly in a watery voice, blinking large green eyes, "and you see an island, say: 'When we get there, food will be ready for us.' Name what food you wish and that is what you'll find on the beach waiting for you. When you are thirsty do the same. When you want to swim, think of whatever fish you like. That is what you will become. You have more power than I tell you now, enough power to—I will not say! But if you remove that shell, then you lose everything and will likely die. Go now, selfish one, before I decide that I gave you too much." The witch used a flipper to throw dirt into Etao's eyes, and when he rubbed them clear he found himself sitting on the beach where he had arrived on the island. He rinsed his mouth with some sea water, spitting out foul bits of pandanus cone that had got stuck in his teeth, then he smiled out at the world, laughing a little as he fingered the piece of turtle shell hanging from his neck. He let the sun warm his skin, and when his mind had eased from the encounter with the witch, and he could feel power streaming through his body and his mind, he shouted into the sky, "I am Etao, the best of the best, and I will never die! Now I will have some fun!"

The Frigate Bird

JEBRO AND NUKE SPED northwest, the hull of their father's boat slapping fast through the calm water, the engine droning, almost whining, leaving a bubbling wake to gently wash toward small jungled islands dimly visible to starboard. Black terns flew low and fast, some alone and others in tight groups. A flying fish shot out of the water and crossed the bow. The red sun lost its fire and became a pale blur low over the Pacific, sometimes revealing a bright point of light from behind fractures in a rising wide dark bank of clouds. Below the distant clouds, scattered flashes of white on the ocean foretold a coming wind. Above, the clear sky showed increasing blue, and to the west, low across the leaden surface of the lagoon, a few stars still shone against the purple ending night.

Jebro whistled to get Nuke's attention. "Rain today," he said.

Nuke nodded, looking east at the clouds massing there. "Should we still try for Tar-Wōj?"

"I don't think it will get too rough—why, are you scared?"

"Ōrrōr!" Nuke shouted, rolling his *Rs* to utter the Marshallese exclamation of disgust. "Nothing scares me."

Jebro grabbed two warm Pepsis from his duffel bag. "I'm proud to have such a brave little brother," he said, tossing Nuke one of the cans. "Bravery is half of what a young man needs in life."

Nuke, smiling a little, studied Jebro's face for a moment. "What is the other half?" he asked.

"A fear of your older brother." Jebro ducked as Nuke opened his can and sprayed him with Pepsi. "Ōrrōr!" he shouted, and turned the boat sharply so that Nuke slid hard into the side and nearly dropped his can. Jebro held up his own can as if it were a weapon, then lowered it when Nuke began drinking the rest of his.

The misty blow from a dolphin caught Jebro's attention as he splashed himself clean with water, and when he looked closer he saw two of them. "They must be sick," he said, pointing. "I heard that's why they come inside the lagoon, to get well someplace safe from sharks, or they might be coming to die."

Nuke mumbled something then looked at the sky. He burped and tossed his crushed can over the side. "What about the helicopters?" he asked after a while. "What if they see us?"

"Tar-Wōj is where I was born," Jebro said, flexing his chest. "It is our rightful land from the line of our great-grandmother. We will defend it. If the Army tries to make us leave, then we dig bunkers and attack them and shoot down their helicopters with our slingshots until they accept defeat."

Nuke laughed. "They have guns and missiles."

"We know kung fu." Jebro raised a death claw and high-kicked his foot at Nuke. "Owaaaa!"

Jebro had his eyes on the dying light of a star he knew lay over Tar-Wōj at this time of year. Very soon the star would be gone, but when the bow was straight on, he looked back, as his grandfather had shown him how to do, and saw that his stern was in line with two light poles at opposite sides of Ebeye's southern end. The less space he kept between the poles, the truer his course. When the poles became too distant to see, then the gray-green bump of an island two away from Tar-Wōj would soon come into view and he would navigate off that. It was impossible to get lost, being inside a lagoon, but he would save time and fuel by being precise.

The last time he had been to Tar-Wōj, not long before leaving to live on Ailinglaplap two years earlier, he had gone alone in a small wooden boat, fifteen horsepower. It was owned by an old man who had fished with it until his eyes caked over gray and he could no longer see. The old man claimed he could still navigate just by feeling the movement of water under the boat, but his family was careful not to let him try. Jebro had gone that day, against the law, without his father knowing, out of respect to tend Ataji's grave. It had been three years since the wake—he was thirteen when Ataji died—three years since his father had scolded him on the sixth day of the wake for refusing to get in the boat to leave. With so many people on Tar-Wōj, living good and fishing and catching birds for six days, the Army trying nothing to get them off because they must be afraid of Ataji's ghost—Jebro thought, why leave and go back to Ebeye? "The shit island," that was the name Ataji had for Ebeye. But on the sixth day, after small white stones were leveled over the grave, when all the others got in boats and left, Jebro finally did obey his father. He did not want to be left alone.

When he returned, three years later and not too worried anymore about being there alone, feeling as though he should have come sooner, he found the wooden cross tipped over and hidden under vines, the bottom of it and some of the back having rotted out. Just a few chips of green paint remained inside the carved lettering. The white rocks and pebbles once covering the grave were scattered. He set the rotting cross back upright within a pile of some of the rocks and sat beside it, unsure of whether or not he should recite a prayer.

Jebro had graduated from the Queen of Peace Catholic School, eighth grade, as far as any boy on Ebeye was allowed to go. He had taken his communion and all that, but he never really understood much about it and especially had trouble sitting through a mass in church. He tried to listen, but in the end the words meant nothing to him. He stopped going after he left school, and although his father said he would learn in time and come back, Jebro did not think so. Ataji had never gone to church. Neither did lots of people and they did not lose themselves to Satan, not most of them anyway as far as Jebro could tell.

While he had sat on the ground by the cross and thought of what to say, he saw, soaring motionless high above the island, a frigate bird, an *ak*, and it made him smile because it reminded him of his grandfather. Ataji had said that you could take a young frigate bird and make a home for it in a tree by your house, and as long as you fed it well it would stay there and grow big and fly around the tree and never leave. That bird would be happy because it knew no other life, but if you caught an older frigate bird and you wanted it to stay you would have to tie its leg to the tree. Even if you gave it all the food it wanted, as soon as you untied the line that bird would be in the air and gone before you knew what happened. Ataji had joked that he was that kind of frigate bird, so old and for so long used to going where he wished, that if the Army wanted to keep him on Ebeye they would have to tie him to a tree.

Now, a little more than two years later and in his father's boat, heading back to Tar-Wōj, Jebro hoped to see a frigate bird again, to tell his brother: *See, there is your grandfather, and nobody tells him where to go.*

Nuke lay his head on his backpack and stretched out his legs. Jebro would let him sleep, even though he had looked forward to talking with him along the way. He remembered himself doing the same thing, sleeping on the few trips to Tar-Wōj he had taken with his grandfather. He had fallen asleep listening to Ataji speak of patterns of clouds and waves and stories of the old days, and when he woke, Ataji would still be talking. Jebro did not remember much and wished now that he had stayed awake. He liked to think that whatever his grandfather had said had somehow found a way inside of him.

Jebro rummaged through his duffel bag and pulled out a three hundred test nylon handline wrapped around an H-shaped piece of plywood. Guessing that pink and white would be good colors this morning, he chose a small feather lure from a bunch that were stuck by their hooks to a styrofoam block. He fastened the lure's monofilament leader to a pigtailed swivel at the end of the handline, let it out about twenty yards, and slowed the boat until the lure was running through the water at a natural speed. The trip would take longer if he trolled, but he would save gas. It cost almost thirty dollars to fill the two six-gallon cans, and he had to buy six dollars worth of oil too—all the money he had saved from his work on Ailinglaplap. If he and Nuke didn't catch a couple of good-sized turtles on Tar-Wōj—one of them, as was the custom, had to be given to Kabua, the *Iroojlaplap*, Paramount Chief—he would be penniless until his got his first paycheck.

He began pulling a little on the lure to make it skip every once in a while, hoping to get a mackerel or maybe a rainbow runner, but he liked knowing that anything could happen. Once, when he was about Nuke's age, he and his grandfather had hooked a rare sailfish inside the lagoon. It broke their light tackle right away, but it was almost worth losing the lure just to see that kind of fish jump full out of the water.

There were many good ways to fish, but to make money, Jebro knew going after tuna was the best. To do so you needed a boat big enough and fast enough to chase the schools through treacherous ocean swells and wind-whipped water, and you needed a huge cooler full of ice so that you could remain out all day. Once in a while a man would try to build a boat like this, but if it was not his plywood hull unable to withstand the constant pounding, or a bad design causing him to capsize, it was always trouble with the engines or their hardware. He might wait months for a new part, if he could afford it, and in that time something else always rotted or rusted or seized or got "borrowed." Somebody might offer to sneak something over from Kwajalein, but a boatman could not count on that too often, especially now with the searches being so thorough at the checkpoint. Even if he found parts, not too many people knew very much about fixing things. Jebro knew of a man once who had put together a boat so poorly that the stern snapped off when he mounted the engines. Those who did own decent boats, knowing the risks and expense of trying for fish, more often used them as water taxis, taking people between Ebeye and Kwajalein for one dollar a head. It was an embarrassment to Jebro—who did not doubt his elders when they spoke of Marshallese being at one time the greatest fishermen and navigators in the world—that Ebeye had many more broken boats rotting on land than good ones floating in its waters, and that most of the fishing done by Marshallese these days was done by children with cheap Japanese monofilament wrapped around dented beer cans. A few men owned surround nets to use on the reef, but with most of the atoll off-limits, all the available good places fished out quickly.

The price of gas made even the most trouble-free boats cost too much to operate, and Jebro had wondered once if a man might be able to chase tuna in something like one of the old Marshallese sailing canoes. It seemed impossible, since the schools changed direction so suddenly, but he knew that men in the past had managed somehow. As he backed down a little more on the throttle, having neared a small pile of diving birds, Jebro thought that such a canoe would be ideal for a weekend trip to Tar-Wōj. Maybe someday he would build one and learn to sail.

The boat passed just beside the diving birds, but Jebro didn't get a bite from any of the mackerel that darted around just under the surface. The birds rose as suddenly as the baitfish dived, squawking loudly as they all shot north in pursuit, leaving the water littered with feathers and tufts of dander and dotted white with their droppings. Jebro studied their flight for a moment, knowing the mackerel would soon get ahead of the baitfish, surround them so that they formed tight balls, then strike the balls as they drove them up to the surface where at once the birds would renew their assault. With a slow boat the trick was not to follow right behind the birds, but to anticipate where they were headed, where the baitfish would rise. Sometimes you might get a clue that would tell you which way to go, but most of the time you just had to guess.

Jebro's guess was wrong, but the school was moving slow enough so that he caught up and made a decent pass. When he felt the nylon line jerk tight around his fingers, sending a twitching vibration up his arm, he turned the boat sideways to the fish and cut the throttle. Nuke opened his eyes, looked once at Jebro, then followed the line into the water. The fish was small, maybe one pound, and it skipped twice on the surface before Jebro flipped it into the boat at Nuke's feet. Its tail flapped frantically for a moment, then the fish lay still, its gills opening and closing as if it were out of breath. The dappled distress pattern on its silver flesh grew darker and more distinct.

"Gut it," Jebro said and began rewrapping the handline. Nuke pushed at the fish with his toe. He looked as though he wanted to go back to sleep, but after yawning he held the fish upside-down in his hand and removed the hook. When he had the fish gutted and beheaded and back in the boat, Jebro had him cut the meat into good-sized chunks for dipping into a tub of soy and pepper sauce he had brought. He wanted to set the lure again, but because of the power outage on Ebeye, he had no ice to keep the fish fresh long enough to cook later that day.

His star having long ago faded from sight, Jebro looked back to Ebeye for a bearing then got the boat headed again for Tar-Wōj. When he stared at the spot where the star had been, he suddenly remembered the shooting star he had seen earlier and the strange feeling it had given him. The memory seemed old, as if it had happened many years ago, and the more he thought about it, the more it seemed that he had seen nothing at all. His mind soon wandered onto other things, such as the approaching storm and the cigarette now burning between his little brother's lips.

Having Fun

THE SURF CRASHED NO less heavily on the reef, and Etao could not see Jemāluut waiting outside with the canoe. The position of the sun showed that not much time had passed during his encounter with the witch, so he did not hurry. When he was waist deep in the water, he brought to mind the witch's words, and when at that same moment he created the mental image of a parrot fish, he found himself, his fishy self, swimming over the reef as if nothing were more natural. He passed easily under the breakers, riding the undertow, darting now and then to chase smaller fish and to nip at their tail fins, stopping once to nibble at some coral polyps, and when he could see the bottom of the canoe, its outrigger smacking the surface, Etao thought: *pako*, and he elongated into a tiger shark. He passed the canoe with an eye out of the water and saw Jemāluut sleeping. For a joke he butted his head on the hull, waking his brother, then he circled threateningly while splashing water into the canoe with his tail. Jemāluut tried to scare him away with shouts and paddle slaps, but when Etao would not leave and had taken a small bite out of the bow, Jemāluut cut the anchor line and raised the sail to escape.

Etao changed back into himself and grabbed the back of the canoe. "Hey brother!" he shouted, poking his finger into Jemāluut's back. "Are you leaving without me?" This startled Jemāluut so much that he fell into the water. Etao pulled himself into the canoe, and since it was already under sail, it was leaving Jemāluut behind. "Hurry, brother! I see a tiger shark! Hurry hurry, it's right behind you!" Etao slacked the sail and waited for his frantic brother, who, once in the canoe, chattered and shook and would not speak until they were far from Bikar.

When Jemāluut finally questioned him about his trip to the island, Etao began changing parts of himself, just for an instant at a time, into something else. His head became a sea urchin, then flashed back to normal. His hand a hermit crab. His legs into bolts of lightning. Jemāluut would rub his eyes, and squint, but Etao kept a straight face while telling him that he had found no witch on Bikar, no magic, nothing but coconut crabs and a pool of sour water. Then, for a full count of six, Etao changed into the tiger shark and snapped his jaws. Jemāluut screamed, backpedaling with his feet so fast that he slipped and hit his head on a cross beam. When Etao changed back to normal, laughing so hard that he cried, Jemāluut yelled, "It was you, you liar, you sorcerer!" He pointed to the shell hanging from Etao's neck. "You took the magic for yourself, robbing our father—give it to me!" Jemāluut lunged at the shell, but as though it were too heavy, he could not lift it from Etao's neck.

Etao, still laughing, ducked to the other side of the sail and tried to tell his brother how they were better off abandoning their father, saying: "We were born with no toes on our heels!" To help his brother understand that they were better off exploring new places and playing with the magic, Etao said, "The smartest eels have many holes. Life is best when anything can happen!" But Jemāluut would not listen and, giving up his pursuit of the shell, he moved to the far side of the canoe and would not open his eyes except to look out at the water.

Etao studied the wind and the current versus the direction and width of the swell, and the ripples on the water, knowing the ways uniform ocean swells and currents are shaped and reflected and bent by islands in subtle ways to reveal their location. He took note of the distance of traveling birds—not the fishing ones—from the sea and the number of white ones compared to the number of black, and from all this and a number of other signs, he created in his mind a perfect picture of the sea and set his course for Utirik, where he would further test the power of his magic.

At the first sight of Utirik, Etao called out, "When we arrive there will be a bunch of the sweetest bananas ready for us on the beach!" Just as he predicted, they found a wonderful bunch of bananas. "See," he said to Jemāluut, "We can never again be hungry."

"But this food is from your sorcery," Jemāluut said after carefully biting one of the bananas. "How can I be sure they won't become rocks in my stomach?"

"Those who sail toy canoes close to the lagoon beach have no worries," Etao said, "and little of anything else." Only because his brother had feared it, Etao turned into stone one of the bananas Jemāluut had eaten, and, howling with laughter, he poked and prodded and tickled him until he was laughing almost as hard, but not as happily, and vomited it up.

After filling his stomach, Etao set a course by the stars for the island of Lodo at Likiep atoll, and when the next morning he and his brother could see the island rise up from the horizon, Jemāluut shouted, "When we arrive there will be two clam shells full of cool drinking water!"

"I don't think magic is contagious," Etao said, "but we'll see."

Jemāluut kept a hopeful look on his face until they were at the beach, then he frowned when he saw no shells full of water. "Maybe they sit a bit farther inland," he said.

Etao called out, "I want two giant clam shells full of coconut toddy!" The two shells, just as he ordered, appeared in the shade not far from the canoe. Etao ran cheering and dunked his head inside one and sucked up enough toddy to become very drunk. "We can sail again tomorrow," he said. "I want to explore this island now, see what can happen here."

Jemāluut agreed that it was good to spend a night on land, but he didn't want to join Etao exploring. "I need to rest," he said, "and to think about how to live with a sorcerer brother. Only yesterday I was the eldest son of a powerful father. Now I can never go home, and I'm nothing but the victim of magic jokes."

Etao changed his brother into a crab. "Maybe you'll want to dig a hiding hole while I'm gone." He took a final slurp of toddy, and as he began down the beach, he called back, "You'll return to being yourself as soon as you have one happy thought." Jemāluut's little pincer thrust a pebble in Etao's direction.

A short way past a bend, at a corner spot on the lagoon side of the island, downstream of the trade winds coming from the ocean, Etao found a line of five men fishing with poles for mullet. The toddy had made Etao hungry, and since pole fishing was one of his greatest joys, he asked the first man he came to if he could borrow his pole to catch a fish.

"Get your own pole!" the man said and gave Etao a push.

Etao, drunk, fell on his butt. "I swear as soon as you get a bite you will change into a rock!" He went from the next man and then to the next, and each time he was told to go away. "All of you will turn to rocks at the first bite!" At his words, all five men got bites and immediately turned to stone.

Etao went further up the beach and asked a young boy for his pole. The boy agreed, saying, "Here, maybe you can show me how. Nobody else will."

Etao removed the strand of seaweed the boy had been using for bait and rebaited the line with the rear of a hermit crab. When he had caught a few mullet, Etao told the boy to fetch some wood to make a cooking fire.

"What is wood for making fire?" the boy asked.

Etao realized that people didn't know yet about making fire. "Bring dry wood and I'll show you," he said.

When the boy had gone into the jungle and come back out with the wood, Etao taught him the trick of twirling a stick to make fire. The boy was so fascinated with the fire that after they had cooked and eaten the fish, he demanded that it belonged to him and insisted on taking it home. "How do I carry it?" he asked. "It hurts my hands."

Etao tossed him half a coconut husk. "Scoop a little of it in here," he said.

Not long after the boy had left, Etao heard a woman screaming: "My house! My house! Who is this red demon eating my house!"

Etao ran inland and found a small village, its people staring in horror at the screaming woman and her burning house. Other huts quickly caught fire from windblown embers, and the people, having no experience with fire, ran in circles around the burning houses and stabbed at the flames with spears and tried to scare them away. One man with two spears charged into his house, and then he ran back out howling because his hair had caught fire. His neighbors chased him around and beat his head with sticks, and not until the man had fallen from the beating did the fire go out, leaving his head bald and smoking. Etao had never seen anything so funny, and when he could speak between his fits of laughing, he shouted, "Your houses are old and dry and need replacing! Let them burn, and get out of the way!" But the people, wailing about sentimental attachments to their old houses, could not see the logic in Etao's words and cursed him when they learned from the boy where the fire had come from.

"Kill the demon-bringer!"

The people charged at Etao, and because he loved a good game of chase, he turned and ran back toward the canoe. "Push out!" he shouted ahead to his brother. "Set the sail and get paddling too!" But Jemāluut was still a crab, bouncing up and down with his pincers in the air and his eyes wide on the rumbling running mob. "Think about not getting stepped on!" Etao shouted. "That is your one happy thought!" Jemāluut changed back with just enough time for the two of them to escape the island—donk donk donk—just as three spears bounced off the canoe. Etao sailed away laughing.

Etao and Jemāluut sailed from Lodo at Likiep to the island of Taroa at Maloelap atoll. When they found a group of women there, alone plaiting mats, Etao suggested to his brother that they could seduce them. Etao then made a small fire, and he told the women how it was good for cooking food and for keeping warm on rainy nights, and he warned them against touching it, saying, "Watch out, it bites!" While the women stared fixedly into the flames and made sleepy, dreamy remarks about its beauty, Etao and Jemāluut jumped behind them and got busy. Afterwards, the women said they were ashamed that they had been seduced so easily, by trickery, and ran away to their village—but not before filling their plaiting baskets with coals from the fire.

Shortly after their encounter with the women, Etao and his brother found themselves in the path of men carrying palm logs across their shoulders. "Hey!" one of the men shouted, "You scroungy tramps better get out of our way!" He and his companions pushed and bumped Etao and Jemāluut into some bushes.

Etao shouted after them, "You'll never get those logs off your shoulders!" Just as Etao said this, smoke was seen rising from not too far away.

"Look!" said one of the log men. "Something is happening at our village!" They took off running.

"Let's watch!" Etao said, and pulled his brother along. When they got to the village they saw all the houses on fire, and the men were twisting this way and that trying to get the logs off their shoulders, but all they could do was fall, one by one, and watch their women run screaming around the houses. Other men came running and when Etao and Jemāluut were identified as the culprits responsible for everything wrong, it was time for the brothers to run.

"Kill them!" the men shouted, but the brothers were quick and were off the island before their chasers could catch them.

Etao let out a whoop, then proudly said, "Now the people of Maloelap as well as Likiep want us dead!"

When the brothers later arrived at Majuro, after making themselves unwelcome at several other atolls, Jemāluut saw a beautiful woman there, the daughter of a chief, and instantly fell in love. "Work me some magic," he said to Etao. "I'm tired of running around these islands and being chased around these islands, and I want this woman to fall in love with me so I can join her family and stay here in Majuro."

Etao shook his head. "Love magic is something different," he said. "You must do it yourself or what good is it? If you want her for just once or twice, maybe then I'll help you." But Jemāluut insisted that Etao help him gain love, and so Etao finally agreed. "What do you think she believes is more attractive," Etao asked, "a dolphin or a turtle?"

"A dolphin, I'm sure!" Jemāluut answered.

"Okay, then here is the plan: I'll change you into a dolphin and myself into a turtle. We'll swim by this woman—you leaping and twirling over me—and when we see her applaud the show, then I'll change you back and I think she will love you."

"Do it!" Jemāluut demanded. "I know for a fact that she's on the beach right now!"

Etao did the transformation, and he and his brother made their way along the shore. When they got near the woman, Jemāluut began his leaping and twirling, but, instead of applauding, the woman jumped up and down and pointed her finger and shouted for men to come quickly with their spears. "Throw! Throw!" she screamed. "I want that dolphin for a feast!" Men ran out of the jungle and into the shallows and launched their spears, and while those that hit Etao bounced off his hard shell, Jemāluut was struck several times and lost his ability to swim straight. His blood began clouding the water.

Etao changed Jemāluut back before any more spears could be thrown. At once the woman screamed, and called for the men to rescue Jemāluut. When they had dragged him up the beach, she cradled his bleeding body in her lap and pressed cloth into his wounds. "I'm so sorry, so sorry to have brought this on you," she cried.

"You're a terrible brother!" Jemāluut shouted out to Etao, who was still a turtle. "I couldn't hate anybody more!"

"I think you will live," Etao called back, "and since you got what you wanted, you should be thanking me instead!" Etao did not want to hear his brother anymore. "Keep the canoe," he shouted, then dived and swam quickly out of the pass and into the ocean.

Etao tried swimming as a shark and as a marlin and even as a whale, but he soon decided that there was no better way to go than by sailing a canoe. He found one he liked at Mili, and tricked the chief into trading for one made of *kōn̄e*, a beautiful wood that will not float but shines dark like a deep swamp when polished. When the chief got inside the *kōn̄e* canoe, which Etao had set in shallow water on top of a coral head, he raised the sail, moved forward just a little and right away started sinking. The chief's hands snatched at the air as he cursed Etao, and then his voice gurgled for just a moment when his head went quickly under as if his toes had refused to release the canoe. By the time he bobbed back up, Etao was sailing away fast in the chief's canoe, shouting, "You should learn to see with more than just your eyes!"

Tacking northwest, Etao sailed to the island of Tar-Wōj at Kwajalein atoll and lived for a time within a hidden village of magical dwarfs. The dwarfs were very handsome, having very long earlobes and fine tattooing, and, as did their kin at other atolls, they had the ability to make themselves invisible to humans. They often shared fishing secrets by speaking to the people in dreams, and sometimes, if a woman was exceptionally beautiful, one of the dwarfs might appear to her and seduce her, always presenting her with perfumes and foods and mats finer than anything made anywhere by ordinary mortals. If a human child was unusually gifted, the mother would be suspected of having spent too much time alone in the jungle.

One day Etao invited one of the younger dwarfs, his friend Ņoniep, to play a game of hide-and-seek. "I should hide first," Etao said.

"No," Ņoniep said, "I want to hide first." But Etao had already run away. Ņoniep searched in bushes and looked up trees and looked underwater on the reef, but all day long he could not find Etao. He grew hungry and climbed a pandanus tree, then reached out for an exceptionally beautiful fruit. Every time he thought he had it in his grasp, the branch with the fruit seemed to move a little higher. When he was at the top of the tree and far from the trunk, stretching as far as he could, he and the branch and the fruit tumbled down through the leaves. Just before hitting the ground, the branch and the fruit changed into a laughing Etao who landed on his feet. Ņoniep landed on his back and lost his breath.

"I win!" Etao shouted. "Now how about a feast!" The food came as it always did for Etao, in the shade of palms hanging over the beach. Ņoniep picked himself up and caught his breath enough to cuss Etao for tricking him, but when he saw the impressive feast that Etao had called forth, he very quickly found enough good humor to sit on a drift log and start eating.

Just as Etao sat down to join him, the white seabird named Keār spiraled down from the sky and landed high on one of the leaning palms. "Your father, Wūllep, is very angry," Keār called down to Etao. "He waited and waited for you, and now he knows you stole his magic."

Etao laughed up at the bird. "What do I care? I have more power, and he is nothing but a blind old worm!" He tossed boiled limpets into the air and caught them in his mouth.

"No, you must listen to me, Etao," Keār said, and flapped down to perch in front of him on another log. "When you didn't go back, your father's angry shouts were heard by Ļajibwinām̧ōņ, evil spirit of the North. Together in his canoe they sailed to the invisible island of Ep, the island of your father's birth. He has great power there, and Ļajibwinām̧ōņ is teaching him black magic and curses to bring demons and sickness and evil, a revenge on this world because he hates it so much." Keār rustled her feathers and turned one eye directly at Etao.

Ņoniep had stopped chewing, although his cheeks still bulged with food. He stared at the bird.

"Give me that piece of shell from around your neck," Keār said to Etao. The white reflection of clouds was sliding across the wet black surface of her eye. "I'll give it to your father, and he'll leave this world for another." She opened her beak as if to receive the shell.

Etao tossed a limpet into Keār's open mouth. "You should eat then sleep then we can play a game of hide-and-seek. Do you play?"

"He cheats!" Ņoniep shouted through his mouthful of food. Etao shouldered him off the log.

Keār shook down the limpet. "You don't understand, Etao—"

"I do!" He stood, dancing away from Ņoniep, who kicked at his shins. "If you give a troublesome shark your foot, it will only become hungry for your leg! You can't stop evil by giving it power. You give this shell to my father and then—no telling. Better that it stays with me." Etao took a mouthful of coconut toddy and spit a sharp stream between Keār's eyes. He lifted Ņoniep, still kicking, by the ears and put him back on the log, warning him with a stare not to try anything.

Keār flew screeching to the top of Etao's head, gripped his hair, and leaned over with the point of her toddy-splattered beak on the bridge of his nose. "Listen!" she insisted, "Wūllep only wants to go back to the stars. I know, I hear him—every day he tells this to Ļajibwinām̧ōņ. If you don't give me that shell, then you are as much responsible for your father's evil as he is!"

Etao reached up and gently invited Keār to perch on his forearm. He held her in front of his face, smoothing back her feathers. "You listen," he said, looking to both Ņoniep and Keār. "My father is an idiot, a fool made evil only by the meddling of this Ļajibwinām̧ōņ. He only uses my father for his power at Ep, and if I were to give you this shell, then I'm sure it will end up around Ļajibwinām̧ōņ's neck, not my father's. Give them time and I'm sure they will come to hate each other, destroy each other, or at least leave each other." Keār made to speak, but Etao pinched closed her beak. "You are a brave little bird, and your soul is pure, but I think it is a demon you will become if it is demons you keep after." He let go of the bird's beak and fed it a limpet. "Go concern yourself with gliding on currents in the sky and diving for the quickest little fishes, and when you want to smile and laugh come see me for games and tricks to play."

Keār hopped from Etao's arm and landed on the drift log. "You are a fool, Etao," she said. "Life is not all playing at games." She opened her wings and with a little bounce she flapped off the log and circled over Etao and N̦oniep, spiraling higher. "Watch out," she warned, "things happen fast." She flew up over the trees, a white blur fading into the bright blue of her sky.

N̦oniep stared at the spot where she had disappeared. "What if she's right?" he asked. "What if your father really means to kill the world? What if you don't—"

"You know nothing of this," Etao said, his hand over N̦oniep's mouth, "so just forget what that bird told me and think instead about trying not to lose every time we play hide-and-seek. That should be your only worry." N̦oniep pushed away Etao's hand and reached for a handful of limpets, but before he could touch them Etao made all the food disappear. "Now, one more game before dark."

N̦oniep thought for a moment then said, "I will play once more, but this game will be like a bubu, a divination. If I can't find you before dark, then you are right and the bird is wrong, but if I do find you, then you are wrong and you must do what the bird asked. I won't play any other way." He turned his back to Etao.

"I will never lose, so I agree to this bubu of yours." Etao ran through the jungle, skirted around N̦oniep's village, and, after taking his canoe from its hiding place, sailed quickly through the pass and away over the ocean.

The Growl

RUJEN WAS WALKING with his friends and had passed halfway through the pier checkpoint when he realized that he had left his boots on the *Tarlang*. He worked back through the flow of the crowd and back to his seat, only to stand in the aisle and stare at the vacant spot where he had set them down. He could not remember if he had seen them after returning to play his trick on Caleb, and not only did the remaining members of the crew not know anything about the boots, none of them seemed to care. Rujen had paid forty-six dollars for the steel-toed boots (an American coworker had got them for him at Sears in Hawai'i) and he was required to wear them at the plant. Now all he had was a pair of rubber slippers, one red and one blue, and not twenty dollars in his wallet to buy a pair of the cheap, so-called Bozo boots a Marshallese was allowed to get at the General Stock. His good socks had been in the boots too. He left the *Tarlang* quickly, scanning feet.

He did not see his boots on any feet or in any hands or in any baskets of the bicycles quickly leaving, and when he arrived at his own bicycle, a red Cyclone which he had parked the day before in a concrete bike rack near the checkpoint's barbed wire fence, he saw that someone had pulled it flat on the ground—his front rim, still in the rack, now shaped like a taco. Passersby whistled their condolences, got on their own bikes, and rode away, speaking to each other of other things.

Bending the bicycle upright straightened the rim some, but the spokes had come loose and a few of them had popped out. Despite being wholly aware of the futility of what he was about to do, Rujen still got on his bicycle and tried to ride away. He fought a losing battle for balance and forward progress, cursing his bicycle when the bent rim wedged rudely within the forks and he could go no farther. He teetered there for just a second, pushing down hard on the pedal, but it would not move. Then he lost his chance to catch himself and fell to the side and bruised his hip.

Up quickly, angrily, he dragged his bicycle by the handlebars and spun it around into a short fat palm tree near the street. The chain came off the sprocket. A guard on the pier sat in a rolling chair outside his shack, looking amused, holding a red thermos between his legs. A yellow forklift, beeping, carried freight behind him. Marshallese men on bicycles gave Rujen plenty of room as they went by, none brave enough to make eye contact.

A good man did not deserve so many troubles in one morning, Rujen thought—sewage percolating up his sink, an embarrassing argument with Jebro, his seat taken on the boat, his boots and socks, now this. His disbelief of all things superstitious thinned into a suspicion of dark powers conspired against him. He pulled his bicycle away from the street and then grabbed another one from the rack. It was a lady's blue Schwinn, rusty, with the seat low like he liked it. The pedals squeaked. Rujen rode slowly, intensely inconspicuous—squeaking up 6th Street—not the way to work—thinking it would be clever to go a different way to mislead . . . outfox. . . . He soon recognized the absurdity of his thinking and what he was doing, but he kept going.

Rujen knew he ought to be getting straight to work, and he knew that stealing on Good Friday was an act he would have to embarrassingly confess at church, but he pedaled on as if in the back of his mind he knew his effort were propelling him toward some necessary reward. In all his years of working on Kwajalein, he had always gone from place to place with a purpose, never, as he did now, just going no place at a slow pace without any sense of consequence. Somebody might already have reported him to the police as a crazy, bicycle-bashing bicycle robber, but he didn't want to think about it.

The housing area Rujen passed through, on Pine Street in the direction of George Seitz Elementary School, transmitted a sense of energy from its whirring air-conditioner motors. The street was empty. Varied brands and sizes of bicycles were parked outside the two-story duplex homes, some in racks and some against tree trunks and some flat on the ground or on their kickstands. Shaggy ironwood branches caught a weak wind up very high and kept dim what lay below, their fallen needles forming thick brown carpets between the homes. *Wind*, Rujen thought, it was good to see a wind coming after three hot nights without it.

The sound of breakers crashing on the nearby reef made Rujen look, but he couldn't see them. Another row of homes lined Ocean Road behind Pine Street, and behind them would be the beach, the reef, and then the ocean expanding to join the horizon. The people of Pine Street could view the ocean from their second floors, and that would be nice to do in the morning, he thought, to sit up high in the air-conditioning and behind a pane of glass, watching the breakers and the rise or fall of the tide.

Rujen crossed 4th Street and looked quickly both ways to see if he was being watched as he rode into the elementary school's large covered hallway. His squeaking pedals were amplified by the confined space—block walls, concrete ceiling, yellow fixtures casting a surreal light from above a concrete bench that ran the length of the hall. The tires squealed, echoing when he skidded to a stop, and the kickstand cracked loudly as he pushed down hard to break its rusty hold. He was not hiding, just stopping because he didn't know what he was doing.

He found most of a paperless blue crayon, tooth marks on it, and began rolling it between his fingers as he sat down. The bench was low, and the doorknobs across the hall were low too. The rooms had no windows, just block walls painted tan, and dark brown doors with numbers on black plaques at the top. Rujen sat across from Room 6. One end of the hall was open to 4th Street, and at the other end was a left turn into space Rujen couldn't see.

With his knees up near his chest and his eyes fixed on the low doorknob of Room 6, he thought of his own childhood on Tar-Wōj, of Father Nicholls who taught him some math and how to read. He could not remember his first days with Father, and because he was born close to the end of the war, he remembered nothing of the Japanese or of the American invasion. His earliest memory, from when he was about five, was of running in the direction of an incredibly loud airplane that flew low over the island. He had waded waist deep in the lagoon, he remembered, reaching with his hand as the plane banked toward Kwajalein and flew out of sight.

When not at his lessons he would make toy boats and play hide-and-seek with his friends, and listen, at night before sleep, to the traditional stories, and stories of the Japanese and German days, but what he really liked was looking through magazines, catalogs, anything with pictures in it of the world outside Kwajalein atoll. He especially liked magazines with maps, and saved those pages he would need later to guide him around the Earth. Some of the maps were of cities—Istanbul, Philadelphia—and some of them just showed places like Harvard or Central Park, but he had several maps of the entire planet—round ones, square ones, some better for giving the names of many places, some better for showing mountains, gorges, and rivers—he even had a map of the moon and one of the stars. His maps were secret things, to be viewed in secret places and never shared. He kept them dry and safe and tied within a piece of tire inner-tube he found on the beach. He would hide the package inside the hollow of a *kiden* tree. At times, when he had the maps spread out, he would pretend that he was looking down from an airplane, bringing the maps close to his face as he dived in for a closer look.

Now, in the hallway of the Kwajalein elementary school, Rujen's hand had warmed the blue wax and worked it into a lumpy ball. He looked up from the ball and across to the low doorknob of Room 6 and thought of the children who turned it, inadvertently polishing it, and he tried to imagine what dreams they too might hold, as he once did. He felt, right then, a strange, quick impingement of dread, but it passed before he could understand what caused it or why. Then it returned, and in that moment he foresaw these children at his present age, really not such a long time from now, and in that time, his vision of it extending not much further, he also foresaw a day in the lives of these children become women and men, himself no longer among them, his memory forever forgotten, all of himself wiped as clean away as waves and wind erasing sandpiper tracks on a beach.

Such dire thoughts surprised him and he laughed nervously, waiting for them to vanish, but as the surprise wore away, and the thoughts did not, and the wax became crumbly within his clammy hand, he stood and quickly paced right then left, frustrated because at the same time he found himself struggling for a defense from within his faith in God, he could not stop reckoning that he, in fact, possessed no immortal soul, no soul at all, and that his life meant nothing.

Rujen clenched his fists, one so tight over the wax that it pushed out from between his fingers, and although it was not his intention to do so, when the yellow lights went out all at once and the hall became much darker than it had been, he heard escape from his throat, from behind his teeth, one quick, explosive growl, a burst of noise so unfamiliar to him that he walked away from it and did not stop until he was out of the hall and well under the sky.

He was not a weak man, he reminded himself severely, and he was no coward. He had a family, people who needed him, two sons he cared for deeply. He stood in front of a little restroom building, angry that he had come there, for no good reason, and wished that he could start over the last hour of his life. The best thing to do, he quickly decided, was to get back on the bicycle and get to work and get his mind away from ideas put there, he insisted, by some force of evil needling him this day—and if that evil did exist, he determinedly proved, it was evidence enough that he did indeed possess a soul, and it was that soul, his soul, that gave his life value and meaning—and to believe otherwise about his soul was the surest way to forfeit it. There was no reason to think about the subject anymore at all.

He was not looking straight ahead when he reentered the hall, and he was just about to the bicycle when he saw—first hearing footsteps—that he was not alone. A tanned white woman approached from the other end, and as Rujen's steps faltered when he saw her, she slowed too, her wooden heels scuffing, her arm pressing a stack of colored papers a little closer to her chest. He realized that his fists were still clenched, and as he relaxed them, feeling crumbs of wax fall from his hand, he smiled. "Hello," he called out, his voice louder than he wanted it to be.

The woman, middle aged but having jet black hair, smiled warily in return, glancing down at a set of keys she was flipping through with her thumb. She wore a yellow dress and a wide black belt. A square black purse hung from her shoulder.

Rujen stopped at the bicycle, but pulled his hand away just as he reached for it. He stood there smiling, sweating a little, and noticed that he had smeared blue crayon on the stomach of his overalls.

"Can I help you?" the woman asked, having stopped at the door to Room 5. Her nose moved slightly as if she were checking the air.

"I'm all right," Rujen said, "I'm just thinking. . . . I—"

"Well," the woman said, turning the key in the lock, "you'll have to find someplace else to do it. Is that your bike?" She stood with the door open at her back, one foot over the threshold and the papers still pressed against her chest.

"No," Rujen said, "I came walking." He stepped past the bicycle and walked in the woman's direction. She moved farther into the classroom as he passed, watching him, not returning his smile. When he had passed by and then heard the door close behind him, Rujen jogged back and jumped on the bicycle. The pedals squeaked loudly past the woman's room, but he didn't care if she could hear him. He then welcomed as a friend the ocean breeze—first one in three days—that hit him as he came out of the hall and bounced onto 4th Street.

The same guard was still at the pier, but he paid no attention as Rujen slipped the bicycle back in the rack. It was not necessary to mention the incident at confession, he decided, as he hadn't really stolen the bicycle, only borrowed it, because he returned it and no damage was done. He might even bring some WD-40 from work, at night after church, and oil the pedals just to set things right. He looked once at his own bicycle—all he needed was a new rim: A decent used one could be found at the dump, and it was only a matter of spending one of his lunch breaks to go get it and put it on. It would cost him nothing but a little time. He set off on foot toward the sewage plant, knowing that he would be almost an hour late for work, and that he would have to answer for not having any boots, but all in all it was still morning and the day had every chance of being good. His optimism flagged only slightly when one of his rubber slippers, the blue one, busted a strap and he stubbed his toe. He simply tossed the red one after the blue and kept walking, looking down to avoid rocks.

The air had that rain smell. Rujen hoped it meant a storm was coming, not so much wanting rain, but cooler air to break the unusual, hot stagnation that had settled in for much too long this time of year. Then he thought of his sons, on the water, and frowned when he looked up at palm fronds that waved and clattered in gusts of rising wind.

An American boy on a bicycle, a deep-sea fishing pole sticking out of a tube on the back, shot past and turned his head, staring Rujen in the eyes as if for a moment he thought he recognized him. Rujen smiled, nodded hello, and then two more riders whizzed past and turned right just in front of him, their tires sliding when they left the asphalt onto a wide patch of sand and gravel that led to the Small Boat Marina. The three boys appeared to be racing and hit their brakes hard when they reached the back of the building, one of them crashing sidelong into a palm tree, causing a cooler to tumble off his back baskets and cans of beer to roll out amid clear plastic bags of ice that burst and scattered cubes. The boy who lost the cooler checked his knees and elbows as he retrieved the cans and ice, and then the other two, cussing and pushing, ended up fighting and fell to the ground. Rujen walked on at a steady pace, chuckling at the scene, feeling better about himself the nearer he got to work. There he would have things to do, people to talk with, and time to forget that ugly moment when he found himself growling over the existence of his soul in the hallway of the elementary school.

The Boys

TRAVIS KOTRADY HAD reserved the morning boat—it was his to drive if he wanted—but halfway to the marina, his friend, Boyd Lutrell, had challenged him to a race. Winner got to drive. Loser hauled the gas, enough cans to stay on the water all day because Boyd had a reservation for the same boat that afternoon. Kerry Zeder raced too, but he had to know that he wouldn't get to drive. Not only was he just two months out of Alabama and didn't have a boat license, let alone an ocean endorsement—and didn't know how to fish except maybe for catfish or whatever else—the only reason he was allowed along was that he got his older sister to buy a case of Oly beer. Travis didn't mind Kerry, and even considered him somewhat of a friend, but Boyd was picky about who he fished with, superstitious about who was bad luck and who was not. Kerry, being a red-headed hick, was bad luck, no doubt about it, until last night when Boyd had trouble finding somebody old enough to buy the beer.

Travis led the race as they passed a Marshallese in front of the marina, and something weird like deja vu made him look at the guy—he didn't recognize him and shrugged it off—then Boyd hole-shotted him on the turn and won by a tire length. Kerry crashed. If he hadn't, and he hadn't lost the cooler off the back baskets of his bike, Boyd might have been just mildly obnoxious about winning, but now with Kerry down picking chunks of gravel from his knees and elbows as he smartly gathered up the beers before anybody saw, Boyd stood over him cussing angrily—probably his version of a victory celebration.

"Quit bitchin' and load the boat!" Travis shouted, pushing Boyd away from Kerry, who looked like a clown now that sweat and dirt streaked the white zinc oxide pasted to his freckled face. Boyd lunged back at Travis and they both fell over, almost kicking Kerry in the head as they went down. Boyd was taller and bigger, but Travis was more athletic, in better shape; in a fight they'd be a pretty even match, but this was not so much a fight as it was a wrestling match, and when one of the beers shot out from under them and burst hitting the bottom of a drain pipe, that was the end of it.

"Dick," Travis muttered.

"Get the damn gas, loser."

Travis brushed himself off, and after Boyd headed away with the poles and gear, he helped Kerry with the cooler before he went around to the office and signed out the boat. The boat was free, as was the gas, two of the many perks that living on Kwajalein had to offer. Kerry stood with Travis in the office even though Travis had already told him to go put the cooler in the boat, probably because he didn't want to be alone with Boyd. Kerry was about Travis's height, more chubby than he was stocky, but if he kept lifting weights he might get the confidence he needed to stand up to somebody like Boyd—not that Boyd acted like a punk all the time. He could be a decent guy once you got to know him. Still, Travis wasn't happy about losing the race to him. Not that he wanted so much to drive—really, he preferred working the lines—it was that he knew Boyd would act like he was King Shit for the rest of the day.

The three boys, Boyd driving, Travis and Kerry gripping rails on opposite sides of the center console, sped along the lagoon side of the east reef and kept near the calmer water close to the islands, passing at one point a pair of dolphins seemingly headed straight for Kwajalein. They veered away from Ebeye to avoid trash that might foul the props, then back again into shallow water past the tiny jungled islands of South Loi, North Loi, and Gugeegue. Rounding the corner at Ningi, the last island before Bigej pass, they picked up an ocean swell and a face full of wind. Dark clouds approached from the east, already unleashing sheets of rain in the near distance. A strong current made the swells tight and steep, and the twin seventy-horsepower outboards screamed as they caught air coming out of the troughs.

"Ain't you gonna slow down?" Kerry asked.

"Not likely," Travis said.

"Pussy," Boyd added, then whooped as the boat flew up the face of one large swell and landed neatly on top of another.

The boat pounded through the pass as showers of cold saltwater shot over the sides, giving Travis gooseflesh. The spray clouded his vision so that he could hardly see the red and green buoys that leaned sharply in the current and marked the way to less chaotic water in the open ocean. He kept his shivering knees bent to better absorb the shock of the pounding boat, looking past Boyd, who mindlessly jabbed his palm into the already maxed throttles. Kerry struggled to remain half inside one of the red foam life jackets, the muscles on his forearms looking ready to snap from his death grip on the console's rail. When the boat cleared the pass and began to bound up and down the slow ordered rollers of the open ocean, Kerry released one hand just for a moment to get himself fully inside the jacket.

Boyd looked over to Travis. "So . . . which way?"

Travis pulled out a pair of binoculars from his bag in the center console, put the lens caps in his pocket, and scanned the surface of the ocean. Finding nothing, he wet his nostrils with saliva on his pinkie, sniffed the air, then said as seriously as he could, "East, straight at the storm."

Kerry fumbled to tighten the straps on his jacket. He looked very scared. "Y'all must be crazy," he said.

"I'll drink to that," Boyd said "I'll drink to that right now."

Contact

ONE DAY, LONG AFTER his warning from Keār and during a time of drought in the season of no wind, while being pursued by many angry chiefs and their warriors, Etao was paddling near Butaritari in the south when he saw the largest canoe he had ever seen. He had heard of such a canoe being sighted once near Bokaak but he didn't believe it—not until now. The canoe had two levels like a Marshallese sleeping house, and five large white sails that drooped like sagging breasts. The sides of the canoe were so high above the water, especially at the front and back, that paddling it was impossible—not a wise design—and at the top of the center of three tall masts was a man in a basket who jumped up and down and pointed at Etao.

"Yes yes, you fool!" Etao shouted, holding his paddle over his head. "This paddle idea is very good at this time of year—if you didn't make such a clumsy canoe!"

When he came alongside, Etao saw that the canoe was full of scroungy sailors, all scurrying around like desperate bugs topside of a drift log too long at sea. They pointed and chattered as if they had never seen a decent canoe before, but they didn't know how to speak, only able make strange noises like birds do when bored from sitting too long on their eggs. Some had skin red like the skin of a cooked pig, and a few others had skin as pale as that of Lijepake, the witch of Bikar. One was as black as the sky at night. Most had hair on their faces, like coconuts stripped in thirsty haste. They looked very hungry, unclean, and they wore so much cloth that when the wind finally did come, their skinny bodies would surely be blown straight off their canoe.

Etao looked into the mens' sunken, bruised-looking eyes, and saw a kind of fear he had never seen before, a hungry fear like that on the face of an abandoned dog or a runt too often denied its turn at the teat, but it was also a menacing fear, an almost cunning fear.

He stared at a piece of cloth that drooped from a pole at the back of the boat. The cloth was red, as if dipped in blood, and in the center of it was a crosswise design like that of a *wapeepe*, a navigational chart used to teach children. The chart, the design of it, was the color of clouds at sunset, but it had no lines showing the currents or any marks for islands. Such a useless chart—not even good for teaching anything to children—and such a stupid nasty crew and a canoe that could only be dreamed up by the worst of fools. . . .

"Oh!" Etao shouted, laughing. "You must be my father's demons! Finally! Who else could have conjured this mess?" Etao stood up in his canoe and danced, swiveling his hips while he sang loudly of what he would be doing to the demons if they weren't so grub-ugly.

For a finish to his dance, Etao lifted the rear of his loin cloth and crapped in the water. "Look look!" He shouted, pointing. "A fish! Quick—get your poles, throw your nets—a feast!"

The demons stopped their chattering and looked down, their faces blank.

"Mine always float," Etao said proudly, "and I think this one might find land faster than you do."

Etao grew tired of insulting demons who were too stupid to know it. He splashed himself clean and turned his canoe to paddle away. "This current," he said, pointing to shiny wisps that stretched like hairs across the calmed ocean, "will take you close by Butaritari. I am going there now and if you come later—before you die or go crazy from drinking sea water—then maybe I'll play some tricks with you."

The people at Butaritari suffered from thirst and hunger because of the drought, and it was made worse because the chief took from everyone else as if it were a season of plenty. Eventually though, even the chief couldn't get enough to eat. When just before sunset Etao paddled onto the lagoon beach, the chief ran over and demanded that he give him all his food as a tax for landing on the island. "But I'm all out too," Etao said to the panting chief, whose once tight, fat belly now hung in numerous flabby layers like many hungry smiles. "All I bring is myself."

"Then maybe we eat *you*," the chief said. "What do you think of that?" He poked Etao with his stick. "You better give me something—whatever it is you got."

Etao hung his head and walked toward the village, the chief fast behind him. "To respect you as the high chief that you are," Etao said, "I give you my life, my meat, so you can survive this drought and breed many good sons just like yourself." He stopped at a sandy spot and told the chief to have his men dig an oven.

"Uh—uh," the chief stuttered, "We don't eat human beings—I only—"

"No no no," Etao said, drawing the outline of the oven with his toes, "this is the custom everywhere else—I guess you never heard, living so far south—man meat is the best, the favorite meat of the Irooj, the highest chiefs. You are Irooj—yes?—or maybe you—"

"Of course I am Irooj!" the chief bellowed. Then he called for his men to dig the oven.

After smooth stones had been dropped on the wood and the fire stoked hot and high, Etao shouted, "More wood! I want this oven hotter than hot!" More wood was added and the flames rose higher and higher as night arrived, and when most of the village had gathered around the fire and their whispers rose distinct above the chattering pop and hiss of the burning wood, and the light from it pulsed as breathing light and sparks flew up as short-lived stars dancing at their deaths, Etao circled close by the flames, his face white with ash, his finger pointing out at the crowd, his voice deep and his eyes wide and unblinking as he chanted again and again:

> *Why do you not eat, people, when all around sits all this food?*
> *Why are you hungry, people, when meat is fresh and ready for eating, people?*

The people looked at each other, some speaking angrily, others defensively, and a few crept away.

The chief stood and put his arm around Etao and proclaimed, "Etao has given us a secret to life—his life—and I hope some more of you follow his generous example so that we here at Butaritari can survive this drought just as well as our neighbors to the north."

Etao called for more and more wood, and not until morning when the oven glowed bright with the color of a rising sun did he say it was hot enough. "Now," he said sadly when the first ray of light broke across the sky, "I must cook."

He asked some men to remove the ash from the oven and to push the stones flat with a stick, then, with all of the islanders watching and the chief waving his hand over the oven to feel its incredible heat, Etao threw in some taro leaves then got in and laid flat on his back. "Ooh hot! Quick—cover me so you won't hear my screams!" They covered him with palm fronds and buried him in a hurry.

The chief and his men sat by the oven waiting for Etao to cook, arguing about who would get a leg or an arm or if the rump would be as tasty as that of a pig—but when the sun climbed straight overhead and the men had taken to sucking their fingers and chewing their nails in anticipation of the meal, Etao sneaked up behind them and shouted, "I am done cooking—so now eat!"

The chief fell face-first into the sand at the sound of Etao's voice. His men jumped back and raised their spears. When the chief scrambled to his feet and hurried behind his men, he pointed his finger at Etao and shouted, "Get get, you ghost! Get over to Ewerōk, island of the dead, where you belong!" He grabbed two rocks and beat them together and shrieked to scare Etao away. He encouraged his men to do the same.

"Wait!" Etao said. "It was only a trick, something I learned at Enewetak. Dig out the oven and see what good things you find inside." A loud bratting blast flapped the back of Etao's loin cloth and a rank reek invisibly but palpably fogbound the area. "See," he said, "no way can I be a ghost."

The men dug out the oven and found it full of cooked dolphin and bird and fish, and in between there was taro and breadfruit and pandanus and coconut, enough food to feed the people of Butaritari for several days.

"How is this possible?" the chief demanded. He speared himself a dolphin steak out of the oven. "Tell me how you did it."

"It's just a trick," Etao said. "A child could do it." He stepped back as people pushed forward to get their share. "Feast feast!" he said. "And then we'll see what happens."

The chief and his people ate so much—all of it—that they fell asleep around the oven and groaned in their dreams. The sun went down and the stars came up and most everybody slept until the sun woke them at morning. Having eaten so much the day before, they were very hungry right away. "More food," the chief grumbled, throwing a pebble at Etao who sat down by the water. "Do that trick again."

"No," Etao said, "I think I'm leaving." He stood and stretched, facing the lagoon. "Maybe I can teach you the trick if you want to learn it."

"Teach me!" The chief demanded. "I'm more hungry than ever!"

Etao had another fire built inside the oven, and when it had burned down to coals and the stones were baking hot, he placed some leaves on top and told the chief to lie down. "As soon as you are buried you'll see what to do. A simple child's trick."

The chief got inside. "Ahhh! It's hot!"

"Ignore it, my friend." Etao covered and buried him in a hurry, then he went and sat back down on the beach.

After a while the chief's brother asked him, "How much food do you think he'll make?"

"He's a very big chief," Etao said, "maybe even enough to feed *them.*" He pointed across the water, to the large canoe full of demons he had seen earlier. It had just entered the lagoon. Three smaller paddling canoes, none of them built with an outrigger, towed it along.

"What kind of way is that to paddle a canoe?" Etao asked, but the chief's brother had already run away, and all the other villagers hid behind trees or ran inside their homes.

The demons towed their large canoe to a shallow spot near the island and dropped a huge anchor that looked like two fish-hooks tied back-to-back. In their little canoes they paddled for Butaritari, and when they came ashore Etao greeted them on the beach and remarked, "You must belong to a turtle clan!"

The demons wore tight fitting shells on their chests and backs, and their heads were topped with what looked like smooth gray coconuts. Their feet were covered—hard with no toes like a pig's feet—and every part of their bodies except for their hairy faces were completely covered in red, white, or yellow cloth. Half of the demons carried useless spears that were round and hollow at the ends, but the other half had sharp flat spears made from some sort of stone that caught sunlight like calm water at midday. They looked even more frightened than when Etao had seen them on the ocean. One of the demons carried a stick with a piece of red cloth at the top—the yellow navigational design in the middle—and when he stuck it in the ground just up from the beach, all the other demons got on one knee and mumbled something up to the sun. Then one of the demons chattered at Etao and then at the not-too-well-hidden people of the village, pointing to the cloth and then the land, repeating several times what sounded like, "Espanya . . . espanya."

"Hey," Etao said, "remember me?" None of the demons seemed to recognize him. He walked toward who he thought was the chief demon, the one who spoke. This demon had strange fluffy red feathers sprouting out of the coconut thing on his head, and when Etao got close enough to look into his bloody brown eyes, close enough to catch his foul demon stench, the demon took off his coconut hat and offered it to him.

Just then the chief's brother came out from behind his tree and told Etao to get away. "Keep your hands off it!" the brother ordered. "I am the one who's getting that thing." He took it and put it on his head. "Okay now," he said to the demon, "what else you got from that big canoe?"

The people came one by one out of their hiding places, and the demons gave them little gifts like flat reflective stones and soft pieces of colored cloth. The demons could not speak with words, but they made it known, by making scooping moves with their hands, that they were very hungry and thirsty. And the people, pointing to the oven and smiling and making their own scooping moves with their hands, made it known that food was going to be ready very soon.

"Give me some help," Etao called, beginning to dig out the oven. "I think your chief is eating everything for himself!" This got plenty of men working fast, but when they got to the bottom and pulled away the leaves—the chief's sweaty red body had bloated to an incredible size and both his mouth and his bulging eyes were stuck wide-open. Some of the men screamed and all of them ran away, and when the demons ran over to look, Etao jumped inside the oven and tossed out the chief. "Now you can eat!" he shouted, but the demons leaped back, some of them falling down and kicking sand at the corpse while they screamed just as loud as the men who had run away. "What a bunch of useless demons my father has made," Etao said, as he walked down to his canoe. "They don't even have a taste for man." He sailed away to islands far south and into Polynesia and modeled for statues further east on Rapa Nui, and when he heard quite some time later of a place where many mysterious things were happening at an incredibly fast pace, he decided he should go there and so it was that he sailed to America.

Part Two
Suicide Messiahs

Land means a great deal to the Marshallese. It means more than just a place where you can plant your food crops and build your houses, or a place where you can bury your dead. It is the very life of the people. Take away their land and their spirits go also.

—From a petition sent to the United Nations by Marshallese leaders

Ļāmoran

IT TOOK MORE THAN two hours for Jebro and Nuke to cross the lagoon to the west reef, and in that time the leading edge of the dark and swollen, almost purple bank of clouds had followed them and come just about directly overhead, so thick at the top and sloped into the clearing above it that Jebro thought it looked as though he could stand up there and scoop out a cool blue handful of sky. Rain approached from below the clouds as a tangled blowing hoard of long gray hairs, obscuring sight of everything to the east. Half a mile west in front of the boat lay a string of lush green islands, each on a fine white carpet of sand. Their green shallows seemed stained black in spots where coral groves disrupted the sandy bottom.

"You know which one is Tar-Wōj?" Jebro asked his sleepy brother.

"The big one?"

"Right—can you see the rocks that come out a bit and curve toward the pass? That was built long ago before the Americans came, before the Japanese and the Germans too, even before us Marshallese. Do you want to hear the story?"

Nuke hunched forward over a cigarette and lit it with a match. "Tell me."

"Tell me first why you smoke."

"Everybody smokes, even girls now."

"Not me."

Nuke grinned. "Maybe you're scared."

"Okay, give me one then."

"You'll smoke it?"

"I can't have my little brother thinking of me as a coward. Besides, I haven't seen you in two years—we should do everything together while we have the chance." Jebro throttled down and the boat settled low into the increasingly choppy water. He held out his hand.

Nuke shook his head and gave Jebro a cigarette. "Usually it's the older brother giving the younger his first smoke. Maybe," he said, grinning, "inside, you are not as much of a man as I am."

Jebro put the cigarette in his mouth and stared blankly at Nuke. "Am I supposed to wait for lightning to light this?"

Nuke handed him a large book of blue-tipped matches. Printed on it was a missile streaking toward the Kwajalein lagoon. "You know how to inhale?" he asked, blowing smoke.

"I'll watch you and learn." Jebro lit his cigarette then turned the throttle. He put the matches in his pocket. He had tried smoking when he was younger, and maybe he would be a smoker now, but at ten cents a cigarette (now twenty-five cents) he could not have afforded to addict himself even if he had wanted to. Over time, sucking those things just seemed like a ridiculous thing to do no matter what. Of course, there were many ways to get smokes besides paying for them—bumming, trading borrowed things, finding butts, asking Americans at the pier for quarters—but if you were into it for good what you needed was a connection on Kwajalein where packs sold for seventy-five cents. Nuke had packs, and not only did he for sure have no Kwajalein connection, he also didn't have one bit of money. Jebro had heard of the Reimers warehouses being broken into not long before he came back to Ebeye. The thieves got several cartons of cigarettes and some boxes of Japanese bubble gum, getting in through a bent panel of the tin siding. He had thought about confronting Nuke with what he suspected, but he decided not to.

"So tell me the story of the rocks," Nuke said.

"Wait now, I want to enjoy my smoke with you." Jebro leaned back, a look of mock euphoria on his face, and exhaled smoke through his nose. He tried, but he couldn't suppress a spasm of coughing.

Nuke giggled. "You are a crazy brother," he said. "Are you sure you know how to catch turtles?"

Jebro coughed up another burst of smoke and flicked his cigarette into the water. He thumped his bare chest and said, "I am the best."

A light but stinging rain arrived in gusts as Jebro killed the engine and guided the boat onto the beach at Tar-Wōj. Sounds of surf rolling pebbles and wind shaking trees swept away the echoing hours of constant mechanical noise. The island was narrow in the middle and wider at the ends, a little more than one mile long with a few tall coconut palms swaying with the wind just above the broad tops of *pin̄pin̄*, lantern trees with heart-shaped leaves and swollen yellow fruit. Two white birds high above the treetops hovered on an air current; like kites they seemed tied to the island. Lower, vine-tangled jasmine and mulberry trees cast shadows against dense thickets of screwpines and flowering shrubs and bushes. Some of the closer palms leaned over a scalloped, bone-white beach strewn with coconuts and lines of driftwood. The beach extended left and right around to the ocean side of the island, some of it shaded by heliotrope trees which stretched thick dark branches at crooked angles low across where *wūjooj* grass drooped over the sandy highwater berm. There, pennywort creepers and purple morning glories wove their way into an expansive barrier of salt-resistant *kōn̄n̄at* shrubs, their thick fleshy leaves poking through a tangled mat of hairlike, bright orange *kaōnōn* vines.

Jebro tilted the engine and jumped into the shallow surf. "You pull while I push," he said. They got the boat high on the beach, and at Jebro's insistence they covered it with vines and fallen palm fronds. "The helicopters will never see it."

"So do we cover ourselves with palm fronds too?"

"Sure, tie some around your waist and on your legs, and while you're doing that I'll set up our tent." He held out a frond but Nuke, laughing, slapped it away.

A blast of wind brought heavier rain, and to the sides of the island Jebro could see the last patches of blue being quickly eclipsed by the storm. He took a gray tarpaulin from his duffel bag and used driftwood to make a small lean-to. "There was a house inside there," he said to Nuke, pointing to the jungle as they huddled under the tarp, "our family's old house, but the jungle swallowed it quick after everybody left and not much is left. Later, I'll take you to Ataji's grave."

He and Nuke sat in the sand without speaking, sharing a Pepsi as the rain drummed harder overhead and silenced the cricket noises that had been coming from the jungle. Wind-whipped waves washed higher up the beach, leaving short-lived semicircles of foam. They slapped violently against the nearby formation of large black rocks that curved a little way into the lagoon.

Jebro patted the sand next to him and looked across the length of the island. As the first son of the second son of his grandfather, who had been an *aļap*, clan chief, at Tar-Wōj, Jebro had rights to a share of land. His rights at Tar-Wōj, however, were *bōtōktōk*, patrilineal, and so were not that great. His children would have even lesser rights at Tar-Wōj, and their children would have none. In Marshallese culture, a man's primary land rights descend from his mother, from his mother's clan, which by birth he belongs to. Women and their female offspring forever retain the land, while their male offspring, despite their tenure as rulers of the land, are forever destined to have their male descendants move on. By this custom, Jebro's greatest claim to land was at Rongelap, on the island of Mālu, where his mother and her clan, *ripako ran* (shark clan), once had lived.

On Ebeye, Jebro had no land rights. To live in the house, his father and the other workers staying there had to pay rent to the Trust Territory government. On Ebeye, the land did not support very much life, boasted no crops, few pigs, no ground water, no jungle, no grass, no stands of fruit-bearing trees. The people's lives were sustained not by the land but by money flowing in and then out like the tide, leaving in its wash so much trash and skeletons of things, like cars and washing machines that never lasted but by accustomed use made themselves necessary. Jebro saw that Ebeye was land made ugly, but for many Marshallese it was also New York, Tokyo, Hong Kong, Manila, the closest a Marshallese might ever get to experiencing the life such places offered. Ebeye had television and a movie house—rural atolls did not. Ebeye had new and exotic foods, electricity, beer, discos, drugs, cars and trucks, and missiles flying overhead, and it held the possibility of working for good money on Kwajalein, working for America, the most powerful nation on Earth. Even Jebro, however much he recognized Ebeye's obscenity, could not reject what it offered him. Ebeye, for Jebro, was like a shark on whose nose he rode to avoid its teeth.

Jebro had known of his rights at Mālu for as long as he could remember, as most Marshallese children, no matter where they were located, relocated, exiled, or resettled, were taught very early their *jowi*, the designation name of their *bwij*, their clan, and taught from this what lands were theirs to call home. Clanship gave people the responsibility to share food and shelter with other members of their clan, without exception, and by doing so they ensure that they will be treated in kind. In this way there were many places a Marshallese was welcome to live, and it was by this custom that Jebro had lived at Ailinglaplap for two years. Some Marshallese though, but not too many, especially some of those in the urban centers of Ebeye or Majuro who had acquired some bit of money, maybe through owning a successful store or having a high government job, rejected their clanship and behaved selfishly. They cared not for their land or for their clan, but cared only for money. These people were said to have sold their souls.

Jebro was proud of belonging to his clan, and he was proud of the bond he had with the land at Mālu. As the eldest son of his mother, an eldest daughter, he could even be an *aḷap* someday, but he would never live there. Mālu was poisoned by radioactive fallout from the sixty-six atomic and hydrogen thermonuclear bombs detonated nearby at Bikini and Enewetak. Jebro might live and die without ever setting foot on his rightful land at Mālu, but knowing that it was there, that he belonged to it and it to him, gave his life profound meaning and position.

Jebro also felt a bond with Tar-Wōj, his *ḷāmoran*, patrilineal homeland, and as he sat on the beach with his brother, in violation of a foreigner's law, he felt not only the power that having a right to be there gave him, but also a responsibility to the land, to be a part of the life it sustained. He had heard a man from Enewetak tell a story once of when he was a boy. The man said that at dawn, only one day out to sea after being taken from Elugelab island, his *ḷāmoran*, he had seen appear a giant cloud and the morning sky had become ablaze with reds and pinks and shades of orange. He had thought it was the most beautiful sight he had ever seen, but in a minute came incredible thunder and it would not stop. When he was told that the cloud and the thunder and the colors were from a bomb, he began to be sad, and when he learned some months later that what had once been his rightful land, his inheritance, had become nothing more than part of a gaping crater in the reef, almost two hundred feet deep and one mile around, he knew right then that the bomb had destroyed part of his soul.

Jebro's mother had also told him a story of the bomb, which was also the story of how she came to Kwajalein atoll. She said that as a little girl on Rongelap, one morning just before dawn, she saw from a window what she thought was a moon rising in the west. It was so bright that trees, the ground, the lagoon, everything became awash in its reddish glow. Not long after that a tremendous wind blasted in, so strong that some homes were badly damaged and even some of the trees were blown half out of the ground. That seemed to be the end of it, and everybody knew it was from an American bomb, but they were safe from this one, they knew, because they had been evacuated before some of the bombs and this time they were not. She was sick that day, remaining inside, and a few hours later she watched a strange dark cloud, a yellowish cloud, blow over the atoll. An ashy powder began to fall. No one knew what that was, and the other children played in it while it formed a two-inch layer on the ground. Some people thought the powder might be valuable—it was rare—and they collected it in wash tubs. Later it rained, the powder coming down from the sky in the rain and washing into the cisterns. The drinking water turned yellow. It tasted bitter. So did the fish caught that day, having been powdered while in water at the bottom of the canoes.

By that night people began to vomit. Their skin and their eyes and their mouths became inflamed, burning hot. Iia, who had stayed inside and was already feeling sick enough not to want to eat, did not suffer as much as many others, and when everyone was evacuated by seaplane to Kwajalein two days later, she only had to put up with some diarrhea, vomiting, and a little burning and itching. They were confined to a Navy ship in the Kwajalein lagoon, while doctors took their blood and samples of their skin and bone. Iia said she watched the faces of her friends and relatives become red with pain, and after about ten days the hair on their heads and their body hair was falling away, their burned skin was peeling off in patches, their fingernails were becoming discolored and falling off, their fingers bleeding.

Because they were never warned or evacuated, and the Americans had to know which way the wind was blowing, some of the people of Rongelap complained that they had been poisoned on purpose, so that the Americans could test what happens to people as a result of their bombs. She never believed it. In 1966, when Jebro was three, his mother and the other surviving exposed people from Rongelap received eleven thousand dollars each from the American government. She bought Rujen a pickup truck. She bought herself a Japanese washing machine. She was one of the lucky ones, she said, never suffering from the thyroid cancers that eventually grew in most of the other children exposed that day, but then she always had that trouble having babies, and sometimes, Jebro knew from hearing what he was not supposed to hear, she had jellyfish babies, what some Marshallese women called monster babies because they looked inside-out, and finally it killed her.

"Shit," Nuke said, looking out at the gray rainy sky.

"No," Jebro said, "rain is good, better for catching turtles."

"Maybe they'll come on the island and think they're still underwater." Nuke crushed the Pepsi can he had been holding and threw it into the jungle. "Did you hear that?" he asked. "I think I hit a bird, or a . . . I heard something."

"You heard me fart."

Nuke covered his nose and mouth with the bottom of his shirt. "Atomic bomb," he muttered, leaning as far away as he could without getting rained on.

Jebro took the handline and a green papaya from his bag. He also removed a length of thick monofilament that had a 7/0 hook at the end. "This is my secret turtle-catching technique," he said. "I give it to you, but don't ever tell anybody else about it." Jebro looked into Nuke's eyes, waiting for a response. Nuke just smiled. Jebro pinched his leg.

"I promise!"

"Eṃṃan, good. Now watch close." Jebro cut the papaya into quarters and used three fingers of his six-fingered hand to scoop out the black mass of seeds. He tossed the seeds and the pulp into the surf, then threaded the hook through one of the quarters so that the barb poked out. Where the leader was knotted at its end, he clipped on the handline's pigtail swivel. With a spare length of handline he tied a fist-sized rock at the top of the leader. "Here." He handed the rig to Nuke. "Hold this while I play out the line. Jebro coiled the line in large loops and hung them over his palm. "Follow me out to the rocks," he said. "Now is a good time to get started."

See What Can Happen

Long ago but not long after Wūllep fell from the sky, his rival nephews, Ļanej and Ļewōj, came down to Earth for a short time and to all living creatures they gave unique markings and colors. Fish were given special beauty, and when Ļanej and Ļewōj traveled to Buoj island at Ailinglaplap, they showed the people how they too, by the art of tattooing, might become beautiful as well. "Everything will pass after death," they said, "but the tattoo will live on."

A triangle covering Ņoniep's upper chest represents a canoe and is filled with a pattern of tightly-arranged double concentric parallelograms. The triangle is bordered by straight black lines affixed with smaller solid triangles representing shark's teeth. The teeth point away from his body. Also on his chest are a series of raised scars, put there by stabbing a palm leaf midrib through his skin and lighting it on fire. He did so in mourning for his people. Only he remains.

Another triangle is created by lines running from his armpits to his navel. This triangle, indented slightly at the nipples, represents waves reflected by land and is filled with a pattern of horizontally aligned zigzag lines. A horizontal band extending from just above his navel to just above his pubis is symbolic of the sky and is filled with a pattern of wavy marks representing clouds. Partially intersecting the sky and running through the waves and into the canoe is a vertical column that represents a mast. This area is filled with curving lines symbolizing rainwater, the essence of life, and at his solar plexis, within the mast, is an area of open-ended rectangles having their ends bent slightly down. These marks at his solar plexis show that Ņoniep is powerful with magic.

Ņoniep's back is marked with another triangle to represent the sea and another band representing the sky. On his arms are bands of shark's teeth, and on the sides of his legs are vertical lines intersected with ovals to represent intertwined sling plants—Ņoniep's boast of sexual prowess. A dark band across the top of his buttocks is filled with a turtle shell pattern. Long ago, an artist had hammered the tattoos into his skin with a chisel made from an albatross wing bone. The black dye came from charred coconut fibers. The entire ceremony took twenty-eight days and resulted in a fever that nearly killed him.

Ņoniep wears a belt of many cords, each woven with narrow pandanus fibers dyed white and black, spiraled in a checkered pattern around a sennit core. Three corners of a clothing mat, patterned in motifs similar to his tattoos, are tucked into the back of his belt, while the remaining corner passes through his legs and is tucked in at the front. When he was a boy, he pierced his earlobes with a shark's tooth and slowly enlarged them by inserting increasingly larger rolls of leaves. The loops of Ņoniep's earlobes have now become so large that he can pass them over his head. Around his neck is a string of dolphin teeth. His topknot is tied with a beaded length of *atat* bark. He is so old and wrinkled that his face looks like a dark rock. This is the last day of his life and it rains. He sits on a sitting mat, chanting knowledge into an extraordinarily tall breadfruit tree. Webs of bright orange *kaōnōn* vines drape over him as a protection against demons.

Over many days Ņoniep had focused on the navigators' science of astronomy, chanting into the tree the secret Marshallese names for the pole stars, for Procyon and Betelgeuse, the Magellanic clouds and Corona Borealis, the Andromeda galaxy and the fog in Perseus, names for countless other stars and for constellations of such faint magnitude that even Western navigators do not recognize them. Ņoniep chanted the positions and movements of these stars and constellations, explaining their relevance to the seasons and to the winds and the yearly storms and droughts. He chanted the names of islands each star finds from Tar-Wōj, and from those islands he named the stars leading to farther islands, and when he had created a network of stars and islands extending thousands of miles in all directions with his chants, he chanted the names of opposing stars that would lead him all the way back home. To this knowledge he added the swell science, explaining how to glean information on position from even the slightest ripple on the ocean's surface. He chanted the *kōkļaļ*, sea signs that revealed to a navigator his proximity to a particular island, among them a glassy streak on the water by Bikini; Limkare, a sand bank north of Rongerik; Jouilobok, a gull by Wotho who flies very high to dive incredibly fast after prey; a sailfish by Lae that can never be caught; sharks attacking tuna by Kili; a sea serpent by Namu; Loromak, a frightful creature near the Toen-Loromak passage into the Kwajalein lagoon.

Ņoniep chanted into the tree of how to build *wa*, outrigger canoes: The *waļap*, large enough to carry fifty people; the *tipn̄ōl*, for ten or twelve people and used primarily for ocean fishing; the *kōrkōr*, a three-person canoe for paddles or sail. He chanted of the *mwijitbok*, *taburbur*, *malmel*, *tojeik*, and *jekad* hull designs. He took several days to chant the voyage-long sea chants. He chanted riddles and proverbs and stories and sang all the songs he knew. He chanted of ways to make kites. He chanted of the *ekjab* spirits, many of them primordial, some of them human, who inhabit trees and rocks and reefs and sometimes appear as birds or creatures of the sea. Many of these ekjabs should be honored with feasts, and so Ņoniep chanted of the proper times to respect them, among them: Jarlo, a hibiscus tree at Namu who, by dropping a leaf, advises navigators of when to begin their voyages; Jemāluut, Etao's brother, whose spirit entered a silvertree at Majuro; Joṃanebuōn, a stone in a water hole on Kwajalein, now covered by a windmill; Lǫweenwōn, a coral head in the Kwajalein lagoon who gives protection against sharks; Likaamijājjāeņ, the glistening stone at Rongelap; and on many other islands many other mysterious basalt stones, some now gone—toppled or roped and dragged into the ocean by angry missionaries.

Ņoniep chanted of the Spanish who claimed the islands and promised life through Christ and gave death by syphilis; he chanted of the Germans who became rich by forcing the Marshallese to work at making copra for them, the Germans, bringing mumps and measles and TB, who punished and tortured those not working as ordered; he chanted of the blackbirders, slavers like Bully Hayes who often snatched an entire island's population; he chanted of Christian missionaries from Boston and Hawai'i who forbade the people from chanting the chants and practicing the magic that taught the ways of navigation and healing and proper living; he chanted of the Japanese who came and pushed out the Germans and worked the people even harder and brought so many settlers that at one time there were more Japanese living in the islands than Marshallese; he chanted of the Americans who brought the bomb and jellyfish babies and *Happy Days* on TV. Ņoniep chanted into the tree the names of plants good for making balms to put on burns, of medicines that heal.

Now, knowing how very soon he will die, Ņoniep chants of the demons who paddle from the west, sent by Wūllep and Ļajibwināṃōņ, intent on stealing his soul. He sees them as he revisits a dream: Ṃōñāļapeņ, a hideous rat-like creature whose coarse black hair hides a secret sucking mouth at the back of his head, whose many bony legs click like crab legs at the bottom of the canoe; and Kwōjenmeto, half man, half enigma, his enormous head glowing from an internal fire, his tight gray skin shining with the prismatic sheen of rotting meat. N̦oniep is old. He is tired. He is brave, unafraid, but he wonders if he will have enough strength for this, his greatest fight.

N̦oniep finishes his chanting, tosses off his protective coat of kaōnōn vines, and, led by a forked walking stick, moves stiffly but with practiced silence through the rain-soaked jungle to the lagoon shore. He finds Jebro sitting under a tarp with his brother, Nuke, and creeps, invisibly, to a spot not less than five paces away. While he is anxious to reach out and inspect Jebro's soul, to grab just a little of it to put inside the tree, he waits, studying Jebro's face, admiring the potent kindness he exudes. For a moment he ignores the ugly, frightful things he must face this day.

As if to remind him, a crushed Pepsi can flies from Nuke's hand and strikes N̦oniep square in the face.

So ready is N̦oniep to fight demons, so coiled are his nerves in anticipation, that in between the time when the can hits his face and before it falls to the ground, he leaps out and is barely able to stifle his battle cry of the crazy diving nightbird.

N̦oniep slips back into the jungle, suddenly embarrassed, worried. Soon he will engage Wūllep's fiercest demons, and yet he cannot prevent being struck in the face by a boy armed only with an aluminum can.

But as he calms his nerves, and his ancient mind becomes more attuned to the complex energies around him, he becomes aware of another, more intimate relevance to the odd chance of getting hit in the face in the same instant that he dropped his guard. He knows of the way things happen by the influence of other things, and just as the presence of certain fish throwing themselves on the beach reveals the presence of a particular predator, getting hit in the face by a can points unmistakably to the presence of energy that could be coming from only one other being.

Focused now, N̦oniep works toward the source of that energy, hobbling all the way to the north corner of the island, where he pauses, his dwarf body knee-deep on the reef in front of a dark tide pool. Thick raindrops make crowns on the water. Without looking, he jabs the forked end of his stick into the pool and pins a blue-spotted grouper. "I win!" he shouts. "Our game of hide-and-seek is finally over and you lose!"

Etao rises from the pool and pushes the stick away from his neck. He wears a Lakers basketball jersey, number 33, and a pair of gray cotton gym shorts. His feet are bare. He leans over Ņoniep, his brow furrowed by a look of exaggerated curiosity. "What happened to your face?"

"I am old, you fool, as old as anything on this island. What did you expect after so much time?"

Etao sneers, his white eyebrows bunching toward his nose. "I want to know how you found me . . . how—I never lose!"

Ņoniep smiles at his long-gone friend, seeing that other than his clothing, his looks have not changed. "If one seeks long enough," he says, "he finds, and now, if you remember the rules of our game, you must give that magic shell of yours to Keār."

"Keār," Etao growls, "that is how you found me, how you got into my dreams and made me come here by some spell—admit it!"

"Hand over that shell and then maybe I can give you some of my secrets."

"You forget," Etao says, shaking his head, "that you were supposed to find me that night, so—"

"You cheated! You sailed away so you lose!"

Etao laughs. "I know you're angry, but that's not the way the game works. I think we have a tie, at best."

Ņoniep reaches for the shell with his stick but Etao dances away. "Give me that shell! Something terrible is about to happen!"

"We should have one more game," Etao says. "I think some play will be good for you."

"Wait! Don't hide from me!" But Etao has already run into the jungle, leaving Ņoniep knee-deep in rising water on the reef.

The Pair of Dolphins

THE SLIME FLOC ON the first RBC was shaggy with a brown to gray color, looking good, but in spots it had sloughed off into the liquor and that meant something was wrong. It was a common problem, probably a pH imbalance caused by some industrial chemicals entering with the influent. After determining the pH, Rujen could mix in some lime or acetic acid, maybe dilute the tank with effluent. It was a decision he could make, but he always checked first with Andy, his boss, just to be sure. Rujen was a Waste Worker I, and even though his job description said he was only good for cleaning and disinfecting, skimming, or shoveling sludge cakes, he was a quick learner, a safe worker, and Andy let him handle more important things. Rujen spent most of his time taking care of the RBCs (Rotating Biological Contactors that look like paddle wheels) and collecting samples from their tanks. If needed, he could also remove the headers and flush the orifices, replace the seals and bearings, and even help measure oxygen demand. It was a job that not only required Rujen to sometimes do hard sweating labor, but also a good deal of thinking.

When Rujen was a small boy on Tar-Wōj, before the missionaries built outhouses, he and everybody else did their toilet business on the north-end reef where the tide and current took it out to sea. Some customs were observed, such as a father not relieving himself within sight or sound of his eldest son, but these were easily accommodated with so few people living on the island. Next to breathing, maybe it was the simplest part of life. Anybody who thought too much about it was probably crazy.

Ebeye's first toilets were Japanese *benjos*, stilted platforms extending over the lagoon, but when Rujen and all the rest of the mid-atoll people had to move to the island, the Corps of Engineers put in a real toilet system with saltwater flushing. The system pumped raw sewage into the lagoon, exiting an outfall a few hundred feet from shore. As Ebeye became more populated, as more and more people flushed more and more waste down the toilets, the pumping station had to do more work than it was designed for and it eventually failed under the increased load. The sewage had to go somewhere, so it escaped right in front of the island. It was a horrible job to fix that broken pump all the time and to fix the broken mains, but for money some people were willing to do it.

With Ebeye so crowded it was hard to observe the customs related to using the toilet, but Rujen and some other men had made arrangements with each other so that they did not have to relieve themselves within sight or sound of their sons. A house might have many visitors after meal times, and although everybody knew what was going on, they pretended not to be aware. It was better that way, and sometimes it was funny because two or three men might show up at the same house at the same time and have to pretend that they came to play cards.

When the sewage pump was not working, people still had to go—no stopping it, no saving it for another day—so they had to find someplace outside. With more than eight thousand people living on one-tenth of a square mile, finding a private place to go took some work. Peeing was easier because you could do it quick, sometimes looking like you were just sitting on your heels. But if you had to move your bowels, most of the time you had to wait for dark. Rujen sometimes used the reef, as lots of other people did, but having a crowd out there with their pants or panties down led to all sorts of trouble—and gossip—so if it was crowded he found another spot. The breakwater on the lagoon side was good and dark, lots of boulders he could drop his stuff between, but he had to remember to bring a flashlight or risk stepping in somebody else's mess. In daylight, he could see clumps of toilet paper and turds all over the breakwater, waiting for wind or waves or rain to wash them away. Rujen's friend Jiem sometimes spread his arms and joked that the breakwater looked as though it had been strafed by a "giant shit-bombing shitbird."

Even if the pump was working, many people did their business outside anyway because toilets did not exist in many of the homes, and having a toilet meant you had to wait for quite a while sometimes before it was your turn. Rujen's joke was that the government would soon issue rubber plugs to the people of Ebeye, and then there would be Marshallese swelling like balloons and exploding all over the place.

The sewage pump always broke if there was diarrhea going around—so many extra flushes shock-loading the system—and when that happened, those afflicted emptied their guts wherever they had time to get to, sometimes not very far from their homes. Not only was diarrhea messy, it was noisy too and if you heard it close by your house you knew the smell would get you soon. Rujen had learned, from working at the Kwajalein sewage plant, why so many extra people got diarrhea when the pump broke down. It was because of flies. Ebeye had so many flies that people jokingly referred to them as the Ebeye Air Force. Diarrhea was caused by tiny little protozoa, little diarrhea demons (so he had named them after looking through a microscope at work) and when flies landed on some diarrhea, as they liked to do, they picked up these little demons and passed them on by landing on your food. You could not avoid flies during the day, swarming around garbage piles and people as seabirds do over schools of fish, and they were not shy about flying around your mouth or your plate of spam and beans. You could get worms that way too (one kind of worm got so big that it stuck out your butthole just like the rubber plugs Rujen joked about), and you could get even more parasites or sickness from flea and mosquito bites or from getting bit by a rat. Diarrhea might seem funny at first, but it could get violent and sometimes it killed people, especially babies and old people, and when it started it took a long time to go away no matter how fast they got the pump working again.

Rujen also knew that spilling raw sewage into the lagoon was unhealthy, the cause of skin infections, and it spread sickness through the fish people caught (he and his household never ate fish caught from Ebeye). For years he had mentioned to authorities that Ebeye needed a new system, one that treated the sewage, but not until just recently had anything been done. A concrete oxidation ditch and clarifier was being built by Filipino contractors but it was nowhere near operational. Promised money had yet to be released from the United States for "phase two," all the rest of the work that had to be done. A new freshwater system was also planned and so were improvements to the power plant, but until then the power was out more than it was on, and the Army sold to Ebeye freshwater barged from Kwajalein. More than anything Ebeye needed a decent hospital, one with real doctors and medicines like the one that took care of the Americans at Kwajalein. This new hospital was promised, and to ease the overcrowding a causeway was planned to connect Ebeye to its uninhabited neighbor islands, maybe even as far as Kwajalein, so that people could take a bus to work.

Someday Ebeye would be as nice a place to live as anywhere, and while Rujen had always believed this, and had always been a strong believer in progressing to join the modern world, he could not help but suspect on this troublesome day of his, Good Friday, that things had never progressed forward at all but backward, upside-down, inside-out, and it seemed almost prophetic to him that the ancient Marshallese had used the word *epjā* (from which the Americans had derived Ebeye) to name the island where he lived. *Epjā* was short for *epliklik jā:* Mostly capsized.

Whatever things were bothering Rujen this day, he didn't have to think much about them once he got to work. That was one of the benefits of having a job. Most Marshallese on Ebeye did not have jobs, and many of these people were among the most unhappy. So many young men killed themselves, and it was a fact that almost all of them were unemployed. It was not that they were not cared for—because Marshallese custom ensured they be given food and clothing and a place to sleep—but that they had nothing to do all day but sit around, drink when they could get it, or roam in circles in search of change and smokes. Nobody relied on them, nobody could make any use of them, nobody asked for their advice, and as if by some design, their idle minds found troubled thoughts, while their idle hands found rope and learned to tie a noose.

Rujen had felt awkward about clocking in late, and especially about not having any boots, but one of his Marshallese coworkers (Sampson, an old man from Lae) had told him about a pair of boots in the shed where they kept the chlorine. The boots were dry and cracked and splattered with tar and three different colors of paint. A spider bit Rujen's toe when he put them on, and the cushioned insoles were so rotten that he had to rip them out. The boots chafed his ankles, hurt the bare bottoms of his feet, and as he stood over the RBC tank, testing the pH, he rose up and down on his toes and worked his feet this way and that to soften the leather. Heavy rain had come down earlier, but now the wind had mostly died and the flat gray sky released only an occasional spray. Still, the catwalks and decks were slippery, and Rujen had to be careful moving around because the bottoms of the old boots had been worn smooth. He missed the cool wind, and while he didn't wish his boys to be out in rough weather, he hoped for at least a small breeze to return by night to combat the humidity brought by the rain.

Five-point-five on the pH tester showed the liquor to be more acid than it should be, and while Rujen stared at the rotating wheel of the RBC, the spots there where the slime had sloughed off, he tried to anticipate whether Andy would want to dilute the tank or just add some lime. Inside the tank, within the dark turbulent liquor being churned by the RBC, it was a hellish world where millions of bacteria and protozoa were employed to devour organic material and even each other, all in the process of eliminating anything that might cause disease or pollution. A perfect balance of conditions had to be maintained, and if the balance was upset, then the whole tank might become black and foul smelling, and certain kinds of bacteria would dominate and rob the water of all its oxygen. Andy called this a septic condition, Rujen called it death water.

Sometimes Rujen looked through the microscopes in the lab, seeing all the different kinds of bacteria that were shaped like strings of beads or like springs or ladders. Fungi and nymphs and pupas and tiny rat-tailed maggots lived in the liquor too, but the protozoa, like little demons, were almost frightening things to see. A chart on the wall gave them names. Some of them looked like rays and others like jellyfish or urchins, and one called *litonotus* looked something like a porcupine puffer fish. The ones that caused diarrhea looked like blobs. All of the little creatures were ugly, foul, sometimes deadly, but by taking advantage of their endless mindless nastiness, Rujen and his coworkers treated the incoming sewage, and when they achieved the proper balance, they made it pure again.

Andy Thygerson, Supervisor of Wastewater Treatment, was tall and heavy, and in his jeans and boots he walked bowlegged like a lanky cowboy. He was over forty, single, and he spoke loudly through a mouthful of crooked teeth and braces. At times, especially if somebody new was around, he would stand on the skimming bridge that spanned the sedimentation tank and shout, "Smells like money to me!" He would always laugh as if it were the first time he'd said it. Today he complained about a hangover and wouldn't let anybody turn on the lights in his office.

Andy's office stood high like a ship's wheelhouse, having large windows that looked over the rectangular array of tanks and the sludge bed and the Kwajalein lagoon beyond them. Rujen stopped at the top of the concrete stairs and looked, for the third time since coming to work, across the lagoon into the gray distance where lay Tar-Wōj. Jebro and Nuke should have arrived long ago, now probably in the thick of the storm and the wind that left Kwajalein, and while Rujen still worried about the helicopters and patrol boats and Jebro maybe losing his opportunity to work on Kwajalein, he was surprised to find himself, overall, actually feeling good about his sons being at Tar-Wōj against the law. He joked to himself that maybe it was his father's ornery spirit vexing him this day, causing his troubles, putting ideas inside his head. Ataji had often threatened to haunt the islands, not willing to let even death stop his fight. "Better you, I think, than the devil," Rujen spoke softly.

When Rujen opened the door to the darkened air-conditioned office, he found Andy sitting at his uncluttered metal desk and laughing into the phone. Crawford Pelton, the lab guy, a balding man in his late thirties from Las Vegas—so thin that Andy had nicknamed him Tape, short for tapeworm—sat on a high stool by the coffee machine. He wore, as usual, a highwater pair of gray slacks and shabby brown dress shoes over black socks that had fallen down around his ankles. One of Crawford's hands picked his teeth while the other filled his cup. Rujen had never cared much for Crawford, mostly because Crawford liked to get bossy whenever Andy wasn't around, often telling people, especially the Marshallese, to do small, mostly janitorial tasks while he stood by and watched. Rujen remained polite to him though, careful never to reveal his dislike.

Just the desk, the stool, some shelves packed tight with manuals, and the counter where stood the coffee machine was all that furnished the office, and on the walls amid schematic diagrams of systems and equipment was a tool calendar by the door, and over the desk was the badly stuffed head of a cougar Andy had shot in Utah.

"Hang on a sec," Andy said into the phone. He looked up at Rujen. "You ever eat a dolphin?"

Rujen had, but he didn't favor the greasy meat. "It's not so good."

"C'mon, really?"

Rujen shrugged. Andy swivelled around in his chair so that he faced the wall and continued his conversation. Crawford's dark, sunken eyes, half-closed as though he were half in a trance, peered over his steaming coffee at Rujen in a way that Crawford often looked at people, as if they were under one of his microscopes. Crawford never said much, and it seemed as though he thought it was perfectly normal to stare at people without speaking.

Rujen stood by the door for a few moments, working his feet around in the boots, but when it seemed as though he could actually feel Crawford's gaze boring into his mind, he pushed back against the door and helped himself to half a cup of coffee. He was just about to mention the pH problem to Crawford when Andy spun back around and hung up the phone.

"So," Andy said, looking once at Rujen and then at Crawford. "Get this. Hansen down at the power plant can't find a couple of his men—two Marshallese—anyway, his truck's gone too and he's gettin' steamed, right?—so after a while here comes his two Marshallese bringin' back the truck, comin' back all wet and gettin' Hansen's seat wet too, and they say to him—get this—*'It's okay, we were just fishing!'* "

Andy laughed so hard that his chair squeaked. He slapped the top of his desk. "*'It's okay, we were just fishing!'* So Hansen, you know, he's playin' along, he says, 'Catch anything?' And the two guys kinda just look at each other and down at the ground, you know, and one looks up and says, 'Couple big fish,' as if they caught some snapper, right?—but Hansen gets it out of 'em that really what they got was a couple dolphins, you know, like Flipper—I don't know *how*—"

"Rocks," Rujen said, smiling. "That's how you catch dolphins, by hitting rocks."

"Why not use a spear or something?" Crawford asked. "I mean, really—"

Andy squinted at Rujen. "You're shittin' me—rocks?"

Rujen saw that he was misunderstood and laughed. "You don't hit dolphins with the rocks, you hit rocks like this, underwater." He knocked his fists together. "It makes them dizzy—you know how they see by sonar. Marshallese have known a long time how to hit rocks together and trick dolphins to the beach."

Crawford set down his cup. "It's illegal, right? You can't kill dolphins—it's like whales."

"Hansen wondered the same thing," Andy said. "But, see, his guys didn't do any butcherin' yet, nothin' like that. They just dropped the dolphins in that turtle pond over there by the Comm. Center—I guess keepin' 'em fresh for later. That's why they needed a truck. Anyway, I'm sure somebody'll come along and say what's what with the law. Meantime, Hansen's got those Marshallese scrubbin'—"

"I don't think that's the law," Rujen said. "I never heard anybody say not to catch dolphins, not to catch anything except . . . you know, Marshallese used to say don't catch some things because it was poison, or some things if it was breeding season, but—"

"U.S. law," Crawford said. "I think it's U.S. law."

"I don't know," Rujen said, looking up at the wall clock. "Maybe for this that law is not so . . ." His lunch break was in half an hour. "The pH in number one is five-point-five," he said to Andy. "You want me to drop some lime?"

"Yeah . . . drop some lime, you know how much." Andy headed for the coffee machine. "'*It's okay, we were just fishing,*'" he repeated, chuckling as he let Crawford fill his cup.

Rujen dropped his cup in the trash can, noticing just as he released it that it was still half full. It landed bottom down, cradled by crumpled papers, not spilling a drop. He took it to be a sign that his luck this day was changing for the better, and although he now had no bicycle, he thought very strongly that he should try walking fast so that he could have his lunch down at the turtle pond.

Smoke

THE MASSIVE BLACK stones of Tar-Wōj curved some thirty yards into the lagoon and looked as if they had once been level and fitted tightly together. Now wide gaps and fractures allowed the lagoon water to wash freely between them. With a few treacherous leaps, however, it was still possible to walk from one end of the formation to the other. Jebro jumped onto the first stone and nearly fell off. "Watch out," he said as he extended a hand to his brother. "Slippery."

The rain came down in intermittent sheets while the wind, still pushing waves against the stones, gusted less and less as if the flat gray underbelly of the sky was having trouble catching its breath. Carefully, the two brothers walked out to where the stones started curving to the left and stopped. Jebro handed Nuke the line's end and told him to kneel, then, gripping the knot where the nylon met the monofilament, he swung the baited papaya and the weight three times around his head and let them fly. The rig splashed some twenty yards from the stones and sank to a sandy area fifteen feet deep. Maybe fifty yards of slack line remained. "Now we go back and wait." Jebro said. He held the rope high as he worked his way back off the stones, and when he reached the lean-to he handed it over to Nuke. "I think you should be the one to hold the rope."

Nuke wrapped it tightly around his hand and stood ready, his eyes focused on the water where the bait had gone down. Jebro laughed. "Relax, little brother, it takes time. Sit."

Nuke sat next to Jebro, the rope still taut going into the water.

Jebro took it from him. "Hold it like this," he said, letting the rope go slack. "If you wrap it around your hand you might lose some fingers, and if you keep it tight, then you won't hook the turtle."

Nuke took back the rope and fumbled to remove a pack of cigarettes from his backpack. "You have my matches."

Jebro reached into his pocket and handed them over.

Nuke struck one, then another. "The matches are wet!"

"Sorry, just let them dry. You can smoke again tomorrow."

"I can't do that." He looked annoyed, as though Jebro had asked him to stop breathing.

"I have some other matches in my bag—waterproof ones."

"Good, give them to me."

"I have only three, and we need them to make a fire tonight. Wait till then."

"No way can I wait that long."

"Okay, I'll give you one match—just one." Jebro took a film container out of his duffel bag and pinched a wooden match from it. The head was green, with a white tip that would spark if scratched on any rough surface. He struck it on the zipper of his shorts and cupped it in his hand.

Nuke leaned over and lit his cigarette.

Jebro stuck the match in the sand. "Keep your cigarette away from the rope."

"Of course—do you think I'm stupid?"

"No, but I lost a fish once that way. Do you want to hear the story of the stones now?"

"Okay, tell me."

Jebro leaned back on his elbows and shook rainwater from his hair. "All right, listen: This island is haunted, especially this spot here by the stones. So—"

"Who are the ghosts?"

"Just listen. Long ago, before Marshallese found these islands, a race of dwarfs lived here on Tar-Wōj. They were great fishermen and lived a good life. One day a sorcerer flew in on a canoe—"

"Wait—how can a canoe fly?"

"I said he was a sorcerer. He used magic. So he flew in on his canoe and he told the dwarfs he would help them build a great city. They told the sorcerer—"

"What was the sorcerer's name?"

"His name was Nuke—now be quiet and let me finish the story. The dwarfs said they were too busy fishing and making canoes to build a city. So the sorcerer used his magic and made fish jump onto the beach. He said he would provide for the dwarfs, give them fish, make breadfruit and coconut fall from the sky already cooked. He did all that and the dwarfs had no excuse for not building the city." Jebro pointed to the large black stones. "The sorcerer flew these stones in on his canoe and dropped them on the beach. Have you ever seen stones like these anywhere else, on any other island?"

"No."

"So you see this story is true. The stones are from magic. The sorcerer instructed the dwarfs to pile the stones in the lagoon, to build the city up out of the water—"

"Wait—it makes no sense. The sorcerer just could have used his magic to build the city."

"He did it that way because he was evil. He wanted slaves. He made the dwarfs work very hard, and they did so for many generations. They forgot how to fish, and forgot their customs and their religion. When the city was finished, the sorcerer told the dwarfs that they wouldn't be allowed to live inside. Only he could live there and the dwarfs would have to serve him and pray to him if they wanted food. The dwarfs grew very mad at the sorcerer. *Raar maijek leo im mane*—They ganged up on him and killed him."

"What happened to the city?"

"These stones are all that's left. The rest is buried under the sand."

"Eban!—I can't believe that!"

"Iñña̅—It's true!"

Nuke looked at the short, smoldering end of his cigarette. "What am I going to do when I want another cigarette?"

"Wait until tonight, when we have a fire."

"I told you, I can't wait that long."

"If you were a fish, I'd know what to use for bait."

"Just let me keep one match, for later."

"No, we need them for fire. There is only one thing you can do. How many packs do you have?"

"Plenty."

"Okay, light another cigarette from the one in your hand. I can help you baidtōn̄tōn̄—chain-smoke."

"That's a waste."

"What else can we do?"

"Build the fire now."

"But the helicopters will see the smoke."

"Ōrrōr." Nuke lit another cigarette, and stubbed out the other in the sand. He and Jebro shared it without speaking, and then Jebro lit another one. He puffed once and passed it to Nuke.

Nuke pointed with the cigarette to the line of stones. "So what happened to the dwarfs?"

"They all died. They had forgotten how to catch fish and how to open a coconut. The sorcerer had provided for them too much, and after they killed him, they all starved to death. Their ghosts still haunt the island. Do you believe it?"

"Where did you hear that story?"

"Ataji told me when I was your age, not long before he came over here and died. We sneaked over here one day to catch a turtle, like we're doing today, but he fished a different way. We walked out to the end of the stones and put rocks inside a breadfruit so that it would sink. While we waited, he told me the story."

"There was a hook inside the breadfruit?"

"No hook, no rope. When a turtle came for the breadfruit, Ataji dived in and tried to flip it over so that he could push it to shore. But he was too old. The turtle cut him with its claw. You should have seen him splashing around out there, cussing at the turtle. I had to turn away so he wouldn't see me laughing."

"That's a story I can believe. I only remember him a little, but he was always angry. I'd hide from him."

"He was only like that on Ebeye. Out here, or on the water, he was different. You better light another cigarette—that one's almost out."

"Okay. So, why not use breadfruit for bait, go diving for the turtle?"

"I could. I know many ways to fish. Today, I want to fish with a rope." Jebro nibbled at one of the papaya quarters. "I use this instead of breadfruit because turtles can't resist it. They smell it and go crazy. They have to eat it no matter what—cannot stop, and then they get hooked. Can you think of anything that works like that on a young man?"

"Biiibi—pooosy." They fell over laughing.

"That's not what I was thinking." Jebro slapped Nuke on the back, causing him to cough. "Hey, what do you know about bibi anyway?"

Nuke cleared his throat. "I know plenty."

"Right, I saw you talking to Emly the other day."

"Ōrrōr! Errūbrūb ledik eņ—that girl farts all the time. I have no idea why she likes me."

"Because you look like me, very handsome."

"Ōrrōr." Nuke looked out at the water. "If your papaya is such great bait, why don't I see any turtles going crazy out there?"

"I also learned from Grandfather to be patient. We waited all morning before a turtle came. But no need to worry—my papaya will bring one soon." Jebro took a drag from the cigarette and passed it to Nuke. "Quick, light another one."

"This is stupid."

"What else can we do?"

"You should have kept my matches dry."

"You should have brought more."

The wind suddenly dropped to almost nothing, while at the same time a torrent of thick raindrops began falling straight down. From not too far away came the muffled whump of a helicopter, becoming louder. Jebro glanced quickly at the fronds and vines covering the boat. "It will never see us," he said, patting his brother's shoulder. "We are invisible now."

The Breadfruit Tree

ETAO IN HIS LAKERS jersey and gym shorts splashes through the jungle and tries to hide by disguising himself as a rock, but Ņoniep finds him right away. Etao tries hiding as a crab and then as a breadfruit high atop Ņoniep's extraordinarily tall breadfruit tree, but just as before Ņoniep pelts him with a handful of pebbles and shouts, "You lose!"

Etao drops from the breadfruit tree and scowls at Ņoniep. "Maybe you are the one who cheats!"

"Nonsense! Now hand over that piece of turtle shell!"

Etao shrugs. "I cannot. We had no wager on today's game."

"You must! Listen for once, and when I explain—"

"Explain to me what's going on with this tree. I can tell you have been up to something here." Etao jumps four times his height into the air and swings from a branch, startling a bird from its nest. It splatters Ņoniep's nose.

Ņoniep wipes a wet hand across his face and spits. He leans forward on his stick, takes a deep breath, and bites his lower lip as he stares into space. Raindrops plunk and rattle surrounding leaves and fill muddy puddles at his feet. "Okay," he says, "the tree is a good place to begin. Just listen, then you have to help me. You see, one day a young man will use this tree to make a very fine canoe, so I put inside a little piece of my soul. I will put inside a little of his soul too, and in the meantime I have been filling the tree with all my knowledge. It is terribly important I do this because—"

"Did you tell the tree any stories? Did you tell it anything about me?"

"Yes, I told many stories, even some about you, but listen—"

Etao lets go of the branch and lands in front of Ņoniep. "I'm sure I have some stories you didn't tell, so you should be the one to listen now." Etao clears his throat.

"Etao, this is a waste of time!"

"Impossible!"

"Let me explain what—"

"Quiet! You'll spoil my story!"

Ņoniep grinds his stick into the jungle floor. "Hurry then, please, we have little time."

"I told you: Impossible! Now listen, this is one of my favorite stories." Etao turns to the tree. "I will tell you how people came to have necks, because a long time ago everybody's head sat right on top of their shoulders. So one day I am down south, at Ebon I think, and I challenge this chief to a game of hide-and-seek. He seeks and he seeks all day, but I'm very good"—Etao looks back to smile scornfully at Ņoniep—"and after a while he becomes so thirsty that he's almost crazy, and he thinks he's really lucky when he finds one of those holes in a coconut tree where water collects, but the water is deep down and he has to lean in far to reach it. '*Eguuk!*' that chief yells when he gets all of his head inside, because the water—oh man!—it stinks, but when he tries to get himself out of the tree, the hole closes tight—this is of course because I am the tree, and the hole, you know, that's my butthole!"

Etao bends over and his legs become the trunk of a coconut tree. "See!"

A hole in the trunk clenches tight.

"Now I have this chief stuck good by his head, and he pulls and he pushes and his legs are kicking and he screams, so I swing him side to side, like this, and when I see a good neck made there over his shoulders, I gas him out like this!"

A roiling cloud of curdled air explodes from the hole in the tree and knocks Ņoniep onto his backside. He gasps for breath while at the same time he throws clumps of mud and twigs at the tree now changing back into a laughing Etao.

"Enough!" Ņoniep shouts. "How can you have lived so long and seen so much and still be the same foolish clown? Are you blind to the truth, that not one person, not one plant, one fish, one tree, is safe from the curse of your father's growing evil?"

"If that's true, then it's a very good thing I've never changed!" Etao gives Ņoniep a hand up out of the mud. "So," he says, "that is the story of how people first got necks, something to put a little distance between their heads and their stomachs. My next story is how I taught people about the better use of their genitals. This also happens down south, at Kili—"

"Not now Etao, please!"

"Okay then, some other day when you aren't so busy I'll come back and finish the story." Etao turns and begins walking away.

"Wait!" Ņoniep reaches out with his stick and whacks Etao's heel. "You can't leave! I have no 'some other day,' only today . . . and I need your help. Today, Etao, this afternoon, I will have my last living moment, and then I must die."

Etao stops, stands still, then turns around. He frowns for just a moment then smiles again. "So you want me to finish my story?"

Ņoniep pokes his stick between the threes on Etao's Lakers jersey. "You *must* promise to help me."

"First I *must* finish telling your tree my second story. And because this is your last day, you should relax, enjoy it, make it a good day if not your best one. That's the only way I can think of to help you."

"I need you to give up that piece of turtle shell, Etao."

"First, my story, then I will be the one to decide what other help I give you, and I don't see this shell ever leaving my neck—I can promise you that for sure."

"Etao—"

"So I'm down south like I said—and this is in the time before necks—and a man keeps begging me for food. He knows I can make food appear, so he won't even try fishing and he gets very hungry because all he does all day is beg me. This man has a wife and she's really something, so one day I tell the man to bring his wife and I'll make some food for them. I take them far from their house and I make for them a fruit tree like you never saw before—the best fruit I ever made and so sweet that even though I tried I can never make it again. I tell the wife to climb and get some of the fruits, and when she gets up high I point between her legs and I tell that man, 'Look! Look at that gash on your wife! Run back and get some medicine!' You see, people in those days were not very smart, and none of them knew anything about each other's genitals. Well, that lazy man badly needed his wife's help to survive so he ran away quick for the medicine, and as soon as he was gone I told his wife to come down and I really showed her how to use that pudendum of hers. When the husband came running back and he saw what I was doing to his wife, his mouth dropped wide open and he had a heart attack right there and died."

Etao leaps up to a thick spreading branch of the breadfruit tree and bounces so hard while he laughs that showers of water come loose from the leaves, and ripe and unripe leathery-skinned breadfruits, oblong ten-pound green or yellow bombs, come crashing down and land with heavy wet splats at N̦oniep's feet, some of them splitting wide open to reveal the mealy yellow pulp inside. "Life was pretty boring for people before I showed them about sex. Now who can live without it!"

N̦oniep stares angrily at Etao. "I've had to live without it for a very long time."

"And you say you are about to die. See what can happen!"

The noise of an approaching helicopter causes N̦oniep to look toward the lagoon beach. "Come with me, Etao," he says. "I want to show you the young man who will build a canoe from this tree."

Ņoniep pushes through the jungle and Etao follows.

"Those two on the beach?" Etao says. "I saw them already and they have a power boat. If anything is foolish, it's your thinking that they need a canoe."

"Have you forgotten how much you used to love sailing?"

"Yes I have—because now I've learned to fly like a missile. Nothing compares."

Ņoniep stops and faces Etao. "Maybe it was you who gave the Americans knowledge of the bomb! Maybe it was you who—"

"I had nothing to do with the bomb," Etao says, pushing Ņoniep along. "You should know that's not my style."

The sound of coughing from the nearby lagoon beach is just audible against the rumble of the passing helicopter. Ņoniep warns Etao with a look to be quiet and creeps to a spot beside the lean-to. As the helicopter passes, the brothers' voices become distinct. Ņoniep points out Jebro to Etao.

"Quick, give me another one to light," Jebro says, holding the short smoking butt of a cigarette.

Nuke hands him a fresh cigarette. "We should just build a small fire."

"The helicopters will see the smoke."

Etao elbows Ņoniep in the ribs. "I think if you put some of that smoker's soul in your tree it might catch fire."

Ņoniep frowns. "I—it must be you, your presence always causes trouble. Jebro never smoked. . . ."

"Jebro? That's a name for a youngest brother. His family must not be very bright."

"The name suits him well. He has the qualities."

"You're going to create the first tree that's an addict."

"It means nothing!" Ņoniep hisses. "I'm sure he has a reason, and whether he wants to smoke now or not—it makes no difference to me. I have admired his soul ever since he was inside his mother's womb. Now I need a little piece of it."

"Those six fingers on his left hand must mean he was born to hold a lot of cigarettes."

"Quiet! I need to be careful." N̦oniep moves his hand toward Jebro, beckoning with his fingers, gently as if rubbing a cat's purring throat. At the back of Jebro's head emerges a clear fluid-like ball and it rolls on the air, gently pulsing, into N̦oniep's palm. He cups the ball in both his hands and brings it close, one hand on top to keep it from floating away. Within it are faint whorls and dancing beads of prismatic light. "I can tell now why he smokes," N̦oniep says. "Everything is fine, wonderfully pure." With the nail of his pinkie he gently teases the soul until it releases a little part of itself, a small round ball about the size of a fish egg. Then, with a little push, N̦oniep sends the remainder of the soul back inside Jebro's head, and with the little piece of it in his hands, he slowly backs away. "Come to the breadfruit tree with me," he says to Etao, "and when I put this soul inside then we can talk about your father and what to do about his demons."

Lunch Time

Walking fast over the gravel back road worked some painful blisters into Rujen's feet, and the cracked leather of the old boots had also rubbed raw parts of his ankles. He began sweating heavily about three-quarters of the way to the turtle pond, and to keep cool he tied the top part of his overalls around his waist. Just a very faint breath of humid air sometimes wavered tree leaves and palm fronds along his way, while the overcast sky hung low like a damp gray sponge dripping infrequent single drops of water. To Rujen's right the slack wind allowed the lagoon's surface to glass over and purl, and in the watery distance it blurred smoothly into nothing but clouds at the horizon.

Rujen heard a bicycle approaching behind him, and when he turned around he was surprised to see that it was Lazarus, a nephew of his from his sister's family. Lazarus, a few years older than Jebro, was a young man whose greatest asset in life was his winning smile—and he used it for all it was worth. If some Americans came to Ebeye looking for girls, Lazarus was there to help them, of course getting himself some beers and smokes and maybe a good plate of restaurant food in the bargain. When missionaries and other visitors came to Ebeye for the first time, Lazarus was there to grab their bags and help them into a taxi, and if because Lazarus was so quick in helping them that one of their bags got left behind—then Lazarus might end up with some kind of reward for returning it safely.

Lazarus was a schemer, a scrounger, a Johnny-on-the-spot wherever some little profit was to be had, and it was not uncommon on Ebeye to hear somebody say, "Your Lazarus smile can't fool me," or "Watch out, that boy has a Lazarus smile."

"Hello, Uncle!" Lazarus smiled broadly as he skidded an adult's tricycle to a stop beside Rujen. He wore a new white T-shirt and khaki shorts, sunglasses, a nice-looking wristwatch, and a new pair of Adidas on his feet, all obviously bought on Kwajalein. The seat on the tricycle was the largest Rujen had ever seen, with multiple black springs underneath.

"You sure look good," Rujen said, turning Lazarus's hand so that he could see his watch, a Titus, not very cheap. "So tell me how you got here on Kwajalein and have all these fine things. Tell me why the police aren't chasing you right now. This should be the best story I've heard all year."

Lazarus took a long look around then leaned in close to Rujen's face. "Ok, I will tell you, Uncle, I really got it good. Have you seen me on Ebeye the last few weeks?"

"No, not for quite a while."

"That's because while it was still dark one morning I sneaked over here by walking the reef—you know I do that at times to get some things . . . some goods . . . and take them back to Ebeye—well, this time I met a girl, a real honey I tell you, and when we get married then I'll be living over here as an American, and you—all my family—can visit anytime you like!" Lazarus, beaming, crossed his arms over his chest and nodded his head proudly.

Rujen was old enough to know when something sounded too good to be true. "So who is this honey of yours?" he asked. "Not some schoolgirl I hope, some girl whose father might be wanting to squash you."

"No no no, she works at the bakery, Melody—"

"Melody! My lord—" Rujen could not help but laugh. He had seen Melody the baker—an incredibly large white woman, the largest he had ever seen.

"What?"

Rujen stifled his laugh. "So she bought you these things? I thought you might have stolen them."

"Ōrrōr! Of course she bought these things. And for the last few weeks, because her roommate is back in America for a while, she's been hiding me in her apartment where all day with the air-conditioner as cold as I like I can eat anything I want and drink cold Michelob and take all the bubble baths I want—and I watch the television on her big puffy couch and when she gets home—*ōttōt!*—I give it to her Marshallese style, all damn night!"

Rujen laughed along with Lazarus, thinking that his nephew might really have fallen into some luck. Maybe that woman would marry him, and if she did then Lazarus of course would become an American. Whatever was going on between them now though, the clothes and things and the living together—that, Rujen knew, could get them both into trouble. "So the maids never see you? I'm surprised this gossip never found its way to Ebeye."

Lazarus looked serious for a moment. "Promise to say nothing, not until I'm an American. Come now, say it."

"You can trust me, Lazarus. I promise to say nothing, but I hope you know that because you are the man, that when you marry your American wife she will become a Marshallese, not the other way around."

"You lie!" Lazarus looked around as if for help. "I can't believe—"

Rujen laughed. "I'm joking—of course if you marry an American then you become one, I think."

"Good," Lazarus said, not laughing at Rujen's joke. "Just remember to say nothing until I'm a citizen. The maid for Melody's apartment, you see, she's one of my aunts—from my cousin's family—and I had to . . . uh . . . give her some things so now she knows to be quiet too." Lazarus lifted the front end of the tricycle and let it bounce back down. "I tell you I really got it good . . . but so much hiding in that apartment is hard for me, Uncle. That's why today I'm taking a tour, working my legs a little."

"If the police see you then your whole game is up."

"What do they know from one Marshallese to another? I can tell them I lost my badge, that I work as a janitor. Besides, do you really think they can catch me?" Lazarus, smiling, raised one of his new Adidas.

"I hope the best for you." Rujen checked the sturdiness of the three-wheeler's large rear basket. "Can you give me a ride up to the turtle pond? Just up the road."

"Anything for my uncle Rujen. And because you promise to keep my secret—no charge!" Lazarus shook his head to show that he was joking.

Rujen got himself standing in the basket and gripped his nephew's shoulders. "When you drop me off," he said, "you better get back into hiding. Maybe you can think of your poor hard-working uncle while you take one of those bubble baths."

"And I'll toast you with a Michelob at the same time, but first I better go one or two times around the island so I can have some sore legs to soothe in that bathtub."

When Rujen got out of the tricycle basket at the turtle pond, he stood for a few moments in the road and watched Lazarus pedal away. He chuckled, admiring the brazen confidence of his nephew, and tried to remember if there were any times in his own youth when he might have been of a similar mind. The only memory that came to him, though, was his stealing a bicycle just that morning. And then for no reason, almost as if the thought had been forced on him by some other mind, he found himself wondering whatever had happened to the maps he had collected when he was a boy. He could not remember, but just trying to made him feeling strangely uncomfortable, and to think about something else he turned his attention to the turtle pond.

Four little boys and girls ran up and down the pond, jumping at times and squealing. Their mothers, three of them, faced the water from a picnic table under the boughs of ironwood trees, the place where Rujen usually sat to eat. On the near side of another picnic table, partly camouflaged by shrubs, was a teenage couple sitting face to face, their heads bent over and brows nearly touching as they spoke.

The concrete pond, a manmade oasis lagoon-side of the Comm. Center and the Range Command building, was no bigger than a basketball court, oval shaped, with a sunbleached, blue mermaid in the center who drooled what was supposed to be a spout rising from her mouth. Within her shaded waters lived mullets and rudder fish and surgeon fish, unicorns, sea cucumbers, starfish, perches, wrasses, butterfly fish, and at times as many as four or five turtles but this day only one, a large adult male, maybe one hundred and fifty pounds, whose dark brown shell carried a thin rug of bright green algae as he made slow, wide orbits around the drooling mermaid. But what Rujen mostly looked at, as he sat down under a short stocky palm and took off his painful boots, what he was sure must have brought him here even though the sky could rain at any moment and he had no bicycle, was a pair of one hundred pound dolphins also making slow circles in the pond, passing the turtle every so often, gaining the manic attention of the children and the passive looks of their mothers, and sometimes, if the dolphins swam close by, a smiling glance from the teenagers. One of the dolphins listed to its left like a half-sunk boat, either sick or wounded, and as its partner nudged it along, the action of both their flukes caused curling eddies of water to trail behind them.

Rujen studied the chipped wet face of the mermaid, suddenly wishing that it was he who had caught the dolphins. It made no sense to him, especially because he didn't like the taste of their meat.

When Rujen pulled off the tight dry boots and leaned his back against the palm, his feet began throbbing with such force that they seemed to be separate living things. His ankles were raw, one of his toes was badly swollen by a spider bite, dried blood caked another toe where he had stubbed it while walking to work, and the bottoms of his feet were so badly blistered they looked as though they might have been held over a fire.

The danger of infection, how quick it might spread from a simple cut into something deadly poisonous, brought to mind images of people who neglected their sores, some losing limbs or dying from blood poisoning. It was more than enough incentive for Rujen to bandage his feet as soon as possible and to use an antiseptic to keep them extra clean. The stores would not sell him any such medical supplies, but the first aid kit at the plant had plenty of peroxide and bandages, and Andy was good about letting his Marshallese workers take from the kit as much as they needed.

Rujen thought for a moment that soaking his feet in the pond might help them feel better, but the dark water and the pond's gurgling filter reminded him of an RBC tank. He decided it was not a good place to put his open wounds. The lagoon was just across the gravel road, cool saltwater to clean and toughen the skin, but the thought of putting on the boots again to pick his way down the breakwater's jagged boulders, or even standing, was enough to keep him sitting on the ground, however uncomfortable it was. He felt annoyed, not just by the condition of his feet, but also by an increasing uneasiness he could neither explain nor push from his mind.

Marshallese workers were allowed to buy lunch at the Kwajalein Snack Bar, and for a long time that was where Rujen had gone, but maybe because Ebeye was so crowded, and the *Tarlang* was so crowded, and he dealt with so many people all day at work, one day a few years ago he had come to be alone at the turtle pond and, except for rainy days or bank days, he had come every working day since. To spend forty-five minutes alone within his thoughts, his eyes closed most of the time but not sleeping, was a good peaceful thing to do, and, at times unexpectedly, he could also imagine the company of his wife—now almost nine years dead. At first he found himself reliving old conversations or picturing some fine moments they had shared, then one afternoon he was surprised to hear Iia say that he made good sandwiches, and from that time on it was not uncommon for Rujen to ask things and get answers in return. He knew it was just his imagination playing tricks with him, and thought that maybe it was a childish thing to do, but he could not deny that it was the time of day he most looked forward to. Sometimes, he had to stop himself from speaking out loud.

Today, though, when he closed his eyes over the orbiting dolphins (and a mother stopping her child from throwing a rock at them) what he heard was not Iia's pleasant voice but the confusion of a hundred nagging voices, fevered gibberish goading him to confront what had been troubling him all day—not only his stolen boots, his bicycle, the sewage in his kitchen sink, or even the question of his soul, but all that and some mysterious other thing that made it all related, something bigger, and now it seemed as though coming to the pond on a rainy day had become part of it, and wishing that he had caught the dolphins had become part of it, but the more he thought about it the more uncomfortable he became as he approached discovering what it was, and right then to chase those thoughts away he opened his eyes and bit his lower lip just as one of the dolphins, the sick looking one, made a terrible raspy sound as it blew mist out of its blowhole.

Being at work and even enduring a painful walk had taken Rujen's mind off of whatever was haunting him, but being alone, just as he was when he rode off on that stolen bicycle, was all it took to get him thinking about nothing else. He knew now, too late, as he sat on the damp ground and winced at the pounding of his swollen feet, that he should not have come to the pond, that he should have known from his experience at the elementary school that it was no good for him to be alone this day, that he should have gone to the snack bar.

Rujen took another long look at the dolphins, wondering what there was about them, if anything, that could possibly make his coming to the pond something more than a foolish exercise in pain. He could think of nothing, except the pathetic thought that right now he was just as stranded as they were, which he was, in a way, as he could not walk back to work either barefoot or in the boots. He made up his mind to forget about the dolphins, to forget about whatever else was bothering him, and to find a ride back to the plant where he didn't have to think about much at all, just work. He could go over to the Comm. Center and call a taxi van, but because it was a rainy day it might take too long for one to arrive so far out in the island's industrial area. He might also call Andy, who had a truck, but he would have to wait until Andy got back to the plant after lunch and that would mean being late to work twice in the same day. The best thing to do was to go over by the road and wave down a passing truck or van, but with his feet still throbbing pain Rujen figured he better wait just a minute or two more before standing.

He glanced down at the paper bag beside him, his sandwich inside—canned tuna with mayo and whole, miniature sweet pickles between three pieces of bread, plus Cheeze Whiz—and a cold Pepsi wrapped in shop rags. He opened the Pepsi, deciding to eat just half the sandwich, fast, before moving over by the road.

Rujen used to make his sandwiches on Ebeye, mostly potted meat or chicken leftovers, but late last year Andy had agreed to do him a favor by taking some money to stock the refrigerator in the breakroom with sodas and enough meats and garnishes for Rujen to have a different kind of sandwich every day. The breakroom also had a rice cooker, hot plate, dishes, and even a knife set—a birthday gift mailed to Andy from his mother. Andy said the knives were probably a joke but he wasn't sure. The knives, set in slots on an orange, simulated tree trunk wooden block, all had large, multicolored plastic handles shaped like different kinds of fish. Rujen's favorite was the rainbow trout, not because he liked the fish but because the blade was sharp enough to make clean, thin slices and flexible enough to spread with. The food Rujen had Andy buy was three times cheaper than it would be on Ebeye, so it was a good way for Rujen to save some money, and it was also cheaper than eating at the snack bar. Andy wouldn't take money from his Marshallese workers to buy any beer or cigarettes, or any kind of things like batteries or watches that might get confiscated at the checkpoint and get him in trouble, but if somebody needed some aspirin or shoelaces, little things like that, he did not mind doing them a favor. Rujen thought he should ask Andy this afternoon to buy him a pair of socks.

An overweight man and his slightly smaller wife, both sweating and red in the face, parked their bicycles against the tree Rujen leaned on, crowding his elbows with their tires so much that he had to scoot forward. Rujen looked up at them but they didn't look down and walked past him as if he wasn't there. When the couple reached the fast-becoming-crowded edge of the pond, held hands, and began to make chirping noises, Rujen couldn't help but laugh, seeing that they were calling to the dolphins. It felt good to laugh and to smile, and for a moment, his mouth alive with the good taste of his sandwich, Rujen felt the tension within him start to recede.

His improved mood, he should have known, was not destined to last, and what killed it was that he could not help but overhear what a few people near him were saying about the Marshallese men who caught the dolphins. One older woman with a pinched face and chapped feet inside flowered sandals said twice while shaking her head, "*Filthy . . . ignorant*," while the man beside her explained to another, likely her husband, that Marshallese at one time were cannibals. It angered Rujen that those people would say such things, especially with him sitting just a few feet away, and to himself he echoed that word "*ignorant*" when he heard the woman's husband blame Marshallese for the pond's disappearing turtles, while at the same time a man in another group was saying that he knew of people who came at night to release the turtles before they could be stolen and eaten by Marshallese. Rujen was not certain that Marshallese never took any of the turtles, but he did know that Crispin Lastimosa, the pond's volunteer caretaker whose job it was to catch more turtles when they disappeared, sometimes took one of the turtles for himself to barbecue with friends. The dolphins, meanwhile, and the pond's current turtle, continued in somewhat tighter circles around the drooling mermaid.

Rujen admired Americans and he got along with them very well, and it was easy for him to forgive them when sometimes they acted superior to Marshallese—which in some ways, especially technological ways, he had to admit that they were—but he did not like it when Americans spoke of Marshallese as if they were stupid, or spoke to him painfully slow and simple as if he had a hard time understanding things. He could speak two languages, while most Americans he knew could speak only one. Some Marshallese *were* stupid, though, Rujen again had to admit—Caleb Aini came to mind—but a lot of Americans were stupid too, and Rujen knew he was at least smarter than the angry woman who was saying now that dolphins, in fact, were probably more intelligent than humans. He wondered, as he discovered that the crowd at the pond was of the general opinion that the Marshallese who caught the dolphins should be arrested, whether or not he, as a Marshallese, might soon become the object of their anger.

"That you, Keju?"

Rujen looked around the bicycle wheel on his right and smiled. It was Foster Rick, a man whose family Rujen knew from church. Rick was in his late forties, narrow shouldered, and thin everywhere except for a low protruding belly that, when he slouched, looked like a small ball hidden under his shirt. He wore his tube socks so high and tight that they looked like they might tear at the ankles. All Rujen knew about him outside of church, besides his habit of calling people by their last names, was that he was a civilian employee of the Army. He stood holding his bicycle, glancing from Rujen to the pond. Rujen could see two of himself reflected in Rick's mirrored sunglasses. "Eh Rick," Rujen said, "how you doing?"

Rick held his mirrored gaze on Rujen for a moment. "You involved with this, Keju? I mean, were you one of the guys, the fishermen?" He lowered his kickstand and crouched down by Rujen.

"I just came for lunch," Rujen said, raising his sandwich. "But do you mean about the dolphins? I think—"

"I had no idea anybody ate dolphins, not anybody, not—You don't, do you? That's not something you do is it?"

Rujen finished the last swallow of his Pepsi and looked past Rick's face to the dolphins. "It has a pretty good taste, like duck I think." Rujen immediately felt uncomfortable, not sure why he just said that.

Rick cringed, his face suddenly creased with wrinkles. "Man! Why—How can you eat dolphins?"

Rujen saw that several people were now looking at him, the only Marshallese at the pond, and he thought then that he preferred it when they acted as if he was not there. "But I don't eat them now," he said loudly, giving Rick's bare white knee a friendly slap, "that was a long time ago, when I was—Japanese days, you know." Rujen thought that was a bad lie, worse than his first one, as he was too young to remember any Japanese, but Rick didn't catch it. Rujen heard his word "Japanese" being exchanged around the pond.

The teenage couple he had seen earlier passed by in front of him and Rick, and the way they walked, heads bowed, holding hands, glancing back at their once private spot now crowded with people, reminded Rujen of a picture he had seen of Adam and Eve being banished from the garden of Eden.

"I don't know," Rick said, "Japanese, Marshallese, whatever it is, now Colonel Spivey has wind of it and he wants to negotiate with the fishermen and the Marshallese liaison. So typical—like everything has to be an international incident when all we have to do is—Anyway, that's the task he gave me—to go find whoever did it, the fishermen, you know, and bring them up to headquarters so we can work something out, get this settled before something stupid happens."

"What do you mean, *negotiate*? Those guys don't want to negotiate—they just want to eat."

"Who?" Rick asked. "You know them?"

"No, I'm just saying—I'm sure they only want to eat." Rujen put what was left of his sandwich back in the paper bag. "Rick, I tell you, no bullshit—Marshallese don't go looking for dolphins, chasing them in the ocean, but it's a Marshallese custom that when you see a dolphin come inside the lagoon, that's a gift. If you refuse to take it then you get bad luck—that's the custom. No *negotiations* can change this. Just let those guys have these dolphins and I think soon everybody here will forget about it—they will have other things to worry about." Rujen surprised himself by taking that position. One way or the other, he didn't think he cared what happened to the dolphins. But now, something felt right about what he just said, like pedaling a three-speed bicycle and feeling the ease that comes with shifting into a better gear.

"Keju, you know I can respect that, different societies and all, that kind of thing, but it goes both ways, right? You see that, right?"

Rujen busied himself by loosening the laces on one of the boots.

Rick said nothing for a short time, then finally, "So you have no idea who caught the dolphins, not at all?"

"No," Rujen said, gingerly pulling the boot over his foot.

"Okay, well, so I guess I'll go ask around, see what's the scoop."

Rujen started on the other boot. "I'll see you at church. You going?"

"Yeah, church, I better have this wrapped up by then. Take it easy, Keju." He wiped his sunglasses with the bottom of his shirt, then rose and turned to walk toward a group of people by the edge of the pond.

"Sure," Rujen said, not loud enough for Rick to hear him, "you take it easy too." He stood, carefully, and as he walked on the sides of the boots, heading for the road, he thought how glad he was to be getting away from so many bad feelings and sour faces, and while he now felt strongly that the dolphins should be dealt with according to Marshallese custom, that no American had any rightful say about it, he also could not help but accept that it was not his affair to meddle in. He had, after all, his own issues to deal with, not the least of them being that nagging uneasiness he felt about some distress, some mystery, which it seemed he didn't have either the ability or the will to face.

A Real Good Feeling

KERRY ZEDER HAD NOT vomited for more than an hour and lay still as corpse by the bow. He was mostly on his side, arms tight over his stomach, and the side of his freckled face was sunk deep into a red foam life jacket. A small black fly crawled around the corner of his open mouth. As the Boston Whaler trolled up and down the slow ordered swells, heading back under gray skies for Bigej pass, Travis spent some time wondering whether Kerry's fly had hitched a ride all the way from the marina or if it had been lured two miles out to sea by a barf-encrusted lip. The icebox was empty of fish and so was the horizon as far as the binoculars could see, and just as Travis endured the dullness by studying the fly, Boyd entertained himself by steering the boat with his feet. They had grown up together, Boyd and Travis, all the way from third grade when they and their families had come to Kwaj in 1972. They fished, they fought, they played every sport except tennis and bowling and volleyball; they egged the cops every night before Halloween, drank beer behind the Teen Center and on all the beaches and on the lawn at the Richardson Theater; they knew how to break into the base of the radar on Mount Olympus and that was where they took their chicks. In less than two months they would graduate, and in the fall Travis planned to go to community college in Honolulu to study aviation mechanics. Boyd didn't have a clue; maybe he would stay on Kwaj and work construction. For now though, they mostly fished, and sold their catch to the Marshallese at a dollar a pound. The boats were always free and so was the ice and gas—profit guaranteed.

Travis crumpled his empty Oly can so that it would sink, tossed it, and turned around again to face the lures. He felt Boyd press another cold one into his neck and grunted his thanks as he reached around without looking and took it. The morning storm had been fierce but it was also brief, and even though the overcast conditions that followed were usually good for fishing, neither Travis nor Boyd had spotted the slightest hint of a tuna school or even any floating debris that might hide some wahoo or mahimahi. They had tried heading farther out, but with Kerry getting so sick, once puking *inside* the boat, Travis had convinced Boyd that it would be better to troll in for calmer water and try the "hot spots" along the drop-off by Bigej.

For the random strike of a large yellowfin or a wahoo, Travis had rigged the two poles with concave Jet Head lures, one with pink and white skirts and the other with green and yellow. On the two handlines he ran small feather lures for mahi or rainbow runner. The feathers ran just outside where the white water of the wake turned to blue.

Maybe because he had been staring so long at the water behind the boat, numbed by the drone of the engines and the beer and the hardly changing pattern of the wake, Travis did not move or even speak when he saw the marlin's dorsal rise behind the most distant lure. It was such a welcome new thing to watch—the dorsal riding higher, the round black eye, the bill slashing—"Marlin!" Travis finally shouted, reaching for the pole just as it flexed away from the boat and the 12/0 reel began brattling away line. The marlin kicked up high, fell on its side, then dived out of sight.

Boyd jammed the throttles forward to set the hook, and when Travis glanced back, dropping his beer as he grabbed hold of the bench, he not only saw Kerry's tumbling legs and feet, but also heard what must have been his head hit hard as he rolled from the bow and into the center console.

"Enough!" Travis said. "It's on." Boyd idled the boat and left the wheel to bring in the opposite pole. Travis hauled in both handlines at the same time, leaving them piled among the gas cans. The marlin continued to take line in long fast bursts, and to keep the reel from overheating Travis doused it with a bailer of water.

Kerry rose unsteadily from in front of the console. "Y'all can just stop mess'n with me, okay?"

Boyd jumped back to the wheel and turned the boat so that the marlin was straight behind. "Dis ain't no *Abalama* crik fishin', boy," he said to Kerry, waving him out of his forward line of sight.

"Huh?"

Travis saw that Kerry had no idea what was going on. "Marlin, Kerry," he said, "we hooked a marlin—just watch."

"A fish?"

"Dumbass," Boyd said.

Travis reached back and gave Boyd a shove. "I remember when you didn't know jack shit either." He looked to Kerry. "One time when we were kids Boyd caught a remora and he thought it was a shark."

Boyd shoved him back. "*You* told me it was a shark."

"You believed me."

Travis poured another bailer of water on the reel and watched the angle of the line rise toward the surface. "He's coming up. Watch, Kerry."

Less than eighty yards to stern the marlin's shiny, faintly striped body broke half out of the water. Its inverted stomach lashed around like a long wrinkled tongue as it whipped its head in an effort to shake the hook. Then with several rapid strokes it brought itself fully upright—"loosen the drag!" Boyd shouted—and with its tail it danced almost fifteen yards across the surface of the water. An instant later it splashed out of sight.

"Three hundred pounds," Travis said.

"Four," Boyd said. "Maybe more."

Kerry stared at the spot where the marlin had gone down. "I'll be . . ."

Travis saw that the reel was losing too much line. "Circle it," he said to Boyd.

Boyd turned the boat slowly to starboard as Travis positioned the pole in the holder so that it aimed to the side.

"Go—before he runs deep," Travis said. He began gaining line on the reel as soon as Boyd eased forward on the throttles. Spiraling in on the marlin was a good way to gain back a lot of line, but it risked catching up to a very fresh fish with a very dangerous bill. Travis thought they had timed it just about right, and after maybe ten minutes of reeling that put a burn in his forearm and shoulder, the line was almost straight down from the boat. "Stop," he instructed Boyd. "Time to bring him up." The pole bent farther over the water each time the boat rose on a swell, the green 130-pound monofilament quivering with the strain, but the marlin did not run.

"You drive," Boyd said to Kerry, guiding him around the console by his shoulder.

"Wha—"

"Just leave it in neutral and turn the wheel when I tell you." Boyd gave Kerry a slap on the back and had to place his hands on the wheel. "Don't screw this up."

"Gone," Travis said, slapping the gunnel. "Damn."

Boyd reached over and tested the limp line. "What'd you do?"

"You tied the knot."

"Bullshit! Bring in the end."

"You bring it in."

Boyd shouldered Kerry away from the wheel. "Why don't you do it?"

"Just reel in the line?" Kerry burped, looked as though he were fighting to keep down his stomach, then he recovered and sat next to Travis by the reel. "I just reel it in?"

Boyd put the boat in gear.

Travis showed Kerry how to guide the line. "Go ahead, I'll catch the end when it comes up. And five bucks says its all curly like a slipped knot."

Boyd reached over his hand to shake. "My five bucks says its clean, like you had the drag too tight."

Kerry reeled in the line, no more than forty yards, then Travis told him to stop. He studied the end—two serrations and an angled cut—then he held it up and said, "Shark."

"Yup," Boyd said, squinting at the line. "It's a draw then. Bastards are everywhere these days, some kind of population explosion."

"What kind of shark?" Kerry asked.

"Good question," Boyd said. "Why don't you stick your face under there and see?"

"You need to stop try'n to rile me, 'cause—"

"Probably a tiger," Travis said, mimicking an attack with his hands. "A tiger shark probably chomped the line while going in for the marlin."

"Boy," Kerry said. "I know we didn't ketch the marlin and all . . . but that sure was a sight. I near crapped my shorts when he came out of the water like that."

"Now I know what I been smellin'," Boyd said. "I bet you crapped your pants way back—"

"Shut up," Travis said. "Grab us some beers, and since you like driving so much let's forget the hot spots and cross the lagoon over to the west reef. I got a good feeling we'll get some action there, a real good feeling like all of a sudden I'm psychic or something."

"Yeah," Boyd said. "This place is shit luck already." He pushed the throttles forward and brought the rising bow in line with Bigej pass. Less than an hour's journey separated them from Gea pass between the islands of Gea and Nini, five miles south of Tar-Wōj.

Good Friday

JEBRO AND NUKE SAT shoulder to shoulder under the lean-to, sharing another cigarette, watching a circle of terns dive now and then amid mackerels boiling the surface of the lagoon. The rain had long since stopped, and the air was so still that a layer of smoke hung under the tarp in imitation of the gray sky above. Nuke tried passing the cigarette to Jebro, but Jebro wouldn't take it. "You're on your own now," he said.

"Good," Nuke said, absently playing with the rope that ran limp into the small surf. "You were just wasting my smoke."

"Do you want to hear another story?"

"More ghosts?"

"No, about something that happened when you were younger."

"Tell me."

"There was a boy who hanged himself one day—"

"Lots of boys hang themselves."

"This is different. Listen. He hanged himself inside a shack behind the beer bar that used to be by the dump—"

"He was drunk."

"I don't know, maybe, but he—"

"They're always drunk when they hang themselves."

"Yes, I think so, but listen. Some other boys found him, four of them, and they saw he had a pack of cigarettes in his shirt pocket—"

"It's a cigarette pocket, that's what it's for."

Jebro gave Nuke a push. "Who is telling this story? Listen, this is weird. The boys took the cigarettes and ran away. Within a month, all those boys had hanged themselves too."

"It happens all the time. I don't think the cigarettes had anything to do with it. Where did you hear this?"

"I knew one of the boys, the last one to die. He was my friend. I saw him one day on the pier and he told me the story. I remember him saying, 'I'm afraid I must be next.' A week later he was hanging from the roof of his house. Can you believe it?"

Nuke nodded and flicked sand with the slack rope. "I'll tell you a story now." He looked into Jebro's eyes.

"Go on, I'm listening."

"About three months ago, a boy in the house behind ours tried to hang himself. Did you ever know Kool?"

"No, I don't think so—maybe. I know the family there—they have several children. What do you mean he '*tried*'?"

"He tied his rope to a beam inside the house, but when he jumped off a table, the beam broke. Termites had made it weak. He wasn't hurt, but the roof had a big hole after that and then a storm came. The house got all wet and the father was so mad that he made Kool go live somewhere else." Nuke took a drag and blew the smoke out his nose.

"That's the whole story?"

"No, Kool died—it ends like that. At low tide he walked the reef over to Epjā-dik and climbed a coconut tree. Then he jumped."

"Look!" Jebro pointed toward the water.

"What?"

"I saw a turtle come up for air. He was far, but headed this way."

Nuke stood and held the rope with both hands, the short cigarette clenched between his teeth.

Jebro tugged him back down. "Relax, it will be a while yet. When you see it take air near the bait, then get ready."

Nuke lit another cigarette and leaned his head on Jebro's shoulder. He took a light drag and held the cigarette so the smoke would rise outside of the lean-to. Jebro put his arm around Nuke and said, "I think it's strange how turtles live in the water but have to breathe air. They lay their eggs on land too. Have you ever seen a turtle lay eggs?"

"No."

"They come at night and crawl way up the beach. By morning they are so tired they almost die trying to get back in the water. Most of the babies die when they're born—they run down the beach and birds get them, and fish get them too because their shells are still very soft. It's like they can never decide which world they want to live in, so they try and live in both. I think it would be very hard to live as a turtle."

Nuke let the cigarette fall from his hand. "I can't smoke anymore."

"It's okay, you tried." Jebro threw sand over the still burning cigarette and waved the lingering smoke away from the lean-to.

Nuke grimaced. "I feel sick."

"It'll pass. Just relax and think about something else. Tell me, why do you think so many Marshallese boys hang themselves?"

Nuke made a drinking motion with his hand. "Too much Budweiser."

"That's all?"

"Maybe they want to die like Jijej Kuraij. The missionaries say that Jijej sacrificed his life to save the world."

"Interesting. I never though of it that way."

"I still think it's mostly because of too much Budweiser."

"I'm sure that has something to do with it, but I think there's more." Jebro looked at the water, and then he looked down at the rope. "Many Marshallese boys' lives are full of boredom, full of nothing but nothing. Ebeye has so many noises and cars and people and—it's strange—but the more things crowd around our boys, the lonelier they become. They have no reason to keep living, nothing to look forward to."

Jebro threw a chunk of papaya in the water. "We've lost too much knowledge of how to be Marshallese, our land too and all those things that used to keep us busy, like fishing, building canoes, teaching the ways of navigation—all our old magic. I think now we try to copy the Americans, but we can never have the life Americans have. Marshallese boys are in a hole between two worlds, and maybe the rope is a way for many of them to get out."

"You know some other way out?"

"Well, when I lived at Ailinglaplap, I went to one of the outer islands, Wotja. Old people there try to live according to the old ways, but so much has been forgotten, and they can't support themselves without canned food and bags of rice. They have to sell copra to stay alive, and the work is very hard on them. I lived there for a couple months, but it's no good unless everybody does it. An island needs children, young men and women, strong fishermen with good boats, not just elders husking coconuts. I left because I was bored, more bored than living on Ailinglaplap or Ebeye."

Jebro drew circles in the sand with a stick. "So that's not a good way anymore. Marshallese can never live like in the past. But I see it like this—I'm a fisherman, maybe not as good as Marshallese fishermen used to be, but I know a lot. I'll take that Kwajalein job and do the Americans' dirty work, but I won't be some worker with a fishing hobby. I'll be a fisherman whose hobby is a job making money. I have my own life, not one the Americans give me. To them I am just a slave, nobody. I take the job because money is a necessity these days—that is how it has to be—and I can't make enough by fishing, not yet. Someday I'll build a good boat and do nothing but fish all day, and I'll teach others how to fish too. That's my way out of the hole. How about you, Nuke, have you ever thought what you'll be doing some years from now?"

"I never thought about it."

"Tell me when you think of something. Until then, anytime I go fishing you can come with me if you want. I will teach you, and we can learn new things together."

"I know where we can steal some wood to build a boat."

"We don't need to steal. But yes, we should start thinking about a boat. That would be something: The Keju Brothers' Fishing Company."

Nuke laughed. "We better not fish for turtles because we won't make very much money!"

"Ōrrōr, have patience. I saw a turtle very close only a minute ago."

"You have good eyes. I haven't seen anything." Nuke leaned forward to scan the water. "Jebro, tell me something. Did you ever try to kilaba—kill yourself?"

Jebro smiled as he reached over and mussed Nuke's curly wet hair. "One time I was going to, but when I was tying the noose, I discovered a great fishing knot."

Nuke knocked away Jebro's hand and laughed. "Is that the same knot you used at the end of this rope?"

"Of course."

The rain plunked steadily on the tarp, and Nuke leaned his head on Jebro's shoulder as he looked out with half closed eyes at the water. Jebro ate the rest of the papaya and threw the rinds into the lagoon. Rivulets of water ran down from the jungle and through the sand on their way into the shallow surf. One, then two helicopters clamored by.

Nuke jumped out of the lean-to. "Won!—Turtle!" he shouted. "Right over the bait!"

"Yes, I saw it. Get ready. This is what will happen: It already smelled the papaya, and now it can't help but try and eat it even though it can see the hook. Keep the line slack. The turtle won't go for the papaya with its mouth—it will try and knock it free from the hook with its claw. The rope will get tangled on its flipper—I don't know why, but it always happens that way. When the turtle tries to swim away, the rope will run the hook right into its flipper. Just keep the line slack and give it more when it starts going out. I'll tell you when to pull back. Can you—"

"Quiet, you'll spook the turtle. I understand." Nuke stood ready, and it was not long before the rope started to go out, slowly at first, then faster. He looked to Jebro.

"Not yet, not yet—NOW!" Nuke jerked back on the rope. "Hold it! Don't let it get a running start!"

Nuke knocked over the lean-to as he stumbled sideways. The rope stretched tight, dripping beads of water as the turtle broke to the surface with a large flapping splash. The rope ran fast out of Nuke's hands. "*Aiii!*" He dropped it and pressed his burnt hands against his wet shirt.

Jebro dived for the rope, dug his heels into the sand, and kept the turtle from gaining any more distance. He got up in a crouch and began to haul it in. "Here, you do it."

"I can't, my hands are hurt."

"I can fix your hands later. Here." He held out the rope for Nuke, who took it. "Lean back. Good, good, pull like this: Side to side with your elbows out. Now you're doing it."

Nuke trembled as hand over hand he hauled in the turtle. His face expressed pain, but his lips were smiling.

Jebro ran into the shallow water. "Pull it right in front of me. Good, you're doing good, just a few more feet."

Jebro grabbed the turtle by one of its front flippers. He hauled it up the beach and turned it upside down. It flapped madly for a moment then lay still, breathing loudly, snorting. Nuke ran over. "We got it! We got it!"

"Yes, you did a good job. It's not as big as I wanted—maybe ninety pounds, a young one—but there's plenty of meat."

"How young?"

"I don't know, maybe your age. We should have a Pepsi now and relax."

While they sat on the beach in front of the turtle and shared a Pepsi, Jebro took a clean shirt from his bag and cut strips from it to cover the rope burns on Nuke's hands.

The turtle was hooked in a soft spot where its flipper met its shell. A narrow stream of blood ran into the sand. A film of mucous covered its eyes and fell in drops like thick sticky tears.

Nuke touched the flipper with his bare toe. "This turtle is crying."

"No, that's what happens when it comes out of the water. Its eyes need the salt."

"Maybe we should take out the hook."

"I think you're feeling sorry for the turtle."

"No, but—this is my first turtle. I learned with this one, and I can catch turtle any time now. Maybe it learned too—maybe it has learned how to avoid the hook and the rope. I think it deserves to live for helping me learn to catch it. Is that—do I—can we put it back?"

Jebro pondered the loss of the turtle, all the time it took to catch it, then he was satisfied with what he gained. "Are you sure?"

"Will you be mad?"

"It's okay. Like you said, you learned. Tomorrow we can try for another turtle. Go ahead, help it into the water and say good-bye. We can go visit grandfather's grave, then take the boat into the ocean and catch tuna. They bite very well on these kinds of rainy days."

Nuke carefully removed the hook and dragged the turtle into the shallow surf. He flipped it over and the turtle shot away, leaving a cloud of stirred-up sand. "Yokwe—Love to you," he said. "You don't have to sacrifice your life for me."

A Feast

Ņoniep judges the light within the jungle and knows that he must prepare to die. Alive he is much too frail to defend his soul from Wūllep's two most malignant demons, not at all fit to prevent their corrupted host of stolen souls on Ebeye from increasing to reach a critical, catastrophic imbalance. He has done more than he had hoped to empower the breadfruit tree, and he is encouraged by what he has seen within Jebro's soul, but Ņoniep knows these things mean nothing if he cannot save his own soul and Ebeye from the coming flood of evil.

Now, as a ruffled Etao flits from tree to tree gratifying himself with the nesting wives of birds out fishing at sea, Ņoniep works to solve the puzzle of how to convince his friend, this immortal grandson of a benevolent creator and motherless son of a blinded, hateful worm, to part with the piece of shell his father so insanely needs to leave this world and return among the stars. Only now, Ņoniep feels the full weight of the responsibility he must bear, and to prepare himself he wishes with his last living moments to fill his being with peace and the power it brings, to enjoy the simple pleasure of a meal and the company of a friend. Maybe after a bellyful of good island food, he thinks, Etao will listen.

"Etao!" Ņoniep shouts over the squawking, flapping, and cooing in the branches above. "Stop this nonsense and come share a meal with me."

Etao spreads his wings and dives, snatching a single strand of hair from Ņoniep's topknot as he screeches by. He banks left, executes a perfect stall, then becomes himself again and tumbles laughing to the ground. "Tar-Wōj is going to be full of baby birds with white eyebrows like mine!"

"And when they chirp for their father, where will he be?"

"I heard you say that you wanted food." Etao shakes a few feathers from his hair and they drift down on top of a picnic table that materializes in front of him. On the table appear bags of Ruffles and Doritos and two tubs of Jesus Lobo's WOW!lapeno dip and three steaming Pizza Hut pizza boxes and a paper-plateful of Double Western Bacon Cheeseburgers and four kinds of milkshakes in large chrome tumblers—clear plastic Silly Straws stuck inside. Etao studies the feast for a moment, then he winks and brings forth an ice-encrusted beer keg, two frosty schooner mugs on top beside the black plastic tap. "I'm sure you never ate like this before!"

Ņoniep frowns at the feast in front of him. "I already prepared some food, real food, not this . . ."

"No better food exists in all the world!"

Ņoniep shakes his head. "There is a pleasure, a special taste, Etao, that you can enjoy only with food prepared for you by the caring, thoughtful hands of a friend. Even you should see the value of this."

"I see ice cold beer and three-meat pizzas. What you got?"

"That's not the point!" Ņoniep pokes Etao away from the table with his stick. "I took the trouble to prepare a good meal, and. . . . *Aiaea!*—just make all this go away and come share my food. I promise you it's better." Ņoniep turns away and begins walking toward a pandanus tree where, within the hollow created by its stilt-like prop roots, he has made his cookhouse.

"Okay, Mister Thoughtful Hands," Etao says, "but I'm bringing my beer."

Ņoniep looks back as Etao pours himself a mugful of dark stout beer and blows off a head of foam. He catches the bittersweet scent of it on the air, pauses for a moment, then says, "Maybe you can bring me one too."

Etao laughs, pours Ņoniep a beer, then makes the rest of his feast, the picnic table and the keg, disappear. He follows

Ņoniep to the pandanus tree and sits on a woven mat that Ņoniep has unrolled over the muddy ground. The design on the mat is identical to the pattern of tattoos on Ņoniep's chest.

"Coconut crab," Ņoniep says, smiling as he unfolds a collection of warm taro leaf bundles. "Roasted in their shells until the steam from their meat made them whistle. The sauce is the only secret I take to my death, so enjoy. And we have octopus, boiled in coconut milk, and these limpets I know you like. Wrapped in those banana leaves is some breadfruit baked with arrowroot and coconut sap. I'm sure you haven't eaten like this in a very long time!"

Etao, his mouth full of coconut crab, stares back at Ņoniep. "It's good," he says when he has swallowed. "Okay, it's better than three-meat pizza."

"The cold beer is good too." A light breeze begins rattling softly through the jungle, wafting mingled scents of bark and flowers and mud. Ņoniep settles sideways on the mat and sips his beer between bites of food. He tries to relish each sound, each smell, each taste, and enjoy the beauty of each tree, each bug, the gauzy spiderwebs, the blue-black pattern on the back of a land crab, the shapes of shadows within which he has always lived. Even the sight of Etao sloppily filling his happy face with food is something pleasant to see. The moment becomes a kind of mellow rapture, a sacred trust between himself and all that surrounds him, a mood whose perfect timelessness makes him forget it has to pass. Which happens in the instant some birds raise an alarm and flap away across the great green underbelly of the canopy above. Leaves in their wake fall swaying toward the ground. The sound of rustling brush and snapping twigs comes from the south, soon mingling with the sound of approaching human voices.

Ņoniep blinks as if waking from a dream, then raises a finger to his lips. "They're back from the cemetery," he says. "Keep quiet now."

"I never said a thing! Besides, our language is nothing but the music of the jungle to them."

"I want to hear them, Etao. Keep quiet so I can hear them speak."

"I never said a thing!"

"Shhhhh!"

Jebro pushed through the brush into the clearing and Nuke followed. The breadfruit tree stood near eighty feet tall, its smooth gray trunk rising straight up almost twenty feet before three broad branches forked exponentially into the fruit-filled oblivion of green at the top. Where the branches curved upward they had the wrinkled look of lizard skin, as if the branches were at times flexible. Birds hidden within the tree's broad, long lobed leaves sang unseen. "This is the tree where they say he died," Jebro said. "It must be. Have you ever seen a breadfruit tree so tall?"

"Only the fruits sometimes in the stores." Nuke kicked at one of the fallen breadfruits with the ball of his foot. It struck the trunk of the tree with a heavy thud and rolled back a ways to reveal a shallow, caved-in gash.

Jebro picked it up and held it with a leaf so that the sticky white sap wouldn't get on his hand. He stripped away a narrow band of the leathery green skin and said, "You can boil these in seawater, fry them, bake them, cook them any way you want. You can burn the flowers too, to chase away mosquitoes. And the sap is supposed to make a good glue for building canoes." He tossed the breadfruit into a muddy puddle and put his hand on the trunk, expecting it to be cool. It felt warm, and a light tingle, like something he might feel after an ant bite, caused him to pull his hand just an inch away. He looked up and down the length of the trunk and into the leaves, catching the stench of stale tobacco rising from his sweaty shirt. He wondered if his grandfather had come on purpose that day to die, here under what was probably the island's most impressive tree.

When he was at the cemetery, where vines and grasses wavered like a green sea over the crumbling remains of square and cross-shaped headstones, most of them made of concrete blocks once slathered white with mortar, Jebro had been angry that Ataji's wooden cross had rotted away, but now, his hand an inch away from the tree, he suddenly became comfortable with the thought that the cross, like Ataji, had dissolved into the island and become a part it, nourishing new life that would grow and then die to nourish again. Maybe it was a good thing that the cemetery had become overgrown, no different from the rest of the landscape—a better place to be buried, a better place to remember dead relatives, rather than someplace where leveled ground and ordered lines made it look like some sort of packaging. He touched the tree again, feeling the faint tingle he now believed to be life, and turned to look at Nuke. "Usually a breadfruit tree is crooked, all over the place," he said, "but this one is straight in the trunk so I think somebody—maybe even grandfather—once took care of it and trimmed it so that it would be good for the hull of a canoe."

Nuke laughed. "How can you make a tree grow straight? They just—"

"You can. I can't say how, exactly, but you can make plants and trees do all sorts of things, and I think you have to talk to them too, like maybe this tree was told to grow just right to be a canoe." Jebro knew that would get another laugh from Nuke. "You laugh, but maybe if you study an old canoe you might see some parts that are curved at the same angle as those branches up there."

"Tree," Nuke said, pointing to the tree, "I tell you to grow some good outboard engines so Jebro and I can build a fishing boat." He put his hands on his hips and stared at the tree as if waiting for something to happen.

"Did you hear that?" Jebro asked.

"What?"

"I heard the tree say, '*Nuuuuke, come closer. I want to drop a breadfruit on your head.*'"

"No," Nuke said. "I heard it say, *'Je-ebro, this is grandfather's ghost inside the tree. . . .'*"

"It happens, you know, peoples' ghosts living inside things—ekjabs, that's what you call them. Grandfather warned me once about an ekjab here, a bush that used to be a mejenkwaad, a baby-eating vampire." Jebro pointed to a bush behind Nuke. "I think it's that bush right behind you." When Nuke turned around, Jebro picked up a breadfruit and tossed it over Nuke's head so that it would land at his feet.

Nuke jumped back, stumbled, and fell on his butt. "Ōrrōr!"

Jebro ducked behind the tree, laughing as he dodged a wild assault of breadfruits coming from Nuke. Some splattered against the trunk and some sailed past to crash into a dense thicket of pandanus trees where, from within, a sudden catlike wrawl filtered out and caused Nuke to drop the next breadfruit he was about to throw. "What was that?"

"Who knows? A cat maybe. I think the island has cats."

"I never heard a cat make a noise like that."

"Go look then," Jebro said, nudging Nuke toward the pandanus trees. "Maybe a mejenkwaad is back there."

Nuke twisted away from Jebro. "You go look," he said, rubbing his bandaged hands together to remove the gummy breadfruit sap.

"We better get going. We need time to catch some tuna and get back before dark." Jebro looked once at the pandanus trees, then, whistling, he motioned for Nuke to follow and led the way out of the clearing, stopping once to look at the remains of wooden homes and houses, his birthplace, now just rot and rusting nails on the floor of the jungle.

Ņoniep laughs again as Etao pulls another stringy yellow piece of ripe breadfruit from his hair and drops it inside his mouth. "That boy is some lucky shot," Ņoniep says after watching the two brothers leave the clearing. "He hit me too, with a can."

"Lucky for him I decided not to change him into a rock—only because this is your last day and I know you're his friend." Etao makes the keg reappear and holds out his hand for N̦oniep's empty mug. "Now," he says, "before you keel over let's get drunk and finish this food."

By the time all the food is gone and the keg has settled into a pool of mud created by its condensation and blown-off foam, N̦oniep and Etao lie side by side on the mat, massaging their bellies to help along their painfully swollen guts.

"Do you know, Etao," N̦oniep says sleepily, "what I think is really beautiful?"

Etao makes a little bubble of spit grow round over his lips. It pops. "How about a skyhook by Kareem Abdul Jabbar? Nothing compares to the form of that shot when he does it just right."

"I'm sure you have a rare taste for beauty, but I was thinking of the different moods of daylight, where each time of day is a different spirit I have known in my life. Even when it's cloudy like this, the light is familiar—a light I've known before. This kind of light makes me think of somebody half asleep, resting comfortably while they wait for something important to happen."

N̦oniep takes hold of Etao's wrist. "Etao, my friend, something important really is going to happen, and I need to be serious with you about your father."

"If you say one thing serious to spoil my drunk, I'll make you barf."

"Etao, listen, even if your father left this world right now, I still have to fight the demons he already sent—and to do this I'm willing to die and risk my soul. But what's most important is to get rid of Wūllep so that his evil will stop for good, and this can't be done without your help."

Etao turns to his side and leans on his elbow. "Stop thinking about all that! Drink more beer, dance, sing—do anything—whatever it takes to make this day a happy one. You might even decide to die some other day, so you can have some more fun first—and then I can really help you."

"You don't understand!"

"Barf time!" Etao laughs madly as he pokes and prods N̦oniep's belly, then, just as N̦oniep feels a surge of stinging stomach juice rise up his throat, Etao suddenly relents and begins swatting blindly at a flapping of wings overhead. He falls on top of N̦oniep.

"Keār!" N̦oniep struggles out from under Etao and stands, leaning heavily on his stick. Above on a low branch of the cookhouse sits Keār. Her white chest billows with short fast breaths. The surrounding jungle is vaguely reflected in her blinking night-black eyes.

Etao looks blearily up at the bird. "I was looking for you earlier up in the trees."

"The demons are almost here," Keār says to N̦oniep, rustling her wings. "Have you told Etao?"

N̦oniep clears his throat. "I tried, but . . ."

"But he got drunk instead," Etao says. "And with a little more time I'm sure I can make him forget all the nonsense you filled him with."

Keār swoops down, screeching angrily, and circles once around Etao's head before landing back on the tree. "You can't ignore this any longer! Think of all the suffering being caused by your father because you won't return that thing hanging from your neck!"

"Please, Etao," N̦oniep says. "Just think—"

"No, you think!" Etao stands and leans over N̦oniep. "I told you long ago that your plan won't work, that you'll give even more power to my father and that scoundrel L̦ajibwinām̧ōn̄, but in all this time you only listen to the prattling of this stupid bird!"

"Enough!" Keār shrieks. She flaps down to perch on N̦oniep's shoulder. "I have heard enough of your—"

Etao pinches her beak. "No, not enough!" he says. "Don't you know what happens to me if I take off this shell? Don't you care that by trying to get rid of Wūllep that you might be getting rid of me instead? No! You, N̦oniep, you call me 'friend,' but you don't care about me at all! You only think this world will be so much better without Wūllep, but you never think how it might be without me! And I can tell you now that this world will be worthless without me. Who will crawl up your nose when you sleep and give you those dreams you need to wake up with a smile? Who will keep your women wiggling their hips under you if it's not me they see in your eyes? Who tricks you with illusions to keep you guessing and laughing at life? Who do you think keeps turning the world upside-down and making it crazy so you never get bored? I'm the only one who does these things, and without me and my power not even the birds will sing—they will all moan like Keār and then die because what bird will go out and fish if there's no fun in it? Without me, life is nothing more than a sad, sexless, boring wait for death, and if you two really want my help, you two sour-faced sea slugs, I tell you that you should have some fun like I tell everybody to have some fun, and I'll help anybody—anybody!—do that. But you two!—you're just as bitter as my father—so you might as well swim right over to Ep to join his side because maybe you don't know it, but you're really doing his work for him."

"No, Etao!" N̦oniep shouts. "You're wrong! My whole life I have fought against every damn thing Wūllep does! And maybe people know how to dream and have fun and laugh and how to have sex without you being involved. Maybe you just get in the way!"

Etao lifts N̦oniep up by his armpits and with a powerful breath blows Keār off his shoulder. She tumbles backwards, up through the canopy and out of sight. Etao's eyes take on a mischievous slant. He speaks in a calm voice. "I have done nothing but help you ever since I got here, and still I think you fear a smile might make your lips fall off your face. Now you insult me, even when you know I could change you into a snail if I wanted, but just to show you that I have no hard feelings, I promise to help you with one thing I know you hope for." Etao grins, a string of saliva stretching between his slightly parted lips. "I'll make sure those two friends of yours really need to make themselves a canoe!" He sets N̦oniep down and tickles him viciously until he cannot help but laugh.

“Good-bye, my friend,” Etao says when he has quit his torture, then he pushes Ņoniep on his butt into a pool of mud.

Ņoniep struggles to get to his feet. His topknot has come undone. “Etao, no,” he says, pushing away hair so that he can see. “Leave them alone.” He reaches to grab the bottom of Etao’s jersey but just as he touches it, Etao changes into a bird, a blue-faced booby, and does a running, squawking takeoff to circle twice around the clearing before he vanishes into the sky.

The Ocean

From the back of the boat heading south, Jebro looked left at the narrow band of gray-blue afternoon sky below the last of the clouds on the eastern horizon. A good wind crossed the lagoon from the east and churned up whitecaps that made the going slow and bumpy, but as the boat cleared the southern tip of Tar-Wōj and headed west into the pass, Jebro was able to increase his speed with the waves following behind. Nuke sat forward, cringing each time the aluminum hull dug in and a cold spray of water shot over the bow and soaked him. Beyond the foam-green shallows of the pass lay the dark ocean, not as choppy as the lagoon but rippling and bulging as though it were some vast slab of muscle.

The coral-covered bottom sliding by under the boat dropped off into deeper shades of blue, and as Jebro cleared the pass he looked north and west across the ocean for any signs of fish. He knew he would have to go south no matter what—even the ocean outside this part of the atoll was off-limits because of the missile tests—but he wanted to see first what he would be missing. He saw no birds in those forbidden directions, no fish, no logs or debris that might be good to troll around, only waves and sky. Five miles south by the island of Nini was the off-limits boundary, and Jebro figured that if he was at least headed in that direction—no signs of fish that way either—then he would have a better chance of avoiding trouble if he was spotted. Returning to Tar-Wōj might be a problem, but he planned to do so at twilight when a small gray boat sailing a gray ocean on a gray day would be very close to being invisible.

"Rocket," Nuke said, pointing southeast in the direction of Kwajalein.

Jebro looked, missing the rocket's rapid climb, but able to see a tall plume of white smoke extending from the horizon into the gray overcast sky. He had seen these kinds of rockets go up many times before when he was a boy on Ebeye, and knew they were called weather rockets, but he had no idea what they did to the weather. "Some missiles coming tonight," he said over the high-pitched drone of the engine. "They usually come whenever you see weather rockets late in the afternoon."

"I know that already," Nuke said. "I probably know more than you about missiles and those kinds of things."

"Okay, if you're so smart then tell me why they call it a weather rocket."

"I think it gets up there and takes a picture, and then . . ." Nuke looked for a moment at the white trail left by the rocket. "They get the picture back, maybe like you get a television picture, and if the weather is going to be clear then they radio over to America and tell them to shoot the missiles at us."

"Hey, that's pretty good thinking." Jebro looked east at the widening band of blue sky rising from the horizon and saw that with the increased wind, the chances were good for a clear night. "I never thought much about it but now that I remember, it's true—they only shoot the missiles at us when the weather is good. I wonder what happens if the Communists decide to attack America during a storm—what will they do then?"

Nuke laughed, wiped the salt spray from his face, and said, "I don't know if America can beat the Communists, but they're getting good practice if they want to bomb the crap out of us!"

"And tonight we camp inside the bull's eye."

The white plume of the weather rocket began to fragment and drift, and as Jebro glanced occasionally at the remains of it he refit the turtle handline with a lure and let it out the back of the boat. He tossed another handline and lure to Nuke and told him to let it out on the other side. "Tie the end of it to the boat," he said, "but keep it about halfway out."

For almost two miles the brothers trolled along without speaking, Jebro scanning the ocean ahead for any sign of birds or debris. He had not brought much food, so whatever they caught would have to be their dinner, but even if they got no fish he was sure that back on Tar-Wōj they could easily find some coconut crabs or beach crabs to eat, or be able to catch red perch at night from the ocean beach. The breadfruit was there too, and Jebro remembered some spots Ataji had showed him where he could gather limpets. Then, just past the south end of the sandbar by Tōñle island, Nuke yanked back on his handline and fell forward onto his knees. "Fish fish fish!" he shouted. He sat down and leaned back with the taut nylon rope held close to his chest. His arms jerked from the pull of the fish.

Jebro relaxed his grip on the throttle and the engine settled down to a patient gurgling. "Why are you staring at me?" he said. "Bring in your catch before a shark gets it." Water slapped at the sides of the boat as it rode up and down the two- and three-foot swells.

Side to side, in the way Jebro had shown him how to pull in the turtle, Nuke hauled in a black-fin jack of about five pounds and flipped it into the boat. He kneeled over the flapping fish and held it down to remove the hook. "Oh," he said, looking back at Jebro with mock sympathy. "Only me? You didn't get a fish too?"

"No, I guess you're the great fisherman in the family now. But what do you want with that poison fish?"

"You lie!"

"You eat that fish and your whole body will go numb—it happened to a man I know. Toss that thing and set the lure back out."

"I still caught you," Nuke said, and with two hands gripping the tail he threw the dark slimy fish over the side.

"It's my fault," Jebro said as he turned the throttle. "I was too close to the reef." He took the boat farther out, almost willing the ocean with his eyes to offer some clue that would reveal the whereabouts of tuna, mahimahi, or wahoo. For luck he trailed his magic finger through the water. At times he thought he saw something, but the ocean was only playing tricks with him. He noticed the wind had picked up, still coming from the east and carrying the scent of the atoll's exposed, algae-covered reef, and the farther he went out, away from the lee of the islands, the choppier the water became. The swells got a little bigger too.

Then, from the corner of his eye, Jebro glimpsed a distant blur he knew to be birds. He saw it for only a second, southwest of Kā island less than two miles away, but the image was familiar: Fast-moving birds dropping down to feed. When he looked straight on he saw nothing, but he knew they were there and he felt, just slightly, the chill of adrenaline trickle through his body. This was the kind of fishing he liked—a strategic hunt for schools of big, fast-running fish. "Keep looking for birds," he said to Nuke, who sat absently flicking his line into the side of the boat. "If you spot some before I do then you can drive the boat on the way back to Tar-Wōj."

Jebro watched the birds rise again, just a brief, hazy darkness above the distant water, but he said nothing. Finally, Nuke shot out his arm and pointed. "There!"

"Good eyes," Jebro said, and he gave the engine full throttle. "You found a nice-sized school—headed this way but moving fast." He could tell by the activity of the school that it was *ļōjabwil*, what Americans called bonito and Hawaiians called *aku*. From so far away the birds looked like a cloud of flies, rising high to chase their prey and then disappearing as they descended on the water to feed. Jebro envisioned himself and Nuke cooking several fish over a campfire that night on Tar-Wōj, but right away he thought that imagining such success might bring bad luck, so instead he concentrated on where he should be to intercept the school. Because of its speed, he knew he would only get one or two passes, so he headed far enough out to catch the school if it cut more west, but not so far that he would lose his chance to catch the school if it veered in the direction of the reef.

As the boat rose to the top of a swell, and Jebro took advantage of the height to study the movement of the school, he saw a brief gleam of white. A little closer, high on another swell, and he saw that it was a boat—Americans. "We're not alone out here," he said.

After the first three passes Travis and Kerry had four twenty-pound tuna whipping their tails against the inside of the icebox, and now the last pass added one more, another twenty-pound tuna on Kerry's handline. The instant Kerry pulled it into the boat, Boyd dropped his beer in the drink holder and brought the twin seventy-horsepower Evinrudes close to full speed for another run at the fast-escaping school. Travis put a life jacket under his butt on the back bench and pressed one of his bare feet against a metal pole that supported the gunnel. Next to him, thick blood ran from the wounded gills of the blue and silver bullet-shaped tuna as Kerry, struggling to stay seated, fumbled to rip out the 5/0 double hook. The blood spattered Kerry's face and knees, and dropped onto the deck where it mingled with chips of red paint and rust from the gas cans. So much blood made the fish slippery, and it slid out of Kerry's hands and back into the ocean when he turned to toss it underhand into the icebox.

"Jesus Christ, man!" Boyd shouted, slamming closed the icebox lid with his foot. "That was twenty bucks!"

"Just drive," Travis said, not looking at him. "Shit." He didn't like losing the fish, but overall Kerry was doing pretty well for his first time out, and Travis could see in his bloodshot eyes the pain of a lesson learned. "Yeah," Travis said, forcing a smile. "I remember doin' that once."

Earlier, when they had first come through Gea pass, they had searched south within legal bounds, but all the birds they had encountered were heading northwest and it was not too long before Travis and Boyd agreed to follow them, into the mid-atoll corridor. They caught up to the school several miles west of Nini, and a weather rocket shot up from Kwajalein in seeming celebration as they landed their first fish. Heading out-of-bounds was an easier decision for Travis, his reservation of the boat ending at twelve thirty, so now, should they be spotted, it was Boyd who risked getting his licence suspended.

The fiberglass boat beat across the waves like a skipping stone, the empty gas cans clanging against each other at every landing, the poles lurching and rattling in their holders whenever the lures came flying out of the water. Just ahead, hundreds of sprinting birds suddenly descended on an ocean become boiling with thousands of frenzied tuna, their mutual prey being an incredibly fast but defenseless shoal of tiny scad. The slaughter inflicted upon the scad was so heavy that the water in many places was splotchy with blood, although any damage done to their million-strong shoal—itself feeding on miles of animal plankton in turn eating other light-loving plankton at the surface—was likely to be relatively small.

Boyd pulled back on the throttles and brought the boat upwind beside a busy part of the school, timing his turn to port so that the lures would pass through the feeding tuna and outside of the wake. It was a good pass, and the two poles got strikes right away. "Keep going," Travis said, hoping to hook up on the handlines but they remained slack. He and Kerry reeled in the two fish, both making it successfully into the icebox.

"We got company," Boyd said. "Marshallese."

Travis tossed his lure back in the water and looked ahead. Maybe a mile away was a small boat, obviously Marshallese because no fishermen from Kwajalein would take such a craft so far into the ocean, especially, Travis soon noticed, since it had just one engine.

"They ain't supposed to be out here." Boyd said, coming around again on the school.

"Neither are we, dipshit."

"Yeah . . . but—"

Kerry's pole hit on the pass, but when he reached for the reel he accidently hit the antireverse lever. The line spun out of control and rose from the reel in whirling loops, then dug in and abruptly stopped, wedged within a big bushy knot, a bird's nest. Kerry held both his hands at the sides of the reel, not touching it, and looked over to Travis, his eyes wide and his mouth moving slightly but not speaking.

Travis shook his head and stepped over to take the line, but Boyd jammed the throttles into idle and got there first, shouldering Kerry out of the way. He began bringing in the fish by hand, piling the 130-pound line in a mess at his feet. "You're such a goddamn fuck-up!" he said.

"I'm sorry. . . . I . . ."

"A *sorry* sack of shit—that's what you are."

The unpiloted boat lurched sideways down a swell, and Boyd, cussing at Kerry, dropped the line in order to catch himself as his knees slammed into the gunnel. Before he could regain his balance Kerry shoved him back down. "You shut your mouth!"

The tendons under Kerry's forearms became taut as he balled his hands into two shaking fists. His face and neck became a deep crimson red that glared out from between runny splotches of white zinc oxide. Boyd rose, grinning, and turned sideways as if preparing for a kick.

Travis wedged himself in front of Boyd before he could strike. "What the hell's your problem? Just drive the damn boat!"

Boyd pressed his chest into Travis and jabbed his finger at Kerry. "Fucker hit me!"

"You had it coming," Travis said, feeling Kerry's weight against his back. The boat lurched again and the three of them stumbled into the console. Travis glanced across the water and saw the school leaving them behind. He stared into the angry slits of Boyd's eyes. "Look," he said, "the hell with this—you assholes wanna forget about fishing and fight, or do you wanna make some more money?" He stepped aside, not sure what might happen.

The two glowered at each other for a moment, then Boyd said, "Yeah," and backed away. "You ain't worth it, not right now."

"Eat my shit," Kerry said to Boyd's back, standing his ground as best he could in the rolling boat.

"Shut up," Travis said. "C'mon—I think we still got a fish on."

Travis hauled in the fish, just a ten-pounder, while he had Kerry wrap the line around the flat plastic flare box. As soon as the fish was in the boat, Boyd hit the throttles and sped northwest after the school. It would take too long to untangle the reel, so Travis tied it out of the way under the gunnel. Three lines out would still do well.

"Sorry," Kerry said, "about the reel. I didn't mean to—"

"Don't worry about it." Travis opened the cooler and handed out beers, Boyd muttering thanks without looking back. He tossed his empty up in the air and it sailed back to land in the wake.

Ahead of them, the Marshallese boat—an aluminum skiff, really—had positioned itself so that it was in line to intercept the school. As Boyd closed the distance between them, heading, it seemed, to fish the exact same upwind pile of now diving birds, Travis saw that of the two Marshallese in the skiff one, the driver, looked to be about his own age. The other was small, just a little kid. They sat, as nothing above the skiff's low sides gave them anything to hold on to if they stood, and each time they rode to the bottom of a trough they seemed to disappear, only to rise again as if coming up from under the water. The older one held up a hand and waved. Travis waved back.

"Shit," Boyd said, slowing the boat. "He cut me off!"

"Just go left, between those two piles."

"This is bullshit." He spun the wheel hard to port.

"Easy!" Travis said. "You're gonna cross the lines."

After the turn the skiff lay behind, in perfect position for a strike, and within seconds the driver hooked up. He idled his engine and began hauling in the fish, side to side, with a grace and speed that Travis had to admire. The driver looked back, and then the younger one started jigging his line, soon falling forward to struggle with a fish of his own.

Boyd brought the boat between two piles, passed them at slow speed, then turned downwind. But, as if prompted by the human intrusion, the squawking birds rose and the tuna stopped boiling, and the lures were left to troll through lifeless water made slick with fish oil and bird droppings. The birds raced west, and Boyd pushed forward the throttles to chase. Behind, the two Marshallese had landed their fish and kicked up a good wake heading east away from the school. "All ours now," Travis said.

Boyd glanced back. "Sayonara," he said.

The boat drew even and kept pace with the birds, running along for what seemed like too long a period to wait for the feeding to begin again. Then suddenly, in tight formation, the birds banked hard to the right and raced back the way they came, leaving the boat headed into an empty, open ocean. By the time Boyd got the boat turned around, having to make a wide semicircle to keep the lines from tangling, the birds were nearing the Marshallese skiff, which still maintained a good speed heading away from them. The black cloud of birds flew directly over the skiff, passed it, then not much farther on finally stalled and descended to feed amid water once again boiling with tuna. The skiff caught up, slowed, and rather than head for the upwind edge, turned to port in front of the fast-approaching Boston Whaler and nearly stopped. The frenzied school, as if the Marshallese had foreseen it, doubled back right on top of their lures. The skiff moved forward just enough for the lures to rise then stopped as both fishermen hooked fish.

Travis became certain, watching them work their lines, that they had known all along that the school was going to make a U-turn to the east, and that they had predicted again that the school would double back. He laughed a little, thinking right then how bad he wanted to ask those Marshallese what secret they knew and he did not. "How do you think they did that?" he asked Boyd. The skiff was less than a hundred yards away.

"Cut me off again? Watch this."

"What?" Travis didn't take his eyes off the Marshallese fishermen, still wondering what they knew, but then the skiff seemed much too close to be straight ahead at such a speed, and he felt a prickling chill form at the base of his skull and shoot rapidly down the length of his spine. He looked quickly at Boyd. "What are you doing? Hey!"

With the skiff only yards away, its two occupants stopped hauling in their lines and stared in a kind of blank, paralyzed confusion at what was bearing down on them. Boyd slowed just enough to keep the boat from skipping in the turn then cranked the wheel hard to port as he dropped the throttles into idle. A huge spray of water, shaped like the webbed dorsal of some immense sailfish, shot out from under the Boston Whaler, rose near fifteen feet in the air, and landed with an audible splash square in the middle of the little skiff, which rocked and swivelled as its two passengers were swept onto their backs. "Bull's eye!" Boyd roared, and powered away after the school now once again on the run. The two Marshallese sat up quickly, the younger one raising both his middle fingers and shouting something Travis couldn't hear. The older one scrambled to regain his line.

Travis punched Boyd in the shoulder, dodged his wild return swing, then hit him again. "That was total bullshit! You dick!"

"It's just a little goddamn water! Get the fuck off me!"

Kerry, having been tossed into the gunnel by the sharp turn, gripped the back bench as he stood back up. "You gotta be the biggest asshole I ever—"

"Fuck you, redneck."

Kerry's jaw muscles tightened, his brow furrowed, then his face softened into something almost like pity. He looked over at Travis and asked, "Why are you friends?"

Travis looked away from Kerry and thought for a moment, watching the distancing image of the skiff, its two fishermen again bringing in their lines. He turned to Boyd, who stared stone-faced at the birds speeding west. "What the hell's gotten into you?" he asked. "I think you better let me drive."

Jebro was still hooked into his fish and hauled it in as fast as he could, angrily determined that the Americans racing away be close enough to see him catch it. He could see one of them looking back. But when he saw Nuke, who having just lost his fish sat quietly up at the bow, his lips trembling and his eyes focused on the water sloshing around their gear, Jebro suddenly lost interest in the fish and dropped his line. It ran back out and pulled tight on the stern cleat where he had tied the end of it. The aluminum boat, its engine continuing to idle smoothly, sat low in the ocean and listed to one side. Each wave that slapped against the sides brought a little more water onboard, enlivening the two tuna caught earlier. The nearest island, Tōn̄le, lay almost two miles away. "Start bailing," Jebro said, tossing Nuke a gallon Clorox jug which had its top cut off. "But stay as far forward as you can—and be careful not to lean on the sides. Pull my bag up there too." He was angry, maybe more angry than he had ever been, but he took a deep breath and tried to keep his cool as he got to work with the other bailer.

Jebro could think of no good reason why the Americans had swamped him, unless, simply, that they were of the type who enjoyed being cruel. The act replayed itself in his mind—the hateful face of the driver, the other two staring slack-jawed as if in a trance, soulless, the whole thing seeming to be a sudden, fleeting contact not with other human beings but with some kind of evil. Then he remembered how, earlier, he had peered below the water with his mask to see the shoal of scad doubling back under itself, how by that he knew which way to go and how he had laughed when he pointed out to Nuke that the Americans and the birds were speeding off in the wrong direction. Yes, the Americans were jealous that they had been outsmarted not only by some stupid little fish, but also by a Marshallese. They had fancy poles and reels, a fast boat, but seeing the greater value of what they lacked made them want to hurt those who possessed it. Having a good reason now for why this had been done to him, Jebro was more angry than he had been before. He bailed faster, looking up every so often at the American boat fast becoming nothing more than a white speck in the gray-blue distance.

The boat slid up then down a randomly large swell, causing the two gas cans to clang together at the same time a wave splashed heavily over the side. "Ayyyyy!" Nuke shouted, holding out his hand as if it might stop another wave.

Jebro winced at the amount of water that entered the boat, more, certainly, than what they had just bailed out. Not wanting Nuke to see the sudden fear he knew showed on his face, he turned away and bit the tip of his tongue until the pain got him thinking calmly again. "This is not so bad," he said, splashing a little water at Nuke. "Just keep bailing."

The best way to avoid sinking, Jebro figured, was to get the boat moving forward and then to pull the plug so that the water would drain out the back. He turned the throttle but the boat, being so heavy, hardly moved. The handline, he noticed, still had hold of the fish and it worried him, not so remotely, that he was now trolling for sharks. He then gave the engine full power, and as he reached down to pull the plug, the bow rising slightly with the forward momentum, he suddenly faced the error of his judgement when the entirety of the water in the boat ran aft, submerging the stern, and the ocean curled in like a broad blue hand and pulled the boat down. What he felt then, besides a kind of stabbing, desperate shock, was an overwhelming sense of embarrassment for having done such a foolish thing in front of Nuke. He only had time to release the steering arm as the engine sank sputtering away and to look once into the eyes of his frightened, flailing brother before he found himself with nothing to hold on to and up to his neck in water. As the boat slipped completely under, at an angle as if rolling down a ramp, and he and Nuke and a few things were left bobbing up and down the windblown swells, Jebro thought that he should know what to do in such a situation, but all his mind produced was an incredibly vivid image of his fish, still on the line, being dragged to the bottom of the ocean.

The Matter Is Very Involved

Ņoniep sits at the southern tip of Tar-Wōj, having some time ago watched Jebro and Nuke vanish into the southern distance. He is alone, at peace despite his recent failings. He admires how the wind blows back the tops of waves breaking on the reef. When he closes his eyes he sees by the sight of a sea bird the demons who come to steal his soul. They enter the lagoon from the west, paddling between the islands of Ļabo and Murle. He is disgusted looking at the demons, so he looks at the waves again, breaking just as they did when he was a boy such a long time ago, and he is comforted by knowing they will continue to break long after his death, through many lives to come.

A splash in the water in front of him is followed by a little red *kur* fish who leaps far onto the dry beach, too far for it regain the water. The shadowy form of a larger fish cruises by, denied its meal. The *kur* fish pumps its tiny gill plates up and down, but it does not flop around as fish on land usually do. It seems as though the fish has accepted its fate, content to trade its life for the satisfaction of eluding its predator. "I will help you, little fish," Ņoniep says. "You are too much like me." He stands, carefully holding in his right hand half of a coconut filled with sea water and a large, deadly venomous cone shell. He walks over to the *kur* fish and with his left hand he picks it up within a small mound of sand. The fish does not seem to notice, its eye wide and staring at the sky. Ņoniep carries it with him as he wades out into knee-deep water on the slippery, pockmarked reef. A small current runs from the lagoon and into the ocean.

A smooth-bottomed, urchin-free depression in the reef appears to be a suitable enough place for what Ņoniep is about to do and he stops. "Good luck," he says to the fish, and slowly sinks his hand below the water. The pile of sand disintegrates, leaving the fish upright and cautious for just moment before, with a flick of its tail, it darts away. Ņoniep thinks irrationally for just an instant that he might escape along with the fish, which causes him to chuckle, then he bends his knees until he lightly falls into a sitting position inside the depression. The surface of the water lies even with the apex of the triangle tattoo on his chest and splashes at his neck.

The fleshy, white-and-orange animal inside the cone shell is not very happy, Ņoniep having starved it for so long and kept it confined within half a coconut. He drops the shell into his hand and teases the animal out with hot breath and his fingernail. He sees the part he is looking for, the long thin instrument which injects the potent venom, and after one last look at the sky and the ocean and his island home he presses the animal to his chest until he feels the hot sting of the poison. He tosses the shell.

The pain is less than he had imagined, fast becoming more of a spreading numbness. Already he can feel his heart's troubled beats. He sings,

Who can I be? Who can I be? Who can I be?
Love is beautiful. Love is beautiful.
The matter is very involved. I try to explain it . . .

Before he can finish, Ņoniep, last of his people, falls face-first into the water and dies.

Part Three
Long Dark Night of the Souls

If you hear birds crying at night, ghosts are approaching.

—Marshallese saying

The Pair of Demons

THE DEMONS KWŌJENMETO and M̧ōñāļapeņ paddle their canoe between the islands of Ļabo and Murle then head south for Tar-Wōj, island home of Ņoniep, the dwarf they have come to slaughter. Ļajibwināṃōņ has commanded them to steal his soul as well, a gift for Wūllep, whose filthy grip will turn it foul. Then, Kwōjenmeto knows, things will happen fast.

In the canoe Kwōjenmeto has the back position, his large, bulbous head glowing so brightly it hides his eyes and mouth. Webs of pale blue veins, like tangled worms, lie collapsed under the slick gray veneer of his skin, which folds in and out of greasy rolls on his chest and gut as he leans to work his paddle. The water at the bottom of the canoe is oily and dark, and it is covered with a thin, frothy yellow scum where it surrounds Kwōjenmeto's swollen fin-like feet. But for his head he seems nothing more than an enormous bladder tied into the shape of a man and filled with a thick putrid ooze.

Kwōjenmeto does not want to rid the world of people. Really, he prefers their abundance, a world overrun with people—so many of them when crowded becoming so miserable, desperate, and dull that the theft of their souls becomes so much simpler to do. This, his only purpose, to forever increase his masters' poisoned host, earns him no reward and not the slightest satisfaction, although at times he gets a certain fuzzy feeling when in his travels he happens again upon those he has condemned, by his silent skill, to live out their lives as vacant, soulless shells.

Kwōjenmeto prefers to prey upon the weak, the young, the lost, although at times his masters demand he steal from those, such as the dwarf, who are too keen to lose their souls without a fight. Kwōjenmeto has no taste for blood, no great skill at killing, and for these occasions he brings M̧ōñāļapeņ, the half-witted abomination whose lust for carnage is just as valuable as his tall, rat-like ears, with which he can track from great distances any living thing by the signature beating of its heart. M̧ōñāļapeņ has been able to track Ņoniep ever since sunrise, revealing his exact position, and as a reward for his obedience he will be allowed to suck on Ņoniep's heart before the sky is dark.

〰〰〰

Large, slick white lice move within the stalks of M̧ōñāļapeņ's coarse black hairs, feeding on each other's young. Around his snout and double-jointed mouth are scars, some fresh, all from ignoring the sharp, broken edges of his victims' bones. His teary eyes are small and blue, pale like low sky on a sunny horizon. His pink teeth, serrated half-moons and daggers, lie back in rows within his raw red jaws; a few long teeth on the bottom are nearly horizontal, soon to be pushed loose and replaced by those behind. The secret sucking mouth at the back of his head has no teeth, only a wrinkled sphincter for an opening. His arms, leathery like the neck of a turtle, are short and end in blunt brown claws that make it hard for him to work his paddle. The effort makes corded muscles ripple across his shoulders and strain taut at the bottom of his back, where his hairy flesh bulges over a bony pelvis that sprouts six exoskeletal legs, each bearing a broad, crooked blue stripe. The legs, diseased with hard tumorous growths at the joints, are long, giving M̧ōñāļapeņ an intimidating height when he stands atop his pointy, spear-like feet.

What drives him to kill is not the hot taste of blood and flesh and marrow, but the cold taste of shame and guilt, an addiction to it so intense that his only solace when not killing is to weep and grind his teeth as he wallows in self-hate and a deep disgust of his existence. He whimpers now, hearing the distant echo of Ņoniep's beating heart, and chews raw the flap of rubbery scar tissue surrounding his mouth. Suddenly, he stops paddling, hearing Ņoniep's heart grow faint, falter, skip, ultimately cease after a series of three rapid beats—death. He turns to Kwōjenmeto and emits a shrill squeaking howl, feeling a desperate rage, approaching panic.

Kwōjenmeto calmly indicates an understanding of what has happened. "This Ņoniep is a smart one," he says, "but his soul will not escape me as easily as his flesh did you. I know a thing or two, you know, of souls and how to find them."

M̧ōñāļapeņ does not care. His anticipation for the dwarf has grown too strong and it must be satisfied. Some other life must now take his place. He shakes the tears from his face and with manic, awkward strokes he propels the canoe forward in a different direction, ignoring Kwōjenmeto's protests, weeping loudly as he pulls toward the nearest, ripest, most easily taken beating heart.

Showdown at the Sewage Plant

FROM WHERE RUJEN sat on a padded metal chair inside the employee breakroom of the Kwajalein Sewage Treatment Plant, his eyes aiming down at the thin black socks that covered his heavily bandaged feet, he knew he could not be seen from the window. His hands shook just slightly if he did not keep them clasped together between his knees. He felt as if he had drunk much too many cups of coffee. The nervous beating of his heart seemed to him to be almost louder than the broken fan blade clacking within the air conditioner on the wall. To calm himself he closed his eyes and took slow deep breaths.

Rujen's feet were swollen, hurting, and it bothered him that Crawford, the boss now because Andy had decided to go home and sleep after lunch, had taken all afternoon before going to get a pair of his own worn black socks instead of taking Rujen's money to buy a pair of normal white ones from the store, and it especially bothered Rujen that Crawford, who wanted to make Rujen finish his shift, had said that Andy had never mentioned that Rujen could leave early to attend the Good Friday service at church; but what bothered Rujen the most, what made him nervous and his heart beat too fast, was an inability to put behind him all the things that had been bothering him all day—the sewage in his sink, his stolen boots, his bicycle, the dolphins even (he had no idea why they troubled him), and, although he thought he had settled the matter, there persisted the nagging question of his soul—and the feeling that all of it was somehow connected, pointing to something larger he ought to know, and what made it worse was a sense of pressure that seemed to pin him constantly at the edge of understanding exactly what it was, neither allowing him to face it nor push it from his mind.

For just a second some part of the mystery seemed to clarify, like an almost-dawning awareness of a long-forgotten name, but then it became vague, melting, oddly, into the memory of an often-told story from his childhood on Tar-Wōj. He had first heard the story from older boys, but his mother would tell it too, probably to keep him from wandering away at night. She said that before the war between America and Japan, there was a group of young Marshallese men at Lae atoll, very close to Kwajalein, who called themselves the Disciples of Satan. They stole chickens and other small animals to use in their rituals, and because of their contact with the "evil worm," as his mother referred to Satan, they all died in strange and violent ways or lost their minds. The story did not end there, though, because the ghosts of the ones who died began to roam the islands at night, snatching the souls of children and tempting others to commit suicide and join them. It was a true story, Rujen later learned, at least the part about the Disciples worshiping Satan. Some of them had died strangely too, and Sampson, the man from Lae who worked at the plant, had told Rujen that one of the Disciples who had lost his mind, a very old man now, still wandered around Lae, sometimes wearing a shabby Japanese soldier's uniform.

Rujen was puzzled as to why he would suddenly recall the story of the Disciples, then he remembered how he had felt one time, while under the spell of his youthful imagination, when he was sure they were after him. He had been having a little *raprap*, diarrhea, not too bad, and had gone outside late that summer night to use the new outhouse the missionaries had built. The moon had already been down for hours, and it was during a period of doldrums, he thought, because he clearly remembered no wind or crashing breakers, only a soundless, overcast darkness which blackened into infinity all the houses and the palm trees and the jungle, even the lagoon and the ocean, making it seem as though nothing really existed as anything at all beyond his face until he reached out with his fingers and touched it. He had brought a small metal penlight with him, a First Communion gift from Father Nicholls, but the perfect darkness and the quiet was so unreal, almost hypnotic, and despite his urgent mission he could not resist the simple adventure of blindly picking his way along the short path that led to the outhouse, slowly lifting his feet up high and swirling his arms so that he could imagine he was floating through some endless, disconnected void. The illusion was broken by the sudden cry of a bird, an unnatural, high-pitched cawing as if the bird had gone insane. Once the sound of it echoed away, the night was quiet again, even more quiet, and Rujen stood still, instantly aware that he was not alone, and then, never before more certain of anything in his life, he knew the ghosts of the Disciples had come to get him, to steal his soul, and that they were watching him, that they had been watching him the whole time, either from their hiding places in the black air or while slithering toward him along the ground. With his thumb he eased forward the switch on his light, held it at arm's length, and saw the sanctuary of the outhouse just a short distance away. Although he fully expected to be snatched as soon as he took one step, he knew that he had no choice and bolted for the whitewashed wooden door ahead, losing sight of it as his beam slashed up and down. He crashed into the door and felt around for the handle on the wrong side, but finally he got it open and spun inside, only to fear at the last second as he jammed down the latch to lock out the Disciples, that he might have run straight into a trap and that if he turned around, in his final living moment, he would stare straight into the angry, disembodied face of a long-dead Disciple and that would be the end. He reached back with his hand and felt the uneven, right angle of the bench, then he looked with the light—only a tin bucket of dirt, the bench, and its black hole in the middle. His bowels roiled and growled, and he could not hold them back much longer, but just to be safe he first shined his light down the hole, quicky judging the relative, unsupernatural safety of the slick stuff amid dirt and scraps of paper at the bottom.

Rujen laughed softly, remembering how frightened of the Disciples he was at the time, and in a way he could see how his mysterious troubles this day had triggered that memory, but something else had happened then that he could not remember now, nothing specifically related to a silly fear of the Disciples, but something else which was important and which for some reason he thought strongly that he needed to remember. He searched among what other details he could remember of that night—the humidity, the stink, his body wet all over with sweat, his running back home . . . no, to the ocean . . . while whipping a small stick back and forth as if the sound was a protection against evil, as if he was striking . . . why was he going to the ocean? . . . Had he been upset about something, not just scared? . . . Yes, before that: A piece of paper in the outhouse, sheets of paper for wiping pushed onto a nail, something to do with the papers . . . pictures of—but Rujen could not remember, and it was stupid, maybe even evidence of insanity, he thought, to think that pictures on wiping paper inside of an outhouse, so long ago, could have any importance to anything whatsoever. Just having to think about it angered him, and it angered him that this day, basically no different from the last and so many before, was a day to cause him so much grief and trouble for no damn reason at all. He should have gone fishing and camping with his sons, breaking the law, just as Jebro had suggested he do. That thought buoyed him a bit, to think that at least his sons were out enjoying their lives, not sitting in the employee breakroom of the Kwajalein Sewage Treatment Plant with hurting feet and wondering about toilet paper, perhaps going insane, thinking only half in jest that maybe one of those Disciples had actually finally found him.

Andy had said that Rujen could leave at three, so that he could arrive at church early enough to watch the children of the catechism class reenact Christ's journey to Calvary, but Crawford's refusal to let him go had caused him to linger and now it was past three thirty. Rujen had known all along that he was not going to finish his shift, no matter what Crawford said he had to do, but it took some time for him to buck himself up enough to do it. Finally he stood, determined to leave, and tested his feet, which he had wrapped in one entire roll of gauze each, over bandage pads, because of Crawford's lousy black socks. He judged the pain to be reasonably bearable, then padded down to his locker in the washroom, stripped out of his overalls, and, after a few strong shots of Right Guard instead of a shower—and a glob of Vitalis worked into his hair—he put on the nice Hawaiian shirt and black slacks he always wore to church. He clipped his ID badge so that it hung on the outside of his breast pocket. As he buttoned his shirt he noticed that his hands continued to shake just slightly, but he hoped that once he was on his way to church, away from Crawford, his nerves would begin to calm. He also hoped that once he got there, inside a holy house—a sanctuary—the rest of his troubles might be lessened or even dispelled through prayer and by the presence of Christ. Having no other option, he put the old boots back on his feet, this time the fit being much tighter but not chafing because of the well-padded bandaging.

At twenty to four—still plenty of time to arrive before the four thirty service and, as required of him as an usher, to arrive half an hour before then—Rujen walked back up and used the break-room phone to call himself a taxi. His fingers, as he spoke to the dispatcher, idly traced the contours of the orange tree trunk that held Andy's set of knives, the ones with handles shaped and painted like different kinds of fish. After he hung up he looked out the window. He saw no other workers and left the room again, expecting to slip away unseen. But as soon as he shut the door quietly behind him, running a comb through his hair at the same time, he turned around and felt a sudden twinge of guilt as he faced Crawford coming down the walk-way. Crawford, carrying a mop at arm's length as though he was looking for another man to use it, stopped and opened his mouth to say something, but Rujen gave him a look, probably much more menacing than he intended it to be, which sort of froze Crawford in mid-thought, his mouth hanging open, his own stupid black socks puddled around his bony white ankles, his mop dripping a little water.

The only way out was to go past Crawford, but Rujen felt awkward, unsure of what he should do. His dislike of the balding, skinny little man was becoming more obvious, he was sure, the more he looked at him. He got the idea that he should let Crawford make the first move, then, almost causing him to laugh, he envisioned himself and Crawford as two desperados, like in Western movies—Rujen with his comb at his side and Crawford with his mop, each waiting for the other to draw. Rujen thought he might say something funny to ease the tension, something Western, but he did not want Crawford to think that he was foolish. "I told you," he said. "Andy said I can leave early." He slid his comb into his back pocket, behind his wallet.

Crawford kept his distance, saying nothing. He moved the mop to his left and supported his weight on it, leaning at such an angle that he looked as though he might fall over. If somebody kicked the mop he would certainly fall over.

"So I guess I'm going now . . . to church," Rujen said. "And I come back tomorrow morning." Rujen took a couple of slow steps toward Crawford then quickened his pace, looking straight ahead. He had to turn sideways to get around the mop, to his right so that he would not have to look at Crawford's face. He passed him, saying nothing, and headed for the stairs.

"I hear you want your boy working here," Crawford said to Rujen's back.

Rujen stopped, letting the words replay in his mind, realizing by Crawford's tone the insinuation of something beyond a casual remark. At first, he was jarred into fearing that his actions might be harming his son's future, his own too, then he reminded himself, recalling the moment, that Andy had clearly given him permission to leave early, and besides, he knew that Andy sometimes made jokes about Crawford behind his back, that Crawford had no final say about anything—Andy did, and

Andy was the one who had hired Jebro, not Crawford, who seemed to take some sick sense of satisfaction from inflicting his own unhappiness on other people. Rujen felt a rising anger, but he resisted the urge to tell Crawford exactly what he thought of him. Instead, when he turned around he forced a smile and said, "Yes, Andy is starting Jebro on Monday. You'll like him, a very good young man. He makes everybody feel happy, maybe even you."

Crawford looked a little stunned, obviously not hearing what he had expected. "Yeah," he said, looking down as he thought of something to say. "Yeah, so I guess you can go then, if Andy said."

Rujen waited a few seconds but Crawford would not look him in the eyes. "Thanks again for the black socks," he said, then turned back around and headed down the stairs. When he reached the bottom he noticed that a good wind had continued to increase during the afternoon and that the sky had cleared in the east and overhead, promising for the first time in several days a good cool night for sleeping, which was a relief. He also could not help but notice, as he sat on the rounded yellow head of a fire hydrant in front of the building and waited for his taxi, that the nervousness within him, almost an accustomed presence now, still caused a slight shaking in his hands. He hooked his thumbs into his front pockets, took a deep breath, and leaned forward as he exhaled to see if he could see his taxi coming down the road.

Shark Clan

JEBRO STARED INTO the wide, frightened eyes of his brother as if his gaze might be a lifeline between them, keeping his body so close that he sometimes kicked Nuke's feet as they both struggled to stay afloat on the rolling, white-capped sea. Nuke breathed heavily, working hard to stay as high above the water as possible. "Move your arms slower!" Jebro scolded. Then, less harshly, "Like me, so you save your strength."

Nuke kept thrashing. "I can't!" he insisted, his voice high and cracking. "The waves are too big!"

Until that moment Jebro had been burdened by an increasing frustration with himself, his mind very much rattled by the recent rapid events and unable to focus on thinking of things he knew he should be doing, but when the full reality hit him that his only brother was likely to drown very soon, he realized then as he dunked under a curl of foam and stared into the dark purple deep below, that saving his own life meant nothing if he could not save Nuke as well. He was suddenly overcome, and freed, by a simple clarity of purpose—to find some way off the ocean, together, and not to accept or even think that they might fail. The perfect logic of it gave him an unexpected, almost guilty feeling of exhilaration, as if by choosing to live he was released, maybe as a necessary element of that choice, from all fear of dying.

Encouraged now, Jebro pulled Nuke to his side and kicked hard to keep them both afloat. "Rest a little," he said, "while I tell you our plan." At the crest of a swell he pointed. "We must be almost two miles from Tōn̄le, do you see?"

Nuke only stared at the wind-chopped face of another approaching swell. He turned away from the swell as they rode up and the top of it slapped past their heads. Right behind the swell was a larger one, and the trough between the two blocked sight of any horizon. A series of lesser swells came after. The ocean was cold and gray. Maybe soon, Jebro thought, the wind might push the clouds away from the sun.

While he had been driving the boat, Jebro would have thought that the two- and three-foot swells, not as choppy then, seemed small and almost friendly, but now, having to keep himself and his brother from being drowned by them, the swells seemed large and menacing, almost angry in the way their blue-gray bodies sometimes rolled over white, at best indifferent and dead toward any life they cradled. He plucked a tuft of bird dander that was pasted to Nuke's forehead. "Look," he said. "Look at Tōn̄le and tell me which way you think the current is taking us."

Nuke looked at the distant green hump of the island for a moment, then he pointed to his right and tried to kick away from Jebro. "The gas can!" he said. "It floats!"

The rusting red can, not far away, bobbed on-end.

Jebro kept his arm around Nuke and told him to stop kicking. "The can is no good for a float. The slick water, the gasoline all around it will blind you, but we might find something—a log, maybe something else from the boat. But look," he said, pointing again at Tōn̄le. "You can see the current is taking us north, even a little west away from the islands, but that's not a problem because the atoll up ahead curves to the west too, far west, enough so I think we'll be just like some Japanese fishing floats and wash up onto a beach—some island up there we can't see yet. We should try swimming a little between north and east, this way into the waves a bit, at an angle to the current so we can get a little closer to the islands. The exercise will keep us warm too." He pressed his head against Nuke's, his eyes focused to where the late afternoon sun was a white glare behind the gray mass of clouds moving west. "So listen, our plan is to stay afloat and stay warm by swimming, but take it easy, okay, so we save our strength because we might . . ." Farther downstream of the current, Jebro saw part of his duffel bag riding the swells, the gray canvas bulging where some air was trapped inside. He also saw one of the gallon water jugs, half submerged, not far from the bag. ". . . because it might be dark when we reach an island—but look, do you see my bag over there, and the water jug? I think I can make a float. You have to swim, though—we have to go get it." He released his arm from Nuke and they faced each other, treading water, this time Nuke moving his limbs more slowly.

Jebro noticed that Nuke's hands were missing the strips of cloth bandages he had put on after catching the turtle. He reached over and checked the wounds, pink and white slices across his palms.

"What about sharks, Jebro. I'm scared of—"

"Hey!" Jebro shouted. He nudged Nuke's shoulder and smiled. "You told me today that nothing scares you, remember? Besides, what is our clan?"

Nuke managed a smile in return. "Ripako ran," he said. "Shark clan."

"So you see we're the sharks!" Jebro showed his teeth. "All the sharks in the ocean respect us and won't eat us—our mother told me this before you were born and she would never lie. We can swim like sharks too, like you see them going slow all the time, never in a hurry, saving their strength. So let's go, swim with me over to the bag, easy like I said—just watch me."

Jebro began a lazy sidestroke, facing Nuke, and Nuke did the same but having a little trouble keeping his head from being washed over by the swells. "Roll a little onto your back at the top and ride down," Jebro coached him, "so you can keep breathing and not get a face full of water."

Nuke adjusted his stroke—doing better. He looked ahead at the bag then thoughtfully to Tōn̄le moving slowly by, then he looked at Jebro. "But when it gets dark how can we see any islands? We might swim right past. Are you sure about the current?"

"The current is strong, moving us fast for now, and when we get close we can smell the islands and hear the waves breaking, and because on this side of the atoll the east wind is blocked by the islands, it will be calmer as we get near—so we're safe from getting pounded when we have to swim over the reef, no matter how dark it gets. We might even get spotted by a helicopter before that, anytime now, or those American boys might see that our boat disappeared—maybe they'll feel guilty and come look for us."

"Ayeee! They want to drown us, those shits. I swear when I get back—"

"No," Jebro said, scanning the water ahead of him. "I thought that too, maybe that they could even be evil, but I think now . . . well, they still owe us—they owe our father a boat, more than a boat I think because they owe us something too, and they better make it right, but I don't know, maybe it was just a bad joke—like some boys are cruel that way, you know, not thinking—they did it for laughs, because they were jealous we beat them to the fish, and they thought we'd just get wet and be too scared of them to keep fishing. Why would they want to kill us? They'd have to be wūdeakeak, insane."

"One time I heard of some wūdeakeak Americans on Roi island, those guys who work the big radars, and the police put them in jail for screwing pigs."

Jebro laughed. "I heard that too, a true story, but that's a different kind of wūdeakeak, because those men living up there have no women—not even one woman lives on that island."

"Maybe like you said those boys aren't really wūdeakeak—just stupid shits—but they better watch out because I still swear I'll walk the reef over to Kwajalein and rock their skulls—whack!—big rocks too."

"I feel the same way—probably I would like to do a lot more than just rock their skulls—but if we do that then the rest of the Americans would see us as criminals and we'd never get another boat from those guys, nothing, so we have to just . . .

We have to get out of here first and then . . ." Jebro smiled, then he pulled a short distance ahead of his brother to reach the water jug. He looked back. "But I think it would be okay to get in a couple good hits if they spot us, as soon as we are safe inside their boat. That would be okay, legal, I think."

"I know which one I want to hit first, that big ugly one, the driver."

"Right, I'll whack him too. But this is funny—just a little while ago we were hiding from the helicopters and then hating those Americans, but how bad would you love to see either of them now!" Jebro opened the water jug and tasted it. "No salt—good."

Nuke kicked ahead to the bag and started pulling up on the canvas.

"Careful," Jebro said, swimming over with the jug. "Some things might still be in there." He held the jug to Nuke's lips and gave him a drink of water, and after another sip for himself he screwed the lid back on tight.

Nuke then slipped one hand under the thick white drawstring that ran through the bag's brass eyelets and with his other hand he reached into the bag. He jerked out one of Jebro's scarred, blue and yellow rubber swim fins, a sliced part of it having been tangled in some loose fibers at the inside seam. The fin was too big for Nuke, so Jebro took it and slipped it over one of his feet. Having one fin made him wish he had two.

As Nuke turned the bag inside-out, Jebro's black plastic film container, the one holding his two remaining matches, bobbed to the surface along with a plastic coil of thirty-pound monofilament leader.

Jebro grabbed the film container and shook it. "Still dry" he said. He grabbed the monofilament too, then he hooked the hole in the middle of the flat plastic spool over his thumb.

"The matches are waterproof, right?" Nuke asked. "You can light them even on something wet?"

"Probably not something too wet, if it's rough enough, maybe. Good matches, and we might need them later. Is anything else in there?"

"No, nothing. But what if . . ." Nuke pointed behind Jebro. "What if you light the gas can on fire?—make a signal."

"Hey, good idea!" Jebro looked for the can but he didn't see it. Then he saw it, maybe thirty yards away. He looked down at the match container for a moment. "What do you think, maybe I can strike the match on the can?—no, too dangerous—or I can move the can out of the gas slick, and with my head under the water—no . . ."

Nuke held up one of the bag's oxidized brass eyelets. "You can strike the match on this maybe, and . . ." He blew on the eyelet to dry it.

"That might work—if I pour all the gas on the water and light it before it spreads out too much." He reached for the bag then stopped. "No, it's still too dangerous, and we'd have to wait, maybe a long time, until we saw a helicopter or a boat, because right now nobody would see it. And it would be too easy to get burned or blinded—no, I better not try."

Nuke squinted angrily at Jebro. "Then let me do it—I can do it if you can't. No way can a fire hurt us with all this water around—and it will save us, you know it will!" He grabbed for the matches.

Jebro pushed away Nuke's hand. "Ōrrōr!—and when they ask me how I was rescued, I will have to say: Well, what I did was burn my little brother as a smoke signal. No, it's too dangerous way out here to try anything with gasoline. And we'll need the matches for a signal fire when we reach land. Otherwise it might take days before somebody finds us."

Nuke frowned. "All you have to do is light a fire—just try it, one stupid match!" He raised his voice. "Do it or we're going to drown out here and die because you—"

"No! We stay away from the gas." He held Nuke by the front of his shirt. "And I promise you will not drown. You will not get eaten by a shark. And both of us are getting back on land. I promise you this like I never promised anything before, my best promise ever. Does that mean anything to you?"

Nuke was quiet for a moment, then he nodded his head. "Okay, I trust you."

"You better. Now watch this." Jebro handed Nuke the water jug and the match container. He took the bag, untied the knots at the ends of the drawstring and pulled it through the eyelets, then, lying on his back, he pulled the bag from the water, wrung it out as best he could, and held it open so that the wind partly filled it. He twisted the back half of it off and tied it with the monofilament so that he had a good four gallons of air trapped inside. He squeezed out a space of about twelve inches and tied another knot, then filled the front half again with air and tied that shut with the drawstring. What he had then was a float shaped like a weightlifter's dumbbell. "The space in the middle is for you, just put you arms over it. The two bags should point out from your armpits.

Nuke tried on the float but it kept slipping up and down his chest or out from under his arms.

"I can fix it," Jebro said. He chewed through the slack end of the monofilament, giving himself a length of about ten feet, and used that instead of the drawstring to close the top. When he had Nuke positioned in the float again he tied the drawstring from one end of the middle space, around Nuke's chest, and back again on the other end, so that his arms were free to swim without the bag slipping away.

Nuke smiled.

Jebro used the rest of the monofilament to tie the water jug to a hole through the waistband of his shorts, enough slack so that it would trail as he swam. Holding it at times would help him rest too. He took the match container from Nuke and placed it within a knot at the bottom of his shirt. "The float will leak over time," he said, "but I can fill it again pretty easy. I tied the knots so I can take them off and on. After a while it will be my turn, or maybe I can think of a way both of us can use it." He gave Nuke a push on his back and pointed which way to go. "Start swimming."

Nuke adjusted the drawstring so that he could lean forward and began stroking, awkwardly at first then finding a comfortable rhythm. The float kept him buoyant but it dragged, making for slower going.

Jebro checked their position again, seeing that they were drifting much more west than he had thought, probably because of the wind and the direction of the swells moving contrary to the current. He was sure that after about ten miles the boomerang-shaped atoll started curving to the west—extending forty, maybe fifty miles west from where they were—but what he did not tell Nuke was that for the first several miles, starting a few islands past Tar-Wōj, the atoll first curved to the northeast, maybe five miles in, and given their course he could see that for a time, probably beginning just before dark, they would lose all sight of land, fight higher seas, and face the brunt of an increasing wind.

The confusing geometries of their predicament—forces of waves against current against wind, the potential distance they might gain by swimming—all played through Jebro's mind but provided him with no secret formula, no solution, only reaffirming what he already knew, the obvious: That they needed to keep from moving too far west, especially now before they might not be able to make any progress at all. He switched the fin to his other foot, so that one leg would not become more tired than the other, and swam close alongside Nuke, realizing then that the current—most likely a tidal current, not one of the stable open-ocean currents—would probably change before very long, in which direction he did not know. It occurred to him that his grandfather would know, but his grandfather's voice was silent, dead, buried with him on Tar-Wōj, which they were moving toward, but at the same time, unable to counter their drift west, they were also moving farther away from it. Jebro looked up for helicopters and saw none. He looked around for boats and saw none. He looked again at Tar-Wōj, his *ļāmoran*, Nuke's *ļāmoran*, and although they would soon pass it by and soon after that be seeing nothing but ocean and sky, the sight of Tar-Wōj gave him strength, and for a while he imagined that just by staring at the island's distant beach he could draw himself closer to it.

Sanctuary

RUJEN HAD LINGERED too long at work and the taxi had not been quick in coming, and now, for the first time since joining the Kwajalein Catholic Church, he was going to be late, probably not late for the service but definitely late for his duties as an usher. He sat on the low, wooden side bench of the crowded taxi van, wedged between two stinking young boys who wanted to sell him a dried-up rockfish. The blond-haired boys looked about nine or ten years old and were probably twins, each holding identical short white rods fitted with freshwater fishing reels, the kind with rounded covers over the spools. The toothy, black-spotted brown fish, pulled from the bottom of the boys' cracked, duct-taped-together tackle box, was about nine inches long, curled by rigor mortis, and held by its ragged tail about a foot in front of Rujen's face.

The speed limit posted on the road, which the driver obeyed, was fifteen miles per hour, not fast enough to clear the taxi of its stench.

"Like buy fish?" the boy asked for the second time. He had some kind of greasy chum smeared into the legs of his denim shorts, most likely from wiping his hands there. His brother's shorts were also greasy with chum, and from the rank smell of it, Rujen guessed it was probably refuse from the butcher's saw long gone bad. More chum caked their tackle box, and a dollop of it was mashed into the taxi floor. Most of the other passengers had their hands over their noses. The smell inside the taxi was so strong it seemed as though the boys had more chum hidden somewhere else, maybe in their pockets.

"No thank you," Rujen said, and leaned back away from the fish. He pressed his legs together, not wanting the chum to rub against his church slacks. The confined space bothered him more than the smell, and maybe as a consequence of that he was beginning to feel oddly removed, somewhat detached, almost as if what he saw and heard was not entirely real but filtered through an unpleasant daydream—a sensation which bothered him even more. He knew his hands would still be shaking just slightly, for no good reason, if he did not keep them held together. He was sweating, just enough to feel it on his neck and chest, not so much from the heat, but as though he were sick. He was not sick, just nervous, not altogether there.

"Fifty cent," the boy's brother said. "Two for dollar. We got two."

"*I* caught two, not you."

"I'm Billy, he's *Dick*."

"Richard!" said the boy with the fish. He reached across Rujen and tried to hit his brother with it. "My name is Richard and I was the one who caught both fish. You can have 'em for fifty cent." He displayed the fish from side to side.

It was the only conversation in the taxi, and except for the two men with crew cuts up front, who looked outside as the van rattled and squeaked up 9th Street past a womens' softball game. The other eight passengers looked to Rujen because, given the offer made by the boy, it was obviously his turn to speak. He could not just sit there, oblivious, as if he hoped to fade from view.

Rujen said nothing, but shook his head, not looking at the boys but from one to another of the passengers watching him—four ladies in back wearing straw hats and holding plastic pails full of sun-bleached seashells, three middle-aged bachelors in swim trunks, and a golfer on the opposite bench who looked a little drunk. They all stared back at him blankly, as if he were somebody inside of a television. He pushed away the boy's arm, Richard's arm, the one still holding up the fish.

"Those fish are spoiled," he said evenly, almost kindly, despite himself. "You can always tell when the eyes turn red like that—but maybe you can use them for bait. Put them in your freezer for next time."

"Nah," Richard said, tossing the stiff fish back inside the tackle box. "'Cause our mom don't let us put fish in the freezer no more."

"'Cause of that eel," Billy said. Both boys giggled. "We caught it on the reef behind our house and that's how we tried to kill it, in the freezer, but our mom found it—"

"And it was still alive."

"It chewed through the peas."

"And it pooped all over!" They giggled again, their red-and-white plastic bobbers rattling against their poles, their squirming leaving a yellowish splotch of chum on each leg of Rujen's slacks. The golfer laughed, then two of the other men in swim trunks did, but three of the four ladies in straw hats, noses pinched, did not. Neither did Rujen, although he did manage a grin before he saw the mess the boys had made on his slacks.

The taxi stopped in front of the airport to drop off the two crew cuts, and because it was not too far across the street from the church, Rujen was eager to get out there as well. He stood, carefully, not touching the boys, and headed for the door. He heard muffled laughter behind him, the bachelors and the golfer.

"You can have 'em for free," Richard said to Rujen's back. "If you want."

Rujen stopped at the door and turned around. "It's okay," he said. "I already ate." He stepped his brown-booted bandaged feet down into the street, feeling a blister squish on the side of a toe, then he smiled and waved good-bye to the driver, Benson, a Marshallese man who had rights to land at Bigej. The stench Rujen got away from seemed to be made much worse by how much better it smelled to be outside. As the taxi rolled on past, and he hurriedly brushed at the greasy globs of chum stuck to the legs of his black polyester slacks, he was right on the verge of laughing at his experience with the two boys—just about to do it now that he was outside, no longer confined—but then the humor of it suddenly escaped him. He did not laugh, and for one futile second he even tried to force it, but the boys and their fish and their little story of the eel—none of it was funny anymore. Now, actually, something was terribly wrong with it all. Now it was going to trouble him, of course, and pile on and agitate all the rest of the things confounding him this day. And did he know why, could he at least understand why, for Christ's sake, did such a stupid little thing have to try his nerves? No, he just had to take it, and sweat, and feel his heart beat faster than it should. And now, although he got rid of the chum, two large greasy spots stood out on his slacks. He brushed at the stains again, all around his slacks. When he brushed at his rear, his fingers came away caked with chum. He had sat in chum on the taxi, mashed it all over the rear of his slacks.

Rujen tried to look over his shoulder at his rear and began to laugh, much too loud. He covered his mouth. He recoiled from the reek of rotten chum on his hand. He felt a piece of it that had come off onto his lip. He spit, and wiped his mouth on the wide collar of his Hawaiian print shirt. None of this was funny. Still, he could not help but laugh—a strange, cheerless laugh, so odd it made him stop, and for a moment he forget why he was standing in front of the airport.

But across the street one hundred yards away, adjacent to the Richardson outdoor theater, there amid tall windblown palms and some gathered people stood the church, a long, almost cross-shaped (one arm shorter than the other) A-frame building with a small chapel attached to the back. The peak of the church's white roof was high, a cross on top, and the sides of the roof extended down to just a few feet from the border of white lily plants on the ground, so that the sides of the church, without walls, were open to the air and, as Father Trotter liked to say, open to the free flow of heavenly spirits.

Sanctuary. And Rujen was going to be late. He ran, brushing, almost slapping at the rear of his slacks, wiping his hands free of the chum on palm trees as he passed them.

Long ago Rujen had Sundays off and he would take his wife and then just his children to the Queen of Peace Catholic Church on Ebeye, but when he was promoted from Waste Worker III to Waste Worker II, four years after Iia died, he had to start working both Saturdays and Sundays to handle the duties normally taken care of by Tony, the American worker who switched to working weekdays. Rujen got Wednesdays off, and for almost an entire year he skipped going to mass, only visiting the Queen of Peace on Wednesdays, and sometimes going to the Kwajalein chapel during lunch just to pray awhile and light a candle for his wife. He had asked Jebro to keep taking Nuke on Sundays (the other Christian members of the household were Protestant, as were most of the Christians on Ebeye) but he knew they often did not go. He thought it would be wrong to pressure his sons—it was better for them if they learned to value prayer and worship on their own terms—and, of course, he could not hold himself up as much of an example, even if he did have to work.

Rujen missed going to Sunday mass, the fellowship of it, but after a while he began to enjoy the times he spent alone in prayer, especially his visits to the Kwajalein chapel. The chapel was almost always empty, and it was such a peaceful experience to pray and then to sit in one of the smooth wooden pews, an electric fan washing air back and forth across his face, the smell of scented wax coming from the wrought iron stand of votive candles, some of them lit and flickering inside colored glass, the kindly blue-and-white Madonna watching over him, chirping birds outside and palm fronds clacking—so peaceful was it that he sometimes fell asleep, never for very long, but long enough so that when he opened his eyes again he felt rested, unburdened even, and very much at peace, certainly ready to accept that sleeping in church was in fact a legitimate religious experience. One afternoon, though, just after nodding off, he felt a hand on his shoulder and it was the new priest on Kwajalein he had heard about, Father Trotter. Trotter stared down at him and told him firmly that he was in a house of God—not someplace a man was free to wander in for a nap. Trotter stepped aside, giving Rujen room, and looked to the door as if that was where he ought to promptly go.

Rujen was immediately embarrassed, and he rose so quickly to leave that he banged his knee loudly against the pew in front. He apologized, as much for sleeping as for striking the pew, but just outside the door he stopped, and as he rubbed his knee he thought he should explain—he was, after all, a Catholic, not just a sleepy Marshallese as Father Trotter obviously assumed—and when he told him this, and apologized again, and said he was only there to light a candle for his wife and because he had to work when the weekend masses were held on Ebeye, Father Trotter's expression softened and he asked Rujen to come back inside and take a seat.

Father Trotter was an older man, from Pittsburgh, he said, and they talked for a while about Rujen's experiences with Jesuit missionaries as a child and with their church on Ebeye, and Trotter asked if Rujen did much snorkeling, which was something he was eager to try. Trotter was a snow skier in his younger days, and he joked that he had the knees to prove it. When Rujen said that he had better get back to work, Trotter asked him to wait just a couple of minutes so that he could make a phone call, to see if there was something he could do about Rujen's problem. Rujen thought he might be calling down to the plant to insist that he be given Sundays off, which was not very likely to happen, but instead, when Trotter returned he asked Rujen if he would like to work as an usher for the five thirty masses held on Saturdays. It was volunteer job, naturally, but it was also official, and it gave Rujen a pass for Saturdays, and any other holy days, such as Good Friday, to stay on Kwajalein past six o'clock when he usually had to leave, when the *Tarlang* made its return trip to Ebeye. Rujen hesitated at first, unsure if he wanted to be the only Marshallese in the congregation. Such a thing had never even seemed possible before. But then he pictured himself, not just a man sitting by himself among strangers and their families, but an usher, standing sharply at the entrance to the fine large church, escorting the well-dressed Americans to their seats—to be an usher was an honor, to refuse it would be an insult. Rujen said that yes, he would accept the job, it was very kind of Father Trotter, and he must have thanked him about a dozen times before leaving and promising to come back later to sign some papers for his pass.

Marvin Cronin was the other usher on Saturdays, and Rujen, as asked by Father Trotter, came a little early that next Saturday (he usually got off work at four thirty) so that Marvin could show him what to do. At the time Marvin was in his late twenties, fit and tan, a professional scuba diver and engaged to Anna, one of the hospital's nurses, whom he later married. Rujen remembered having seen Marvin's picture in the *Kwajalein Hourglass* for having won a racquetball tournament. He greeted Rujen warmly, although he was quick to make a joke about Rujen's suit.

The day before, Rujen had borrowed a black sports coat and matching pants from Elwin Balos, a neighbor of his whose wife had been given the clothes by the woman she was a maid for on Kwajalein. The woman's husband had outgrown them by quite a bit, so Elwin's wife had said, but they fit Rujen reasonably well, the coat just a little long in the sleeves. He owned a lavender shirt he thought was a good match for it, and another man loaned him a thin black tie—the only problem was a matching pair of shoes, which he solved by polishing the hell out of a black pair of leather work boots. He thought he looked fit to be president, but when he arrived at church, Marvin, who wore white jeans and a Hawaiian print shirt (and a small American flag pinned to his collar), sized him up and down and asked, "Who died?"

Rujen had no idea it was supposed to be a joke, and for a moment he thought that Father Trotter must have mentioned something to him about Iia, but Marvin was smiling too much to have asked about a man's dead wife, so Rujen just smiled back, until his curiosity finally got the better of him and he said that he did not understand. He felt a little foolish once Marvin explained the joke, and a little more foolish when the church filled up and he saw that he was the only one in a coat and tie, and, as Marvin pointed out, the only man in black. Rujen took off the a coat. He was sweating anyway.

Marvin joked a little too much for being inside a church, but other than that Rujen liked him very much and even took to wearing his own Hawaiian shirt so that they looked like partners. On that first day Marvin showed him how to seat the older people up front, because they sometimes had a hard time hearing, and how to seat the mothers with babies toward the back or to the sides, so that they could leave if they had to without interrupting the mass. If the church was crowded, he and Marvin had to ask people to scoot over to make room. It was important to greet people with a smile and to make them feel welcome, and it was also important, after he and Marvin gathered the collection baskets, to cover them when they placed them at the foot of the sanctuary, otherwise—and Marvin said it had happened once—the wind might catch the money and blow it all around the church.

Rujen told Marvin, just before mass that day, that he had seen something like that too, on Ebeye, but it had been done on purpose. It was in a Protestant church, during a Christmas day singing presentation, and he had gone at the invitation of his aunts who were members. As the Protestants sang, a plaster atomic bomb was slowly raised to the high point of the church's ceiling. It was a very high ceiling. Painted on the bomb were the words "GOD DESTROYS ALL EVIL." When the singing reached its climax the bomb was dropped, and the entire church cheered as it crashed to the floor where, amid a cloud of plaster dust, it released several hundred one-dollar bills. Marvin thought it was a very funny story and he laughed, much too loud for being inside a church—no matter that mass had not yet started. It was loud enough for people to turn around and look. Marvin just smiled and waved to them. One other thing Rujen learned then, from Marvin, was that if you were friendly enough, you could get away with anything.

After two years as a Waste Worker II, Rujen had the option not to work weekends any longer, but he had gotten used to it, and he had to admit that, rather than return to the church on Ebeye, he liked it much better being a member of the church on Kwajalein. It was vain, and he knew it, but he enjoyed too much the prestige and importance he felt from being an usher there—and was it so wrong for a man to want something in life that made him feel that way? He had made friends too, some of them even inviting him to dinner at their homes after church, but of course he could not go, as he had to be off the island by seven, or at least past the checkpoint at the pier by then, or he would be fined for trespassing. Rujen also enjoyed his relationship with Father Trotter, who taught him the Latin names of the sacred vessels, instruments, and furnishings in the church, and taught him the Lord's prayer in Latin too. Not until Father Trotter had told him did Rujen know (or more probably he had once been told but did not pay attention then) that the blessed ashes placed on his forehead on Ash Wednesday symbolized his mortality, his destined return to dust; that on Holy Thursday the altar is stripped of its cloth to symbolize Jesus being stripped before his crucifixion; and that the reason no mass is held on Good Friday (only prayer, a homily, Veneration of the Cross, song, and Holy Communion) is because mass is a celebration and Good Friday a day to mourn, not celebrate, Christ's death on the cross. It may have been vain to remain with the church on Kwajalein, but Rujen was sure it also made him a better Catholic—he had nearly memorized the various masses in his missal—even if part of his motivation to learn was because he wanted to appear knowledgeable among his American peers.

If Rujen had to pick one thing in his life that defined who he was, other than a father to his children, it would most definitely be that he was an usher at the Kwajalein Catholic Church. If there was one aspect of his life that had never caused him any grief, other than that first day when he had looked a little foolish in a suit, it was most definitely his job as an usher for the Kwajalein Catholic Church. Not one moment in that church had been anything but warm, friendly, and an affirmation of his soul, nor did it ever fail to comfort him, heal him, or be for him a sanctuary from whatever troubles plagued him. No, Rujen had never had one bad moment at the Kwajalein Catholic Church.

The late sun broke free from clouds and beamed down heat as Rujen ran across the lawn. The new light made shadows east of the church and the trees and brightened the color of the grass and the white of the church's roof. The dull thudding of his footfalls seemed too soft to match the pain they caused his feet. Ahead, a small group of men and women and a few young fidgeting children stood close together near the front of the church. They stopped their talking and looked at him running at them. He knew their names, most of them, some of them he considered friends. They were upwind and smelled of aftershave and perfume. Rujen was sweating, breathing hard, running at them, but they had no idea what was troubling him. They looked at peace, relaxed, as if they had just stepped out of a bath. A plump young girl in a yellow dress danced at her mother's leg. He passed them, and he would have said something as he ran by instead of only looking back at them, but he was late, already up on the sidewalk, behind them, and headed inside the church.

With hurting feet it took him farther than usual to stop, and had he not caught himself on the marble stoup of holy water, he would have run straight into the back of a man who stood speaking with Darlene Brinks, Kwajalein's Supervisor of Pools. He stopped just short of the man, so close that the man flinched. The man was Foster Rick, dressed in gray slacks and a green and white striped shirt that looked like Christmas. The stripes were vertical, and made his shoulders look even more narrow than they actually were. His face and arms glowed red with a very bad sunburn. For some reason he held one of the wicker collection baskets, and Darlene Brinks had just put money in it.

"Easy there, Keju," Rick said. He grinned as he wagged his finger back and forth. "No running in church."

"Sorry," Rujen said, working to catch his breath. He dipped his fingers in the stoup and made a quick sign of the cross. The strong smell of rotten chum wafted from his greasy hand. He didn't want to believe that he had just fouled the holy water. "My taxi was—I was at the plant and—"

Darlene patted Rick's shoulder. "Good luck," she said, then she smiled politely at Rujen before heading down the aisle. Rujen took a step after her, to seat her, but he held back at the first pew when it struck him that to usher in his sweating out-of-breath condition was probably bad form. He needed to compose himself, to wash his greasy hands and wipe a wet cloth over the smelly stains on his slacks. The church had no restroom. The nearest one available was back at the airport. He moved to Rick's left, downwind, and wiped his sweaty brow on the sleeve of his shirt. From somewhere near the front of the church an infant's muffled cry filtered back through the soft chatter of the congregation. The church was almost three-quarters full. He looked down the aisle to the altar then back to Rick. "Where is Marvin?" he asked, not seeing his partner. He wanted to know who had seated all the people. "Have you seen him?"

"Cronin? Nah, haven't seen him—probably out on a boat, working. Wife's here though, I think. . . . So hey, let me tell you what—"

"Then who . . . ?" Rujen had to take a breath. He wiped his brow again. "Then you're the usher, Rick? Who—"

"Usher? Is that what you're so worked up about, no ushers?"

Rujen felt out of place, out of time, nowhere near as comfortable as he thought he would be once he got to church, and now he felt worse seeing how badly he had failed in his responsibility as an usher. This was one of the holiest days of the year. If only he had left the plant when he should have, he knew everything would be going fine, his spirits would be improving. Instead, he had wasted his time, because of Crawford—now this. And his feet were throbbing, hot. He never should have tried running. "Sorry, I was late and I—"

"Really, Keju—people can seat themselves, you know. It's not unheard of."

Rick's words stung, and the quiet that followed seemed to linger, thick with their echo, trapped inside the church. Rujen had the urge to fire back with an insult of his own, but this was no place to start an argument, and he could think of nothing good enough to say. He just kept quiet and took it, feeling it churn in with all the other crap he had to take this day. He was going to move away from Rick, but then he hesitated: His eyes, now seeing it clearly, unable to look away from the collection basket in Rick's hands. Taped to the basket was a length of light blue construction paper, and in wide black ink were the words, "SAVE THE DOLPHINS." The O of "dolphins" was crudely drawn to look like two dolphins nose to tail. Several one- and five-dollar bills and a few tens lay inside the basket. Rujen reached out and held the bottom of the blue paper, looking at it as if on a second read he might find something he had missed. The paper shook just slightly in his hand.

"Like I was going to tell you," Rick said. "I found those guys, the ones who caught the dolphins, remember?"

Rujen let go of the paper, leaving a damp spot where his thumb had been. "You want to buy the dolphins from them?" The idea of it troubled him, of course having to compound the nervous irritation he had wanted to escape all day.

"Yeah—well, we thought we might get the guys to be nice about it, forget about it, you know, but they seemed pretty dead-set on eating those . . . gosh, those beautiful, intelligent creatures. The things those guys said—I mean, I can't believe anybody would—no disrespect or anything, you know, but . . ." Rick looked away from Rujen and down at the basket. He shook it. "Anyway, Keju, then Colonel Spivey offers cash money—and boom—two minutes later it's a done deal at a dollar a pound. Everybody happy. No fuss, no incident, and the Scuba Club will take the dolphins out to the ocean in the morning. Far into the ocean so they don't . . . so they're safe. Those two guys probably got the better of us, though, if you ask me. But no big deal, and hell—it feels good, you know, to help out now and then."

Rujen looked again at the money in the basket. "Good good, everybody happy then," he said, but that was not the way he felt. He felt the same way about it as he did when he had left the pond, that the dolphins should have been dealt with according to Marshallese custom. Having that opinion surprised him then, and still did now, not only because he would never have felt that way before, but mostly because he was adopting what would have been his father's opinion, an opinion that esteemed the old ways, which Rujen had always sought to move away from. He imagined what might have happened if the two Marshallese workers had refused to trade the dolphins for money, as his father would have done, but right away he knew they would have gotten nothing, no money, no dolphins, only trouble, which was exactly what Ataji always got.

Rujen saw nothing to gain by thinking like his father, and he reminded himself, while watching Rick toss the money like stir-fry in a pan, that he had no good reason to concern himself with the dolphins—not being affected one way or the other—not personally, but still, maddening him, was that he could not help feeling increasingly frustrated over how easy it was for the Americans to get their way, how the two Marshallese, whether they knew it or not, never had any choice at all. The frustration he felt was the same, he was sure, which he had seen so often turn to anger in his father, but he knew better than to start something like one of Ataji's hopeless protests, certainly not in church, and certainly not if he wanted to keep his job at the plant. That kind of tactic had only made Ataji a bitter man—proud maybe, but very bitter. No, Rujen had come to church to find peace, to unburden himself of his troubles, not to add to them. He realized, though, wiser now, that peace was not just going to come rushing into him as he had so foolishly expected. He would have to earn it. "I guess everything is good then," he said. "No fight about the dolphins is good. So how much money those guys going to get, how many pounds?" He tried to look friendly, interested, trying to ignore how much the sight of Rick holding the basket and its sign continued to really irritate him.

"We agreed to one twenty-five each," Rick said. "But I'll bet you anything those—what are they, spotted dolphins, spinner dolphins? I don't know—they can't be that heavy. But hey, close enough and it's for a good cause. Whatever we collect over that'll go to the Scuba Club for their help, maybe give them a couple hundred if we can." He rocked forward onto his toes, whistling a few notes as he looked away from Rujen and at the group of people standing just outside, closer to the open entrance of the church than they had been before.

Rujen forced a slight smile and looked straight ahead into the middle distance, focused on nothing in particular. He took slow even breaths, trying to clear the troubles from his mind, maybe to accept his fate this day as God's will, but he was far too nervous to accept anything, and far from being able to relax. Having to think of the troubles he wanted to put behind him simply made him think about them more. Having Rick standing next to him didn't help much either. He tapped Rick's arm. "Why are you doing this here, in church?" He realized as he said it that he still wore the smile he had forced onto his face.

Rick shrugged his shoulders and smiled back sheepishly. He held up the basket. "I guess this part was my idea. Spivey wanted to take the cash out of the recreation fund, but I thought it would be better if it was a community thing, if a bunch of us did it. Get a story done for the paper too—'Kwaj Catholics Save Dolphins'—something like that, maybe not exactly that, but something. . . ."

Rick was chewing his thumbnail, probably considering how he wanted his headline to read, when Arch Stanton, who worked in the control tower at the airport, and his wife, Joy, entered the church and walked up to him. They had a son who was about fifteen, Evan, or Edwin, who was already taller than both his parents. He always picked at his face in church. He hung back by the stoup, disassociating himself. The Stantons had never been very social with Rujen, or even talked very much with anybody else. They mostly kept to themselves. Arch spoke to Rick almost in a whisper, facing slightly away from Rujen, saying that he and Joy had "heard," and with a wink he put a sealed envelope in the basket. They headed down the aisle, Evan, or Edwin, following a short distance behind, not one of them looking for Rujen to show them to their seats. *Really, Keju—people can seat themselves, you know. It's not unheard of.*

Rujen laughed, much louder that he should have, which caused Arch Stanton to turn around and stare at him. Some people in the back pews turned around too, eyeing Rujen with disapproval. A week before they might have been smiling if he or Marvin had made a joke and laughed; now they were frowning. Arch looked as if he had been insulted. Rujen raised his hand in apology. "Sorry, I just thought of something funny." He looked back to Rick. "You see, you want to save the dolphins, Rick, but now you will have plenty of Marshallese catching them if they think you Americans will buy them every time!" He laughed again, not as loud, and before he realized what he was doing he reflexively raised his hand to cover his mouth. He leaned back from the chum stench. He caught himself just as he was about to reach up again and wipe his nose.

Rick was not smiling. "Thought of that," he said. He cocked his head to one side and looked at Rujen strangely, in the way dogs looked at people sometimes. "Monday morning Spivey's getting the legal office to draft an ordinance. You smell something?"

"An ordinance?" Rujen did not know what it was, but the meaning was clear—legal office—the next Marshallese who caught a dolphin was going to jail.

"An ordinance is like a law. Damn. . . ." Rick looked around the floor and sniffed the air.

Rujen held the bottom of his shirt over his slacks. He thought of the people who looked at him when he had laughed, and what they must have been thinking of him, a Marshallese, if they were some of the ones who had put money in Rick's basket. Rick had poisoned all of them against him. He was beginning to feel confined again, and not just frustrated and nervous, but much too conspicuous as the only Marshallese around, and as one who smelled. It occurred to him that there might be enough time to jog back over to the airport and get clean, to go there and come back slowly, calmly, and to start over. If he left now he might just make it, at worst be only a couple minutes late. But his feet hurt, swollen and blistered within the socks and bandages and boots, in no condition for another jog. And if he was late Father Trotter would notice—no ushers, no Rujen. Rujen would probably distract him by coming in late. He leaned over to get a look at Rick's watch. He had five minutes, just enough time if he thought it was worth the pain. Then again, Father Trotter's watch might be different. *Really, Trotter—people can seat themselves, you know. It's not unheard of.*

Rick was looking down the aisle. "Listen, Keju," he said. "How about you do me a favor, huh?"

Rujen wanted no trouble, but if Rick was going to ask for money, for Rujen to help "SAVE THE DOLPHINS," he felt he might rip that stupid blue sign from the basket and slap the whole thing straight to the floor. But no, he could do no such thing in church, and people would turn and look at look at him, question him—and how could he explain? He would just tell Rick that he brought no money, tell a lie right there in church and he knew he would. He wished that Rick would go seat himself. "Okay," he said, "What you need?" He looked out the side of the church, toward the airport.

"Well, the wife, you know, she's a little miffed I been out all day on this and, um, if you're going to be standing up here, maybe you could hold the basket for me, for the rest of the people who come in. I really should go sit with the family—if you don't mind. Okay?" He held out the basket.

Rujen shook his head. He did not want to help "SAVE THE DOLPHINS." It seemed strange that Rick would even ask him to, being a Marshallese, the kind of person he wanted to save the dolphins from. "No," he said, not too harshly. "I'm sorry, I cannot—I don't want to be responsible for all that money."

Rick held the basket closer, grinning. "C'mon, Keju, it's no big deal. I trust you."

"I have no place to put it, and no—I can't walk with it during communion."

Rick looked at his watch. "Five minutes," he said. "In five or six minutes just bring it up to me, before Father comes in, when you see him coming up the lawn."

Rujen had said no—twice—and no matter if he had said nothing at all, it should be obvious why he would not want to hold the basket, not want to take part in collecting money to stop a Marshallese custom. And not respecting that custom would bring bad luck. But Rick raised the basket a little higher, almost touching Rujen's chest with it, and suddenly Rujen could not help thinking of shoving his stinking hands straight into Rick's annoying sunburned face, of slamming the back of his head against the wall and quickly, before Rick could shout, stuffing his big fat mouth full of the basket's money. His heart beat louder, faster, encouraging him to do it. So close to doing it. And Rick kept grinning, red-faced as the Devil, just daring Rujen to pound him, outright tempting him to desecrate the church with violence. Now Rujen understood; he could see what Rick was trying to do—to get him expelled from the Kwajalein Catholic Church and hauled before the American court, fired from his job and barred from ever coming back—because he was Marshallese, one of the hated dolphin eaters, one who did not belong. Rujen was not going to fall for this trick of the Devil. It was Rick who did not belong, the Devil with his money basket who was the one who should be expelled from the church, chased all the way out of the Marshall Islands, just as Christ had sent the desecrating money changers running from the Temple in Jerusalem. He stared back at Rick, thinking, deciding after a moment that the best thing to do, actually, was to take the basket from him, take his power, and thereby make the Devil go away and find his seat. This would put an end to his game, and to all of the daylong deviling that had conspired against Rujen, all of it leading to this one critical moment so that he would be given a very good chance to ruin himself, his faith, and his position in the church. But the game had failed. Now it ended, all of it. He took the basket.

"All right, thanks," Rick said. "If they ask, just tell 'em what's going on—see if they want to throw in a couple bucks." He held out his hand for a shake.

Rujen had expected something else from him, for the Devil to make a final play. Maybe it was not going to happen. He did not shake Rick's hand, did not look at it. "Okay, see you in five minutes."

Rick lowered his hand. "Aren't you forgetting something?"

Rujen studied him, saying nothing, The Devil had his one last trick. "What you want now?"

"Well, you came running in here all desperate to seat somebody. . . . Now's your chance." He made an exaggerated motion for Rujen to lead the way, then he grinned his Devil grin, showing teeth, a gold one on the top gleaming behind his chapped red lips. "You *are* the usher, right?"

It was a slap in the face, a final insult meant to push Rujen over the edge, but the Devil would have to do better than that, even on this, one of Rujen's most trying days. He stepped up to Rick, close enough to breathe on him, showing him with a good hard look who was not going to take any more crap.

Rick's cocky grin fell so fast it looked as though it had dropped into his money basket. His grin was replaced by a slack-faced look of awkward surprise. His head twitched once, twice. The Devil was a coward, weak. "I was just kidding there, Keju. I didn't mean to . . ." He tried to smile, failed, and took a step back.

Now Rujen grinned, aware of the fear he had put into the red-faced man. "No no, come," he said, overly polite, as if he too had just been kidding. "I see your family, up near the front." He set off quickly down the aisle, gritting his teeth at the pain in his feet, one hand holding the basket and the other holding down the bottom of his shirt. Rick's footsteps padded behind him.

In front of Rujen the crucifix was covered with a red cloth, as was required on Good Friday, and so were the statues of Joseph and Mary. The altar was bare. The sound of the wind outside and the not-too-distant surf was almost indistinguishable from the sound inside of rustling clothes and low voices. He noticed that the cloth over the crucifix had been blown back some by the wind, exposing Christ's legs, the edge of the cloth being caught around the bend of his knees. It could not stay like that, in violation of the custom on Good Friday, but it looked as though the wind, gently flapping the cloth, might blow it back to hanging straight.

At the fourth pew from the front, Rick genuflected then scooted in next to his wife, Patrice, and kissed her on the cheek. Two teenage daughters were seated beside their mother. Rick reached over and squeezed the nearest daughter's hand. She had braces, and a wire going around her head. Rick looked up at Rujen, "Okay, then," he said.

"Okay, I'll give this back in five minutes."

"Hey, look, if you'd really rather not hold it . . ." He reached out to take the basket.

"No," Rujen said, keeping it back. "I can do it—or what, are you afraid now I might steal your money?" It felt good to play games with Rick, to tease him a bit.

Rick glanced at his wife. "No, of course not, Keju, but—all right, okay, I'll see you in a few minutes then."

"Okay," Rujen said, enjoying Rick's unease. "I'll go up now and save the dolphins for you." He laughed, so softly that probably only Rick heard it. Then he headed back up the aisle, smiling and nodding hello to people he knew—most of them acknowledging him and smiling back—then he heard, just behind him, a woman mispronouncing his name.

It was Michelle Kitchner, seated next to her husband, Troy, and she was waving him to come over. They had been on the island for about a year, and had a son in college who visited at Christmas. Rujen went to her and took a knee in the aisle beside the pew, so that he would not be looking down at her as they spoke. He hoped she would see his correct name on his badge. She was tall for a woman, and when Rujen got on his knee she was looking down at him, into his eyes and not at his badge. Her glistening lips were waxed with almost the same color as Foster's sunburned skin. Her pearls hung in three loops, the lowest well below her breasts. A few fine thin hairs stood up through the powder on her slightly pockmarked face. She smelled powerfully of sweet perfume. "I want to help," she said, showing an exaggerated look of kind concern. "I just couldn't find my money earlier." She fumbled to unfold and separate a five from a ten-dollar bill which she had pulled from a small purple coin purse, which she had taken from a zipper bag of cosmetics, which had come from a tan canvas bag that had the face of a blue-eyed cat stitched into it. She dropped the five into the basket. "It's just wonderful I think, Rueben, that you got involved with this, just wonderful. . . ." She put her hand on top of his, just when he had put it on the arm of the pew to push off and leave. Her touch was light, soft and as annoying as the legs of an insect. Through the veil of perfume Rujen could hardly detect the chum stench on his hands and pants, and maybe she could not either. It was probably on her hand now though, and later, when she smelled it, she would probably remember where she had picked it up. "I mean," she continued, after looking at the ceiling as if to find her words up there. "I was just telling Troy—I believe you two have met—" Troy winked, pointed to Rujen with an imaginary pistol, and shot him as he made a clicking noise. "And um, well, I was saying that I'm sure you people, the Marshallese people, you're just like us, and that some of us, a few of us, do bad things but that doesn't mean all of us are bad. Do you know what I mean?" Her nose twitched, sniffing. She lowered her voice. "I mean, I heard it was the Japanese, anyway, who started the whole thing, feeding dolphins to their Marshallese workers back during the war. Is that true?" She sniffed again, and her lips pursed as if she had bitten into a lemon.

"Right," Rujen said. "It was the Japanese. They made us eat dolphins and now some people just can't stop." He stood, smiled politely as he slid his hand out from under hers, and walked away.

Michelle Kitchner made a little noise behind him, something between a whine and a cough. "You're welcome," she said cooly.

Rujen was not ten feet past the Kitchners when he heard a man inquire, quite loud, about something that smelled. Arch

Stanton confirmed it, saying, "Gotta be coming in from outside, a dead cat out there or something."

No longer smiling at people, Rujen hurried to the back of the church. He leaned against the wall and stood on the sides of his feet. When he breathed in through his nose, he could smell the rotten chum, the smell of long-dead meat. His shirt, no matter how far he tried to stretch it down, did not cover the reeking stains that splotched his slacks. He could feel grease between his fingers. He endured it for no more than a moment more, and after checking to make sure that he was not being watched, he took a couple of the bills from Rick's basket and began wiping his hands. Then, after a short hesitation to resist his guilt, he took two more bills and dipped them in the marble stoup of holy water. First he used the bills to quickly clean his palms and fingers, then he used some more to wipe the sides and then the rear of his slacks. It was a wicked thing to do, maybe a sacrilege, and he had to stop. He used another three dry ones to finish off his hands. He could smell the bills now stinking in the basket. His hands, though, did not feel so greasy. He tried to reason that it was more of a sin to stink up the church than to wash with a little bit of holy water. Except now the stink was still in the church, maybe not so much coming from Rujen but from the money. When Foster Rick got the money back he would surely touch it, and then he would stink as well.

As Rujen leaned back again against the wall, and for no reason he could understand, the wet stinking money in front of him got him thinking again of that night, as a boy on Tar-Wōj, when he had run from the Disciples of Satan. The memory ran its course, leaving in its wake a lingering sense of agitation. He was supposed to remember something, but he could not. It bothered him, it made no sense, and he did not want to think about it.

Rujen was tired, and he had had just about enough of standing, for nothing, so it seemed that the best thing he could do was to find himself a seat. Maybe he would get up again, for appearance's sake, when he saw Father Trotter headed inside.

And he would keep the basket too, under the pew until after church, just to irritate Rick. But just when he had picked out his seat—alone in back on the downwind pew—he saw Napo and Lydia Velasco step through the entrance. They had been in the group outside when Rujen had run over from the airport. They were an older couple, Napo being the head chef at Kwajalein's Yokwe Yuk restaurant. Rujen thought he should seat them, at least do that before he took a seat himself.

Napo smiled. "Hey, Buddy," he said, pointing at the basket. "What you got there?"

Rujen thought of saying what the little boy had said on the taxi: *Like buy fish? Fifty cent, two for dollar.* "It's Rick's," he said. "Foster Rick's. I'm just holding it for him."

Lydia dabbed her fingers in the stoup and made the sign of the cross, then did Napo. Rujen felt a twinge of guilt, but it was a big stoup, and he had only tainted it with money, not his hands, except for that first time just with his fingers.

"You had me worried, Rujen," Lydia said. "I thought maybe you were in trouble, the way you came running here like that. You okay?"

Rujen smiled and nodded. "I was late, that's all, just late."

"Do you know what they say about a man who runs to church? Tell him Napo."

"What Lydia, what are you talking about?"

"It's a saying, Napo—isn't there a saying about a man who runs to church?"

Napo chuckled. "C'mon honey, you don't even know and you're telling this to Rujen?"

Lydia shrugged. "I thought you knew. Irene will know—I'll call back home tonight and she can tell me."

Napo flicked the paper sign on the basket with his finger. "So how is Foster Rick saving dolphins, where is he sending all this money?"

"I don't know, he just said to ask people for money."

"Nah, don't ask me. Tell Foster Rick to pay for it himself." Napo put his arm around Lydia.

The rest of the crowd that had been outside came in then, taking their turns at the stoup. Rujen said hello to the Campbells and the Martinos, people he considered friends, and they greeted him kindly in return. The little girl in the yellow dress waved. She belonged to a couple that was new to the islands, the Zeders, but Rujen had not been introduced. They all headed down the aisle and, genuflecting, they sidled into the nearest open pews.

"You want to sit?" Rujen asked. "Come, I can take you."

"Yeah, let's go." Napo said. "You better get us some good seats too." He chuckled again.

Rujen motioned for them to follow him. "I see where you like to sit," he said. "Front pew, plenty of room." Just spending a minute or two with people like the Velascos, good happy people, was all it took for Rujen's mood to begin improving. People like Rick and Crawford could sour even the brightest of moments, but Napo and Lydia were the opposite of that, their very presence just like Iia's had been, and Jebro's.

About halfway down the aisle, Rujen heard Lydia say something in Spanish, then Napo said, "So, Rujen, you work down at the sewage plant, that right?"

Rujen looked back at him. "Right, down at the plant."

Napo came up beside him and put a hand on his shoulder. In a whisper he said, "I think you might have something—you know a little something maybe on your boots, Rujen. I'm sorry, but I have to tell you that you smell."

"It's the money." Rujen said quickly, his fragile aura of happiness suddenly evaporating, his confidence crumbling. "Foster Rick's money—I don't know why." He held out the basket for Napo to smell.

"Is okay, is okay! Whew, Dios mio, you better tell Foster Rick to stop using his money to wipe his—"

"Napo!" Lydia hissed. "Estamos en la iglesia!"

Napo chuckled, falling back in step with his wife.

Rujen was embarrassed enough to want to abandon the Velascos and find some place to be alone in back. And not only was he embarrassed, he was suddenly feeling the full weight of guilt for having lied in church—for the third time in less than fifteen minutes. Without a doubt, he had lost his right to take communion. They walked by Rick then, and he and Rujen looked at each other. Rujen looked away first, the sight of him, the red devil Disciple of Satan sitting smugly in the house of God, instantly bringing back to him everything that had been troubling him this day. Now he was nervous again, if the feeling had ever really left, angry that he seemed to have very little control over what went through his mind, that one minute he could feel as though he had jumped clear of a deep dark pit, and the next feeling as though he had fallen into it. It made no sense, and if it did not stop he worried he might soon become insane.

He brought the Velascos to their pew and pointed to a space open for them in the middle. As they took their seats, Lydia said something but Rujen did not catch it, because he was not paying attention. He nodded though, and mumbled something pleasant in reply. She might even have been speaking to someone else.

He was looking at the crucifix, the red cloth meant to veil it still gathered to the side of Christ's jutting, slightly bent knees and caught in the space under his nailed feet. It was a sacrilege—or maybe it was not something so serious as that—but still, it was wrong and the cloth needed to be straightened before Father Trotter would have to interrupt the service to do it himself. Rujen was already moving toward the crucifix, having appointed himself, being the only present employee of the church, as the proper person to do it.

As soon as he stepped up into the sacred space of the sanctuary and passed beside the lectern, he knew, without looking back, that most everyone was watching him. He would be quick about it, delicate and respectful. By the simple gesture of fixing the cloth, he would remind them—all those whose minds had been poisoned by the Devil Foster Rick—that he was a thoughtful, valuable member of the church. He would redeem himself for arriving late, for lying, for tainting the holy water, and for bringing into the church the stench of rotten meat. He might, at last, be doing something that would earn him a little lasting peace.

Rujen had never gone behind the altar before, and as he stepped softly past it, head bowed, he could not help feel as though he were in a forbidden place, keenly aware of an energy, a holy presence, that could only be the soul of the church. It accepted him though, he could tell, because he had come on a honorable task, which he would accomplish with the utmost dignity.

But when he had positioned himself under the crucifix, which was much higher on the wall than it appeared to be from a distance, he found that he was too short to get a hand on the bottom of the cloth. The lowest edge of it, hemmed with a double stitch, was about a foot above his reach. The top of it, tight and flat, was draped over Christ's head and arms and was fastened somewhere on the back of the cross.

Rujen's friends, fellow Catholics, even the Devil, all of them had to be watching him now, waiting to see what he was going to do. Each of their hundred muted conversations seemed to speak of him. He could not just turn around now and go back. All he needed to do was make a little jump, unsnag the cloth, and then once the job was done he could walk back down the aisle a different man—and make the Devil, that coward, be the one then to look away first. He put Rick's basket on the floor.

The corner of the cloth hanging below and to the side of Christ's feet, (the ankle wound of the nail, in good taste, was clean, round, bloodless) was the best part to reach for, so he bent his short, stocky legs half down, and raised his short, stocky arms above his head, and, just as he heard the distant, almost dreamlike sounds of a woman and then a man call out his name, he gave it everything he had—and jumped. That was when the moment seemed to slow, a sensation just like the time, years ago, when he had fallen off the back of a pickup truck. Back then, as he tumbled out of the bed and onto the road, he had the time to notice that two lovers had scratched their initials into the chrome on the bumper, LW ♥ KT in rusting crooked letters, and he had seen, although he could not get her attention, the driver in the car behind not looking, and when he hit the ground he had already decided on which way to roll, to the right, escaping by inches the car's dusty, black-walled tires, which spit bits of gravel at him as he rolled to safety toward a plywood fence, which he recognized, before it stopped him, as belonging to a man named Admar. This time, as he left the ground, hands high, on his way to Christ, with a hot jolt of pain moving from his feet and rising up his legs, he was distracted by the sight of termite damage on the back of Christ's left thigh just above the knee—the same kind of small perforations in wood that he had seen countless times before on Ebeye—and at first it seemed almost impossible, a trick of sight, but it was unmistakable, as if the termites had penetrated some divine shield of holiness that should have made this Christ invincible, not just to termites, but fire, an ax, or even a bomb, but of course this Christ was only made of wood, an earthly thing, and even though it had been blessed, consecrated, prayed to, and worshiped, it still needed the care of a craftsman, a carpenter not unlike Saint Joseph, who in the Bible days had raised and protected the real living Christ; but that was not Rujen's most urgent concern, hardly, because he had jumped too high, too close, and when the shockwave of pain that began in his feet ran up his back and up his arms and reached his brain and then his hands just as he grasped the cloth well above Christ's feet, he tensed, reflexively balling his hands into tight, stubborn fists, and he must have only held the cloth for half a second, maybe less, even though it seemed like so much longer than that, but it was time enough to feel it in his arms that his full weight had come to bear upon the cloth, just enough time hanging there for his legs to swing out from under him, and to hear a woman's scream, and to hear the cloth begin to tear in places near the top, not only tearing where it caught on Christ's crown of thorns but also where it was fastened behind the cross, the sound of tearing followed by a small almost imperceptible snap, and then a crunch, rudely sounding very much like someone stepping on a bag of chips, a miserable sound that Rujen wished he did not hear as the cloth tore free an instant before he finally let it go, too late to keep himself from falling back, his feet no longer under him, his eyes having no time to blink as the thorned head of Christ emerged from behind the falling cloth, the head free from the gaunt naked body and falling, tumbling sad eyes over fractured neck amid tiny scraps of wood and a mist of tiny black and tan pellets, termite pellets, which Rujen recognized just as the flat of his back and then the back of his head came crashing to the floor, knocking the wind from him and dazing him, but not disabling him so much that he did not have the presence of mind to reach out with his hands to try to catch the falling tumbling head of his Lord and Savior Jesus Christ, an act which he actually thought might silence all the screams and shouts behind him growing louder, as if catching Christ's head might save himself some dignity he had not already lost, so he reached, despite having no chance at all to catch it—except that when the face of it bounced off one of the kneecaps, chipping the nose, it changed direction, flying over him toward the altar, which allowed him to get his left hand up in front of it, which was not enough to catch it, but he did stop it when three of the thorns on Christ's crown dug into his palm, one stabbing clear through the flesh between his thumb and forefinger, holding there for half a moment, before the head fell and clunked down on the varnished wooden floor beside him, where it came to rest on its ear, as did Rujen's head, at just the right angle so that the two of them looked at each other, and in that other half of the moment, between the initial shock of the trauma to his hand and the onslaught of pain, just before the full horror of what he had done consumed him and as the red cloth sailed down to rest across his feet, the only thought in Rujen's head, a pleasantly distracting, dreamy kind of thought, was that the downcast eyes of Jesus Christ staring back at him, almond-shaped, deep dark brown, the effect enhanced by the newly-flattened nose, were in fact the eyes of a fellow Marshallese.

With a gasp he regained his breath, and on his first attempt to stand he fell back down, his boots tangled within the cloth.

He kicked it away and scrambled to his knees and turned around, picking up the head of Christ as he faced them. Shocked faces. Terrified faces. Crying faces. The sad angelic face of Christ, still serene, suffering in silence the indignity of blood from Rujen's badly bleeding hand smeared across his painted wooden cheek. And now they were spilling from the pews and coming for the Christ slayer, to give him all he deserved, because Foster Rick was not the Devil. The Devil was Rujen Keju. Disciple of Satan. Antichrist.

He stood, dizzy from hitting his head, faint from shock, pain, and the chill rush of humiliation, and for the lack of another place to put Christ's head before he skulked away, forever banishing himself from God and Church and any hope to save his soul from Hell, he placed it upon the altar, only passively aware, while doing so, of knocking loose from the neck a dusting of pellets and a pair of translucent, squirming larval termites, not thinking clear enough to understand in time that the hand he used to wipe away the blood from Christ's cheek was the same hand to smear it there—but realizing, only then, too late, that the blood on Christ's head and his face and upon the altar was why the screaming rose again, from both men and women, and why some of them looked away to hold each other or to hide the sight of Rujen from their children's eyes, and why Father Trotter, in back now with the altar boys, his vestments red as Rujen's blood, had dropped his lectionary and fallen to his knees—and why the men coming for Rujen had stopped, unable to proceed beyond the sanctuary—awestruck—because they knew they faced a demon risen from, no longer headed for, the infernal pits of Hell.

Rujen looked at them but he could not speak. He wished they could see him as the man they had always known, not the evil man, the demon they believed him now to be, but no words of explanation of how it was all one accident after another, or how very sorry he was, would ever get them to see him as anything beyond his desecration of Christ, his defiling of the altar, his profaning of a sacred, solemn day; no words in either language he could speak would ever make these people, once his friends, ever forgive him for the unholy mess he had made, because what he had done required no forgiveness, only guilt, which he bore without resistance, a guilt which caused his heart to beat so hard and so fast that it hurt, in time with the painful throbbing of his feet and the throbbing of his hand, a throbbing and a beating so strong that he actually heard it, his trinity of pain, throbbing and beating to him the insistent demand for his doom louder and louder until that was all he heard and felt, the sights and sounds of the church becoming nothing but elusive blurs, his pulsing pounding trinity flooding him with a loathing of himself, pushing him to cease to be—to expel, to vomit up his pathetic worthless soul.

But when his head became heavy with the weight of his sins, and his chin dropped to loll above his chest, when it seemed as though his soul had gone and left him nothing but his shame, it was then that in the swirling void before him, at the edge of his oblivion, his eyes found two shining points of light, drawing him forth with a soothing glow—they were the eyes of Christ looking up at him from the altar, Marshallese eyes. And they spoke to him. And by the grace of God they offered him a way to redeem his soul, speaking to him of a truth so stunning and profound, so perfect in its simplicity and its ability to heal him and to remedy all the things he had endured this day, that as the sights and sounds of the world came back into being around him, he was sure that by the doing of this simple task he could be no more a devil but a saint, and then he found within himself a gift, the strength to disregard his pain.

There was no reason to remain in church a moment longer, his presence only adding to the misery of others, and he had such an important thing to do, so without looking at them he turned around and ran, no matter that his third step landed squarely in the middle of Rick's basket, his boot getting stuck within the wicker, he knocked it free on a kneeler and kept on running, through a small hallway into the sacristy and from there into the chapel then out onto lawn under the late amber rays of the sun. He ran, with the wind at his back, his pace slowing but never stopping at the bicycle racks by the commuter terminal, where on the run he borrowed one, a men's Schwinn, red, with the seat low just how he liked it. He pedaled fast, ignoring the stop sign at Lagoon Road, racing past the automotive department, his bleeding hand slipping from the rubber hand grip as he bounced onto the dirt road by the gravel piles, his tires kicking up a trail of dust all the way to the sewage plant, where, without detection, he sneaked upstairs into the breakroom and from Andy's knife rack he pulled his favorite, the rainbow trout. He knew exactly what he had to do. And Crawford better bring his mop.

One Down

JEBRO PULLED HIMSELF along with a sidestroke and kicked just ahead of his brother, swimming crosswise to the flow of the current. The east wind was strong in his face and the swells forged past him coming from the same direction. Each time at the top of a swell he saw the distant green blur of Tar-Wōj, and each time the distance between them became a little greater. In the troughs of the swells he saw only water. He heard only the wind and the water. Most of the sky in the east and overhead was clear, pale blue and hazy. The ocean was cold and gray and white because of the clouds still massed over the west heading sun. In a short while the wind would free the sun from the clouds. Maybe two and a half hours later the sun would fall behind the clouds again and set. It was the rising wind and the increasing distance from the lee of the islands and the reef that made the swells half a foot bigger and lengthened the trail of foam behind the ones that foundered into whitecaps. The whitecaps sometimes broke over Jebro and Nuke and washed Nuke back, away from Jebro, because he went wherever the rolling water pushed the canvas float. Jebro could dunk under the whitecaps. The float also caught the wind, and despite Nuke's steady kicking, he was moving forward very slowly. He seemed not to mind the rougher water so much so long as he was buoyed by the float. If not for the float, Jebro knew his brother might have already drowned.

In the whitecaps Jebro had to hold the line he had tied to the jug, to keep it from pulling down his shorts. After a while he retied it to his shirt. He tried to use the fin on his hand instead of his foot, but it did not work. The container of matches had slipped loose from the knot in his shirt and he did not see it floating. Nothing but the empty horizon lay in the direction they were trying to go, northeast, and nothing lay in the direction they were actually headed, more west than north or east. He was not too worried though, not yet, because he knew the atoll was large and up ahead it stretched far to the west (Kwajalein was the largest atoll in the world and he had known that fact even before going to school) and being so close to something so big he did not think they could drift so far west that they would miss it. Soon, although after dark, he was sure they would near some islands, the names of which he did not know. The wind was coming almost straight from Tar-Wōj and brought the smell of the island and the reef. The ocean would become calmer when they neared the islands up west. He would smell them too. He knew the night would have no moon.

Nuke's float was losing air, becoming flatter more on the left than on the right. Jebro wanted Nuke to be relaxed, to keep a clear head and feel confident about reaching land, because this would help him stay alive. "Be ready in a little while," he said. "I will need to put new air inside the float."

Nuke looked at him, worried. "We're going nowhere, Jebro, straight out to sea. You said—"

"It just looks that way, because of the shape of the atoll. You'll see, soon the water will be calm again as we drift back close to some islands."

"If we're going to drift into the islands why not just drift? I'm tired of kicking into these waves." He strained his face to show how hard he was kicking.

"I told you—" Jebro said, his breath catching, "—it will keep you warm, and we'll reach the islands sooner. Do you want to be out here all night? Listen, there's a man on Ebeye, Loeak, and he came fishing out here a few years ago with his friends, three of them, I think, and their boat was not—" His head burrowed through the top of a swell. He spit the wash of saltwater from his mouth. "Their boat was not very good and when they hit a wave wrong, it knocked an entire sheet of plywood off the bottom. Loeak was strong, but he was very fat and he—"

"I heard of that man already, Loeak. He was fat when his boat sank and he was skinny two days later when he swam onto an island. The other three men drowned out here."

"Those men drowned because they hung onto to their fish-box and didn't swim. If you do that you get cold and then you drown. So swim, like Loeak did."

"What do you think, that we have all that fat like Loeak to burn out here for two days?"

Jebro lost sight of Nuke for a moment while riding down the back of a large swell. Then Nuke, wide-eyed, dropped over the top of it and followed him down. Jebro thought it might have been a mistake to bring up the story of Loeak. "Loeak's boat sank much farther out, you know, and he had much farther to swim than we do. And the ocean was rougher. I heard him say he could see no islands when he started swimming. I think he said he was south of Āne-eḷḷap-kaņ, from where you can see those domes for miles, so you know how far out he was if he couldn't see them."

Nuke struggled over a whitecap that turned him and the float sideways, and at the top of the next swell he pointed to Tar-Wōj. "After that one goes away we will see no islands either, nothing, just like Loeak."

"Ōrrōr! That island you see is the one belonging to you, Tar-Wōj, so you better learn to recognize it. And I told you—the shape of the atoll . . . it will come back around in front of us, maybe only a few more hours with this current is all before we get close to land again. I promise you."

Nuke looked into the distance, squinting through the water dripping from his hair. "Okay, I trust what you say, Jebro, but . . ."

"Hey, look who's coming to see us." Jebro pointed up at a large, high-flying frigate bird, an *ak*, gliding toward them from the east. The wide span of its large black wings was middled by a slender tube of a body that tapered down into a long, deeply forked tail. It glided to a spot almost directly over them, turned about slowly and gracefully into the wind, then hovered there so black and motionless that it looked like a bird-shaped tear in the blue exposing the night.

Jebro smiled up at the bird. "Do you know who that is, Nuke? That's our grandfather come to watch over us."

Nuke looked up at the bird then frowned at Jebro. "Maybe you have been swallowing some saltwater, because I heard it gets a person talking crazy like that."

"Crazy, eh? You listen to this." Jebro told Nuke the story of how Ataji had compared himself to an old frigate bird who had to be tied to tree to keep it from flying away, unlike a young one that would stay if it was given food. "And the last time I came to Tar-Wōj one of these birds was flying over his grave. So what do you think of that?"

"I think you better stop swallowing the saltwater."

Jebro's arm was getting tired, so he rolled over to his other side. He swam around the float so that he was facing Nuke again, but now unable to see Tar-Wōj. "Okay, if you think you know so much then tell me why that bird is watching us."

"I think it just flies up there, probably not even looking at us."

"Maybe you don't believe that bird is the spirit of our grandfather, but it's watching us for sure. Those kinds of birds fly up high and look for things in the water, things like logs or palm fronds, any kind of thing some fish might be hiding under. When they see something they want to eat—ssoosh!—they fold back their wings and dive-bomb it." Jebro used one hand to demonstrate. "Sometimes if another bird has a fish they chase it around until it drops it or spits it up. Right now, that bird thinks maybe some fish are hiding under us, like we are a couple of logs, so if you have to pee, watch out, because when he sees your little kukkuk wiggling outside your shorts . . . ssoosh! No more kukkuk."

Nuke laughed, splashing Jebro in the face. "Here, drink some more saltwater you bwebwe!" He stopped laughing just as he saw the rising water in front of him, a heavy roller that broke over white and submerged both him and the flattening float. He came up coughing, spitting. “Shit, Jebro, this float is sinking.”

Jebro kicked over to him and held him around the waist as he gave him a drink of water from the jug. He laughed. “See, you made grandfather angry by not believing his spirit was inside the bird. You better listen to me when I tell you something.”

Nuke’s lips were trembling. “No more jokes. Are you going to fix this thing now?”

“Okay, okay.” He untied the drawstring that belted Nuke inside the float. “Just take it easy for a little while, and tread water like I showed you.” Jebro gave Nuke the drawstring to hold, then pushed parts of one then the other of the sides of the float underwater, finding streams of bubbles that revealed worn spots he planned to pinch off and tie. Nuke did not look comfortable being out of the float, working much too hard to keep his head above the water. Jebro hurriedly untied the three lengths of monofilament from the bag, holding each one between his teeth.

Just then the sun broke free from the clouds and Jebro paused to enjoy the feeling of it on his face. He welcomed it, willing it to fill him and his brother with its warmth before it went away. The sun made the ocean bluer, more transparent, shot through with angled shafts of light that penetrated the darker depths below. He saw the glint of the sun on Nuke’s hair and skin and in his eyes. Despite the sun, Nuke began to shiver. A thin stream of mucus ran from his nose.

At the top of a swell Jebro lifted the bag to fill it with air, not ready for the force of wind that caught it and jerked him forward. His fingers strained to keep a hold on the bag. He could feel in his arms and legs and gut how he had lost some strength since the last time he had filled it. The bag snapped taut, full, pulling him along as he tried to reach up and seal off the end of it. It was hard to manage, too much space in the tall bag catching the wind, and then he lost one hand on it and the bag began to spin, painfully contorting his wrist. He heard Nuke behind him, just barely, a sound of alarm, and when he turned to look, at first surprised at how far the bag had pulled him, he was then suddenly feeling very helpless because there was nothing he could do about the large crashing roller bearing down on his brother, larger than any before, the boiling foam almost blinding white in the new sunlight. Nuke cringed and then it struck him, swallowing him, and a second later it barreled into Jebro, who could not dunk under it with one hand gripping the unruly, windblown bag. He lost his hold on the bag. He tumbled, surfacing several moments later to find himself deep with a trough and facing another crashing wall of water. He still had his fin. He dived and propelled himself under the wave, watching the turbulent white cloud of water roll over him and feeling the jug pull hard against his shirt. When he surfaced again, weak in his arms and legs and out of breath, the first thing he did was to look to where he thought Nuke should be, but he saw only trails of foam like claw marks on the ocean. He shouted, looking in all directions, but all he got in reply was the sound of the wind and the water.

Death ruled the ocean. The ocean itself was not a dead thing, having never been alive, but the life in it existed only as a byproduct of death. Every living thing in the ocean was fleeing from something trying to kill it and eat it, and every living thing was out to suck the life from something else. You could cut open a living shark and it would eat its own guts. The same thing was true of life on land, even with people—if one thing wanted to live then it had to take the life of another, to kill, swallow, and then crap out as much life as it needed to stay alive. Life was a shark eating its own guts, an eel chomping on its own tail, a twisted game where the goal was not to win, because nothing ever did, but to put off losing for as long as possible and to have a good time doing it. Then you were food. And like it or not it was natural that way, the way things had to be, and to be on a boat cutting through blood-stained water, thick within the deathfest of frenzied shrieking birds diving amid the frenzy of feeding tuna—this was to face and accept the truth of it, to be a part of it; it was to be Travis Kotrady who loved above most other things in his life the raw brutality of working a school, the chase, the kill, getting a little bloody, the adrenaline rush he felt when using a club against the snout of a shark when it came too close to the boat after a fish. He couldn't get enough of it—skipping classes, blowing off girls, leaving his teammates a good man short every chance he had to hop on a boat—and at times it even scared him, seeming so evil like some kind of bloodlust, but then he would remind himself that people ate his fish, as was the natural thing to do, and with the right people and maybe a few beers, music outside at the beach and a nice fire in the grill, a good fish dinner was about the happiest, most nonevil thing in the world.

The boat settled into idle, fish on, several miles west of the third island north of Nini, still close enough to the running school to be passed now and then by low-flying birds. The wind was coming up and the waves were getting larger. The sun looked as though it might soon break free of the west-heading bank of clouds.

The fish Travis was bringing in would be the ninth they had caught since Boyd had pulled that asshole-ish stunt on the Marshallese, the tenth fish if Kerry hadn't lost one by ripping out the hook when he had tried too hard to fling it inside the boat. Kerry was looking sick again, burping, probably ready to vomit. He sat on the back bench, hunched over, staring at the water behind the boat. Boyd had one hand on the throttles and the other on the wheel, watching impatiently as Travis brought in the fish. No eye contact. Earlier, Boyd had refused to let Travis drive, nearly tossing the boat when he let go of the wheel to shove Travis away so hard that he almost knocked him over the side. Travis might have gone back after him, but he wasn't so stupid as Boyd to start a full-blown fight this far out at sea. After this though, that was it, Boyd could find somebody else to fish with—and he had a little something else coming too. They had been friends a long time, but friendship had its limits, insanity being one of them. Boyd was getting too damn crazy. Shit, someday he might even get somebody killed.

Travis brought the fish alongside the boat and flipped it onto the deck. The fish beat its tail just like they all did, even though it did them no good out of the water—it was, of course, the only thing their tiny brains knew how to do. Its black eyes, expressing no emotion, seemed lifeless, and as Travis ripped out the hook he wondered if the fish's brain was complex enough to feel any pain. It made no difference even if it did. It was just a fish. He threw it in the open icebox and Boyd kicked shut the lid. The fish's tail beat rapidly against the inside of the box, *batatat-tat batatat atat* like a machine gun, inciting one of the other fish to join it.

Boyd jabbed forward the throttles and took the boat back after the school. The school was still running fast, heading mostly west, sometimes north. Boyd drove without speaking, his eyes fully bloodshot, as much from the beer as from the windburn and salt spray. He was well into the rhythm of what he was doing, almost trancelike in the way he brought the boat just ahead of the school, matched its speed, then slowed to swing the lures through for a perfect pass.

"Fish on!" Travis shouted. Both his pole and Kerry's handline had strikes. As the boat settled back into idle Travis sat half on the gunnel, one hand low on the pole's foam rubber grip so that he could guide the line, his other hand working the reel fast. It wasn't a very big fish. Kerry fumbled with the handline, looking like he might vomit at any moment. He hardly had the strength to bring in his fish.

Batatat-tat batatat atat. Something about the sound of the fish beating their tails was beginning to bother Travis, although he didn't know why. It was a sound he had heard so many times before, a good sound that spoke of a good day fishing, but this time something was different, as if the sound of it should be reminding him of something else he might not want to think about. Then, a few moments later, as he stood to bring in the last few yards of line by hand, he found himself looking at a small whitecap, a part of it that rolled over pink with blood. *Batatat-tat batatat atat.* Distress. *SOS.* The thought came to him slowly, a slight sense of guilt just nagging enough that he felt he needed to do something about it. He was thinking again of the two Marshallese fishermen and their small boat, that maybe, just to be sure, he better get out his binoculars and see if he could find them. It had been the school, too much thinking of nothing else and wanting to stay with it, that had distracted him from any consideration of looking for them earlier. In fact, even right after they got swamped he had been more pissed at Boyd for doing what he did, now that he thought about it, than he was concerned for the Marshallese. He realized, idly focused on the *batatat-tat batatat atat* of the fish beating against the inside of the icebox, that if something had happened to the Marshallese it wouldn't just be Boyd's fault alone. He had to ask himself whether he could live with it if something had happened, or if he could even stand not knowing for sure. Immediately, he tried to imagine that the two Marshallese were all right, that they were still fishing somewhere or maybe back on land. Last he had seen them they seemed to be doing okay. One of them was still hauling in his fish. The little one was giving him the finger.

"What are you doing?" Boyd asked. "Bring it in!"

"Huh? Oh." Travis pulled the fish into the boat, a fifteen-pounder. "Hang on a minute," he said as he removed the hook. "I wanna check on something." He tossed the fish into the open icebox, feeling more than a little buzzed as he turned too quickly to do it, then stepped sideways between Boyd and the bench and grabbed the binoculars from under the console. He scanned the ocean in front of the distant islands, up and down the reef. He could see a short way into the lagoon. Nothing, but it was hard to tell because of the distance and the rise and fall of the boat. He didn't think they would have gone much farther out, not with such a small boat. It had been a while too, and they could be anywhere. He wanted to be sure. "I think we gotta go back," he said. "We gotta go make sure those guys are okay—the Marshallese."

"Man, fuck that—like, where'd that come from?" Boyd fished another Oly from the cooler. "And you saw 'em. They weren't hurt or anything, just a little drenched—a little pissed off too, I guess." He chuckled, pointing at Kerry who finally fell to his knees and puked over the side. The line Kerry had gained on the fish slipped back out of the boat. "You better get that. *Barfweiser* there is just about useless." He opened his beer and threw the pull tab at Kerry, hitting him on the shoulder. "You country fuckin' dweeb."

Kerry seemed not to hear him, his sunburned freckled face gone strangely pale. Travis set his binoculars on top of the console and with both hands he removed the keys from the twin ignitions. He held them in his fists. The absence of the engine noise was like a crowd gone suddenly quiet, waiting for something to happen. Even the fish momentarily stopped beating their tails against the box. Then the radio spit out a burst of static. Kerry wretched. *Batatat-tat batatat atat.* "No more fucking around, Boyd. I mean it. We gotta go back."

Boyd threw up his hands, spilling beer that ran down his forearm. "What the hell, Travis, that was over an hour ago and they're probably already—shit, they could be halfway back to Ebeye already. Don't be a dick."

"Think about it—we only saw them for a few seconds and then we were out of there fast, chasing the school. Did you even look back after that? I didn't."

Boyd looked out at the escaping school. "Yeah, I saw 'em, for a long time after that, and then I'm pretty sure they went back inside the lagoon. C'mon, man. . . ."

"Bullshit!"

"No, *this* is bullshit! Now give me the keys."

The boat leaned sideways down a swell, nearly dunking Kerry's head.

Travis knew this was going to drag on, jawing back and forth, without ever convincing Boyd to do anything but either fight or get back to fishing. At the top of a swell he looked into the distance at the school, boiling again. They had a chance to pick up another eight or ten fish before it was time to head back in. The bow smacked into the bottom of the trough. He saw Kerry's handline still tight, Kerry with his face still over the side, oblivious to everything but his own guts. The fish needed to be brought in before a shark got it. Travis wondered if maybe he was just being paranoid about the Marshallese, thinking the way he did just because he wanted to get back at Boyd for being such an asshole. It did seem kind of remote that anything would have happened to them, especially with the way they maneuvered that little boat so well around the school. They knew how to handle themselves on the ocean, and probably what to do if they were in any kind of trouble. He had heard that the Marshallese used CB radios instead of marine band like the boats from Kwaj. They must have had flares.

Boyd held out his hand for the keys, looking smug, as if he knew Travis was having doubts.

Maybe Travis was only doing it to piss off Boyd, but the more he thought about it, the more it seemed as though that was reason enough. It was worth it to lose such a good school just to knock Boyd down a notch, and to let him know he wasn't King Shit every time he stepped onto a boat. Besides, Travis had to know for sure, to at least make an effort to find the Marshallese, if only to give them some of the fish. They were owed at least that much—part of *Boyd's* share of the fish. And it was torture to keep Kerry out here any longer. Kerry would get a full share too, not half like Boyd made him agree to, just for putting up with so much crap. Travis understood suddenly that there was only one way to make Boyd see things right, or to at least get him out of the way. He would have to be quick, one good shot, maybe two. It was a cheap thing to do, but Boyd had it coming. Not just from Travis but from Kerry, and for what he did to the Marshallese.

"All right," Travis said. "Sorry. Here." With his left hand he held out the keys. He stood slightly sideways, so that he could pivot into his swing, knees bent to keep his balance in the rocking boat. He tried to look passive, defeated, but really his heart was beating so hard that he thought for a second it might give him away.

Jebro dived, searching through the hazy blue and into the purple depths below until he grew faint from lack of breath. When he surfaced his lungs seemed paralyzed—that terrible instant before he finally forced them into gasping air. His exhale was a shout into the wind, unanswered, and when he looked around the barren pointed peaks and carven hollows and saw that he remained alone, he dived again, not sure he would ever come up if he did not find his brother. He did come up, answering the pull of the half-filled water jug tied to his shirt, clinging to what he knew was a shameful, undeserved will to live. He tried to justify it by bringing to mind three faces, the Americans' faces, imagining how it was going to feel, how he might live to show them a picture of Nuke before he crushed their skulls or cut them down with a machete. But when he tried to visualize his revenge, and was unable time and time again to push himself to see and revel in the finish of it, he realized how doing such a thing took so much more than burning hate—it took a touch of evil, or a soul as cold and dead as the ocean, and he could not make within himself a place for either one. To lose his brother and then to have found no mettle for revenge made his life seem worthless, and still, shaming himself, he could not help but think of reaching land, of wanting very much to go on living. And he would, he knew it, just to suffer to face his father, to be forever shunned by his father who had told him several times that morning not to go—and then to sit in some official room on Kwajalein to tell the story, only to hear the Americans explain it as an accident, apologize, and walk away—and even if they did confess and have to take some punishment, some American *justice,* there would be no satisfaction in that, no putting it right, because there was no counterbalance to the taking of a father's son, and nothing, not even revenge, could replace or even soothe the lifelong love and friendship lost between two brothers. This was what he lived for. He shouted again for Nuke, and again and again, only to be answered by the howl of the wind on the water.

Rujen and the Demons

M̧ŌÑĀĻAPEŅ WORKS HIS paddle with vicious intensity in and out of the water, his ears erect and listening, his body shivering with anticipation. He howls, so close now to the boy's faltering heart, a treat that Kwōjenmeto is generous to allow. It is a small delay to leave the lagoon to appease his monstrous pet, but there is a bit of time before Ņoniep's soul will rise. And to reap this boy's soul in the wait—so easy to snatch it just before he dies—will surely please his masters Wūllep and Ļajibwinām̧ōņ.

"Be quick," Kwōjenmeto says. Above them is a frigate bird, seeming to be nothing uncommon until Kwōjenmeto catches the glint of its eye. An ekjab, he realizes, a protective spirit watching over the boy. It is powerless to save him.

M̧ōñāļapeņ howls, but now it is the same shrill howl of a time ago when he was denied the heart of Ņoniep.

Kwōjenmeto sees then, in M̧ōñāļapeņ, that the ekjab is not so impotent as he thought. It has hidden the boy from M̧ōñāļapeņ, the sound of his heart suddenly muffled among the million other hearts beating within the sea. Still, the ekjab cannot hide the boy from death, and with a little trouble Kwōjenmeto might yet gain his soul. M̧ōñāļapeņ trembles, quickly consumed by a rising fury that Kwōjenmeto knows will soon explode. He charms a rope that lies at the bottom of the canoe, sending it flying to wrap itself around the arms and torso of his pet. What's left of the rope binds his legs. M̧ōñāļapeņ's howls then are silenced, when Kwōjenmeto rips a length of hide from the demon's back and gags him with it.

A group of three boulders in the breakwater formed a small hollow where Rujen crouched hiding. Across the road he could see the turtle pond, now just four people there watching the dolphins go slowly round and round. In the middle of the pond the mermaid steadily drooled forth her water. Rujen's hand that held the knife still trembled, the blade pinging on one of the boulders. He knew when he finally used the knife he'd make the trembling stop. Sometimes he thought about what happened at the church. Behind him, the lagoon gurgled through the breakwater with each rise and fall of the waves. He felt he was thinking clearly now, excited, ignoring his pain, and as he watched first one then two of the people leave the pond he came up with a better plan. At first he thought he'd need a hacksaw, but then he thought better of a large pair of bolt cutters, and he knew, as he crept out of his hollow, just how he was going to get them.

Above, the ekjab dips its wings and circles, a dance that indicates its readiness to fight. In a rare moment of humor Kwōjenmeto laughs, so well within his power to easily defeat this flying thing, so amused by this display of selfless courage. M̧ōñā̧lapeņ thrashes around at the bow, his own beating heart the only one he hears, so infected with madness that he'd devour it if he could.

No need for Kwōjenmeto to hear the boy's beating heart to find him, the smell of his approaching death now sufficient. But to take his soul requires he destroy the ekjab first, and to do so might attract others of his kin whom Kwōjenmeto prefers remain as dormant, as powerless, as they have been for such a long and favorable amount a time. And there is another presence that Kwōjenmeto felt recently, an ancient presence of a power he'd rather not attract. He is troubled that he cannot identify it, something yet familiar about it that brings to mind his master Wūllep, but not Wūllep, something more of what Wūllep longs to be. It seems to be growing distant and Kwōjenmeto wants to keep it that way, far away while he tends to what he has come to do. The boy is not necessary. *We'll let the ocean have him*, he tells the ekjab, *let his soul become lost and wander as you try to protect that other one, and then some other time I will find it and pluck it from the water as easily as I might pluck one of these lice from Ṃōñāļapeņ's back*. He plucks one and flicks it up at the ekjab, then with his paddle he pulls the canoe back toward the lagoon.

Now Ņoniep has died to hide from him, to increase his power, but Kwōjenmeto has come to figure what Ņoniep plans to do. Kwōjenmeto need only hide as well, and then to strike at that inevitable moment when Ņoniep, too much always thinking to save others than himself, becomes vulnerable in that hopeless battle he should know he can never win. Yes, Kwōjenmeto will hide and he will wait, and what a sight it will be when Ṃōñāļapeņ, at the proper moment unbound, is free and mad and so utterly enraged and ravenous he might not sate himself until the light of dawn.

Behind him is the boy, and Kwōjenmeto can sense approaching death.

The Ekjab

As soon as Boyd looked down and reached for the keys, Travis let him have it, a good solid shot right below the eye, so hard that Travis was certain in that instant, when he heard something pop, that he had broken the top knuckle of his middle finger. No matter, he pulled back to swing again, but then he saw he didn't need to. Boyd's eyes opened wide for a moment, then they just sort of rolled up into his head as he dropped his beer and staggered back into the console. His beer dropped between Travis's legs, spitting foam. Travis caught him as he crumpled, guiding him so that he fell on his side behind the bench. He wasn't out—just stunned. The fight was gone from him though, Travis could see that in his wounded expression as he tried to pull himself up, his arm slipping out from under him on the wet bench, his brain seemingly unsure which of his bare feet was right and which was left.

Kerry came to life. "Hit 'im again! Hit 'im, Travis!" Yellowish vomit dripped from his lower lip. Still on his knees, his eyes somewhat glazed, he looked almost worse than Boyd.

"I think he's had enough," Travis said.

Boyd slowly pulled himself up by the wheel. He stared down at it, breathing deeply. "I can't believe you fuckin' hit me. You fuckin' hit me! I thought we were friends, man. . . . Asshole." He said the last word weakly, as if he thought too late that it might earn him another shot.

"You're the one being an asshole," Travis said, grimacing as he rubbed his fist. "And you oughta be glad I was friend enough to let you know about it." He tossed the keys on top of the console. "Now drive—we're heading in."

Kerry got himself seated on the bench. "'Bout damn time. And Boyd, you a-hole sum bitch, let me tell you—"

"Knock it off," Travis said. "Let's just . . ." He pointed to the handline. "The fish, Kerry. Just bring in the fish." Kerry groaned, taking the line as if he had been asked to beat his mother with it. The line was short, and when he got the fish in the boat, another fifteen pounder, it was so spent from fighting the line that it hardly beat its tail. Travis unhooked it and dumped it in the icebox.

The side of Boyd's face was already beginning to redden and swell. He looked away from Travis and out to the school now almost half a mile away. "Man . . . I can't believe you. . . ." He started the engines. "Fuck it—you know, you didn't have to. . . . If you wanted to find those guys so bad you shoulda just . . . fuck it, it ain't nothin' to me." He felt around his eye with his hand. "So which way then?"

"Just head straight in. If they're around they're probably trolling the reef, maybe anchored somewhere going for lobsters . . . or spearing maybe. They were kinda heading south before they got to the school. We just gotta make sure." Travis reached in front of Boyd and picked up the binoculars. He put the strap around his neck. Boyd brought the boat facing east and pushed up on the throttles, looking back only once more at the school before it vanished over the horizon behind them.

At over half speed, gunning it at every chance, it took about fifteen minutes of beating hard into the swells to get within a couple miles of the reef, in between the second and third island from Nini, near the spot—Travis wasn't exactly sure—where Boyd had swamped the Marshallese. By the time they got there Kerry had nothing left inside his stomach, just some stringy fluid that came up each time he had one of his dry heaves. The ocean was somewhat calmer, although with the way Kerry was gripping the bench he did not seem to notice. Boyd's eye was swollen partly closed, getting a little purple on the bottom.

Travis told Boyd to stop.

"Man," Boyd said, looking around, "this is pointless, like you actually expect to—"

Travis looked at him coldly, then lifted the binoculars to his face when the boat settled down into the water. He looked south, all the way along the reef and past South Pass, as far as the tip of Carlson island, just south of Carlos. He looked into the lagoon, choppy now, thinking he was seeing about halfway to the eastern reef. He looked north, even west from where they came. Nothing.

Just then the sun came out from behind the clouds, striking the white of the deck and making Travis squint. He thought the best thing to do was to head south—the way the Marshallese were originally headed—maybe catch up to them near Zar Pass by Kwaj, or, if there was time, look around Ebeye for their boat. Then he realized that their little boat would be nowhere near Ebeye. Even with such a late start the Boston Whaler—twin seventies tuned to perfection—would make it to Ebeye long before the Marshallese could get there—fifteen horses, maybe twenty-five, that's all they had and it was an old one, and that boat of theirs would be crawling to get through the chop. The islands to the south blocked sight of part of the reef, maybe where the Marshallese could be anchored or trolling. It was the best direction to go look. Travis didn't think they would have turned around and gone back north. . . . Then again, they had come from that direction. He looked once more with the binoculars, sweeping from just west of north to where the reef bowed inward to the east. Back again, more west, this time the new sunlight catching the glint of something, far away to the northwest, glass maybe. The little boat had no glass. He adjusted the focus, pain shooting through his knuckle as he did it, holding his breath to keep the image steady. It was just the water, slick with something that caught the light, then he saw something else: A brown dot, maybe red.

"Out there," he said. "That way. Go that way."

"What?" Boyd asked. "You see them? They're all right, right? Let's get out of here then."

Travis looked at him. "I don't know what it is, just go. That way."

"*Maaan* . . ." He took the boat in the direction Travis pointed, into rougher water again, stopping after a while so that Travis could get another bearing.

"It's a gas can," Travis said. "See it?" Once he found it with the binoculars he could see it from time to time with his naked eyes. "Over there." He pointed. Kerry brought himself weakly to the console, on Travis's side.

"I see it," Boyd said. "So what? It's just an old gas can."

"With gas in it," Travis said, handing Boyd the binoculars. "Look at the slick on the water. You tell me where it came from, and how something like that just happens to be down current from where you swamped those guys?" Boyd was looking back at one of the islands. "What are you doing?" Travis gave him a small shove and took back the binoculars. "Get us up there!"

Boyd gave it near full throttle and beat through the water until the boat was only a few yards from the can. He dropped into neutral, then reverse to kill the momentum, and brought the boat cleanly alongside the can with Travis leaning over the side to retrieve it. The gas line was still attached. The metal clip on its connector was bent where it had been hooked into an engine. Travis pulled it onto the boat and held up the gas line, staring at Boyd. "You sank their damn boat, Boyd, I'll bet you anything. And if those two guys are . . ." He dropped the can, scarring the deck, and reached for his binoculars. "I knew it, I just fuckin' knew it!"

"It was only a joke, man. I didn't mean to . . . I mean, how do you even know that it's from their boat?"

Travis searched the ocean in a complete circle. "Shit!" He pushed the binoculars into Kerry's chest. "Keep looking," he said, then he shouldered Boyd out of the way to reach for the radio. "We gotta get them to send a helicopter. Or maybe they know something, like maybe somebody already picked them up. Shit!"

Boyd grabbed his wrist. "We're not supposed to be out here, remember, and I got two warnings already. I could lose my license if you tell 'em where we are. You don't even know for sure—"

"Your license? If somebody found those guys, or worse: If they never find those guys—shit Boyd, that's murder, only attempted murder if you're lucky. And I'm gonna get blamed too. You asshole! You know, sometimes you really—" Travis jerked his hand free from Boyd's grip and pressed the button on the mike. "Kwaj Marina, this is Kilo six-two, come in, over."

Static.

Travis repeated the call, twice more, then finally: "Go ahead six-two, this is Kwaj Marina, over." The voice was Kevin Hartley's, a tenth grader who had been working at the marina for about a month. His dad owned the *Moonglow*, a two-masted sailboat they had brought over from Hawai'i. Kevin might know how to raise a sail—he always dressed in polo shirts and Topsiders—but he didn't know jack about power boats. He had run a boat into the ski dock once and blamed it on a bug that flew into his eye.

"Yeah, uh . . . Kwaj Marina—look Kevin, this is Travis Kotrady, and uh, we think a Marshallese boat might have gone down out here, west reef, a few—no, um, three islands past Nini, north past Nini. I don't know the name of the island. Do you copy? Over." He stared at Boyd, wondering how much he wanted to say at this point about what had happened.

A burst of static on the radio, then Kevin again: "Kilo six-two this Kwaj Marina. Who went down? Do you mean they sank? Over."

Travis looked up at the sky as he pressed the mike. "Look, Kevin, is Danko there? Put Danko on the radio." Steve Danko was the supervisor in charge of the marina. He also coached the high school varsity basketball team—both Travis and Boyd were players.

"Kilo six-two this is Kwaj Marina. Danko's not here, just me. Over."

"Look Kevin, call Harbor Control, the Police Department maybe, and tell them to send a helicopter—three islands north past Nini. Two people might be in the ocean—Marshallese. Their boat—I think their boat might have sunk. You got that?"

"Kilo six-two this is Kwaj Marina. Uh, okay . . . that's two Marshallese three islands north of Nini, right? That's out of limits isn't it? Over."

Travis stopped an inch short of slamming the mike on top of the console. "I can't believe this idiot, like he's taking an order for burgers or something." He took a deep breath and brought the mike to his mouth. "That's right, three islands north of Nini, a few miles out, and tell them we'll stay here so they can find the spot. Over."

"Kilo six-two this is Kwaj Marina. Um, just hang on and I'll try and call somebody. Okay? Over."

"Hurry up dammit, and cut out all that Kilo Marina—just hurry up!"

"Okay, Roger."

Travis shook his head. He pulled the binoculars away from Kerry. "Anything?"

"Nah, it's kinda blurry."

Travis checked the lenses and used a dry glove to wipe away a thin film of salt spray. Boyd was looking at him. "Don't look at me, look out there!" He made a sweeping motion with his hand. "And keep the boat into the swells, keep it steady so I can see. Shit."

In front of the console, part of it, was a molded fiberglass seat which was a little higher than the wooden bench in back. Travis stood on top of it, one hand on the frame of the Plexiglas windshield as he scanned the water with the binoculars. All he found was the school, a black blur of birds far away. He heard Kerry suffering through another dry heave. He heard Boyd open a beer, then another. When he looked back he saw Boyd in the process of opening and tossing the rest of the beer cans. "You're pathetic," Travis said. "Two guys might be shark bait out there and you're worried about gettin' busted for beer.

What did you think, that the helicopter is gonna land out here and check the cooler?"

"It's your ass too," Boyd said. "Yeah, and his too." He pointed at Kerry, his head just coming back up over the side. "It was his sister got the beer. He brought it."

"Oh right, this is all Kerry's fault, for getting you stupid drunk. Don't be a—"

"Kilo six-two this is Kwaj Marina. Over."

Travis held out his hand for the mike and Boyd gave it to him. "Give me some good news, Kevin."

"Kilo six—um, Travis? They want to know what you saw. Why do you think a boat sank out there. And that's out of limits. They want to know why you're out of limits. Over."

"Who's he talking to?" Boyd asked. "Ask him who he's talking to."

"Shut up." Travis thought for a moment. He handed the binoculars back to Kerry, who came up beside him, looking weary. "Kevin, do you have them on the phone now? Who are you talking to? Over."

"It's the police. I called the police and yeah, I got 'em on the phone right now. Over."

"Okay listen. Make sure the volume's up. Can they hear me? Over."

"He said he can hear you."

"Uh . . . this is Travis Kotrady and uh . . . we were fishing out by Nini—that's not out of limits—and we saw this Marshallese boat a while back, and it looked like it was having some trouble in the waves—it was kinda north of us, in the restricted area. So I saw it through my binoculars, and then, well, after a while I didn't see it and we thought we better go look . . . to see if they were okay. All we found was a gas can—it still has gas—and we can't see the boat. I think it might have gone down. Over."

"Thanks, man," Boyd said. "Really, I mean it." He was trying to look chummy, his red swollen eye making the attempt look absurd.

"I'm not doing a damn thing for you, Boyd, just keeping things simple. If I have to I'm gonna tell them everything."

Kevin on the radio: "Travis, he wants to know if the last time you saw the boat it was near an island. Do you think they might be on an island? Over."

"I doubt it. Look, like I said, they were having trouble. It was a small boat and the water is pretty rough. They were a couple miles out last I saw them, nowhere near any of the islands. You better send a helicopter to look, and we can stay here in case they get spotted. We can pick them up. Over."

Travis came around the console, motioning for Kerry to stand on top of the seat. It was quiet for a while, just the spit and gurgling of the engines and the slap of the water on the hull. He looked around, thinking that if the two guys were in the water, if they weren't actually alive and well someplace else, they would most likely be swimming toward the islands, but he could see it would be hard going against the wind and into the swells. He figured they probably had some kind of life vests, red or orange, probably easy to spot if he was looking long enough in the right direction, down current. "That way," he said, getting Kerry's attention. "Keep looking that way, around there."

"'Kay."

Then the crackle of static and Kevin's voice: "Travis, this is Kevin again. Over."

"Talk to me, what's going on?"

Static. "Travis? Uh, the cop said he called the Fire Department and they called the heliport, that's the uh, you know, the helicopters, and so they said in about half an hour one of the commuter flights will be at Illiginni, one of the radar sites—it's not far, and then they'll be passing over there and they can take a look. So stay there, they said, and you gotta go to the police station when you get in and make a report or something. They wanna talk to you. Over."

"Okay," Travis said. "We're standing by, and um . . . okay, so do they have our frequency, can we talk to the helicopter? And they're gonna look around for a while, not just a fly-by, right? Over."

"Shit," Boyd said. "I'll bet you anything those Marshallese are already headed back to Ebeye, and now we got helicopters and cops and—"

Static. Kevin: "Travis, uh, I don't know about the radio and all that, but I can check. Okay? Over."

"I think I see somethin' out there," Kerry said. "Up in the sky, some kinda kite."

Travis looked, speaking into the mike, "Yeah, find out now and let me know. Over."

"Okay. Over."

"A kite?" Travis stared where Kerry was pointing, shielding his eyes from the sun. He couldn't see anything.

Boyd grabbed the binoculars and looked. "It's a goddamned frigate bird!" he said. "You idiot. What were you thinking, looking up in the sky instead of—"

"No, wait," Travis said. "Let me see." He took the binoculars. He saw the frigate bird, huge, hovering, motionless, looking very much like a kite. It was almost out of sight. "Something's under it," he said. "It wouldn't be up there like that if it wasn't looking at something—maybe only a log, you know, but we should go check it out." He couldn't see anything under it, but it was far and the water was rough. "Let's go. You know which way, right?"

"Yeah," Boyd said. "I got it."

The boat roared off in the direction of the frigate bird, and with almost a following sea Boyd took the swells at an angle, zigzagging to keep up a good speed and a fairly smooth ride. He'd throttle back now and then, timing his path through the swells. About halfway to the bird, Travis told him to stop. He looked again through the binoculars. At first he saw only the bird and nothing under it. Then, for just an instant, at the crest of a swell he saw something at the edge of his field of vision. Then he saw it again, clearly this time because he knew where to look. A head, the grainy hint of a face—then down and out of sight into a trough. "Go!" He shouted, jumping a little as he pointed. "Go, go, I see one of 'em!"

"One of the Marshallese?" Boyd asked, as if it made a difference in deciding whether or not to go pick him up.

Kerry leaned against Travis in his effort to sight along to the same spot.

Travis slapped Boyd's shoulder. "Go, dammit!" He looked again through the binoculars just as the boat took off, scanning the ocean near and far around the Marshallese. Then the excitement he was feeling turned sour, chilling him, when he realized what should have been obvious right away. His mind replayed Boyd's stupid question: *One of the Marshallese?* It wasn't so stupid. There was only one Marshallese in the water, only one. He felt weak, bending over as a cramp worked its way through his gut. He wished he had found nothing but a log under the frigate bird.

Jebro shouted out Nuke's name again and again, each time pushing violently at the water to propel himself round and round, shouting until his voice was cracking, all for nothing in reply. He fell silent, settling into a gentle kick and stroke, almost floating, feeling somewhat dizzy as the ocean seemed to continue slowly spinning around him. He trembled, his pain of loss, like the sea, attacking him in waves; his guilt, jabbing at him, taunting him with all the different things he might have done, just little things, and Nuke would still be at his side. The sound of Nuke's voice and even his smell remained so present, as if Jebro might only blink and his brother would reappear, laughing. When Jebro thought of Nuke's face, his eyes, his smile, it occurred to him then that he had no picture of his brother—the only one he knew of belonged to their father, an old one slowly fading where it stayed in the framed corner of a painting of Jesus Christ, a black-and-white instant photograph of Nuke as an infant in the arms of their mother, Iia, her smile as wide and bright and proud as the meaning of her name, rainbow.

Jebro rode up and down the choppy, whitecapped swells, staring at the glaring path of sunlight that winked and danced upon the water, and he remembered how his mother had told him that at the first touch of sunset it became the golden path to heaven. He had watched many sunsets after she had died—a boy who stared into the painful burning sun until it had him seeing shapes that changed and oily oozing stains of light: The tiny shape of his mother among a thousand other spirits that swirled through the brilliant reds and yellows, in heaven, and when he closed his eyes she glowed, her spirit staying with him, captured inside of him, backlit by the setting sun. Jebro knew how Nuke had been so special to her, after all the other children she had lost, the brothers and the sisters he had never known. He pictured her, his eyes fixed on the sunshine path of water, and he recalled the songs she had sung when Nuke was feeding from her breast, and he knew he could not bear, and that he had no choice, to think of how much losing Nuke would have hurt her.

But then he did not have think of it, not yet. Because it was then that he saw him, drifting out from where he had been hidden by the blinding million silver glinting chips of light, his head and one of his shoulders just above the rolling surface, floating seemingly lifeless no more than four blue crests away. Jebro flung himself down to the bottom of a swell and kicked, riding it and then the next one, calling to Nuke as he clawed his way across the water, his throat so raw from shouting that it stung, his voice a raspy croaking howl.

Nuke did not respond, but he was alive, though maybe not aware of it himself. His head bobbed underwater and then to the surface, his mouth by some reflex turning to find a little air to breathe, not unlike a fish at the surface of a stagnant, drying tide pool. Jebro grabbed him by the waist and shook him gently, getting from him only the slightest wheezing moan. He was cold, pale, his eyes half open and unfocused. His shallow breathing was not near enough to keep him alive much longer.

A rising warmth pressed at Jebro's chest and balled up in his throat, a welling of the love he felt for his brother, the power not to let him die. He pinched Nuke's nose and covered his mouth with his own, breathing into him and feeling the buoyancy that came with each inflation of his chest.

The turbulent push and pull of the water caused Jebro's mouth to slip, twice—their teeth clacked together—and then Nuke coughed, spitting up into Jebro's face, convulsing as he drew a forceful, deep and rattling breath, spitting again as he let it out to breathe once more. A whitecap crashed over them, nearly tumbling them, and when they were free from it Nuke was gasping for air and crying out in short clipped bursts, trying with what little strength he had to climb on top of Jebro, scratching him and pulling at his hair. Jebro kicked hard to keep them both above the water, using his hands to pry loose Nuke's fingers and pin him close to his body, speaking soothing words into his ear, holding him tight until the panic ran its course and his muscles became as limp and lifeless as before. Nuke was breathing much too fast. He began to shiver. His teeth chattered loud enough for Jebro to hear.

Jebro turned Nuke's head and held him so that they could look into each other's eyes. Nuke seemed almost scared of him, as if what Jebro had been doing was meant to harm him, not to save his life. Jebro smoothed back Nuke's hair and smiled at him, so overwhelmed by the sight of his living breathing brother, so unable to find a thought beyond his pure elation that instead of speaking, all he managed was to giggle, feeling muscles twitching in his cheeks. Nuke's face remained blank, seemingly drained of blood. The dark centers of his eyes were wide, so open as to appear painful.

Jebro's happiness thinned, having to accept, as the breaking ocean swells would not relent, and the wind and current would not slacken, that Nuke's life was far from being saved. "You have nothing to be afraid of," he said. "I made you a promise to get us both on land, and you'll see that I can keep it."

Nuke said nothing, only trembled, his wide eyes looking past Jebro at the ocean. Jebro pinched him, pulling at the little hairs under his arm until he yelped. "Aha, you're not a zombie after all. Quick, tell me how you feel before I pinch you again." He rubbed the top of Nuke's back, to warm him.

Nuke blinked. His voice was weak. "There was a wave, Jebro. I can't remember. . . . I . . ."

"Yes, the wave, the biggest I have ever seen and both of us survived it. You see how strong we are? Nothing will stop us." He moved Nuke around so that he held him with his other arm, riding him partly on his hip.

"I feel sick. Cold."

Jebro used his teeth to take the cap off the water jug. He tilted it so that Nuke could take a drink. Nuke coughed a little as he swallowed, gagged, and then he vomited, slicking the water with a thin gruel, mostly fluid. Jebro wiped his trembling mouth. "It was seawater in your stomach, a good thing you got it up." He gave Nuke another drink and this time he kept it down. He took another.

Nuke burped. He looked behind him and then he looked over Jebro's shoulder. "Where is the float? You . . . you were supposed to fix the float." He clung a little tighter.

"The wave . . . it . . ." Jebro felt embarrassed as he searched around the water for his duffel bag. He did not expect to see it, and did not. His legs were sorely tired. So were his arms and even his back. "That wave sank it, I think, but no matter—I can hold you, and I can swim for the both of us, so we should still get near some islands pretty soon." He wanted to believe it. He had no other choice. He had found Nuke, and he was alive, and it seemed so impossible that after getting through so much he might . . . the ocean might—it was too cruel to even think about.

Nuke looked around for the islands, only Tar-Wōj and next to it, Maan, visible as faint discolorations on the horizon—and not the way they were headed. "Jebro . . . are you sure?"

"I'm sure. Listen, I want you to—can you kick just a little? To stay warm." He relaxed his grip, not quite letting him go.

"Hang on to me, Jebro!" Nuke pulled himself tight against Jebro's side, wrapping his legs around his brother's waist. "I am scared to drown—I know I almost drowned!"

“No no no, listen—we’ll be okay, and I promise I won’t let you go. But I can’t hold you like this all the time. I want you in front me, so we can swim on our backs—I’ll do the swimming for you—and you just kick a little to stay warm. It’s the best way not to drown, I promise.” He pulled Nuke off of his hip “All right, you ready to try?”

“Maybe we should wait. I . . .” He cringed as they rode up one of the larger swells and slid quickly down into its trough.

“We should try, just once to see if works, okay?” He turned Nuke around and slipped one hand under Nuke’s arm so that it crossed his chest and gripped the opposite shoulder. He leaned back, causing Nuke to whine and struggle when right away they plowed into a swell. “Okay okay,” he said as he brought Nuke back upright. “Maybe we can do it a little different, with the jug. He broke the line from his shirt and took a few large swallows of the water, then handed it to Nuke and had him do the same. When he took it back he poured out most of the rest then screwed the lid on tight. “Hold on to it as a float, under your shirt and against your belly, and when we lean back I’ll keep the rest of you up higher this time.” It did work better, with Jebro slightly on his side and kicking deep, able to see the oncoming swells. He could switch sides when one arm got tired. Nuke was a little more relaxed, higher on the water, but still shivering, and Jebro had to keep reminding him to kick. He glanced from side to side, imagining he might find a log, a branch, a frond, any piece of trash that would hold them up. He thought of a log big enough to put himself and Nuke on top, only their legs dangling in the water as they rode into the night, their shirts drying on branches in the wind. He had caught fish by such logs many times before, and had seen them washed up on islands, even several on Ebeye. But all around was the ocean, only the ocean, its churning surface working to enfold them and suck them to its bottom. It did no good to think of logs, it only made things worse. Still above them, motionless, the frigate bird, dipping its wings now and then, never flapping, doing only what little it had to do to keep on watching them. Earlier, the bird had been a source of strength for Jebro, a symbol of his grandfather protecting them from harm; now it seemed as though the bird mocked him, teased him by showing how at ease it was while he and Nuke were in such peril. Jebro began to hate the bird, because it could fly away and perch on land whenever it wished, without so much as a flutter of its wings. He wanted to shout at it and make it go away, but he did not want to waste the strength, and he had to be calm, for Nuke.

The top of Nuke's head rested below Jebro's chin, his shivering body dead weight on the side of Jebro's chest. Now Jebro shivered too. Nuke seemed to drift in and out of a stupor, mumbling things and sometimes closing his eyes. Whenever Jebro told him to keep kicking, he had to repeat himself two or three times, loud, before Nuke would understand.

Jebro's arm around Nuke became so stiff that it hurt just to move it, and he could feel a numbness spreading from his wrist into his fingers, so he switched sides, finding both his arms were nearly useless. He could not let Nuke go, not even for a few seconds just to stretch and rest.

Suddenly his mind offered him an ugly thought, that he might make it by himself, if he did not have to carry Nuke, that it made no sense for both of them to drown—no, it was not a thought of his own—impossible—he would never let his brother go. It was the frigate, the evil frigate taking its sick pleasure in watching them slowly die, hovering there and messing with Jebro's mind. He cursed it silently, finding within himself an extra bit of strength, a little more resolve to keep himself and Nuke alive, just to spite his enemy. He tried to think of something he and Nuke could do with their shirts, maybe two small floats made from the shirts and then tied somehow to the jug—but he saw the cotton of their shirts was too thin and full of little holes. They would not hold air. Their shorts, too short, useless. There had to be something, he had to find some other way, and then, just as he started feeling the added chill of desperation—he reflexively twitched his head and blew a burst of air up across his face, a quick, automatic response to the tinny vibration in his ear, a familiar sound on

Ebeye, the sound of a mosquito or possibly a fly. He did it before he realized it made no sense. He looked up, holding his breath to hear better. Maybe it was not so high-pitched as a fly, but more like the hum of a distant outboard boat. A boat. "Nuke!"

Jebro spun Nuke around and gripped him by the front of his shirt. "Do you hear it? Tell me you hear the boat!"

Jebro kicked, rising as high as he could at the top of the swells, and then he saw it, a small, white shining shape east of them, seemingly heading straight for them.

Nuke saw it too, sort of squeaking as he pointed at it. The water warmed where Nuke's groin pressed against Jebro's thigh.

Jebro raised one arm and waved, shouting even though he knew they could not hear him. Soon, he saw that it was the Americans, the three of them coming fast. He lowered his hand, not just because it grew quickly tired but because he became worried about what the Americans might do. No. He could not believe they came to do more harm, but he also did not believe they came out of any great concern for anybody but themselves. They came to save themselves from their own stupidity, to rescue themselves from a life of guilt. They were his and Nuke's salvation, but still, he had to hate them. It did not matter. He put his hand back up and waved, wondering how they had found him, so far from where the boat had gone down. And then he knew. He looked into the sky, the frigate still suspended there, a huge black beacon over their position. He smiled at the bird, no longer his enemy, always having been the free and roaming spirit of his grandfather.

It was Boyd who first saw two Marshallese instead of only one, pointing out that fact as if it were a vindication of what he had done. He brought the boat skillfully toward them, as fast as he could, but the look on his face said that he still didn't accept how close he had come to being a murderer. He had always been like that, now probably already fooling himself into remembering some other more innocent they-cut-me-off-and-I-had-to-turn-real-sharp-not-to-hit-them version of what had happened. Things never were his fault. It was a good bet that by the time he had the Marshallese on the boat he would be thinking of himself as some kind of hero. His left eye had mostly closed, bruising nicely. "What are you gonna tell them?" he asked Travis.

Travis kept staring at the two Marshallese, worried that at any moment one of them would go under, a shark would attack, that every time they disappeared into a trough they might not come back up. One of them slowly waved, the older one, and that made Travis feel better. "Huh? What are you talking about?"

"I'm saying, you're not gonna put this all on me, are you?—I mean, c'mon, we can say the throttles stuck, and . . . and like you said: They looked okay last we saw them. And we'd have gone back, you know, if—"

"Forget it, Boyd, just get it in your head: I'm done covering your ass on this one. Don't even think about it."

"You already lied to the cops on the radio, you know, and if those guys rat us out then you—"

"Rat us out? Like they would be real dicks to do that too, huh? You'll never get it, Boyd, not even if I—shit, go ahead and lie all you want, just don't expect me to back you up." He looked to Kerry for agreement.

Kerry stood just behind Travis, his cheeks hollow and his eyes somewhat sunken-in and glassy. He held onto the elbow of the console's rail, looking from Travis to Boyd. "I ain't lyin' for you, neither. Nuh-uh, no way Ho-zay. You face up to whatcha done, an' be a man about it."

Boyd jerked around to face Kerry, half his upper lip curled toward his beaten eye and twitching at it. "You pudgy little shit—you p—p–p"

"Slow down!" Travis shouted. The boat was less than forty yards away and closing fast. The two Marshallese held each other, looking as though they feared Boyd was coming to finish them off.

Boyd pulled back to neutral. He turned the wheel so as not to blast the Marshallese with the wake, then circled half around so that he was coming alongside with the bow into the wind and facing the swell. Travis bent under the console to get the first aid kit. He didn't know if it would be of any use, but it seemed like a good thing to have ready.

When the boat drew even with the Marshallese, the engines gurgling loudly as Boyd kicked them momentarily in reverse, Travis hurdled over the gunnel and splashed butt-first into a rising swell, directly in front of the Marshallese. He hadn't meant to do it; maybe it was just an instant reaction to how exhausted the two of them looked, and in a way it could have been because he wanted to distance himself from Boyd—but before he even thought about why he did it he was treading the deep purple water, eye to eye with two shivering people who, for obvious reasons, might really want to break his face. For a short time he was confused about what to do next, because in all the years he had fished the open ocean, he had never swam in it, never even put more than his arms in it, and to be up to his neck in such wild water, so far from land and to dangle his feet so incredibly far above an unseen, seemingly nonexistent bottom was as eerie as it was exhilarating—and while his brain processed this new experience, the two Marshallese, staring at him coldly, quickly passed him by and grabbed onto the side of the boat. The older one tried weakly to lift the other up to Kerry. Boyd stayed at the wheel, only glancing down at the rescue.

Travis felt stupid. "Hey," he said, kicking over. "It's easier to get in through the back, between the engines."

Kerry already had a hold on the little one's arms, and pulled him, more like dragged him over the side, too hard, and failed to catch him before he tumbled noisily to the deck. Kerry fell back too, into a seated position on the bench. A water jug the little one had been holding drifted away around the boat.

"Be careful!" Travis said. "Jesus, see if he's okay." He pulled over next to the other Marshallese, who seemed to have only enough strength to hang onto the boat, not near enough to haul himself up. Travis nodded to him. "You speak English?"

The guy stared at Travis for a few seconds, as if he was trying to figure him out. "What difference it make? I—I need to get inside your boat." His voice was shaking, as was the rest of him. His accent was thick, hard to understand.

"Oh—sorry, I mean, can you come around the back? It'll be easier for both of us." He looked up at Kerry. "Toss me a life jacket."

Travis had the Marshallese hang on to the jacket while he towed him around to the back. At the corner he shouted up to Boyd. "Neutral, keep it in neutral!" They came up between the engines, the Marshallese first so that Travis could push him from behind. Kerry had cleared a path between the gas cans, and as the Marshallese stepped weakly through it he nearly tripped because of the one fin still on his foot. He caught himself on the bench, turned so that he could sit, and took off the fin. An indented ring remained around his ankle. His chest billowed with heavy breathing. He was thin, muscular, not more than five and a half feet tall. The smaller one sat next to him. He was stocky, just a little kid. He was out of his wet shirt and he had Kerry's Hawaiian-sunset beach towel draped over his shoulders. The two of them resembled each other in the face, probably brothers. Both of them had several dark round scars on their bodies, like mosquito bites healed badly. The older one had six fingers on his left hand, a longer, extra pinkie without a nail. They held each other, shivering, looking warily at Travis and Kerry. Boyd stayed behind them, his hands on the throttles and his eyes on Travis as if waiting for permission to leave.

Kerry's was the only towel on board, and Travis realized he should have taken off his shirt before jumping in. Kerry's and Boyd's shirts were relatively dry. "Your shirts," he said. "Give 'em your shirts." Boyd just looked at him. "Hurry up!"

The older one took Kerry's shirt and wiped his face and hair with it. He stripped out of his wet one. Boyd handed his shirt to Kerry, who gave it to the little one, who put it on. On it was printed: "Virginia is for Lovers." It hung on him like a dress. He got back under the towel and pulled it tight, hiding his face. The older one put on Kerry's shirt, an "Almost Paradise,

Kwajalein Missile Range" shirt, now damp. He looked around the boat, his eyes settling on the gas can that had come from his boat.

Travis knelt in front of him. "Yeah, we found that. Good thing too—I mean . . . So are you guys thirsty? You want anything to—Um . . . but, uh . . . I guess we don't have anything left to drink, just some ice in the cooler. You want some ice, maybe the water in the cooler? It should be pretty clean."

The Marshallese looked straight at Travis, his body shivering, obviously not wanting any ice. "Why you did this to us?" he asked loudly, his voice hoarse. "My brother, he almos'—If he—I would have—You don't know, you never think what you doing!" His eyes narrowed, lips trembling. He looked from Travis to Kerry, then he turned around and pointed at Boyd, stuttering a bit before he said, "You—you are no good! I thought maybe you all crazy, but you all just stupid, and you drunk, I can smell all of you drunk! You lucky you don't kill us, stupid asshole! You . . ." His anger seemed to tire him, and rob him of his breath. His shivering chin dropped a little, and when the boat slapped to the bottom of a trough he gripped the bench with both hands to keep from falling over. His kept staring at Boyd, seeming to study the bruise over his eye. Boyd's other eye stared back at him.

Finally, Boyd raised his hands in surrender. "It was an accident, man—I didn't mean to, you know. . . . A few beers, sure, but—"

"Bullshit, Boyd!" Travis wanted very much for the Marshallese to know whose side he was on. "Just tell them the truth: You fucked up. And try saying you're sorry for once. Like Kerry said, be a man about it."

"Shut up, Travis. Shit. If you ain't gonna share the blame—Man, just stay the fuck out of it then." He looked again at the Marshallese. "Look, like he said, I fu—I was wrong, all right? I'm sorry. You want a shot at me or something, take it." He shrugged, feeling around his swollen eye. "Open season, I guess." He put the engines in gear and turned the wheel so as to take a large swell at an angle.

"Oh, that's real great, Boyd," Travis said. "The guy can hardly keep his butt on the bench and you—"

"What the hell else you want me to do? I mean, shit, I can't take back the past, put 'em back in their boat. Give 'em the fish then, I don't know. Shit."

The older Marshallese pushed Boyd in the ribs with his left hand, the one with the with extra finger. It hung limply, swinging. "How come you say it like that, like you don't know you owe me one boat? You owe us some other things too—so that is what you better say to me. I don't care if you sorry. I don't care anything you feel." He seemed to grow disgusted looking at Boyd, and then glanced above the boat, eyeing the frigate bird that still hovered overhead. The sun gleamed on his face.

Kerry used the lull in the conversation to kneel down and let loose with a few dry heaves over the side. His bare back and shoulders were bone white, his sunburned arms looking like long red gloves. Boyd fiddled nervously with the purple rubber skirt of a lure that lay on top of the console.

Travis hadn't even thought of replacing the Marshallese's boat, and judging from the look on Boyd's face, he hadn't either, probably because for them the boats on Kwaj were always free, not something he and Boyd ever worried about replacing if they sank. If a boat broke, if it needed parts or even if the engines got a little old—into the shop and let Uncle Sam pay for it. Kwaj was a fantasy land like that, where almost everything didn't have a price. He knew, but never really thought much about it, that on Ebeye it was the exact opposite, which was why not too many of the Marshallese fished, and why he and Boyd never had any trouble selling their catch to them at a dollar a pound. "He's right Boyd, this is gonna cost you big time. I can't believe you thought you could just give him some fish." Travis laughed.

"Man, you gotta pitch in too, you know, this isn't just—"

"No way Boyd, you sunk it, you replace it, you—"

Kerry rose up from the side and interrupted him: "Shouldn't we be takin' these fellas back home, maybe to the hospital?

Really, cain't ya'll hash this out along the way? I'm about fit for the hospital myself."

"You're right," Travis said. "And get on the radio, Boyd, so Kevin can tell the cops what's going on. Say we found the Marshallese and we don't need the helicopter anymore. And then let's get out of here." Travis turned to the Marshallese. "We called in a helicopter to look for you." He pantomimed one with his hands, realizing as he did it that the guy probably already knew what "helicopter" meant. He looked worried though, at the mention of it.

Kerry sat next to the younger Marshallese and looked down at his hands, an open wound on each one that looked like rope burns. He pulled his hands away when Kerry tried to inspect them more closely. The kid had not spoken yet, hardly even made a sound, and Travis wondered if he was mute. The two of them were shivering less, the back of the boat being warmed by the late, bright beaming sun.

"Wait a minute," Boyd said, holding the mike away from his mouth as if it might pick up what he was saying, no matter that his thumb wasn't on the switch. "What are we gonna say? I mean, let's think about this."

"Dammit, Boyd, just say what I said. What kinda problem you got with that? Here, let me do it."

"No, just hang on a sec. I don't mean only about the radio, but later. Listen, you're all ready to hang this whole thing on me—fine—but let me get it straight: When we have to go talk to the cops, then I'm gonna say we all agreed to go into restricted waters, where these guys didn't belong either—and that's not to excuse what I did, because I'll admit I swamped them, just for a prank and not to hurt them, which is a fact and you all know it—and then you two," he pointed at Travis and Kerry. "Just kept on fishing and didn't say shit about finding them or even checking on them until an hour later, right? That's the truth, right?"

"Yeah," Travis said. "That's exactly right and I'm willing to fess up to what I did wrong, and just because I'm not as much of an asshole as you are, I'm gonna help you replace their boat. They could be dead, Boyd. Doesn't that bother you?"

"I know, Travis. Shit. I'm sorry. I said I was sorry and we can't do nothing to change what happened, but listen—"

They all seemed to hear it at once, the thrumming beat of a helicopter. Boyd saw it first, pointing northeast. It was low, coming fast. Above them the frigate bird rose on the wind, turning slightly to the west, climbing so high and fast that within seconds it was nothing more than a black dot soon to be gone, never once flapping its wings. The radio crackled and then the pilot of the approaching helicopter hailed them. Boyd answered, explaining briefly that they had just picked up the Marshallese. No, no more of them were missing. He said they were doing okay, everything was fine, and they were ready to head back home. Then the pilot wanted the names of the Marshallese. Boyd looked at them.

The older one shook his head, suddenly looking very worried. "I cannot. I just got one job on Kwajalein. My father, he says—maybe they'll take my job for coming here. I cannot. . . ."

"I understand," Travis said. He smiled at him. "Just say any name, make one up. Hey, as far as we know it's the truth, right?" Both Boyd and Kerry nodded.

"Halmar," the older one said. "Halmar Lino and Bwiji. Bwiji Lino." He mussed his little brother's hair, saying something to him in Marshallese.

Boyd had trouble repeating the names, testing variations on Butch and Hamlet. The Marshallese coached him until he got it right, or close enough. He gave the pilot the names, then tried to spell them, then he gave Kerry's, Travis's, and his own name too when the pilot asked for them. The helicopter rose higher as it came above them, its nose pivoting to face them as the pilot positioned it in a hover, downwind, so that the boat was out of its wash. It was close enough though for them to see the rivets on its white skin, the whole thing looking like a fat white insect. It was loud too, and nobody could understand what the pilot said next over the radio. Boyd waved. "Okay, gotcha. Thanks for your help. We better get going now.

Thanks, over." The two Marshallese huddled together, their faces hidden.

The pilot waved out the window, and in the passenger area several men were peering out. They had large gray headphones on their ears and wore sunglasses. They spun out of view when in one fluid motion the helicopter turned its tail on the boat, dipped forward, and droned away, soon becoming as small and as distant as the frigate bird.

"What do you think he said?" Travis asked.

Boyd clipped the mike back on the radio. "I don't know, probably just telling us to get out of here."

"Good idea. Hit it."

"Hold on, Buddy. Things have changed a bit, yeah?—so we all gotta talk and get some shit straight first."

"What? Because all you have to do is pass along some bullshit names, you think—"

"I think if he don't want his name out there, then none of us can go around saying I sunk his boat, right? Kinda takes my balls off the chopping block, don't you think? And we got to get the story straight, that's all." The smug, asshole look was creeping back onto his face.

"Give it up Boyd," Travis said. "No way I'm gonna let you weasel out of this."

The older Marshallese stood up and faced Boyd, his legs unsteady. "You going owe me one boat no matter what. I don't care you say my name, but you—" Travis put a hand on his shoulder and he shrugged it off. "You understand, you owe me—you owe my father, that was my father's boat!"

Travis thought Boyd was going to be a dick; instead, he offered the Marshallese his hand. "Look, I don't even know your real name, and I never said anything about not getting you a boat, okay? I'm good for it, I swear. Ask Travis."

The Marshallese ignored Boyd's hand, staring at him for a moment before he turned away and sat back down next to his brother.

"Jeez you guys," Boyd said. "Give me a break. I just wanna get the story straight, so we all get out of this clean, even you

Travis, because I'll bet you anything they would yank your licence too—probably haul all three of us to court, Kerry."

Travis laughed. "All of a sudden you're acting like you're so concerned for everybody else, when really you're just thinking about saving your own ass. One thing you got right—this guy's getting a boat, and some gear. How much cash you got in the bank?"

"I don't know, man. What about the story?"

"What about it? It has to be the same as I told Kevin and the cops, except now we use those names—which I forgot, but that's even better. So let's hit it, get these guys back to Ebeye before somebody from Kwaj gets over there looking for 'em."

Boyd eased forward on the throttles. "Settle in then, it's gonna get bumpy." He radioed Kevin at the marina to make sure he'd heard the conversation with the helicopter, then headed southeast at an angle to the swells at near three-quarter speed. Only one island in the distance was visible, just barely. It wasn't in the direction they were headed.

Travis stood next to Boyd at the console, but after a while he went back and sat on the bench, next to the older Marshallese who had his arm tight around his brother. Kerry sat on the other end of the bench, holding his arms around his gut.

"So you guys are okay?" Travis asked. "Your brother, do you think he needs a doctor?" He spoke loudly so that his voice would carry above the noise of the engines.

"No, I don't think so. He just need to rest."

"His hands," Kerry said, almost shouting. "He's got a couple a cuts on his hands."

Travis stepped over the bench and got the first aid kit off the console. He handed it to Kerry. "You know what you're doing?"

Kerry grinned. "I got me a Red Cross certificate. An' a patch." He seemed eager to do something besides wonder when the next revolt would happen in his stomach.

Travis sat back down, watching Kerry try coaxing the little one to hold out his hands. The older one had to say something in Marshallese before his brother would cooperate.

Travis nudged the older one's knee. "My name's Travis. Travis Kotrady. We're in the phone book if you need to get a hold of me." He smiled. "And I'm sorry, really—I know that probably doesn't mean much, but . . ."

"Maybe you're okay, not like him." He gestured with his head toward Boyd.

"No, I'm not like him." He grinned, then put his fist up by his eye and pointed a thumb to his chest, letting the Marshallese know who had slugged Boyd. The Marshallese smiled. "So, um, it's all right if you tell me your real name—I'm not gonna get you in trouble. And I guess I kinda should know, in case I need to find you . . . you know, about the new boat."

"Jebro."

Travis didn't catch it. He pointed to his ear.

"Je-bro," he said, louder, his voice still very hoarse. "Je-bro Ke-ju, and my brother, he is Nuke, Nuke like the bomb." He held out his hand and Travis shook it with both of his.

"Cool name," Travis said. "Nuke: That's pretty cool. I like it."

"I'm Kerry." He shook Jebro's hand as well. "I'm the one that found you—I mean, I found that bird over you, and—"

Nuke said something in Marshallese, causing Jebro to laugh. Nuke's face finally peeked out from the towel, almost smiling. Kerry was nearly finished with his hands, using way too much gauze.

It felt good to Travis to hear Jebro laugh. "What'd he say? Nuke."

"He understand your friend is talking about the ak, that bird, but he cannot speak English so good, not yet. He say in Marshallese, 'Freckles is talking about our grandfather.' You see, that bird, he was there long time, waiting for someone to find us. I tell Nuke it is our grandfather because he . . . because my grandfather one time tell me he think like one . . . ak—how you say that bird in English?"

"It's a frigate bird. Frig-et. You really call it a hawk, in Marshallese?"

"Not hawk, ak. Aaaak."

"Haaak . . ."

Kerry and Nuke laughed. "Ya'll sound like a couple a ducks!" Kerry looked at Jebro. "So how ya say 'freckles' in Marshallese?"

Jebro looked suddenly serious, then he smiled. "I think maybe I cannot tell you, because that word is . . . I hope you understand: To say 'freckles' in Marshallese is kūbween ļoñ, but when you say that back in English it mean fly shit." He brushed Kerry's freckled shoulder with his hand.

Travis laughed. "Sorry, Kerry."

"S'all right. Ever'where I go there's a joke about freckles. Now I heard a new one." He shook his head. Nuke's hands were done, bandaged up as though they had third-degree burns. Kerry snapped shut the first aid kit and tossed it into the console's cubby.

The ride was as bumpy as Boyd had promised, so Travis passed out the life jackets to sit on. It was much better, almost comfortable. Travis looked away when he got caught staring at Jebro's extra finger. Jebro held up his hand in front of Travis, the extra finger flopping over while the others remained upright. He smiled, not at all upset that Travis had been staring at it. He seemed to be proud of it. "This finger is magic," he said. "I can bring fish with it." He held it out for Travis to touch. It felt like it didn't have any bones, like pinching someone's lip. Kerry watched intently.

Travis didn't know what to say. He let go of the finger. "Cool."

"Maybe I am the only one in the world with a finger like this. You ever see one?"

"Not at all—I'm sure it's one of a kind."

"Me neither," Kerry said. "But I knew a guy who had a birthmark looked like Woody Woodpecker pushin' a lawnmower."

Jebro didn't understand, but Travis laughed. "Bullshit, man! I'm not gonna believe that."

"I swear! It was on his neck."

"Yeah right. Listen," he said to Jebro. "I was thinking about your boat, where we might find one, and there's gonna be an auction, probably in four or five weeks—something like these kind of boats." He pointed at the deck. "But they're smaller ones, eighteen-footers, Boston Whalers like this one but smaller. Do you know what kind of boat I'm talking about?"

"Sometimes I see them going by. I know what kind of boat. Good boat."

"Yeah, they get new ones for the marina every few years, and then auction off some of the older ones. I saw a few of them stacked up in the lot, three or four of them. They might need some fixing up, but don't worry 'cause we'll help you. What do you think?"

"If you can get that kind boat—eighteen-foot fiberglass—okay then. My boat—my father's boat was metal, like beer can—only fifteen-foot and the engine small too, cannot even chase fish."

"They don't sell 'em with the engines though, only the hull. The marina keeps the engines for parts. We'll have to look around, maybe order one if we have to, 'cause people kinda hang on to their engines. How about Ebeye, any decent engines people might sell?"

Jebro laughed. "Ebeye get plenty engines, you see them everywhere, but nothing works."

"I kinda figured that. Anyway, so when are you gonna be on Kwaj, for that job? We can go look at the boats."

"I start Monday, at the . . ." Jebro looked at his feet. "At the sewer plant. My father work there too."

Travis grimaced. "Really, the sewage plant? You don't have to . . . I mean, what kind of stuff you gotta do there?"

"It's not so bad."

Travis thought about making a joke, something about it being a shitty job, but he decided against it. "Yeah, okay, so maybe next week I can meet you sometime, and we can go look at the boats. It's a sealed auction—that means we have to write down what we want to pay, and the highest one gets the boat."

Jebro frowned. "How much they cost? Maybe your friend, he no like pay so much. My boat was only cheap."

"Hey, don't even worry about that, and it ain't like we're doing you a favor here, remember. Besides, I heard they go for just a few hundred bucks, maybe five or six for one of the better ones. It all depends on how much work they need. Sometimes you gotta refoam the entire hull—it gets water-logged in there. We'll have to take a look, and I'm in good with the boss at the marina too; he's my basketball coach. I bet he'll let me use the shop and stuff."

"Okay, maybe Monday then. You come find me after my work, four thirty, and we go look."

"All right, four thirty, and don't worry—even if we can't get one of the Whalers, we'll find something good, a lot better than that skiff you were running. I promise."

Jebro nodded, smiling. He turned to his brother and spoke rapidly in Marshallese. Travis thought Marshallese sounded like a cross between birds warbling and boiling water. He tried, listening to Jebro speak, but he couldn't tell where one word ended and another began. It seemed like an impossible language to learn. Maybe English seemed like that too, to people who never heard it before.

After a while, once Boyd had the boat cutting through calmer water, both Jebro and Nuke appeared to doze off, their heads bobbing up and down, their eyes only occasionally coming open. Travis tried not to disturb them. Kerry dozed too, only once spitting something over the side. Travis thought about talking to Boyd, but with all that had happened it was kind of nice to just sit back and watch the sun slowly dip back under the clouds, the color of gray seeming to smooth over all the turmoil of the day. As the boat passed into the lagoon between Gea and Nini, he watched slow fat birds return from the ocean and drop into the islands' jungles.

Jebro woke first, less than half an hour later when they were close to two miles from Ebeye. Maybe he smelled the island. Travis could. The sun was not yet fully down, but definitely gone for the day. The twin beams of the green-and-white rotating beacon on top of the Kwajalein water tower, the green being a double beam, were just beginning to sweep through the premature twilight. A Caribou was taking off from the airport.

The *Tarlang* was just coming around Kwajalein's Echo pier, headed for Ebeye.

Jebro stood, stretched his arms, yawning. He gently shook his brother's shoulders and said something in Marshallese. Nuke sort of whined, the same kind of noise American kids made when they get woken up. Kerry helped him stand. Jebro looked at Travis and pointed at Boyd. He cleared his throat. "Tell him to go south, to that small wooden pier, in case they looking for us. You see it?" His voice was scratchier than before.

"Yeah." He pointed it out to Boyd who adjusted his course, slowing to weave his way through a maze of trash that littered the water in front of the island. Jebro looked like he was ready to go back to sleep.

Travis placed a hand on his shoulder. "You gonna be all right?"

Jebro managed a smile. "I think so, except now some people might be upset I never bring the turtle meat I promised."

"Why don't you take the fish?" He kicked the icebox. "It's probably two fifty or three hundred pounds in there, that's three hundred bucks."

Jebro looked insulted. "I don't want your fish."

"Okay, no problem. I just thought . . ." Travis remembered Jebro's skill with the school, realizing how a certain amount of pride was probably involved, how he himself might feel the same way. "I guess I know where you're coming from. Maybe on one of your days off I can swing by with a boat and we'll go fish. The rules say we're not supposed to stop over here, but I'm sure we'll get away with it. You can show me how you knew where that school was gonna come up. Or did you use that magic finger of yours?"

Jebro nodded, smiling now. "Okay, we go fishing sometime, but if you want my secrets, that is worth more than any boat you give me!" He laughed.

"I agree," Travis said. He laughed too. "I got a few secrets myself. Maybe we can work out some kind of trade." It seemed suddenly odd to Travis that he had spent so much time in this part of the world and didn't have even one Marshallese friend. He imagined himself fishing with Jebro, looking forward to it.

Boyd called for somebody to man the bow. The flimsy wooden pier was just a few feet away. It was about twenty feet long, maybe three feet wide, and looked to be made of wood scavenged from crates and pallets. It probably had to be rebuilt after every minor storm. Travis went to the bow. A large group of naked young children played nearby in the shallow murky water, several of them pushing back and forth a rusting fifty-five gallon drum, sort of like a game of rugby. Most of them had dark round scars on their bodies, like the kind on Nuke and Jebro. One boy had a rubber spatula and some of the others were trying to get it from him. They turned their attention to the boat, waving and yelling at it and splashing over to meet it at the pier. On the shore of the island, just up from a narrow yellow beach, some other children had rigged a piece of wood onto half a denuded set of mattress springs. They would run and jump on it, launching themselves into the air, doing three-sixty flips and landing on their bare feet in the gravel clearing. Some of the children doing flips couldn't have been more than six years old. A thin, shirtless, ancient-looking man sat on top of a metal bucket at the head of the pier. The skin on his body hung loose in wrinkled frowns. He rocked back and forth, licking his toothless gums and grinning as he wagged his finger at the boat. His eyes were caked over gray with cataracts, staring blindly at the boat. Beyond the old man and the children was the bustling traffic of rusting Japanese cars and pickups, their cabs and beds packed tight with men. They leaned into the turn of a perimeter road and swerved to avoid potholes filled with muck and then more running children and other cars with missing tires and doors which were obviously abandoned right where they had broken down. It seemed almost like a joke to see so many cars on an island so narrow that it was almost possible to throw a baseball from one side to the other. More cars darted in and out of dark alleys lined high with patchwork plywood walls, the tops and bottoms of the boards rotted away so that they stood at different heights. Some of the boards were green or pink or white, but most were weathered gray. White smoke rose from the dense decrepit interior of the island and from fires outside several nearby tin and wooden shanties, some of their roofs nothing more than black plastic tarps. Around the fires or around wash tubs, women in skirts and T-shirts and some wearing loose, neon-colored dresses sat on mats or on their haunches. A tangled array of power lines draped over the island like cobwebs, many more poles holding up power lines than there were trees. There was no grass or even any soil. Overall the island smelled strongly like something sour burning, maybe like burning rotten fruit, and Travis could smell shit. A pack of barking snarling mongrel dogs ran by the children playing with the mattress; the lead dog, a white one, had the limp body of a calico cat between its jaws. The last dog limped, running on three legs. Like birds suddenly rising after a speeding school of fish, the children left their game and ran after the dogs, shouting and throwing rocks as they passed a collapsed tanker truck, and vanished behind a long and narrow tin-roofed clapboard building. One small naked child remained at the mattress, jumping up and down by himself on the spring-loaded piece of wood. Flies circled his head.

Travis grabbed the pier, worried his grip might pull it over, not at all sure it was a good idea for Jebro and Nuke to walk across it. They scrambled onto it anyway. The wet brown faces of children peered over the sides of the boat, chattering and giggling. Boyd shouted at the one with the spatula not to touch his pole, then looked around nervously, as if the children were pirates after his ship.

Jebro tossed Kerry back his shirt, then said something to Nuke who then held out Kerry's towel.

"S'all right," Kerry said, not taking it. "Hang on to it an' stay warm."

Nuke smiled at him and pulled the towel over his head like a shroud. Boyd's shirt hung below his elbows and his knees. He did not make any effort to return the shirt, and Boyd did not ask for it. It had been his lucky shirt.

"Okay," Jebro said. "We go home now." He and Boyd looked at each other, saying nothing.

"Monday," Travis said. "Four thirty, and we'll go check out the boats." He pushed off from the pier. Jebro scolded the children in the water to move out of the way. Boyd put the engines in reverse.

"Monday," Jebro said, waving good-bye to Travis and Kerry, then he took Nuke by the hand and led him quickly down the pier. By the time Boyd had the boat turned around and the bow was rising under speed, Jebro and Nuke had hurried out of sight.

"That island done give me the creeps," Kerry said. "You see them dogs? An' that creepy ol' man?"

"Nah," Travis said. "What's really creepy is how all those little kids seemed so happy."

Ebeye Nightlife

At dusk Jebro lay on his mat next to Nuke, listening to him breathe. He wanted to sleep himself—his eyes were closed—but the will to live he had instilled within himself remained so strong (as if he were still fighting to stay afloat) that sleep became a step too close to death. He still felt the continuing bounce and sway of the ocean, as if the concrete under his mat were waiting for him to sleep so that it could open up and suck him down. Nuke slept soundly, having done so shortly after Jebro made him a bowl of hot rice and potted meat. Nuke slept with Kerry's towel under his head, his hands carefully rewrapped with about half as much of the gauze.

Jebro got to his knees, taking a few deep breaths before he stood and rummaged through a bucket of his things. The power was still out. The sewage was still backed up. The block-house was dark except for the lanterns burning in the kitchen where the household had gathered to eat, there and outside on the picnic table by the cemetery because the smell from the kitchen drain, despite the shirt somebody had stuffed down it, was too much for some people. Their voices were loud, laughing at things each other said. Jebro had told them a simple story, that the boat sank and that some Americans brought them home. He had gone to lie down not only because he was sore and tired, but also because they kept asking him questions. Jebro might tell the whole story later, how Nuke had almost drowned, how it was the Americans who sank the boat, but he wanted to speak about it with his father first.

The late ferry would be arriving in about an hour, the one Rujen always caught when he stayed late for church, so rather than fight for sleep or endure being the center of talk at home, Jebro decided to take a fishing line to the pier and wait. He whispered a charm into Nuke's ear, one their mother liked to say to them, a protection against demons who prey on those who sleep, then he slipped out through a window at the other end of the house.

The light of day was almost gone, the sky gray and going black. The wind was still strong, good for blowing away the mosquitoes and the smells and keeping a body free from sweat. Plenty of children still played up and down the roads, and some older boys and girls were out cruising, but most people had gone inside. Lantern light and a thousand voices drifted from the homes. Here and there people came out of the homes and headed for the reef, to use it as a toilet. Nearby and far away, babies wailed, cats fought, and dogs barked. Automobiles shifted gears and squeaked and rattled as their rolling tires spit gravel into wooden fences. Flying overhead and unseen, a bird cried, the shrill noise growing faint, only to rise again as the bird came around again for one more pass. The low light made it hard to see the puddles, but they always formed in the same places and Jebro knew them well. As cars and trucks came by he and the other people either hurried or stopped to avoid getting splashed.

Several radios played the same song, coming from the station at Kwajalein, "The Tide Is High" by Blondie. Jebro liked the song and hummed along with it as he walked to the pier, choosing his route so as to pass from one radio to the next. A girl he had liked since his school days was a big fan of Blondie. She had a cassette her American boyfriend had smuggled from Kwajalein, but no player. Jebro liked Dr. Hook and Kenny Rogers. He had a small Panasonic radio cassette player, but only the radio worked. Most of his fishing gear had gone to the bottom of the ocean with the boat, but he still had a few things. He brought with him a length of twenty-pound test wrapped around a Pepsi can and rigged with a swivel and two number-eight hooks.

Into the dark area behind Ben's Coral Reef Bar, which was closed, Jebro followed the music to find a gang of about fifteen boys, a few of their girls with them. Three of them stood sharing a smoke, the rest were crouched by the radio and passed a jug of homemade liquor, something probably fermented from yeast and sugar water. They were Pako Pako, the Shark Gang. When he was Nuke's age, Jebro was a secret member of the Kakūtōtō, the Naughty Boys. They were at war with the Kuuj Kuuj, the Cat Gang. The Pako Pako were allies. He recognized some of them in the group. They invited him to share what they were drinking. He declined, apologizing as he walked past. It was a small insult, which they would probably dwell on for a while because they were already very drunk and there was nothing else for them to do. Later they might make some enemies and fight, forgetting who the enemies were by morning. In the mornings sometimes these kinds of boys were hanging from a rope.

Not until Jebro got to the pier did he realize that he had brought no bait. No matter. He walked to the end and dangled his hooks over the side, jiggling them until they gained the curiosity of a crab that scurried out of a crack in the concrete. It took a few tries but he finally got one, and baited his hooks with one leg each. He was alone where he stood, behind a shipping container, facing out across the darkening lagoon. A few other people waited for the ferry closer to the beginning of the pier. A radio sang out from a parked truck. A portable generator started humming at the power plant, then the sound of people cussing followed the clang of spilling tools. A dim light leaked out of cracks in the tin wall of the power plant. Jebro tied a rock to the swivel and let it fly, the line leaving the smooth end of the can so fast it sounded like a moth at his ear flapping its wings. He pulled in the slack and sat down on a flat-topped iron cleat.

The tide was low and rising. Moonless nights were good for fishing, but the bottom had been fished out for a long time.

During the day it was sometimes possible to catch mackerel or other schooling fish if they wandered by, but at night, on the bottom, there simply wasn't much left but eels and pufferfish, sometimes nurse sharks after trash. It was good though just to have a line in the water, to feel the possibility in his hand. Across the dark water lay Tar-Wōj, and looking in that direction made Jebro feel cheated. Like Ataji, he had gone to claim what land was his by right, to join himself to the land passed down to him from his ancestors, and while he was there he had felt that connection as if it were the beating of a second hidden heart; but now here he was, right back on Ebeye where Marshallese by law were meant to stay, snapped back as if he were a bird with an elastic tied to his leg. Cheated. He promised himself it would not be long before he tried to go again.

Then he looked toward Kwajalein, scanning the water for the ferryboat, imagining his father sitting in the hold and reading the pamphlets he often brought home from church.

What Came Up from the Mouth of the Mermaid

At one end of the Kwajalein turtle pond was a sluice gate, behind it a large pipe that ran under the dirt road and into the lagoon. The gate was locked into position with two large padlocks, but Rujen had cut them with the bolt cutters he took from the utility truck at the Comm. Center. Using the bolt cutters got his hand bleeding again, throbbing under the bandage already sopping red. The pull of the draining water had been strong, and one dolphin, tired and weak, had been sucked down the first time that Rujen drove it near the pipe. When he closed the sluice gate he found that he had drained more than a foot of water from the pond.

Now, knife in hand, he faced the center of the pond, the mermaid there, the other dolphin listing beside her. It looked so close to death that Rujen thought of waiting just a bit. A blue lamp, now only half under the water, cast dappled light onto the dolphin and the mermaid and the water that spilled off her chin. It was a fine night, cool, with a good breeze for sleeping once Rujen put an end to this. He had a strong feeling of energy, as if he were young again, this feeling keeping his mind off his pain. It felt like winning. He stared at the mermaid for a while, the algae that clogged her mouth, the drooling white woman's torso with the body of a fish. She made no sense. He slogged through the water toward her, toward the dolphin. He would not wait because it made no sense. If later he were caught it did not matter. Because this made sense. He wanted to be quick.

"Yokwe," he said, then he drove the knife down. That was when blood came up from the mouth of the mermaid on Good Friday, 1981.

The Kind of Fish You Keep

THE YELLOW LIGHTS OF Kwajalein shimmered to Jebro's left, their glow spilling onto the water. Above them, atop Kwajalein's water tower, the bright green then white dots of the rotating beacon each glared for an instant on their way around, the long broadening sweep of the beams seeming to claim infinity. In front of Kwajalein the lights of the ferryboat were just visible riding on the water. It was a slow boat, an old Army landing craft, an LCM, and probably twenty minutes away. Jebro thought of Travis, wondering how much he could trust him. Americans could be very friendly if they needed you for something, only to act as if they did not know you the next time you saw them. Jebro knew Boyd could not be trusted, but he thought Travis was different, Kerry as well. He would find out for sure soon enough, and if they tried to get out of replacing the boat, then Jebro was not sure what would be the best thing to do. He had already broken the law, and he had lied about his name. This was what he needed to speak with his father about.

Two small tugs on the line brought Jebro's rear end off the cleat. He crouched, waiting for another, the one he would pull back on. It was probably a puffer or an eel, but until he saw it, it was fun to imagine that it could be anything. *Tug*—Jebro yanked back, feeling the weight and fight of the fish. He piled the line between his legs, bringing it in fast before the fish had a chance to wedge itself inside a hole. It was decent sized, putting up a good fight, and when he hauled it over the side he was surprised, almost to the point of cheering even, that he had caught a red perch, a real fine catch for the pier. It was a good eating fish too, but he knew better than to eat anything caught in the lagoon around Ebeye, the sewage outfall being so close to shore. He unhooked the fish and tossed it back. Then he tossed the rest of the crab. Too disheartening to fish just to fish and to have no use for the catch.

He coiled his line back on the can and sat down again to wait for the LCM, watching as headlights revealed more and more people arriving on the pier to meet it. Their voices carried on the wind, as did smoke from their cigarettes and the sounds of barking dogs and cars and music, and then from somewhere the sound of breaking glass, probably rocks thrown at bottles. Above, clouds moved swiftly past the stars, incredibly bright because of the streetlights being dark. But not as bright as they would have been from Tar-Wōj. The headlights of cars circling the island's dark perimeter road seemed like sentries, keeping people and things contained within. Sometimes for a second the headlights revealed the people squatting on the boulders of the shoreline breakwater. The people came and went, some of them holding flashlights that flicked on and off.

An American man, maybe fifty years old, and his teenage Marshallese girlfriend strolled up to the end of the pier, holding hands. They did not see Jebro where he sat on the cleat. The man leaned the girl against the shipping container and ran his hands up her skirt. She giggled. Jebro slipped quietly away from them, headed to where the LCM would dock. He saw one of his uncles there, Nelu, and some other people he knew, so he held back in the darkness, not wanting to endure their questions. By now most everyone would know he had sunk his father's boat. Ebeye had very few secrets, none within families.

When not much later the gray and dented metal LCM bumped sidelong to a stop, Jebro moved forward, squinting against the spotlights that beamed down on the pier. He watched as the workers filed off, jugs of fresh water and carry bags in their hands. He practiced in his mind what he would say to his father, thinking it would be best to begin by saying plainly that his boat had sunk at sea, so that his father would ask right away about Nuke and be glad to hear he was asleep at home. Then Jebro would tell Rujen everything. But he did not get the chance. Because from the first to the last worker who stepped off the ferryboat, not one of them was Rujen Keju.

Trespassing

AROUND THE BACK OF the Calibration Lab Rujen stumbled through the dark and weeds, keeping away from the road and struggling to hold the slippery plastic sack of flesh from sliding off his back. His two fists held the end of it over his shoulder. The thumb of his tightly bandaged, thorn-punctured left fist pointed up, too swollen and disabled to close over his fingers. Crickets chirped, and the wind soughed through the shaggy branches of ironwood trees behind him. It hurt his neck if he looked up at the stars. Earlier, the bicycle he had borrowed had thrown its chain and he had crashed. The master link was lost. He had left the bicycle inside a Quonset hut at the Boy Scout camp. The handlebars were crooked after the crash. His church slacks and his nice Hawaiian shirt were torn, stained dark in a few places from blood mostly not his own. His elbows and his knees were scratched and bleeding from the crash. His cheek was scratched and bleeding too, but that was from even earlier when he had fallen off the rocks, into the lagoon. His boots were heavy, soaked through with saltwater that stung his wounded feet. The sack had a few holes from the crash. Fluid from it leaked down the small of his back and into his slacks. He had taken the sack from a trash can at the turtle pond. He had washed it in the lagoon before he filled it with the flesh. That was when he fell. At some point he had lost his ID badge. He had lost the knife too, the rainbow trout, but the blade was bent already and dinged and dulled from jabbing and hacking through so much cartilage.

Near the boat shacks by the Round House, a defunct domed radar site, he dropped the sack and unzipped his fly to urinate. He stood beside an open shack that covered the upside-down hull of a catamaran. His hands, he noticed, no longer trembled. His heart no longer beat unnaturally fast. When the bicycle had crashed, he had not blamed it on some force of evil out to get him. His mind was no longer plagued with nagging voices he could not understand. He did not want to think about what had happened at the church. He thought only of going home. Just as his urine began to stream, headlights washed over where he had been walking. It was a police truck, approaching slow along the nearby gravel road. The truck bounced over a rut as it passed the amber lights of the low wooden shelter where stray cats were gassed. The body of the truck was flat white, with black tar slathered on its seams to prevent rust. A red bulb sat dormant on top of the cab. Rujen wondered if the police were looking for him. They could only know of half of what he had done, only of what had happened at the church, that and the crime of missing his boat, making him guilty as a trespasser. The only evidence of his other crime was in the sack, there and a carcass somewhere drifting at the bottom of the lagoon, probably being eaten. Rujen held his breath as the police truck rolled along not far away. The lone policeman inside looked straight ahead, his white face made green by the low light coming from the dashboard. He drove past and kept going, gone out of sight. The night was dark again, noised with crickets and the wind, and the metallic chime of windblown ropes twanging the masts of several nearby sailboats.

Rujen zipped up his fly and threw the sack back over his shoulder. He felt as though he had been beaten badly in a fight. He had no idea of the time, but figured it was not so late that he would miss the midnight boat to Ebeye. He put one painful foot in front of another and plodded toward the pier, keeping away from the lights and the road as much as he could. The smell coming from the sack was strong, but it was a good smell, even though he knew he did not like the taste of the meat. It was a good smell because in a strange, backward kind of way, the insanity that had driven him to possess it—the same insanity that he had feared all day would grip him—was the one thing that got him thinking now that he was more sane than ever.

Not much farther past the marina, and just past where that morning his flip-flop had busted a strap, he turned left to face the security checkpoint at the pier. He headed for the door. The building was rectangular, about the size of a trailer with its windows painted over black. It was attached to a small store, the Bargain Bazaar, where on Mondays and Wednesdays Marshallese workers could buy second-hand toys and clothing donated by Americans. Both buildings fronted the much higher harbor watchtower. A wall-clock visible inside the Bargain Bazaar showed just after nine o'clock. Rujen had been quicker than he had thought. He opened the door, bouncing a little as he adjusted the sack's position on his back, then stepped into the light.

The policeman inside the checkpoint wore a badge that said his name was Oliver Shrevell, but Rujen knew that people called him Oly, like the beer. He was a large man, with pale cheeks so fat his small, thin-lipped mouth looked something like a butthole. He sat behind a long metal table, a soldier magazine in front of him. The walls were white, as was Oly's shirt and the high ceiling racked with bright flourescent lights. The tile floor was gray, flecked with green, indented in spots where the legs of tables once had been. The room was quiet except for the hum of a window-mounted air conditioner, empty of people except for Rujen and Oly. Oly tiredly raised his blue-green eyes from the magazine and asked to see Rujen's badge.

"I'm sorry," Rujen said, shrugging, "but I lost it. I don't know where."

Oly frowned, studying Rujen more closely. "Are you drunk, been drinkin'? You look a little strange. How'd you get so damn tore up? And what the hell you got in that bag? Shit stinks to Hell."

Rujen heaved the sack off his back and set it on the floor. "Fish meat. You want to look at it?" He opened the sack's wrinkled top.

Oly leaned forward as best he could and peered inside the sack. He grimaced. "What kinda fish is that?"

"What kind you think?"

"Is it from a shark? That how you got all cut up, catchin' a shark?"

"No, no shark. I had an accident. I fell off my bicycle, and I fell inside the lagoon."

"Right," Oly said suspiciously, nodding, looking at Rujen as though he was trying to figure something out. "What's your name?"

Rujen said his name, last name first, which was how the police always liked to hear it.

"Yeah, I done figured it was you." Oly's chair squealed across the tile floor as he pushed back from the table and stood. He adjusted his gun belt over his paunch, squinting down at Rujen. "You're that fugitive lunatic been runnin' around, who caused that ruckus up at the church—tearin' down the Jesus and rippin' off his head and God knows what else. Right, bicycle accident—buddy of mine said that mess of yours looked like the work of the devil himself, blood all over the damn place and blood drippin' off the altar like some kind o' satanic damn kind o' antimass! Jesus, I mean, what the hell got into you, boy?"

Rujen felt flushed with guilt. He had tried not to think about the church, and now, unprepared, the consequences were about to catch up with him. He twisted shut the sack and worked to tie the top into a knot. "That was an accident too." He glanced around. "So what, I am a criminal now? What is the charges?"

"Well no, no charges or nothin'—though for the life of me I can't imagine why nobody pressed any—but no, no charges, except you're late, you're trespassin', and I'm gonna write you a ticket for that. Oh, and this was left for you by the priest—probably wants to hook you up with one of them ex-or-cists." He chuckled, holding out an envelope that he took from a drawer. On the envelope was Rujen's name written in Father Trotter's handwriting.

Rujen snatched the envelope out of Oly's hand and put it in his torn top pocket.

Oly stared coldly at Rujen for a moment, then he took a ticket book and pen from the drawer and held them close to his face. "Job site?" he asked sternly.

Rujen absently circled the toe of his soggy boot around a wet spot forming beside the sack. "Sewage plant."

"Supervisor?"

"Andy Thygerson."

Oly wrote with his hand low and tight on the pen, shoulders hunched, brow furrowed. It looked almost as if it were painful for him. "Badge number?"

"Oh . . . I don't know. Maybe . . . I think it started with a seven. Seven, two . . ."

"Right, you lost it. You gotta get a new one tomorrow then, and they charge you, ten bucks I think, because you lost the last one. And fifty more bucks for this. Here." He handed Rujen the ticket. "Lucky for you a water taxi's gonna be here in about half an hour, comin' for that crew worked late on some concrete pour. Go ahead, then. Take a seat with 'em out back—but don't you be rilin' them boys with no more o' whatever satanic mojo-hoodoo bloody shark shit neither, all right?"

Rujen tried to ignore Oly's insult, to contain the anger that had been building ever since Oly had first opened his mouth, but as he stared down at the yellow, two-part ticket in his hand, repeatedly reading the line marked VIOLATION: ***Trespassing***, he suddenly saw how incredibly backward it was, how it made no sense. How could a Marshallese be trespassing on a Marshallese island? The ticket filled Rujen with an unbearable loathing of the ignorant man who had written it. He waved the ticket in front of Oly's face, nearly slapping him with it. "Maybe you better pay *me* fifty bucks! *You pig.*" He spoke the last two words softly, not quite prepared to say them until they were already out of his mouth.

Oly's buttocks-like cheeks flushed red. "Don't you get smart with me, you freak fuckin' lunatic!" He started to come around the table, but he got wedged between it and the wall.

Rujen was already walking away, dragging the dirty wet sack, not once looking back as he pushed through the door at the other end of the room.

"Son of a bitch!" he heard as the door shut behind him.

"Asshole face," Rujen muttered, not loud enough for Oly to hear him.

The dimly lit waiting area in back of the checkpoint was like a patio, with a wooden roof and several wooden benches. Some of the benches—an aisle between them allowing access to the door of the Bargain Bazaar—faced the high gray concrete wall of the harbor watchtower; other benches faced the calm, light dappled water of the harbor and lagoon. A short fence between the checkpoint and the watchtower was topped with curls of barbed wire, as was the fence surrounding the gated entrance to the two-lane concrete pier. The *Tarlang* was tied to the pier, and behind the *Tarlang* was another boat which held in its open bay a yellow submarine. Behind them in a line were three smaller LCMs, a water barge, tug boats at the bend, and at the end a crane. To the left of the pier were two thirty-foot patrol boats in berths.

At the far end of the patio a group of seven or eight Marshallese men sat on two benches they had turned to face each other: The work crew who had a water taxi coming to get them. They all looked at Rujen, obviously having heard most of his exchange with Oly. Rujen knew every one of them; one man was his cousin Alfred. He said hello to them, displaying his trespassing ticket as an explanation for what they had heard, then he sat on a bench near the checkpoint door, not much in the mood for conversation. The crew seemed to understand his wish for privacy and bent back in on a card game they were playing. Their voices were low, backgrounded by the creaking of mooring lines and the grating of the boats against rubber tires chained to the side of the pier.

Rujen leaned back against the bench and breathed deeply, eyes closed, feeling all the different pains in his body sing the various stories of his day. The throbbing of his feet seemed about to burst his soggy boots. Sweat stung the wounds on his arms and legs and face. The fingers of his punctured left hand were almost numb, feeling only cold and pressure as they tapped the envelope in his pocket. He was not ready yet to read it. It was only purgatory not to read it, only minor torment to put off learning of his banishment from Father Trotter's church. *You will take your punishment from almighty God, Rujen Keju.*

He brought to mind Father Trotter fallen to his knees, having to witness Christ's head bleeding upon the altar, the members of his church frozen in the aisle and in their pews in fear and horror and in disgust. It did not matter that it had been an accident. It did not matter how bad his day had been. He saw no way to make amends. He had hurt Father Trotter, maybe his dearest friend, just as much as he had hurt his church. And now, once the story of what Rujen had done quickly spread, it would become as much a part of his identity as his name. People would hate him and they would pity him, and everyone from Andy Thygerson to Caleb Aini to even his own sons would never think of him the same. And if the Americans ever learned of what he was bringing home with him this night? It would make them hate him so much more. They would not care to hear him speak of his insanity, how he had been divinely guided by the eyes of Christ to redeem his soul by the taking of a sack of flesh.

When he thought again of the shining, Marshallese eyes of Christ, the image of them became so vivid in his mind that he feared for a moment he was once again about to go insane. Then, his eyes still closed and staring into the eyes of Jesus Christ, he felt creep over him an uncomfortably familiar understanding of this man whose image he had thoroughly disgraced, an understanding that it seemed he had no right to possess, an understanding of him not as savior nor as a god nor as the son of God, certainly not as part of a termite-riddled crucifix, or even very much as having anything at all to do with the rituals of the church, but an understanding of him as a man, for the first time understanding Christ's words and teachings and the stories of his life as not just Bible verses to learn and to recite, but as the life of a man, a once living breathing man whose ancient land had for so long been occupied and dominated, not so unlike the islands of the Marshallese who had no choice but to submit to the Spanish then the Germans then the Japanese and now the Americans, as Jerusalem had to submit to Rome in the time of Jesus Christ, a man alive in a world of war who dared to preach of love and kindness and sharing, the same virtues long held by Marshallese before they ever heard of Jesus Christ, a man in some ways maybe very stubborn like Ataji Keju, a man who would take beatings and bullets and die defiant before falling in step with anything other than what he believed was right and true. For Rujen to understand Jesus Christ this way was to come to an understanding of himself, not just as a man but as a Marshallese and as the son of his father; and for Rujen to have beside him now what in that moment of insanity the eyes of Christ had told him he should take in order to redeem his soul, to know now the importance of having the strength to take it, this assured him that he would survive this day not in shame and not to care that so many people would hate him or pity him, because in the end he had been true to himself, to his people, and because he had done exactly what his father would have done. In the morning he would read Father Trotter's letter.

Rujen heard a familiar Marshallese voice inside the checkpoint, angry words followed by Oly's angry growl and furniture grating across the floor. Another man cussing and then a thud, a crash like a chair slamming the wall. Then the door flew open, or rather it was banged open with a man's head. The man was Rujen's young nephew Lazarus, wearing only his new khaki shorts, drunk, in handcuffs, being shoved ahead of Oly and another policeman, a shorter man who wore a small wig not well matched to the rest of his hair. Half his white shirt hung outside of his trousers. His wig was a little crooked, too far forward on his head. He and Oly spun Lazarus around so that he was facing Rujen. "Uncle!" Lazarus shouted, managing an awkward smile. Partly sticking out of the leg pocket of his khaki shorts was a ticket identical to Rujen's. The older policeman removed Lazarus's cuffs and gave him a shove just as Rujen stood.

Rujen was knocked back down on the bench with Lazarus sprawled on top of him. He struggled out from under Lazarus, holding his nephew's arm to keep him from taking a swing at the policemen.

"Uncle?" Oly asked, grinning at Rujen. "I shoulda guessed you two were related, cut from the same damn fucked-up cloth that's for sure."

The other policeman laughed with Oly, tucking in his shirt as they went back inside the checkpoint.

"Any time," Lazarus said when the door had shut. "That big guy wants to fight me, I'll fight him any time he wants." He settled down on the bench, his feet out and arms spread wide.

The work crew shuffled over, asking what was going on. Alfred sat on the other side of Lazarus, while the rest stood or sat sideways on the bench in front. Alfred was about Rujen's age, but thinner, and he wore a beard that covered most of his face. Rujen admired Alfred's padded leather boots.

"Aiaa, you look terrible, Rujen," Alfred said. "What have you been doing? And you, Lazarus, nobody has seen you for weeks. Where have you been?"

"Tell them," Rujen said. "Tell them what you told me about your new girlfriend. Did she kick you out?"

“Hey,” Lazarus said, reaching up to gently touch the cut on Rujen’s cheek. “You been fighting too!” His breath was sour with the smell of beer. He looked Rujen up and down. His eyes were bloodshot. “Ōrrōr, looks like you lost.”

Alfred leaned across Lazarus and pinched a dark spot on Rujen’s sleeve. “I think so too. Is all of this your blood?”

“Why are you soaked?” Lazarus asked.

Alfred let go of Rujen’s shirt, now studying his pants. “Who were you fighting with?”

Rujen fastened an undone button in the middle of his shirt. “Maybe I look like it but no, I was not fighting—just an accident, nothing to talk about. Tell us what happened with you, Lazarus. Where are the rest of your clothes?”

Lazarus brought his arms off the back of the bench and rubbed his wrists. He looked once at Alfred then at Rujen, frowning. “That policeman stole my watch, that fat one. He told me they have to take it back to the store, but I know he’s going to keep it. I tried to kick his table on him but I fell down, and then that other one grabbed me so I tripped him on his ass. They hit me couple times but it was nothing. Next time I beat them both.” He sniffed the air, looked around, then reached over and tugged at Rujen’s sack. “What you got in here?”

Rujen saw everyone looking at him, looking at his sack. “Just some ke.”

Lazarus grinned. “I think I know where you got this—Melody told me about them—and today you were there at the pond—I took you there. I never knew you were so sneaky, Uncle!” He laughed. “You should have told me of your plan—I would have helped you, just for something to do.”

“I never really planned it. So tell us, what’s going on with you and Melody?”

“Who is Melody?” Alfred asked.

“You know what she said?” Lazarus asked Rujen, then answered, “She said that later tonight some friends of hers were going to throw those ke into the lagoon.”

“I heard something too about those ke,” Alfred said. “It was some Marshallese from the power plant who caught them, for some Americans who are buying them to keep as pets. You really are sneaky, Rujen."

One of the other workers laughed. His name was Kinoj. "*Boolshit!* How can you keep those things as pets?"

"You can," Alfred said, "I saw it on the television. A place in Hawai'i where they keep some ke in a big pool and they do tricks. They get a fish every time they do a trick. So maybe some people here want to do the same thing."

"Boolshit," Kinoj said, reaching over to slap Alfred's shoulder. "Who told you this story?"

"You know the guy, Jeton, he works as a janitor at the headquarters. I saw him at the snack bar this afternoon."

"That guy is always telling boolshit. I remember once he said the Colonel wanted to paint everything on the island brown."

Lazarus seemed not to be listening, his eyes staring blankly at the watchtower wall. Rujen nudged him. "Come now, tell us your story."

Lazarus looked away from the wall, slowly focusing on the people around him. "Okay," he said, his word followed by an overly dramatic sigh. "If you really want to hear it, but my story is a sad one." He took a moment to look seriously at each member of his audience, then his eyes settled on Alfred. "You haven't seen me because I've been hiding over here, living over here with my American girlfriend. I—"

Alfred whistled, while some of the other men cheered.

"Tell them who she is," Rujen said.

"She works at the bakery," Lazarus said. "Melody, she—"

"That Melody?" Alfred asked, laughing, the others laughing too. "That big girl who works there?"

Lazarus looked hurt. "You think she's funny looking?"

"I always wondered what it would be like with her," Kinoj said. More laughter. "Was she a virgin?"

"Of course," Lazarus said. "And—ah, forget it, if you are just going to laugh at my story . . ."

"No no, go on," Rujen said. "Sorry." He shhh-ed the others.

Lazarus waited a moment, eyeing his audience. "So I really had it good living here, all the best food and beer and living in her nice air-conditioned apartment with the bathtub and big color television, and maybe in a few days I was going to ask her to marry me—I was going to become an American. So I really had it good, and today I rode all over the island on her tricycle, and this afternoon I even went bowling—that kid working there never even asked me if I was Marshallese. Nobody said anything, just like I was an American already. And so tonight—"

"What was your score?" Alfred asked. "I did the same thing once."

Lazarus shrugged. "I never kept the score but I hit plenty, maybe five hundred I think."

Alfred nodded, tugging at his beard.

"So after bowling I went home for some Michelobs, and when Melody got there—*ōttōt!*—I started giving her a real good time, first in the bathtub, but—well, after that in her big bouncy bed and I think somebody must have complained about the noise because that bed was really squeaking, and she was howling I swear just like that siren that goes off every day at six o'clock!" Lazarus laughed now, howling in imitation of the siren as he bounced up and down on the bench.

Kinoj reached over the bench and slapped Lazarus's knee. "You said this was a sad story!"

Lazarus suddenly looked serious again. "It is. I only laugh because that was what I was doing at the time, before the police came."

"Sorry sorry, go on. I want to hear the end of this." Kinoj smiled.

Lazarus waited for Kinoj's smile to drop. "So when the police knocked, 'Police!' they shouted, Melody got really scared. And her face all of a sudden turned bright red—I never seen anything like it! She rolled off the bed and started walking in circles, bent over and holding her arms across her tits—like this—like she thought maybe they could see her through the door—so stupid. I had no idea what to say to her. So then she looks at me like it was my fault, like I was the one howling—maybe I was making some noise too, some whooping you know, but not so loud as that—then she put her mu'umu'u on backwards and inside-out and she opened the door. I hid under the sheets with another Michelob, listening to her trying to lie that she was alone being quiet—so stupid. All she had to say was her boyfriend was there, and they would have thought I was an American and told her to stop howling. Instead she made them suspicious, so they kept asking questions—and then, you know how sometimes if you drink it wrong beer gets up your nose?—I couldn't help it and I sneezed—three times! Right away she started crying almost as loud as she was howling, and then she was telling the police how sorry she was for breaking the law and she kept saying, '*Please don't tell anybody, pleeeease!*' Then it was her—can you believe it?—Melody was the one who pulled the sheet off me! What kind of girlfriend is that?"

Rujen saw that Lazarus was genuinely hurt, and he tried not to laugh along with the others, but he couldn't help it, not when Kinoj made the siren sound, and with Alfred off the bench and turning circles to mimic Melody covering her breasts.

At one point Lazarus seemed almost about to laugh as well, but he steeled himself and waited for the laughter to quiet. He refused several pleas to finish his story before he finally continued. "So Melody was crying and crying, still holding her tits real tight and looking scared like she was the one they were going to send back to Ebeye. And what could I do? I was sitting there naked with beer and snot on my face, and those policemen were just standing there looking at me like I was some kind of demon before one found my shorts and threw them in my face. Melody didn't even say good-bye, didn't even look at me, when they dragged me out of there and took me to the jail. And I never got my shoes, all the clothes and things she bought me, only these shorts and the watch—now that is gone too." He held up his ticket. "All the time I spent over here with her and all I get is this ticket, trespassing, fifty bucks—so you see my story really is a sad one."

Rujen put his arm around Lazarus. "Yes, your story is sad, but someday I think you'll laugh about it too, maybe with your next American girlfriend. No need to worry about it."

"You should try that girl at the laundry," Kinoj said. "I heard she likes Marshallese."

"Not her," one of his coworkers scolded. "She's already married. Try that girl who works the snack bar at Emon Beach. One time she gave me a free ice cream."

"Boolshit," Kinoj said.

Lazarus was looking at his ticket. "I hate this thing," he said. "What's the difference if I come over here?"

Rujen showed him his own ticket. "Look," he said, smiling. "Your uncle is a guilty trespasser too. And my sons, Jebro and Nuke, they are also trespassing tonight on Tar-Wōj."

"Your sons better be carful," Alfred said. "There's a mission tonight—I heard the missiles are coming about eleven o'clock."

"Who told you that?" Kinoj asked. "Jeton?" Alfred laughed with him.

"Those missiles never hit Tar-Wōj," Rujen said. "Always more north. My sons will be fine. Right now I bet they're catching coconut crabs or fishing."

"Good," Kinoj said. "I like it when boys like yours go trespassing on the outer islands. All boys should go if they have the chance, instead of just laying around and drinking." He slapped Lazarus's knee.

"Maybe we all should go," Alfred said. "We should go live on those islands and tell the Army to shoot their missiles at Ebeye instead!" Kinoj and the others, not laughing, seemed to be giving Alfred's proposal serious thought.

The drone of approaching outboard engines signaled the arrival of the water taxi. Its lights were visible coming around the pier. "Come," Rujen said to Lazarus. "Help your poor old uncle carry his ke down to the pier." He stood, the pain in his feet worse now that he had rested them.

Lazarus pushed himself up from the bench and slapped his ticket across his thigh. "How could I have been trespassing when she invited me to stay with her? It makes no sense. I am *not* going to pay this thing." He tore the ticket into several pieces and tossed them high over his shoulder.

"I know," Rujen said, watching the pieces flutter to the ground. "I was thinking the same thing. It makes no sense."

"Just a few more days," Lazarus said, "and I think I would have been an American. What shit luck."

"Maybe someday you'll get another chance," Rujen said. He handed Lazarus the sack. "If not, you know, it is not always so bad to be a Marshallese."

War

In the lee of Tar-Wōj in darkness Ņoniep rises within a shallow part of the sea and becomes aware, his soul alive within his ghost, his once magical body now dead and wholly carnal down below. He sees, but not by light, that a massive swarm of triggerfish, black ones, has already eaten his eyes and lips and the long-lobed ears he took so long to grow. With no lips he looks as though he grins. The fish have opened a hole in his gut and fight to get inside. A pair of nurse sharks linger, but they seem too shy to take their share. Ņoniep is confused, frightened as he rises and sees the stripping of his tattooed flesh, but then, when he ascends into the wind and the waves caress his soul, he finds waiting for him his spirit canoe, and it speaks to him, reminding him of who he is and of the souls that he has died to save.

He paddles now, stroking through the pass and into the lagoon, his canoe riding cleanly on the water and leaving not a ripple in its wake. His paddle strokes are deep but meet with only a slight resistance. It is by the stroking of the paddle, just by the rhythm he creates, that the goddess Lippidjowe graces him with speed. In the sky he sees the stars as suns, one farther than another into liquid purple infinity. Their light is glossy wet and blue. His whole world is cast in different shades of blue, his vision startlingly clear and able to focus on things near and far in the same precise detail. The extent of his vision is limited only by the curvature of the Earth, not at all limited by the night. He has no sense of smell or taste. He can touch, feel the water and the wind, but they are neither warm nor cool. His hearing is acute like his vision, but does not range as far. His ghost is simply what he wishes it to be, an image of his former self. He knows he could just as well take the shape of a cloud or a rock or inhabit the body of a tree. His soul is like a fluid ball, fragile, yet alive with the power that only his death could bring. He looks across the water, searching for the demons who are out to rob him of his soul, Kwōjenmeto and his beast, M̧ōn̄āļapeņ. He does not see them, but he knows them well enough to know they must be hidden, disguising their approach. By now they surely smell his soul.

Ņoniep trains his reaching gaze on the darkened slum of Ebeye, the demon blighted island he more aptly names Meļaļ. He knows these demons by their names: Jibukra, the leprous demon sitting naked on the beach, the water lapping at her thighs and soaking up the puss that dribbles from her wounds. Jibukra's slick is glassy on the water where the children always play. She gratifies herself with the stiff and bloated body of a long dead eel, pausing now and then to expel a gurgling sigh as she gives birth to hoards of flies. Lowat, his spiny limbless body lying in a milky puddle, swelling then deflating like a pufferfish. The swamp of his rotten mouth breeds mosquitoes, escaping in a cloud with every wheezing bubbling breath. Kidudujet, like a flying fat-lipped trumpetfish, a demon gifted with the skill of kissing sickness into every sore his snout can find. Lejron̄, like a sea slug, whose gassing anus fills the air with a rancid stench of death. Kuran̄, Loojwa, Komle, Malūen, Jiruullōn̄, Wōnoot, Lomonlalok, Kamrōk, demons who bring on coughing, chills, fevers, headaches, the sea-ghost sickness, brain damage, weakness, heart attacks, and parasites. The *eakeak*, ugly little snot-nosed goblins whose beaked mouths spit out rot and chew on things until they fall apart. The *mejenkwaads*, hungry ogress demons that suck the life from babies' navels, making once-plump babies as thin and wrinkled as their grandparents, doomed to die and lose their souls before one year of life. The *kijon̄ran*, a clan of rat-like demons who urge the people to indulge in excess, who now urge a group of boys to drink until they vomit in the road. One boy is left behind and falls down in his vomit. The *kijoñran* dance around his body, calling for the roaming *kakwōj*, demons tutored by Kwōjenmeto in the art of stealing souls. Their long and filthy fingernails poke and prod the weak, the drunk, the drugged, the lost, the dying sad and hopeless, gently scraping out their souls, a harvest for their masters, the evil Wūllep and his cohort Ļajibwinām̧ōņ.

Into this Meļaļ, this playground of demons, Ņoniep goes alone. He is strong, his soul vibrant with the knowledge and the powers he has taken all his life and now his death to cultivate. But it may not be enough. Not alone, not without Etao giving Wūllep what he wants, not enough against this army of evil to bring the stolen souls of Ebeye back to purity, to return the ones belonging to the living, to guide the others on to Ewerōk, home of the souls of the dead, where kindness and plenty, not pain and darkness, can be theirs forever. It is a desperate quest to save so many thousand souls, when all Ņoniep's powers might not even be enough to save his own.

The gentle people of Ebeye, their tiny island barren as a sand spit, more filthy and more crowded than almost any other place on Earth, have managed to live in peace, to find happiness at times despite their plague of demons, and as much as such a life allows; but all too clear is Wūllep and Ļajibwinām̧ōņ's design, to increase the host of blackened souls on Ebeye until their numbers exceed all others—to win the balance to their evil side and revel in the sudden mayhem it will bring. Soon neighbor will hate neighbor, the containment and the crowding and the mindless boredom will suddenly become too much, and then the people of Meļaļ, no more the gentle people they once were, will as one, like rats trapped too long inside a box, become vicious, cruel, and violently insane.

Closer now, Ņoniep hears the squalling tortured souls of jellyfish babies, a beacon to finding all the other shriveled blackened souls seething in a pile in the middle of the dump. The souls are veiled by the rancid smoke from smouldering heaps and pits of trash. Three swollen blistered corpses of dogs lie around the souls like offerings. The dogs are being eaten by a swarm of rats, many more rats than there are souls. Ņoniep looks away from the souls and finds their ghosts, among them the ghosts of boys who died by suicide, circling round the island in a ghost truck, seeding evil visions in the minds and dreams of others ripe to join them. Ņoniep also sees Jebro just past the pier, walking with his limping father. Seeing Jebro is unexpected, unwanted; Ņoniep had hoped to keep him away this night, safely on Tar-Wōj. Something must have happened, but Ņoniep does not have the time to find out what. Jebro puts an arm around his father and helps him home.

Ņoniep turns his attention to the beach and chants a charm that makes Jibukra fall asleep. She slumps, falls back, her head cushioned by a balled-up soiled Pampers, her eel remaining stuck inside her. Her gut heaves with labored breathing and she snores. None of the other demons are aware that Ņoniep approaches. He must put them all to sleep, paralyze them before he can revive and purify the souls. The task is so much easier if the demons do not see him first. Any other way might be impossible, there being so many of them. His luck is going good. It seems almost too good. And it is, because before Ņoniep can begin his charms, he feels an annoying tingle begging him to gaze behind, which he does—his new awareness suddenly revealing to him Kwōjenmeto and M̧ōñāļapeņ, Wūllep's most feared and fiercest demons, coming across the lagoon. Kwōjenmeto paddles fast while M̧ōñāļapeņ at the bow is bound and gagged, his muscles taut and rippling as he struggles to break free. Kwōjenmeto's fulgent head is burning bright, so bright it nearly hides his grin as he reaches forward and rips loose M̧ōñāļapeņ's gag.

M̧ōñāļapeņ opens wide his toothy mouth and howls, a tormented, desperate cry of hate and pain which causes every demon on Meļaļ to look, to shriek in both sympathy and fear. Then they discover what Kwōjenmeto is directing them to see, the ghost and soul of Ņoniep paddling through the shallows near the island, fumbling in his hurried preparations to disable them with charms. Their shrieking rises to a frenzy, angry now, ripe with lusty hatred of the little magic dwarf who should have known he had no chance. As Ņoniep beaches his canoe, the demons fly to him.

The Scream

By the back of the cemetery Jebro tended a driftwood fire, glancing from time to time at his father, who slowly bandaged his wounds while sitting on a bucket outside the washroom. The power was still out. Jebro's uncle Nelu cut meat by lantern light on a table near the kitchen door. Both Jebro and Nelu had insisted that Rujen find the doctor to sew closed the wounds on his hand. One wound was clear through, clotted black with blood. And he would need some medicine, the red antibiotics, to fight off infection. Rujen had said that he would wait until morning, when he could go to the hospital on Kwajalein, which was obligated to treat him because he had hurt his hand on the job. He had said no more about how his injuries happened, nothing about where he got the meat, nothing except that his boots were stolen and that he had a bicycle accident. "Later," he had said to Jebro. "After I clean up we will talk." He looked beaten, and he walked as if he were a man twice his age. Earlier, when he had asked Jebro why he was on Ebeye and not Tar-Wōj, Jebro also said very little about his day, only that the boat had sunk and that Nuke was well and sleeping. He agreed with his father that later would be a better time to talk.

Inside the house some people snored. In other houses people snored and sometimes babies cried. Traffic on the roads was light for a Friday night, the lack of power leaving nothing very much to do but sleep. The fire was large, popping, beginning to coal, its heat driving red ants and roaches out from under the gravel near it. The wavering light of the fire reached into the cemetery and danced over an old white dog who slept with her back against a concrete cross. Jebro remembered playing with that same dog when she had been a puppy, around the time Nuke was born. It seemed odd that the dog had become so old so soon.

Nelu brought a tray of meat and set it on the gravel by the fire. He and Jebro leveled the coals and set up the grills, two racks from old refrigerators and part of a heavy screen that had been used to sift rocks from sand. Nelu was a few years younger than his brother Rujen, and he had long curly hair that fell almost to the middle of his back. He was a member of the Hippies gang that gathered at the Kitco bar. They smoked marijuana from Pohnpe when they could get it. Sometimes Nelu worked as a laborer for AIC, the construction outfit on Ebeye. "Let the grills get hot," he said. "So the meat will sizzle. I always like to hear that first sizzle."

Rujen hobbled over from the washroom, his bandaged feet in socks and Nelu's rubber slippers. "Come with me, Jebro," he said. "Nelu can cook while we go over to the log and talk. I heard some missiles are coming too, maybe we will see them."

Nelu frowned, obviously disappointed that he would have to wait even longer to learn what had happened with Rujen and Jebro.

"Are you sure you want to walk?" Jebro asked his father.

"Just sit here by the fire," Nelu said, looking for something to sit on.

"I can make it to the log," Rujen said. He headed slowly in that direction.

The fat, sunbleached log was less than a minute's walk from the house, and had drifted onto the island years earlier. A storm had pushed it far enough up so that it sat just like a bench on the side of the road at the northeast bend of the island. From the log it was possible to see both into the lagoon and out to sea. It was a good place to sit and talk and feel the breeze. On a night like this, when the streetlight above the log was out, it was also a good place to look up at the stars. Most of the top of the log was whittled almost flat from peoples' carvings upon carvings of names and hearts and sharks. Other spots were smooth, slightly indented from so many people sitting. The sides were covered with more carvings and painted graffiti, every gang on the island claiming the log as their own. Jebro let his father pick his seat first, then he sat beside him. The wind was strong in their faces, wet with salt spray coming off the ocean, smelling faintly of feces that had been deposited on parts of the reef still exposed.

"Long time now, I never really looked up at the stars," Rujen said, wincing as he leaned back. "Do you know the name of that one, that group there?" He pointed with his bandaged hand.

Jebro laughed. "Of course I know that one—Jebro, king of the stars. 'When Jebro rises he makes all the people happy.'"

"The night you were born I saw Jebro winking at me, straight overhead, and I knew that had to be your name."

Jebro groaned. "You always tell me this story whenever we look at the stars. Tell me what happened with you on Kwajalein. How did you get hurt, and how did you get that bag of ke?"

"Wait. How about those stars over there? Do you know what that group's name is?"

"Kouj, the octopus. He holds the ax that killed him."

"How about the American name? Do you know what the Americans call it?"

"No, what?"

"Okay then, I'll teach you. That is Orion, the hunter. You can see he has a bow and arrow, and he has a knife in his belt."

"Maybe, but I think it looks more like an octopus. What is Jebro then, what do the Americans see in Jebro?"

Rujen thought for a moment. "It was something, but I can't remember. When I was a boy I had a map of the stars, many maps of all kinds. On the star map the stars were connected with lines, making all the shapes. But all I remember is Orion and one called Scorpio, the one in summer we call Tūmur. Do you know what is a scorpion?"

"Yes, with the poison tail."

"If you look at Tūmur you can see a scorpion too. I also had a map of the moon, like a picture. I thought for a long time the moon had water because the map said it had seas." Rujen laughed. "You know, I was wondering all day whatever happened to those maps I had on Tar-Wōj, a big stack of them, and then—it was when I crashed on my . . . on this bicycle I borrowed—right in front of one of those portable toilets at the Boy Scout camp. When I got back up that was when I remembered."

Jebro had lost what his father was talking about, watching a gang of boys pass quietly behind the log. "You remembered what?"

"My maps. One night I found my maps in an outhouse, in the toilet pit and nailed to the wall for wiping paper. I remember being so mad that I ran away from home, but when I got to the ocean there was no place left to go!" He laughed. "I think now that maybe it was my father who put my maps in the outhouse, to teach me something."

"Why did you collect maps?"

"Like you used to collect rocks and shells, I think, to look at and play with. But when I was a boy I really thought I was going to visit all those places on my maps."

Jebro laughed. "Even the moon and the stars?"

"No, maybe not those places."

"Do you know that group of stars?" Jebro pointed.

"What is that?"

"Iju-pilo, the blind woman led by her daughters. And I think that one next to it is a needlefish but I forget the name."

"That one looks like a canoe. See the outrigger? I bet that is a canoe."

"I think it looks like a bird."

Rujen looked to be deep in thought for a few moments. "The important ones are all the sons of Lōktañūr, the brothers of Jebro and Tūmur. If you know all those stars you know when to plant things and when is a good time for sailing to different islands and when to get ready for storms. Do you know which one is Lōktañūr?"

"No."

"I thought I knew where to look, but I forgot. Maybe she is not around this time of year."

"Your father would know. I think he knew all the stars."

"Yes, he was very smart with all the old knowledge, all about the stars and the swell science and sea signs. He could tell if a storm was coming even if the sky was sunny. I wish I had learned from him." Rujen fiddled with the bandage on his hand. "So tell me, what happened with you and Nuke out there?"

Just then the streetlight overhead flashed on, as did lights all over the island. Radios played, static blared from televisions, washing machines started spinning, fans rattled, startled animals ran, and from near and far came the pop and sizzle of sparks—an entire carnival of electric sound that caused several people in the nearby homes to cheer. Farther away a woman screamed, a terrible scream almost as if she were being stabbed.

"Hey!" Rujen said, looking around. "Good thing!"

Jebro looked back up into the sky, squinting. Because of the light overhead he could not see the stars, only three flaming streaks of light, warheads leaving trails, headed for the heart of the lagoon. That woman kept on screaming.

Bull's-Eye

ETAO SOARS THROUGH the clouds like a god, boasting of his godhood high above the choppy Kwajalein lagoon. He has bug-eye goggles strapped to his face, white cotton wristbands on his wrists. His number 33 jersey, home gold, flaps against his cool, dampened skin. The wind sings past his ears. Streaks of vapor run off his goggles and fly off his face. Out of the clouds the goggles reflect stars. Below him, on darkened Ebeye's grimy beach, the ghost of Ņoniep battles demons. Ņoniep cannot defeat so many, only try to hold them back with charms. He slowly fails. One demon, Jibukra, is almost close enough to lick his soul. She licks the air, flashing teeth, edging closer. Behind her, an army of demons howls. Ņoniep stands by his spirit canoe, paddle raised, chanting so fiercely that his ghostly image wavers.

Farther away from the island, Etao sees the bright burning head of the demon Kwōjenmeto, who paddles easily to hold against the current of Ņoniep's charms. Potent Kwōjenmeto is the largest drain on Ņoniep's power, the demon from whom he has the most to fear. Bound tightly at the bow of Kwōjenmeto's canoe is his enraged pet, M̧ōñā̧lapeņ, who strains and trembles as he struggles to break free. M̧ōñā̧lapeņ's teeth gnaw and tear the scarred, rubbery flesh of his lips, making a bloody bubbling mess of his mouth as he wails of the hearts he has failed to devour. M̧ōñā̧lapeņ has gone insane with hunger, a ravenous danger even to himself. He is no longer useful to his master Kwōjenmeto. Kwōjenmeto is calm, so obviously aware of

Ņoniep's dwindling power, pooling his own for the disgrace he must deliver.

Etao waits, enjoying the drama down below, laughing at the seriousness of all the players. They do not see him flying through the clouds; they are too concerned with each other's charms and howlings to hear him laughing. Soon Etao will enter the game, when what he knows is coming will make his entrance something to remember. While he waits, to prepare, he flies away to a cloud he judges to be at the distance he desires, and with a giant, godlike hand he levels it flat. Then he flies a little higher, half again the height of his body, and punches a hole through another cloud over his head. He drifts down and stands on the leveled cloud, waiting, several paces between himself the hole above. He adjusts his goggles, cracks his knuckles, and bends from side to side for a little calisthenic stretch.

The cloud on which Etao stands glides across the sky, carrying him to a point almost directly over Kwōjenmeto and M̧ōñāļapeņ. This is when his moment comes, his timing perfect, when three warheads break into the atmosphere and streak red-hot toward the lagoon. Etao snaps his fingers and the lights of Ebeye suddenly blink on, every type of electric thing becoming noisily alive. A woman down there screams. It is all the distraction Etao needs.

Knees bent, with his hands outstretched and his back to the hole, Etao catches one of the warheads and tucks the glowing oblong thing low by his waist. Its heat is like the sun, but it does not burn him, not Etao who once was buried in an oven. He pivots left, his right knee rising level with his waist, his right hand rising with the warhead as he uses his momentum for a strong one-footed leap, his body angled sideways toward the hole, hand high as he releases the warhead with a quick, downward snap of his wrist, sending it on a high arc toward its goal. He lands back down on the cloud, facing the hole as the red-hot warhead drops cleanly through. "Skyhook!" he shouts. He whoops and claps his hands to applaud his own superior skill. One of the other warheads strikes the island of Illeginni, the third splashes into the lagoon after being missed by one of two missiles launched from Meck.

Etao's warhead continues to fall at increasing speed, headed where he had all along intended it to go, straight on target to ruin the lives of two unsuspecting demons. In just an instant, as Etao watches eagerly, the warhead sears through M̧ōñāļapeņ's bonds, slicing open his belly before crashing through the bottom of Kwōjenmeto's canoe. M̧ōñāļapeņ shrieks, looking down as slick white guts bulge out from his wound.

Kwōjenmeto jerks back his fulgid head and looks into the sky, hand raised as though to cast some evil spell at his attacker. Etao gazes back at him, dancing on a cloud, laughing so hard he pees, his urine falling like rain on Kwōjenmeto's face, blinding him from seeing M̧ōñāļapeņ—the beast now free to act upon his insane rage to kill and feed. M̧ōñāļapeņ leaps to the back of the canoe, indifferent to his massive wound, and lops off his master's bright swollen head in one enormous bite. The rest of Kwōjenmeto's body shrivels, his open neck bleating with the sound of gas escaping from a bladder. M̧ōñāļapeņ's spilling guts droop and bloat, piling around his bony legs as he gulps down what is left of Kwōjenmeto's carcass. When M̧ōñāļapeņ finds his master has no heart to stuff inside his secret sucking mouth, he lifts his head and shrieks again.

The canoe slips cleanly under the chop, leaving frenzied M̧ōñāļapeņ tangled in his guts and splashing on the surface. He stuffs the guts into his mouth, no concern for anything but to keep on feeding as he sinks down and out of sight, devouring himself on his way to the bottom of the lagoon. Etao flies away laughing.

The tip of Jibukra's tongue is just beginning to lap at Ņoniep's weary, deflating soul, sticking to it, when suddenly the island's lights flash on and the sounds of things electric start up blaring. Ņoniep falters, startled, but keeps on chanting. A woman screams. Jibukra pauses, watching warheads streaking toward the atoll. Ņoniep only glances at the warheads, desperately knowing how close he is to failing. It is not within him to accept defeat, but seeing it, how near it looms, fills him with a sadness for the souls he knows he cannot save. As Jibukra turns her gaze to Ņoniep and grins, he cannot help but visualize the wave of evil soon to follow his destruction. She opens wide her filthy mouth, thick saliva dripping, and strains to sink her crooked teeth into his soul. It seems to him that he has lived his life for nothing, only to die then lose his soul at the dawn of total evil on Meļaļ.

Before Jibukra's drooling toothy jaws snap tight, the air is shattered with the sound of M̧ōñāļapeņ shrieking, a shriek of pain that causes tremors in the evil forces Ņoniep fails slowly to repel. It seems too much to hope for, to believe the tide of battle might be changing. But like feeling the sudden slacking of an undertow, no longer needing to work so hard to stay afloat, Ņoniep then feels it in his soul that Kwōjenmeto, master demon of Meļaļ, has made some fatal error and now he is no more. The other demons feel the loss as well, wailing in confusion, crying out for their master who to them must have seemed invincible. Ņoniep has no idea what has happened, no time or chance to turn and look. He fears it must be a trick, expecting Kwōjenmeto at any moment to grip his soul. But when nothing happens, and he feels the glow of focused power now flowing strongly through him, he hesitates no longer and takes advantage of the demons' chaos. Stepping sharply forward with his paddle, shoving Jibukra back, he chants to all the panicked demons of Meļaļ:

I charm you away, disappear
I charm you so that you will close your eyes and die
Come on, die. Go die
I step on you and trample you
I throw the magic spears
I stab your eyes so that they decay and close
I fight with you

Ņoniep's power is so much greater than he had ever expected. Jibukra falls into the sand, her eyes blinded. She wails, her body infected with an advancing state of rot. The other demons drop back and try to hide or flee, while in the distance M̧ōn̄āļapeņ shrieks again. Then he is gone. Ņoniep steps backward now with his paddle high, chanting to the souls that he has come to save:

I let myself into the medicine of the north
The medicine of the south
The medicine of the east
The medicine of the west
I extend my hand to you
I extend my soul to you
I make you untouchable, invincible
Grow, grow, spring up and find your bodies or your ghosts
Animate your souls
Awake, awake, those of you who died
See your spirit canoes rise up from the water
Find your guide to Ewerōk, your destiny of paradise

Ņoniep steps forward again and chants destruction to the demons. Stepping back he calls the souls to join him. Forward and back, forward and back, his chants becoming excited then soothing and subdued. Some demons are escaping, others burrow out of reach. Ņoniep knows that for quite a while none of them will face him. A light rain begins to fall, almost like a mist. It makes rainbow halos glow around the streetlights. Jebro and his father hurry under cover by their house. Smoke rises from a fire there. The rain, a magic rain, falls gently on the souls piled at the dump and washes them free of the taint of evil. The rain enlivens them and fills them so that once again they are round and light and full. They rise, thousands of them, many of them returning to the living, others finding long lost ghosts that lead them to the water, where one after another of their sunken spirit canoes rises up from the bottom.

Ņoniep has never been more pleased, his soul beaming as each of the ghosts greets him and thanks him. Into his own canoe he loads the helpless souls of jellyfish babies, still squalling, pained by the vulgarity of their short and tortured lives. When all of the other souls are in their canoes, extending up and down the length of Ebeye, they raise their paddles and cheer for Ņoniep to lead them on to Ewerōk.

Ņoniep slides his own canoe into the water, but before he can paddle to the front of his flotilla, he hears demonic growling close behind him. He whirls around with his paddle raised, prepared to fight, only to find Etao bursting into laughter.

"You look funny as a ghost," Etao says, running his fingers through Ņoniep's face.

Ņoniep is glad to see his friend, proud of him for coming back in this time of need. He stares at the shell still hanging on the outside of his jersey. "I should have guessed you had something to do with this. What happened to Kwōjenmeto and Ṃōñāļapeņ? How did you destroy them?"

"I never even touched them. You did it, you exploded them with your magic. Like you did to this one." He pokes his toe into the liquified remains of Jibukra.

"No . . . really?" Ņoniep studies Etao's smiling face. "I never know when to believe the things you say."

"I saw the whole thing while riding one of those warheads. Did you see them?"

"Yes . . . well, no. Etao, listen to me—you still must give up that piece of shell. You must return it to your father so that he never tries this again. You know he will if he can't go back to the stars."

Etao leans into Ņoniep's canoe and tickles one of the souls of jellyfish babies. It quiets for a moment then continues squalling. He looks up at Ņoniep. "Maybe so much fighting my father all your life, always trying to be the opposite of him, is what has made you into a very good dwarf, a better dwarf maybe than if my father had left long ago. If I return this shell then what will you do? What will others like you do? No, it is better that I keep it, better for people to have someone like my father to fight against. Besides, I am having too much fun with this thing." He flicks the shell with his finger. "Now, how about we finish that game of hide-and-seek?"

"You are impossible, Etao. I hope someday my words make sense to you—before your father and Ļajibwinām̧ōn̄ turn this world inside-out."

"So what about the game?"

"I am dead, you fool, a ghost. What do I need with games when I am going to Ewerōk, eternal paradise for the souls of the dead. I will miss you, my friend, and now I must say good-bye."

"Not even one quick game? I promise not to cheat."

N̦oniep groans. "You never listen. Look around at all these ghosts waiting for me. I am their guide, and we are going to where everything will be peaceful and relaxing for all eternity."

"That sounds like a very boring thing to do, even for you. Maybe you will come back, crazy with boredom, and then we can really have some fun!"

"No, Etao," N̦oniep says as he settles into his canoe. "I am not coming back. But maybe someday you will come and join us."

"Not as long as I can do this!" Etao pulls a pair of goggles from his pocket and straps them on his face. Before N̦oniep can ask him what they are for, Etao shoots into the sky and seems headed for the stars. N̦oniep stares for a while at the spot where Etao disappeared, then whispers a good-bye.

N̦oniep takes his position at the head of the canoes and leads his charges south. They pass a dolphin swimming away from Kwajalein. The ghost and soul of another dolphin, its mate, rides above it. N̦oniep invites the dolphin ghost to follow, but it ignores him and stays close above its mate.

The flotilla travels fast, passing Lib then Namu then Jabwot on to Mili atoll, gateway to the calm, sacred waters that take them on to Ewerōk. The island of the dead is long, dark, quiet, surrounded by a low stone wall, not what N̦oniep had expected. There is no wind, only cool still air. No ghost birds chirp. No ghost crabs crawl. All of Ewerōk seems only ghost trees that form broad canopies, their leaves and branches making not the slightest brush or clack. The island is narrow when looked at from its end, but infinitely dark and deep when seen from its side. N̗oniep instructs the others to wait by the wall while he paddles around to look for the entrance.

Nothing moves beneath the canopies as N̗oniep makes his way around the bend of the island. Then, when he is out of sight of his fellow souls, he finds a spirit sitting on the edge of the wall, his toes drawing circles in the calm flat water. He looks sad, bored even. N̗oniep paddles up to him and asks him who he is.

The spirit looks up slowly, managing a weak smile after glancing once at the squalling souls of jellyfish babies in N̗oniep's canoe. "I am L̗ōrōk," he says, "spirit of the south, keeper of this home of the souls of the dead. I suppose you have come seeking paradise. You have my blessing to enter if you wish, but I would not recommend it."

N̗oniep peers into the dark interior of the island. "Has something ruined Ewerōk? Where are all the other souls?"

L̗ōrōk sighs. "I thought it was a very fine idea, to provide a place for souls where they would want for nothing, need nothing, where everything was provided for them, but all that did was give them nothing to do but sleep. When they wake they are unhappy because they have no use for themselves. That is the nature of a paradise. You may stay if you wish, that is your right. But your eternity will not be a happy one."

N̗oniep feels a rising panic, his understanding of things turning upside down. "But I have brought many, so many souls have followed me here. And I have these babies, tortured souls who are desperate to find peace. How . . . what am I supposed to do?"

"If you are smart, you will lead your group of souls back to the islands of their ancestors, the islands of their children, and their children to come. Let them become ekjabs and inhabit the trees and the rocks and the reefs. Let them fly with the birds and swim with all the creatures in the lagoons and the sea. Tell them to be kind, to take an interest in things and to help people. They can even cause a little mischief if they wish, stir things up to keep the world exciting. Those are the things better suited for the dead, not this tragic place of sleep and boredom."

N̹oniep looks once more at dark dead Ewerōk then agrees with L̹ōrōk's wisdom, already knowing what tree it is he will inhabit—the breadfruit tree soon to become Jebro's first canoe. "Why do you remain here then? Why not take these souls and do what you say?"

"It is too late for them now that they have lost their minds by so much sleeping. I only stay because I know I must warn others like yourself. So I sit here, that is all I will ever do."

"I am going to do as you advise, L̹ōrōk, but because you are so lonely I promise to come back and visit you from time to time. Maybe I can introduce you to my friend Etao."

"Oh, I have heard of him! That would be very nice if someday he could visit!"

"I promise I will speak to him," N̹oniep says as he pushes off the wall to paddle away. He waves one last time to L̹ōrōk before he passes back around the bend.

N̹oniep has quite a bit of trouble convincing the others not to enter Ewerōk, but when he leaves most of them dig in with their paddles and follow. Some of them leave the flotilla at Ebon, some at Jaluit and Majuro. Most of them continue on to Kwajalein, where one by one N̹oniep guides them into trees and birds and fish and rocks and reefs.

By early morning, all that remain with him are the souls of jellyfish babies, still squalling in the bottom of his canoe. As the red sun rises above the pale, cloudless horizon, he paddles them past the misting breakers that shatter on the reef and then out across the ocean. The water is rough, carved deep with troughs and peaked with whitecaps, but it does not impede the progress of N̹oniep's spirit canoe. He paddles into the bright rising sun, racing birds headed out to feed, gaining on a traveling pod of whales. Some of the whales rise and fall heavily on their backs, others rise and spout warm spray that carries on the wind and makes rainbows in the morning light.

Ņoniep calls to them when he nears, chanting into them the power to see him. Gracefully, gently, they circle close by his spirit canoe and he speaks to them, holding up the jellyfish babies for their big black eyes to see. He asks them for their help, and without very much delay they accept his proposal kindly, that to each of the whales' souls Ņoniep will pair the soul of a jellyfish baby, so that over time, with love, they might stop their squalling and maybe even learn to sing.

Acknowledgments

The author would like to thank the following people whose work was consulted in the writing of this book: William John Alexander, Takaji Abo, William Cahill, Byron Bender, Alfred Capelle, Tony DeBrum, Gerald Knight and Labedbeden, Phillip Henry McArthur, Dirk H. R. Spennemann, Gene Ashby and the Community College of Micronesia, Giff Johnson, and August Erdland. Special thanks to Masako for all her help, to Pia for her wonderful art, to Scarlett for teaching me how to read, and to Ian for teaching me how to write.

About the Author

Robert Barclay is a former resident of Kwajalein Atoll and currently lives and continues writing in Honolulu, Hawai'i. This is his first novel. Visit the author at www.Robert-Barclay.com.